IMMORTAL TEMPTATION

IMMORTAL TEMPTATION

DENISE TOMPKINS
OLIVIA GATES
MICHELE HAUF
LISA CHILDS
CARIDAD PIÑEIRO

MILLS & BOON

Published in Great Britain 2014
by Mills & Boon, an imprint of Harlequin (UK) Limited,
Eton House, 18-24 Paradise Road, Richmond, Surrey, TW9 1SR

IMMORTAL TEMPTATION © 2014 Harlequin Books S.A.

Immortal Desire © 2013 Denise Tompkins
Immortal, Insatiable, Indomitable © 2012 Olivia Gates
Playing with Fire © 2011 Michele Hauf
Resurrection © 2009 Lisa Childs-Theeuwes
Nocturnal Whispers © 2012 Caridad Piñeiro Scordato

ISBN: 978-0-263-91404-7

89-0814

IMMORTAL DESIRE

DENISE TOMPKINS

From stable hand to a name on the door of a corporate American office, **Denise Tompkins** has been many things. (Never a waitress, though. Thank-you cards for her sparing the unsuspecting public from this catastrophe can be sent in care of her agent.) Writing has always been her passion, though. And writing romance? An absolute dream come true. Her theory is that a kiss should be meaningful regardless of length, a hero can say as much with a well-written look as he can with a long-winded paragraph and heroines are meant to hold their own. She's no Cinderella, and Shakespeare wrote the only *Romeo and Juliet*, so Denise sticks to women who can save themselves and tortured heroes who are loath to let them.

Denise and her husband live in the South, where all foods are considered fry-able and bugs die only to be reborn in bloodsucking triplicate. Visit her online, at www.denise-tompkins.com, anytime.

To my most amazing agent, Deidre Knight, for the conversations, the conviction and the certainty that I would end up here. You are a force of nature!

Chapter 1

Bailey slammed the bathroom stall door behind her. Sweat dotted her brow. Her limbs ached. A low-grade fever burned beneath her skin. The familiar, flu-like symptoms were worse than normal, but they were secondary to the sexual hunger that rode her like an ever-present addiction. Desperate, she ripped at the button on her jeans and tunneled one hand beneath her underwear. A gasp escaped her as she rubbed the hard little bundle of nerves. Her hips bucked involuntarily. She ground her mound against her hand as the orgasm built. Need curled through her pelvis, and she worked herself harder, faster, not bothering to stifle her soft moan.

Then she crashed into that bitterly familiar invisible wall. The orgasm she craved hung right there, so close but unequivocally out of reach. Primal hunger scorched her veins. She couldn't breathe. No matter what she did, no matter how hard she worked herself over, she couldn't get any closer to that elusive pinnacle.

"No. No, no, no." Body rigid and unfulfilled for what had to be the thousandth time, Bailey thumped her head against the stall wall. Hard. Frustration made her movements jerky as she yanked her hand free and zipped her pants. What was *wrong* with her? She was twenty-three, a normal woman with an abnormally high sex drive that couldn't do more than redline.

An angry tear tipped over her bottom lashes. She always ended up here, denied release and pissed as hell. Every night she worked was punishment, watching strangers connect on the dance floor. They'd mingle, flirt, touch, and then, paired up, they'd go home together. She'd tried to follow that path, tried to take lovers both short and long term. It was so difficult to watch men walk away from her after hours, days or weeks. They left her feeling damaged, thinking themselves inadequate and blaming her for her inability to respond. They said all the right words—"It's not you, it's me"—but the looks on their faces said it all. It *was* her. She inevitably ended up equally as frustrated and even more alone.

Then there were the books, movies, toys—a veritable cornucopia of sexual paraphernalia that had passed through her possession before she tossed it all out, down to the last battery, as defunct. Nothing ever helped. Excluding attempted self-satisfaction when the need grew too strong to deny, she'd given up finding release. It wouldn't have been so bad except for two things. First, she really, *really* needed to get off. And second? That was the kicker. She wanted it to happen with a partner, to share that intimate moment of connection with someone who mattered, to have someone look at her without disappointment or disgust.

Core aching, sex slippery, Bailey stormed out of the stall to the sink.

The other women in the bathroom openly stared. One smirked. Clearly they'd heard what she'd been up to in there.

Screw them. A bark of laughter escaped her. *Maybe not the best term to use.*

Bass from the club's music pounded through her when she opened the bathroom door and stepped into the hall. The thump-thump-thump caressed every nerve ending, driving her need back to fever pitch. The urge to rub her thighs together made her walk strangely. Whatever.

She slipped behind the bar, nodding to her boss. Griff was generally laid-back and definitely easy on the eyes. Over six and a half feet tall with ice-blue eyes, dark brown hair that brushed his collar and a hard body made for sex, he starred in every explicit fantasy she came up with. Lately she had him taking her against the wall, hard and fast. That full mouth would prove unyielding. His blue eyes would dilate. His breath would burn her skin, brand her. Capable hands would—

"Bailey?"

She looked up, unaware he'd moved in so close. "Sorry. What?" Her reply was short enough to sound irritable.

His nostrils flared. "I asked if you were okay."

What was she supposed to say? *Well, Griff, I just had another round of solo sex that didn't work out. Want to take me to your office and bend me over the desk, see if you can maybe work out the kinks in my kink?* Not likely. She wanted him beyond reason, but at what cost? Her employment? His respect? Their friendship? Every cost she came up with was far too high, the sacrifice too great, for a casual one-night stand, and that was all Griff ever offered anyone he bedded. Instead of answering, she closed her eyes and nodded. "I'm fine."

One hand, hot and heavy, rested on her shoulder. "You're sweating."

"Yeah. It's just hot in here." *Really, really hot.* She stiffened as a wave of sensual hunger roared through her. Dizzy, she gripped the bar edge.

Griff's hand tightened on her shoulder. "You're sure."

"Yeah." The single word sounded thready and definitely unsure.

"Sling a few drinks and we'll talk."

"Talk?" she squeaked.

"Yeah." He ran a hand over his chest, his silk shirt shifting sensually over his pecs and revealing the tips of his hardened nipples.

Bailey licked her lips, her thoughts dark as her eyes roamed down, straight to his... *Whoa.* Griff's leathers were stretched tight, the head of his cock clearly defined.

"Talk." The word was harsh.

"Okay." She turned back to the bar, hoping her mind would get back to task and stop tormenting her with images of her boss naked and writhing beneath her as she rode him. He'd pound into her slick heat, his thick shaft spearing her with every thrust. "Yeah, that's not going to work."

"What's that?" the guy across the counter asked.

"Nothing. What can I get you?"

"One rum and Coke. One margarita on the rocks, shot of tequila on the side."

He became the first of many customers, another nameless face she would never remember as she pulled orders together by rote, slinging bottles with a finesse she definitely didn't feel.

Griff slipped through the unobtrusive door marked Private and headed for his office. Every step rubbed the underside of his cock against the leathers he wore.

Bailey was so close to the Change. Putting himself in her immediate proximity had been criminally stupid. Her scent—citrusy with a sharp undertone of mint—coiled around him like an emotional noose. The morbid comparison didn't stop his cock from reacting, though. Self-loathing soured his stomach. He absolutely hated being an incubus, hated this part of his nature, this part that marked him a predator. "Get over yourself," he muttered.

He slowed his steps, relishing the burn of need that settled at the base of his spine. Pleasure and pain began an intimate, familiar dance. Hunger manifested as cold sweat at his nape. A single drop rolled down his neck like a specter's caress.

"You up for a little conversation?"

Griff turned, every movement controlled and deliberate. "If it's not critical, it needs to wait."

Seth, the club's general manager and one of Griff's only friends, looked him over. "Need me to send one of the JABs to your office?" he asked, referring to the women who regularly hung out at the club with the singular goal of adding any of the preternaturally gorgeous men to their list of conquests. They'd been dubbed JABs—Just Another Body.

"Not in the mood."

The other man arched a single brow. "Sure."

"Now's not the time, Seth." Griff slipped into his office, shutting the door with a soft *click*. Hands shook as he ripped his pants open and shoved them halfway down his thighs. His erection sprang free. The silk of his shirt slid around the root and feathered across his balls. He hissed. Bending forward and bracing himself against the edge of the desk with one fist, he gripped his thick length with the other. The first hard stroke—tip to base—drew a grunt from him. He twisted on the upstroke, spreading the single bead of moisture around the heated skin. He pumped faster, eyes unfocused, mind pulling up only one woman's face. *Bailey.*

From their first meeting, Griff had wondered what she'd be like in bed, what she'd look like naked and writhing beneath him, over him, kneeling in front of him. Her carefree nature and uninhibited wild side would undoubtedly make her unforgettable. Guilt tugged at what was left of his conscience. She had no idea what she was about to go through, and he hadn't taken the opportunity to forewarn her. Maybe he *should* get one of the JABs...

"Screw that." He shoved aside the worthless emotion and let his imagination go. The bastard went straight for the kill shot and had the imaginary Bailey on her knees, her mouth closing around his raging cock. He'd grip her head and pump as her tongue did decidedly wicked things. The images grew and layered as he gripped the desk and fucked his fist harder. Increasingly graphic images joined the caress of phantom fingers and sent him over the edge. With a shout, he let go.

The burn of pleasure shot up his pulsing shaft. No time to go for tissues. Griff blindly groped for something, anything. He knocked a ton of shit over before grasping a pen cup. Pens scattered all over the office. His hips surged forward, and he barely caught the first stream of hot seed. The orgasm raged unchecked, even when he tried to shut it down. Every pulse up his shaft forced his body to seek out pheromones from which to feed.

Griff shook through the initial wave of sexual hunger. When it finally crested and turned on itself, it was too much. His knees buckled and dropped him to the floor, the impact echoing through his head. Pain wracked his body. Lust's invisible talons ripped at every fiber of his being. His lungs protested every forced breath. Dark spots marred his vision and made him think lying down might be a good idea. He eased to his side, curling in on himself.

This was the closest he'd come to the pain of the Shift since the actual event over two hundred years ago. It hadn't taken a brilliant mind to figure out this sucked. That it was as bad as he remembered made him shiver as dark, unwelcome memories surfaced.

Hands had groped him, fondling him indiscriminately. Hot breath swept over his skin in the form of moans and gasps he gave and took. Confusion had colored everything, but underneath it? Underneath it had been shame. He'd never been given the opportunity to choose a lover or lovers the night his Shift occurred. His pheromones had done their worst, pulling lovers to him regardless of gender, regardless of preference, regardless of will. He'd taken what hadn't been his to take, and what had been his to give freely was taken against his will.

He wrapped one arm around his stomach and propped the other under his head. He should have taken Seth up on his offer to grab one of the JABs. There was only one reason he hadn't.

Bailey.

Chapter 2

Bailey wiped sweat from her brow. The last two hours had been a blur of bar patrons, strobe lights and that ever-present thump of bass. Every song seemed designed to heighten her arousal. The smell of sex permeated the air, hanging there, mixing with the thin haze of smoke so that every breath teased and tortured.

Cut the crap. You can't smell *sex.* But she could. It was dark and sensual, slightly spicy and full of promise. She wanted to roll around in it, coat herself in those unspoken promises and find a way to unlock the Orgasm Express. The idea of riding that train brought back thoughts of Griff, naked, face buried between her thighs. Yeah, he'd definitely drive that train. "Choo-choo," she whispered. A small smile crooked one corner of her mouth, and she absently traced her upper lip with her tongue.

"You okay, lady?" The guy across the bar eyed her speculatively. "Looks like you could use some company. I'll volunteer."

"Keith, take over." Griff's voice cut through the din. "My

office, Bailey. Now." He turned and stalked away, shoving through the swinging door that led to the back.

"Shit." Bailey ripped off her apron and tossed it in the bin beneath the counter.

Keith glanced her way as he pulled a beer. "Sounds like you're in for it."

"Sounds like that's the case."

"Good luck."

"Thanks." She moved toward the door to the back and, with every step, fought the urge to run. But would she run toward Griff or away from him? The answer drove her through the doorway and down the hall. Her breath came in hard draws and harsh exhales. The silk of her bra rubbed her nipples, tightening them until they hurt. Every sway of her hips rubbed the seam of her jeans against her clit until she struggled not to detour to the supply closet and try, one more time, to make herself come.

"Inside," Griff called out, his deep voice reeling her in.

The smell of sex, thick and decadent, assaulted her the instant she slipped through the door.

"Close it."

No request, just the command. She kicked the heavy door shut with her heel. Despite her wariness, something about Griff's tone encouraged her to purr and rub against his body. The images that followed were definitely not anywhere within the sphere of employer-employee relations.

"Lock it."

Her chin jerked up. "What?"

He moved around his desk and towered over her. "I said, 'Lock it.'"

She turned and laid a hand on the lock, stunned when he stepped in close and settled his hands on her hips.

He leaned down and rested his lips against her ear. "Now, Bailey."

"I—"

"Now." The deep growl in his voice said there would be no arguing, only submission.

Involuntarily arching her back, she ground against his cock. Shock froze her mid-grind.

"That's what I thought was going on." His hands tightened and pulled her closer.

Bailey groaned at the sensation, at the heat pouring off his body. And that *smell*. Sex. Pure sex. Stronger now than ever. Her mind raced through every raw fantasy that involved her boss. She wanted him, craved his nearness, coveted his touch. "Griff, please."

"Please what, baby?" His deep voice rumbled through her back.

"I need..." She shuddered, unwilling to place her well-being in his hands. Trust was hard, mistrust easy. Life had proven that she shouldn't, *couldn't*, count on anyone but herself.

Strong hands distracted her. Fingers feathered over her hips and up, under her shirt, across her belly. Flat palms pressed her against him. His erection pressed into the seam of her ass.

Familiar distrust crowded her desire and whispered, "*Why now and never before?*"

Before she could ask, he bent over her, sealing his chest to her back and placing his lips behind her ear. "You can't get off, can you?" he whispered.

The question burned through the haze of lust. "I... What?"

"I didn't stutter, Bailey."

Absolute confusion dragged the truth out before she could edit her response. "How did you know?"

"Let's just say we have a few things in common."

Those clearly capable hands roamed over her body, clouding her mind again. "Like what?"

"Later." His breath washed over her, hot and suggestive. "What would you say if I told you I could cure your little problem?"

Tilting her head, she gave him better access to her neck. "I wouldn't call it little."

"You'd be right." He nipped her ear.

Distrust tagged doubt, sending it into the arena and forcing her to ask, "Why are you interested in me now?"

"Why *not* now?" When she didn't immediately answer, he placed a kiss against her neck. "You interested?"

She wanted this. Wanted him. Badly. He was worth the cost, whatever it was. Shaken, she managed a stilted nod.

"Let's get those pants off."

With one hand, she fumbled with the button on her jeans. Large hands settled over hers and Griff took over. The slow rip of the zipper mingled with their heavy breathing to create an erotic chorus. The sinfully delicious smell of sex wafted around them, intimate and suggestive.

Griff knelt behind her, fingertips skating over bare skin as he inched her jeans down. "A thong. I approve." He punctuated his comment by nipping her bared ass cheek.

Bailey gripped the door handle so hard her knuckles were white. "What's going on, Griff?"

"So many questions." Another nip. "I'm going to show you what you're capable of, beautiful."

"Something's wrong with me." Even to her own ears, her whispered admission sounded ashamed.

"There's nothing wrong with you that a night with me won't fix."

She tensed. "Arrogant much?"

"It's not arrogance if I can deliver." He traced an incredibly tactile tongue up the back of her thigh and licked the line between upper thigh and butt cheek. "And I can."

What the hell. Worst case scenario, I end up with fodder for my fantasies. Best case? He lives up to his own hype. She shelved her misgivings for the moment and toed her sneakers off at the urging of his hands, making way for him to pull her jeans free. The silk thong slipped away from her vulva with silent promise. Air moved over bared skin. Pleas hung in the back of her throat.

"Patience." Leather creaked. Something heavy hit the floor. A metallic clink followed.

Bailey couldn't take the suspense. She looked over her shoulder and her mouth fell open. Griff had stripped. Completely. And holy shit. The man was more beautiful naked than she'd imagined. Thick thighs were corded with muscle. His abs tightened in a wicked eight-pack as he moved. That chest with its heavy pecs sported hard nipples. Her gaze dragged down his hairless body to his belly button where the thick head of his erection rested. He'd been impressive behind pants. Now? He was large enough to intimidate.

Turning slowly, she forced herself to meet his penetrating stare.

"Bend over the desk."

She moved so fast she stumbled.

He grabbed her by the arm and steadied her. "Easy, Bailey."

"I need..." Nausea made her bend forward and clutch her stomach.

"I know what you need, baby."

She hoped so. Because if this got much worse, she was going to think she was dying.

Griff struggled not to throw Bailey down and drive into her. She clearly had no idea what was going on, but he'd known from the very second they met. *Succubus.* She hadn't matured, though, so he'd waited. Impatiently at times, true, but he'd worked the bar far more than ever before so he could be around her. Somewhere along the way, he'd decided to see her through this. His maturation and shift from mortal to immortal was something he'd never forget and for all the worst reasons. If he could spare her that...

That's all it is. Just doing what I'm programmed to and giving her what she needs. Yeah. Right. He'd craved her from day one. It had started as purely physical before evolving to something complicated. *Not safe. Do this and get gone.*

Bailey clutched her stomach. Sweat sheened her skin, a testament to both her pain and need. He caught her as her knees gave out and shifted her so she lay facedown on the desk. Kicking her feet wide, he moved in closer. Her scent drove him mad. The instinct to power into her without apology made his balls draw up tight as his cock wept crystalline tears. He'd help her achieve orgasm. Then he'd feed until the abysmal memories her Change had dredged up were buried again. Shaking his head, he cursed and stepped back.

Bailey moaned, the sound one of pure agony wrapped in crazed lust. Then she arched her back and presented herself.

He was lost.

Griff moved in behind her. Slipping the head of his cock

into her cleft, he dragged it up and down her wet heat. "Sweet hell," he muttered. "You're so wet."

A hard shiver was her only response.

He leaned forward and pulled her hair aside, laying his lips on her neck. "Only two rules. First, no kissing. Second, no strings attached."

Her only response was to roll her hips in a way that wordlessly translated to desperation and stole his breath.

Gripping her hips, he pressed forward. His cock slid in a fraction at a time. She was so damn tight he was afraid he was going to tear her in half. It took every ounce of restraint to keep things slow and controlled when the dregs of his sexual hunger roared to the surface. He resisted the commands screaming through him to push her hard, to feed, to sate the emptiness that threatened to drag him under. The only currency his nature dealt in when denied was personal pain, so he kept working his way into her. The aches started up again. Heat burned through him like a wind-driven wildfire. Finally, seated as deeply as possible, he adjusted his grip and began slow, rolling thrusts.

Bailey gripped the edge of the desk and hauled herself back on him hard enough that the head of his cock hit her cervix. "Again," she grunted.

"You're not warmed up enough for that."

"Again!" She rocked back on him with such power he stumbled back.

Griff wrapped one arm around her waist, lifting her hips up at the same time he propped a fist on the desk next to her head. "You want it rough?"

She shook in his embrace. "I need it."

"Let go. I'll take care of...this." He'd started to say *you*, but that would have been a lie. "C'mon, Bailey. Let go."

When she went limp in his arms, he settled back, knelt just enough that her thighs rested on his and powered into her. Long, hard thrusts slapped his balls against her clit. He had to hold onto her, one hand on her waist and the other on her shoulder, to keep her from sliding across the desk with every drive of his hips.

Her sheath was so tight, so wet, he thought he'd lose his damn mind. Every quiver of her body translated to pure craving, a need so raw it raked against the most sensitive parts of him. All he wanted in that moment was to experience the power of her release.

But not like this.

He pulled free of Bailey's body.

She dropped her forehead to the desk. "I knew it."

Griff's mouth kicked up at the corners. "We're not done, baby." The empty affection rolled off his tongue with practiced ease. He gently rolled her over. "Hips to the edge."

Propping her feet over his shoulders, he leaned in and settled his hands on her waist. She presented a vulnerable, trusting picture, spread out like an offering. The small, insidious voice in his head reminded him that he didn't deserve her trust. Self-loathing's abyss loomed. His near-dormant conscience pushed him closer to the ledge and encouraged him to leap.

"Not yet." His whisper was harsh and emphatic.

Bailey gripped his arm, misunderstanding. "Finish this."

He drove into her with a single thrust. Reveled in her shout. The hard-pounding rhythm of skin on skin drowned out the club's muted cacophony.

Her nails scored his arms, drawing blood.

The violence in her matched his own. He was too far

gone, too lost in Bailey's response to shut down his own. His cock swelled. *Fuck.*

Reaching between them with unfamiliar urgency, he found her clit. The swollen bundle of nerves was slick with her arousal. He thrummed it faster and faster until her wild undulations forced him to hold her in place. Her cries drowned out everything else until she was all he could hear, all he could see, all he wanted.

Hot seed shot up his cock. *Sweet hell.* He was going to lose himself right here. Right now. He pinched her clit between his thumb and middle finger, flicking it hard. "Now, Bailey!"

She screamed, and that was it. Game over.

Griff's orgasm rocked him, nearly taking him to his knees. He came so hard his eyes rolled back in his head as he buried his cock deep. Then he felt it.

Her sheath tightened around him.

But instead of the anticipated rush of energy typical with feeding, he only got a trickle. He drew in every last lungful of the drug his body needed to survive. The semi-high would tide him over. For now.

Leaning forward, he took her nipple into his mouth. Her skin was salty. The musk of their sex mingled in the air. Yeah, life was fucking good.

It took him a minute to realize his lover was taught under his hands. She trembled, her need a beacon to the incubus within him. "Bailey?"

"I don't feel so good," she whispered.

Then she passed out.

Chapter 3

Griff shoved everything off his desk with a single swipe. Sliding Bailey further up the slick wood surface, he traced a finger down her breastbone. She was breathing in erratic pants, but her color still seemed good. She needed to wake up, though. This was far from over. He might be an incubus, but even *he* had basic standards. Namely, the woman had to be alert and willing.

"Bailey? C'mon, sweetheart. Wake up." He tapped her face gently.

Her tongue traced her lips on a sigh.

"We don't have time for this, baby. Wake up." Grasping her chin, he leaned forward and forced her to focus on him. "Don't go thinking we're done here." The growl in his voice was a surprise, and he was temporarily relieved she didn't hear the passion that resonated through every word.

He grabbed the box of tissues off the filing cabinet and cleaned her up before sliding her jeans on and wrapping her in his shirt. With a quick yank, his leathers were on. Shoes weren't a matter of general decency so he left them.

"Up you go." He grasped her wrist and hauled her over his shoulder in a fireman's carry.

Murphy's Law said the hall wouldn't be empty. The Law held. Seth's door hissed closed as Griff stepped out of his office. The *ifrit*, a rare type of elemental *djinn*, or genie, turned to him, smiling, until he recognized the shoulder cargo. "Bailey?"

"She's fine." Griff started down the hall toward the elevator.

Seth fell into step beside him. Naturally. "What happened?"

"She, ah…"

"You finally fuck her senseless?"

"*What?*" Normally a master of the poker face, Griff couldn't hide his surprise.

"Oh, c'mon. You two have wanted each other from the start. I couldn't stand the chemistry between you without getting a hard-on. Don't tell me you didn't know."

Had it been that obvious? Could everyone see what had started between them? He hoped not. It would make what he had to do that much worse. "Whatever. I need you to cover the bar. I'm going to make sure Bailey's…taken care of." He scanned his thumbprint then punched the up button beside the private elevator door.

"Be careful." Seth's words might have been soft, but they were heavy.

"I know what I'm doing."

"Make sure *she* does." The large man pivoted and stalked away, clearly worried about the woman in Griff's arms.

The urge to call after him, to explain what was happening, burned in Griff's throat. "I don't owe anyone an explanation." He thumped his forehead against the wall, frustrated and unsure of himself. He'd chosen to see her through this, to ensure she didn't become a victim of her nature as he had. Justifying his actions didn't change the truth of the situation. He didn't want Bailey to live with a lifetime of haunted memories and regrets. If he could save her that…

The elevator doors opened and Griff stepped inside. Bailey's hands brushed his ass and he jerked. "Strung tight as a damn guitar." He hit the door close button and widened his stance as the car started up.

Bailey groaned. "Griff?"

"Hang on, baby."

She pushed up, scaling his body.

With her weight shifting, he had no choice but to let her down. *How* he did it, though, was up to him. He gripped her loosely and let her slide down the front of his body, settling her cleft against his thigh. The scent of arousal swept around him, winding through his lungs and reminding him of sunshine and summer and sultry sin. His hips jerked in response. Desire flooded through him, quickly cresting well above record flood levels.

What is it about her? She'd been everything he'd dreamed of—passionate, responsive, wild. His heart lurched, and he lifted a hand to stroke her cheek, the affectionate gesture one that had never come naturally to him yet fit the moment perfectly. He traced her jaw with his fingertips, considering her. "What?"

"I appreciate you trying, Griff." She shook her head and looked down. "I mean, I was closer than ever, but it's just not in the cards for me."

His face went slack. "Excuse me?"

"It's okay. It's me, not you." Her eyes shone with unshed tears. "Don't make me a charity case."

"I... Pity... Don't... What the hell are you talking about?" The way she shook her head and looked away made his chest tighten. Swiftly, without thinking, he slapped the emergency stop button on the panel.

The elevator stopped abruptly enough that they swayed into each other. Baily grabbed his biceps for support.

It was random, the way his body moved. He watched with detached amusement as one hand wound around her neck and fisted in the back of her hair. His free hand cupped her ass and drew her up his thigh. Breaths came hard and fast. Muscles twitched. His nostrils flared.

Color stole into her cheeks to create a pretty flush. Lips parted, she stared up at him.

The emptiness that ate at him with every faceless coupling pushed in. She deserved more than this, deserved more than he could ever offer her. "Won't do this to you, too."

"Do what to me?" Her hands rested against his chest, light but hot.

He closed his eyes and struggled to regain control of his traitorous emotions, particularly the one demanding he protect what was his. *Bailey.*

"Griff?"

Teeth grinding, he slowly opened his eyes and, with an intentionally sensuous smile, shrugged one shoulder. "Shame you're only good for a preliminary attempt."

She crossed her arms and glared up at him. "Wait a second. Are you insinuating that I'm a—"

"Lightweight, Bailey. And I'm not insinuating anything. I'm *saying.*" He arched a brow.

"Screw you, Griff."

"That's what I thought we were doing. Guess I was wrong."

Her lips thinned. "I'm not a lightweight, and for what it's worth? Your reverse psychology bullshit doesn't fly."

He dragged the hand cupping her ass up, under her waistband and back down to cradle bare skin. "Whatever you need to believe, but trust me when I tell you I'm still the best person to solve your little problem."

"So you said, but here I am in almost the same shape as when this, this—" she flapped one hand between them "—*thing* started." She dropped her gaze and thumped her forehead against his chest once before resting it there. "Honestly? I'd hoped you were right."

Griff pulled her into a tight embrace without thinking.

Strong arms wrapped around his waist in return.

They stood quietly, their heartbeats falling into a lethargic beat, counterbeat.

She buried her face in his bare chest and nuzzled.

Such a simple gesture of affection yet it catapulted him into near panic. Unable to stand the strange emotional onslaught, he pulled her head back and bent to nuzzle her neck.

Bailey couldn't breathe. One minute she'd been sure the little interlude with Griff had ended, and the next second he was everywhere, all seeking hands and hungry mouth and hard body. He managed to peel the shirt—*how did she end up in his shirt?*—off before she hit the elevator wall.

A little huff of air escaped her.

She had spent so long wanting him on so many levels. Now she needed him to obliterate the tightness in her chest that accompanied the wanting. The urge to give in, to let him do what he would, pulled at her. *Trust me*, he'd said.

She would. He had promised to fix this, to fix *her*. If anyone could, she wanted to believe it was him, that he wouldn't ever give her that *look*, the one that said she was little more than a broken doll destined for the recycle bin. Glancing up, she licked her lips, her belly fluttering when blazing blue eyes zeroed in on the movement. He made her feel sensual and sexual, desired in a way no other man had. She rested a hand feather-light on his chest. "Griff."

He caged her in with his arms. His mouth homed in on first one nipple and then the other as if they emitted sonar only he could hear.

She pressed deeper into his mouth, reveling in the wickedly talented tongue that flicked and laved, lips that suckled, teeth that scraped. The urge to give herself into his keeping grew painful but stronger, a new emotional muscle being stretched and pulled.

He shoved at her jeans. "Off," he growled.

She wiggled free. "You do the same."

"In a sec." He ran his hands down her thighs and pressed her legs apart, kneeling before her. "Leg over my shoulder." He punctuated the command by hooking an arm behind her knee and working it over his shoulder.

Her protest had barely formed when his mouth found her core. He latched onto her clit and flicked it with the tip of his tongue.

A half hungry, half crazed groan escaped her. She wound her hands through his hair, nails scraping his scalp.

Griff hummed his approval.

One part of her wanted to pull him closer. The other wanted to ride his face like a cowgirl on a mechanical bull. He made up her mind for her when he twisted around and positioned his free shoulder under her grounded leg. Shoving up, with his face buried between her legs, all she could do was hold on.

Skillful lips nibbled and teased, his tongue occasionally flicking the little nerve bundle. A stream of cool air whispered over the hypersensitive flesh, and she twitched like she'd been hooked up to a car battery. Pleasures stacked one atop another until they ran together like watercolors. His hedonistic assault drove her wild. Every calculated touch and measured stroke fed the burn beneath her skin like a well-aimed bellow.

She ground her pelvis against him. "Griff." His name, little more than an explosion of air, whispered just below the desperate, hungry sounds that ricocheted off polished-metal walls.

He didn't answer. Instead he grew more aggressive, drove her harder toward the crest.

Uncontrollable shudders rocked her. She was a slave to the man commanding her body.

The orgasm crashed into her without warning. Hands buried in his hair, she screamed and arched her back so radically only her head touched the wall behind her. Heat suffused her vulva. Her vaginal walls spasmed as she bore down on that relentless mouth.

Griff shoved her legs wider as he surged off the floor. Forearms hooked behind her knees, he slid her up the wall and pinioned her with his chest as he worked at his zipper one-handed. He freed his cock and swiftly lowered her onto the broad head as her orgasm tapered off. One hard thrust seated him. A deep, approving growl rumbled through him when she shouted in surprise. "Again," he said against her ear, his harsh, hot breath combining with the arrogant demand to rake across her skin.

She turned to him, her mouth seeking his.

He jerked his chin away and tried to cover the reaction with intent by leaning back and powering into her with long, deep thrusts. "Just feel, baby."

Bailey wrapped her hands behind Griff's neck and laced her fingers together. Skin slapped skin, an erotic soundtrack to the best sex of her life. A second orgasm loomed, imminent. The way her sex tightened around his thick cock, the ache in her womb, the throb of her clit—everything led to that ultimate release. She rode him hard. Small, desperate sounds escaped every time she slid down his girth. Her thighs tightened around his waist. A strong pull below her belly button drove her toward an unfamiliar darkness and intensified every sensation.

"Oh!" Pleasure crested and crashed over her. Pulling herself forward, she ground against Griff's pelvis as she rolled her hips and took him with rapid, short strokes.

"Yes," he groaned. His brute strength encouraged her up his cock again and again, those shallow thrusts wringing out every ounce of pleasure from the moment.

Strong fingers dug into her ass hard enough to bruise. Every muscle in her body shook. She pressed her forehead against his and closed her eyes.

It was the only way to avoid seeing his hot gaze shutter with the contact.

Chapter 4

Griff draped an arm across Bailey's shoulders after setting her down and restarting the elevator. The contact was light and casual. Nothing they hadn't done a hundred times before. Still, it felt different. It *was* different. There was a connection with her he couldn't explain. He'd just helped her achieve her first full-blown orgasm, and that changed whatever it was between them. It changed *them*.

He watched her distorted reflection in the elevator's polished walls. Her silence unnerved him. She hadn't said anything since he put her down. Instead, she'd retrieved her pants and pulled them on before wrapping his shirt around her upper body.

His leathers lay untouched on the floor. *Too late for modesty.* He kicked them aside as the elevator doors opened and he stepped into his living room.

The Atlanta skyline burned bright through the floor-to-ceiling windows so he didn't turn on lights. Instead, he propelled her through the lavish, if impersonal, apartment and straight to the kitchen where he dropped his arm and went for the fridge. "Want something to drink?"

"Sure." She slid onto a bar stool. "A beer if you've got it."

"I own a bar. My rep would be seriously impinged if all I had was juice." He grinned over his shoulder and found her staring at the cityscape. The grin faded. *Damn.* This was about to get complicated. Not for the first time, Griff wondered what the hell he'd been thinking in taking on her Change. Caustic memories crowded his consciousness and he rebelled, shoving them away. He simply couldn't let her be used the way he'd been used, or use the way he'd used. She needed to survive this and emerge far more whole than he had. History had taught him that some things, once lost, could never be found again. Self-respect floated near the top of that list. The last thing he wanted was for her to end up despising herself. If he could save her the centuries of heartache he'd endured, he would. He'd see her through her Change. No way would he back down just because shit got hard. He rested his forearm against the cool steel fridge and let his head hang forward, loose and heavy. What he had to tell her was going to rock her world, and not like he had in the elevator. Granted, his little planet had been rattled, too, but he was sure that had more to do with her intent to kiss him than the mind-blowing sex.

He'd told her straight up that kissing was off the table. When she'd moved in… Goose bumps shivered across his skin. Nothing, and no one, had come closer to tempting him to break his number one rule. Bailey had pressed against his boundaries and made him reach for her, made him long for the kind of connection an incubus couldn't have. If he was smart, he'd tell her what she needed to know and end this now, let someone else see her through the Change.

He grabbed a couple of longnecks and let out a short whistle.

Bailey looked over and snatched the tossed bottle out of the air. A practiced twist freed the cap. Her expert flick shot it into the trash can. She took a long pull, her throat working as she swallowed.

Griff couldn't look away. Every idea of cutting her loose dissolved. Her borrowed shirt—*his* shirt—had fallen open to reveal a thin line of pale skin from chin to unbuttoned jeans. The swells of her breasts peeked out. He'd fed hard the second time Bailey came. Technically? He should be sated. Reality wasn't concerned with technicalities, though.

Her nostrils flared as she lowered her chin.

He wanted to drag her against his body, skin to skin. Instead, just looked at her, all mussed after being thoroughly pleasured. Then her tongue snaked out to capture a lone drop of beer on her lip. Suddenly there wasn't much thinking left to do. Bottle dangling deceptively loose from his fingers, he started toward her.

She shook her head and stopped him in his tracks. "What's going on, Griff?"

"Come again?"

A cheeky grin revealed her dimples. "I sort of did, thanks."

"You know what I mean." The words were harsher than he intended.

Hurt flashed across her features, stealing the intimate playfulness. Bailey slipped from the stool and moved to the window, presenting nothing but a silhouette as she sipped her drink. Her normally fluid carriage grew concise. Calculated, even. Cold city lights partially illuminated her face when she finally glanced back. "I'd like to know what the hell's going on. You said we had stuff in common."

He set his beer on the bar and tilted his head toward the sofa. "You want to sit down to have this little chat?"

"Not so much."

"I think you should sit."

"And I'm passing on the offer."

"Suit yourself." He stalked to the bedroom. "Such a fool for getting into this damn mess," he muttered, grabbing a pair of satin lounge pants from the dresser and yanking them on.

"I'm assuming I'm the damn mess." Her cool voice came from behind him.

Turning, he found her leaning against the doorjamb.

She sipped her beer and studied him with the same impassive gaze she leveled at customers coming on to her when she worked the bar.

Griff closed his eyes, laced his hands behind his head and pulled. "Shit."

The thunk of her bottle on the dresser made him look up.

Long legs carried her away with a delicious hip-swinging gait.

Time slowed to an impossible crawl and he couldn't react, couldn't move, couldn't even *breathe*. He watched her punch the down button, saw the elevator doors open, felt the loss of her like a physical wound. He didn't want to go there, didn't want to let himself swim through emotions he had no right to feel. But it quickly became apparent he'd swim the murky emotional waters or sink like a stone.

Suddenly he was moving. Across the room between heartbeats, he hooked an arm around her waist and drew her back into the heat of his body.

She stood rigid in his arms. "Let go."

"You aren't the mess, baby." Not a single ounce of give in that curvy body. The doors closed. He held her, listening to every harsh inhale and exhale between them as her pulse pounded beneath his hands. "You're about to find yourself *in* a hell of a mess, though."

"I know you didn't just threaten my job because I screwed you." Her voice, barely audible, shook with unchecked rage.

"What? No." He let her go.

She didn't turn around.

"Give me thirty minutes. I'll explain what's been happening to your body and why I fixed the problem, at least temporarily." When she still didn't face him, he shoved his hands through his hair. "When have I ever steered you wrong or lied to you?" Unwelcome desperation punctuated his words.

"Fair." She turned and moved across the room, taking up her position in front of the window again and crossing her arms. "Besides, you sign the paychecks. I suppose I'll spend my time however you tell me to."

An exasperated sigh escaped him. "Stop fronting, would you? You're not a hard woman. That's always been part of your appeal."

She glanced at him and arched a brow before returning her attention to the view. "You want to spend thirty minutes listing my attributes? Fine. I'm sure my tits have you enamored, but don't forget my eyes. I've been told they're one of my best assets."

Griff's eye twitched. "Quit trying to bait me. This is too serious."

She rolled her head back and forth before looking over at him. "Fine. Go ahead."

A hard knot formed high in his chest, an ache that refused to be assuaged by touch or logic or demand. *Best just get it out there, then.* "If we don't get this sorted out, you're right. You're going to die."

* * *

Bailey pressed the heels of her hands against her temples. Surely she'd heard him wrong. A quick glance at his face said otherwise. The only surprise was that she wasn't entirely surprised. She'd been waiting for this moment. The fear he'd given voice to had painted a patina of dread over her life as her symptoms grew worse.

Several weeks ago she'd broken down and talked to her doctor. He'd run a battery of tests. Nothing more than a few oddities—higher than normal hormone levels, a raised baseline temperature, slightly elevated blood pressure—showed up. As a precaution, he'd referred her to a reproductive specialist. She'd accepted the referral. Then she'd skipped the appointment. She hadn't been brave enough to reschedule. Not yet. Not when she might be empowering a stranger to take something irreplaceable from her again. Not when she didn't have anyone to trust her fears to. Bailey was alone and had never more reminded of it than in that moment.

Hot fingers brushed over her cool skin and startled her.

She moved to the sofa with short, jerky steps and half sat, half fell into the deep leather cushions. "Dying?" She shook her head. "You can't know that."

"Look, Bailey, you're a—"

"You can't know that," she shouted. "You're not a doctor, you're not a...a...you own a freaking *bar!* Unless you've got a magically diagnostic dick, you're not qualified to tell me what's wrong."

Griff shoved his hands in his pockets and widened his stance. "I've been where you are, gone through exactly what you're experiencing. I'd say that makes me pretty damned qualified."

"You can't understand." She looked out over the city.

So alive. It fed her need to feel connected to something, anything. She'd been alone so long. The thought that Griff might be right, that she could die in her small apartment with no one to hold her as she faded, tripped every fear response she had.

History caught up to her when Griff's phone rang. His voice registered, low and slow, as memories abused her in vivid color. She was suddenly four years old all over again. Staring blankly at hands at once so capable and so ineffectual, she shuddered. These were the hands that had held her mother as she died in a dingy efficiency apartment as the phone rang incessantly.

Bill collectors. It had probably been bill collectors.

Death's magnitude had been beyond her comprehension as she waited for her mother to wake up. For two days she stayed with her mother's body.

"Bailey?"

The phone kept ringing. She finally answered, pleading with the only adult she could get to listen to help her. Police arrived. She was taken from her mother, stuck in a broken system of ever-changing homes. Alone. Forgotten. Abandoned.

"Bailey." Griff's voice swept through the fragmented memories, anchoring her in the present.

Griff. She knew him better than she'd ever known her mother, knew what he looked like when he smiled, knew how he sounded with laughter tickling his words.

Her fingers shook violently as she traced the numb contours of her lips. Impulse drove her to press hard enough to split the fragile skin against her teeth. The copper tang of blood hit her tongue. She prodded the wound, hungry for the pain and the proof it afforded. Dark red stained her fingers. *Proof I'm alive.*

"Listen to me, Bailey." Griff dropped to the sofa. Cushions sank under his weight, and she slid toward him. He gripped her wrist. "I can get you through this."

She curled her fingers over the bloodstain and looked up, searching his face. "I don't even know what 'this' is."

His fingers tightened. "Do you know anything about your parents?"

"Not really. I never knew my dad. My mom died when I was little, so I was handed over to the State's foster care system." The scars of time stretched and burned over the deep wounds. She'd learned to live with them, but nothing had ever healed.

"I'm sorry about your mom. Your dad probably wasn't equipped to take care of you, so the State was likely a better choice."

She shook her head. "Don't make excuses for him, Griff. Just don't."

"I'm doing my best to explain what's happening." Letting her go, he rose from the couch and shoved the waistband of his pants down. "See this?"

Bailey glanced at the exposed hip. "It's a tattoo."

"No, it's not. It's called a Marker. Five large says you have one, too."

"I don't have a—"

He cut her denial short when he grabbed her arm and hauled her off the couch.

"Ease up, Captain Caveman," she snapped. "You might buy my time, but no amount of money gives you the right to abuse me. Clear?"

He gave her a gentle shake. "Check your hip."

She pulled free of his grip and undid her pants enough to expose skin. "Nothing there."

"You're female. It'll be on the other side."

She sighed. "There's nothing…" Roughly the size of a silver dollar, a thin-lined circle surrounded a large dot. "What the hell?" She rubbed the unfamiliar red mark, but it wouldn't come off.

"It's your Marker—like a brand. Every species has one. Design and location depend on what you are." Griff ran a hand behind his neck, his biceps bunching.

"What you *are?*" Scrambling to button her pants, she shot him a hard stare. "I'm afraid to even ask."

An ironic, humorless smile lifted one corner of his mouth. "I'm an incubus."

Her jaw dropped. "You think you're a sex demon."

"There's no 'thinking' to it. I know."

"And now you think I'm a…what? Succubus?"

Silence.

Her vision narrowed, graying on the fringes. She backed away from him in a tripping rush, stopping only when she hit the wall. "Look, you clearly cracked the orgasm vault, and I'm grateful. But gratitude doesn't mean I'm willing to buy into your time-share of crazy."

"Crazy, huh? You're suffering low-grade fevers and flu-like symptoms that run the gamut from full-body aches to nausea and vomiting. Orgasm has been impossible, yet you've been horny as hell. And it's all getting worse, fast. I bet you even went to the doctor, and the only thing they found was a whole lot of nothing. Tell me, Bailey. How far off am I?"

Cold, the kind that seeped through bones and turned

blood to slush, started at her center and spread outward. "Stop it."

"No. You need help if you're going to survive the Change from mortal to immortal."

"I-immortal? You're insane," she whispered, shaking her head.

"Immortal. And you're going to wish I was." He reached around her to grab the phone, completely ignoring her flinch. The beep of keys sang across the tension strung between them. "Upstairs." He tossed the phone on the sofa.

The elevator hummed as it ran down and then started back up seconds later. They waited, both staring at the polished steel doors. A faucet dripped in the background. The AC clicked on. Cool air rushed from the ventilation ducts and carried a stale, recirculated smell.

She jumped when the doors slid open.

Seth stepped into the apartment and glanced between them. "What's going on?"

Griff blinked slowly and lifted his chin. "I need you to show Bailey your Marker."

The man stared at Griff, considering. Then his lips twitched. "My Marker, huh?"

"Keep it in your pants, Casanova." He swallowed hard enough that she heard it. "She's entering her Change. I showed her my Marker, explained what is happening. She doesn't buy it."

Bailey rounded on him. "You don't 'buy it' when the waiter pushing dessert promises the cheesecake will never show up on your thighs, Griff. This? If this was a game of hangman, you'd be one silent consonant away from spelling *psycho*."

Seth snorted and began unbuttoning his shirt.

She opened her mouth to object.

Griff spun her around, one heavy arm banding around her and locking her arms to her sides.

She started to argue. *Loudly.*

His free hand settled over her mouth. Chin resting beneath her temple, his breath skated across her cheek. "Bite me and I'll take you over my knee."

Seth paused in the act of shrugging out of his shirt. "I don't care how close we are, man. Bro Code says I do *not* need to know your proclivities in the bedroom."

"She's a succubus, Seth."

"That explains the influx of men in the club. You've put a serious cramp on my love life, sweetheart." He smiled before dropping his shirt.

A narrow, very realistic flame tattoo started somewhere below his waistband and snaked up to lick at his belly button. Reds, blues and yellows ran together and gave the erotic art depth. Every breath made the vibrant ink undulate across his skin like a living thing. He ran a hand down his chiseled abs and traced the flame's edges, following the dark outline without looking.

Her heart pounded. Every shallow inhale and fast exhale burned. She couldn't get enough air. Sagging in Griff's arms, she started to tremble. Cold sweat slicked her feverish skin. It was impossible to drag her narrowing gaze away from those fingers tracing a sensual path along the flame.

Seth's voice, tinny and far away, cut through her awareness. Shouts echoed in her head. She heard her name, tried to respond. Her jaw locked tight and made it impossible to make more than rudimentary sounds. Sight had abandoned her. Then a familiar smell hit her.

Sex.

Terror gripped her as that familiar fever raged unchecked. Her muscles began convulsing.

A heavy body pinned her to the ground.

Whispered words carved through her terror. "I'm here, baby."

Firm hands gripped her arms and held her steady.

Griff.

"Breathe through it with me."

His intoxicating smell wound around her, stoking her senses until they blazed with awareness.

"I'm not going anywhere, Bailey. You hear me? I'm right here."

As her world fractured further and true blackness obliterated her awareness, she caught her breath. She might be going under, but she wasn't alone.

Chapter 5

"Go," Griff ordered, struggling to pin Bailey without hurting her.

Seth snatched his shirt off the floor and shoved his arms down the sleeves. "She going to be okay?"

"If I can get the seizure stopped."

"How?"

"Just go, okay?" He grunted when her fist connected with his chin. "Lock the elevator behind you."

"Don't let her go." The elevator doors slid closed on Seth's parting order.

Griff shifted to get a better grip before scowling down at the woman in his arms. "You need to feed, Bailey."

Her sightless stare roved around the room, unfocused and eerie as hell.

"Dammit." He rolled and wiggled like a preteen wrestler, struggling to get Bailey turned around. "You're going to make me break the rule of two Cs in sex—woman's got to be conscious and consenting."

He maneuvered an arm around her torso and his legs around her thighs. He ripped at her jeans. Long minutes later, after wriggling and shoving with his hands and feet, he managed to get the denim wrapped around her ankles. Mutually slick with sweat, it was hard as hell to hang onto her as he worked his own pants free.

She froze the second his cock brushed her ass.

Blood flooded his groin in a near-painful rush as his body responded to the ever-present need of what he'd become.

Painful keens escaped her.

"Easy, baby." Arms still locked, he rolled the two of them over so he pressed against her back as she lay facedown on the Oriental rug. He hooked a foot in her jeans and shoved them free of her feet before easing her legs apart.

She arched and lifted up, presenting herself to him.

"Son of a bitch." Griff dragged a shaking hand down his face. "I'm not a damn saint, Bailey."

The smell of her arousal hit him like a fist to the throat and left him grappling with his need and his hesitation.

Need won.

He grabbed his hard length and fed it straight into her welcoming heat. Thigh to thigh, Griff refused to fall into the despair that often accompanied his couplings. This wasn't just empty sex. This was Bailey. This was about saving her life.

Liar.

He ground against her, the action earning him a low mewl. She bucked against his long, hip-rolling drives forward. The response wasn't to him, though. Just his body. Any body would have done just as well. She had no idea who held her. He could have been anyone. Still, he didn't stop. He couldn't.

Sick bastard.

"Say my name, Bailey."

No answer.

Anger washed over him at the situation, her body's timing, his genetics, everything. The power of his thrusts increased. His grip on her hips tightened, slipped and then dug in. She'd bruise.

Skin slapped skin as he drove into her again and again. The cold light of the city washed over them and gilded their bare skin in oranges and whites. A siren sounded from the street below. And still that damn faucet dripped.

Griff fought to keep himself removed, to keep this practical. It was a matter of saving her life and extending his. But this wasn't living and he knew it. This was existing. Sex had become a matter of drive-through dining—no flavor, no atmosphere, no experience. Every night was a matter of empty, forgettable calories. He was an excellent lay as a matter of necessity, not because there was any connection with his partner.

A memory swept through him. His rhythm faltered. "Just feel," he'd admonished Bailey. Now here he was fighting that very thing. Hypocrite.

Nothing new there.

He'd give anything to take the advice back.

Because to survive this fate, she'd have to learn to do just the opposite.

Bailey ached. Everywhere. She scrubbed her hands over her face and tried to clear the fog that swirled through her consciousness. Nothing made sense.

She rolled over and right out of an unfamiliar, very high bed. Sheets and a heavy jacquard comforter wrapped around her lower body and created a tangled, high thread count mess. Kicking free, she grabbed the mattress and popped up on her knees.

Griff lay on his side, head propped in his hand as he watched her.

Embarrassed, she dropped low so her chin was level with the edge of the wide mattress.

"All I can think is that this is my favorite version of the Whac-A-Mole game ever—very adult and very naked." Words that should have been playful were impassive.

"What happened?"

He arched a single brow, slow and almost insolent. "This is the first time a bed partner has passed out on the front side of a session." One corner of his mouth lifted. "Now, afterward? That's not uncommon. Should I be offended? By all measures, you enjoyed yourself."

Memories blinded her as they illuminated the dark corners of her mind. Recollections flashed like lightning in a stormy sky, each strike a precursor to the emotional boom that rattled through her with jarring percussion. She traced the small wound in her lower lip with the tip of her tongue. "Why?"

"Why did you enjoy yourself? Because I'm a good lover."

"That's not what I meant."

He closed his eyes and lifted one shoulder in an attempt at indifference. "You would have died."

She slid down the side of the bed and turned, resting her back against the rail.

The mattress lurched. Air moved as he settled beside her. "You feel any better?"

She opened her mouth, closed it and cleared her throat before trying again. "Still a little sick."

"You've got to feed. It gets better after you do."

When she started to object, deny, question him, maybe even argue, he laid a hand on her thigh. "Your Marker's coming in, Bailey. You can deny it all you want, but that ink isn't going away."

"You're crazy."

"I prefer psycho. I'm all about the silent consonants these days."

An unexpected laugh broke free.

Griff gently squeezed her thigh before withdrawing his hand.

The loss of his touch was sobering, the tremor in her voice profound. "This is real, isn't it?"

"Wish it wasn't." He laced his hands behind his head, his pecs and abs rippling as he moved.

"I don't want this."

Instead of meeting her eyes, he leaned his head back and stared at the ceiling. "No doubt, but it's like a kid with brown hair wishing he'd been born blond. He can dye it a thousand times and tell the world to believe what they see, but it doesn't change the truth."

Leaning over, she rested her forehead against Griff's biceps. She'd never seen him this quiet. He was forever in motion—running Desire, working the crowd, unloading a truck, filling in behind the bar or seducing women. Now? Only the steady rise and fall of his chest said he was animate.

She didn't want to leave, but staying here made everything far too real. Besides, hiding wouldn't change anything. "I should probably go."

"You need to stick around in case you get in trouble." He gathered his legs under himself and pushed up, rising with preternatural grace. "I'll be in the office until about three.

You going to finish your shift or do you want to, ah…" A rough gesture toward his bed said what he hadn't been able to articulate.

"It'd probably be wiser for me to finish my shift. I'd imagine Keith's ready to kill me." She accepted the hand he held out.

He hauled her to her feet. "Seth covered for you. When I called down for him, his phone rang through to the bar." Heavy hands settled on her shoulders. "Promise you won't leave without checking in with me."

She bit her bottom lip. "You really expect me to believe this, don't you?"

"You're too smart to deny it." He chucked her under the chin. "It's one of your best assets."

She winced. "Sorry about that."

"No apologies. Just don't leave. And…" He rolled his shoulders.

"And what?"

"If you start getting light-headed or sick, come get me. I'd like to see you through this."

"Why?" She blurted, only to hold up her hand and stop his response. "You know what? Forget I asked. If I need you, I'll find you." Heat burned her cheeks. The idea of popping in and asking him to… Yeah. Definitely blushing. She looked around, her brow wrinkling. "What about my clothes?"

Griff grinned. "Pretty much destroyed. You'll have to wear the uniform."

"Oh, hell no."

Griff leaned against the wall at the end of the bar and watched Bailey take orders, flip bottles and flirt like a pro.

Hell, she *was* a pro. He grinned when she bent over and swept up a fallen towel. Half the men at the bar had to adjust their zippers. The half that didn't clearly hadn't seen the move from behind.

She'd grumbled like mad about wearing the cocktail waitress's uniform—cut-off denim short shorts and a tight, low-cut crop top with the name of the club over the breasts and "You can't help it…and neither can I" across the back. Damn if she wasn't rocking it, though. Men were stacked three deep at her end of the bar, and they were all vying for her attention. She'd emptied her tip jar more than once.

Nickelback came across the sound system, the beat hard and fast. One of the men closest to her held a folded benjamin between his fingers and motioned her forward. Griff read the word "dance" on his lips.

She grinned, shook her head and turned away.

The guy didn't take no for an answer. Instead, he lunged forward and grabbed the back pocket on her shorts.

Griff came off the wall with a snarl, intent on ending the contact by whatever means necessary. He hoped the means involved force. Lots and lots of force. No one else had the right to touch her.

He stumbled to a stop, shock making him lightheaded. Jealousy hadn't ever been his gig, so what the hell was this little pissing contest about? He blinked several times and refocused on Bailey.

She rounded on the customer, grabbed him by the shirt and stared him down before nimbly plucking the hundred-dollar bill from his fingers. The guy's face lit up before giving way to confusion when she crawled up on the bar. Springing to her feet, she started down the bar top with the same hip-rolling gait that had lured Griff into innumerable fantasies. She pulled the pins from her hair. A fast, loose roll of her head flung the loosely curling mane out and around. Then she began to move in ways that were surely illegal.

He couldn't call it dancing because dancing wasn't inherently carnal. What she was doing? It could turn saint to sinner and make him grateful for the lick of hell's flames. She stalk-walked down the bar with exaggerated steps. Men stared at her, open lust decorating their slack-jawed pusses. She was the incarnation of every male fantasy. The way she moved to the music would be burned into their tiny brains and there would, no doubt, be a YouTube video.

Griff growled. Starting tomorrow, cell phones were banned inside the club.

Every few feet she'd stop to grab a beer and toss it to a customer or catch a bottle to pour a shot into an open mouth. Then she turned toward the beer taps and bent forward to pull a draft. Ass out. The crowd came off the chain. Keith and Seth were emptying the tip jars as fast as they could, finally resorting to dumping them into the laundry bin just to keep up.

The guy who'd proffered the cash that got her up there made a grab for her ankle as she passed. Someone yanked him backward and he disappeared under a barrage of fists and shouted curses. Bailey winked and traced her upper lip with the tip of her tongue. A shout went up. Male-fueled sex hung heavy on the air.

Acid churned in Griff's stomach.

The song wound down. Bailey took a bow and blew kisses amid shouted requests for an immediate encore, offers to buy her everything from drinks to diamonds and even proposals of marriage. She laughed it all off before leaping to the floor, high color staining her cheeks.

Her legs wobbled on impact, folding beneath her. Hands out, she managed to break the fall and keep her face off the floor. Bravado she'd worn only moments before fell away. Fresh panic replaced it.

Shouted obscenities and threats flooded the human wake Griff created as he plowed through the crowd. Flipping up the pass-through, he charged toward Bailey.

Seth, who was closest, scooped her up and started for the end of the bartenders' galley.

People on the other side of the bar suddenly realized something was wrong. Yet the music still rocked. Rapidly volleyed questions formed an indecipherable buzz. Laughter rang out somewhere beyond the first three or four rows of onlookers. The party carried on.

Griff met Seth halfway down the chute.

The man gave Bailey over without hesitation. "Help her."

"Plan to." Griff pivoted and started for the private hallway. He tried to ignore the way her scent wrapped around him with proprietary intimacy, the way she shifted toward him without hesitation, the way cradling her in his arms touched the void in him. He clenched his jaw so hard his molars ached. The last thing he needed was some ridiculous, albeit temporary, complication, but that was exactly what this was turning into.

I'll cut her loose as soon as this is over.

He couldn't bring himself to look down.

Loping strides carried him beyond the pass-through and into the crowd. A hard hand landed on his forearm and tightened. Momentary confusion interrupted his mental ranting. He looked back.

The man's face was familiar in that Griff had seen him

tossing money at Bailey. Beyond that, the guy was a complete stranger.

Griff's arms tightened around Bailey. "Step aside."

"Who are you to her?" the stranger demanded.

There wasn't an easy answer. *Boss. Friend. Incubus to her succubus. Lover.* "Nobody special." The thump of his admission took up like a drumbeat in his chest, pounding hard enough to steal his breath.

"Why don't you hand her over? I'm a doctor. I'll look her over, take her to the E.R. if necessary." The guy held out his arms.

Griff shifted Bailey closer to his chest. Her breathing had become irregular. "I don't have time to discuss your Boy Scout badges and charity work. Out of the way. Now."

Shouldering his way through the door, he headed toward the elevator. *Screw this. No way was she going to get behind the bar again. She'd just have to stay in the apartment until she finished her Change. This was such bullshit. No way could she die—*

"Griff." Bailey's voice, sultry and rich, loosened the tangle of his thoughts.

"I'm taking you upstairs." He still couldn't bring himself to look down.

"Good."

The relief in her voice soothed him. *Why?* Examining that little nugget of curiosity would have to wait. He hit the elevator button with his elbow. The doors slid open and he stepped inside.

She turned her face into him and mumbled something against his chest.

"Couldn't understand you, Bailey." The moist heat of her sigh spun him up all over again.

"I need you."

Such a small admission, yet it frayed the edges of his composure as effectively as hemp cut by a dull razor. *Need.* He'd learned the bitter truth about the often capricious line that existed between want and need. Women wanted him. Always. No one needed him. Ever.

From the moment he'd entered his Change, he had been a means to a very pleasurable end for his lovers. He was as much a conquest to them as they were a food source to him. They were temporary fixtures, nameless faces and one-night stands that left him cold. He gave them what they wanted and they left needing nothing else from him. He took from them what he needed. Without him, they would find other lovers. Without them, parasitic thing that he was, he would die.

The years had hammered home the hard facts of his reality. He could rail against the injustice of a lonely life, but to what end? Nothing would change. That meant that whatever fantasies he might privately harbor involving Bailey, they were just that. Fantasy.

"Griff." Cool fingertips fluttered against the pulse in his neck. "Please."

That single appeal cracked the foundations of walls he'd long thought a permanent part of his makeup. He closed his eyes. *Don't let it be structurally irreparable.*

Then he silently uttered a plea of his own.

Please.

Chapter 6

The way Bailey's stomach gently flipped said the elevator had stopped. Finally. Griff's apartment lay on the other side of those doors. She willed them to open. He could end her pain once they were inside. Of course, death could too. *Not going down that road.*

Refrigerated air hit her overheated skin. She sighed. *Relief.* "Feels good in here."

"You need it colder?"

"Not right now." A small moan rolled through her chest. "I can't believe I danced on the bar. The *bar*, Griff."

"It's the nature of what you are working to draw viable partners to you. The sex on the air can impair your judgment, make you a little…overenthusiastic." His fingers twitched. "You were pretty amazing, though. I had no idea you knew how to move like that."

Heat suffused her cheeks. "Neither did I."

He carrier her through the apartment and settled her on the unmade bed, his deft fingers divesting her of her shorts. "Commando? Sexy."

Struggling to keep him in focus, she attempted a smile. "You're a sucker for ass. That's all."

The pained look that flashed across his face made no sense, but she was too far gone to dig into the man's little mysteries. Her nipples ached. The wet heat of her sex burned. Muscles in her abs cramped and released in tiny, torturous contractions. Her legs scissored uncontrollably.

"Two seconds, baby." Clothes hit the floor with a soft thump. The mattress dipped as he crawled up. "What do you need?"

She didn't think before answering. "You."

Griff froze. "What do you need *from* me?"

It was so clear, this distance he kept between them. Boundaries. Seemingly unbreakable boundaries. He continued to redefine them with hard lines and harder words every time she exposed any emotional vulnerability. How could she explain that it wasn't just his body she was interested in? Bodies were a dime a dozen on the dance floor. But he, *he* was different.

Her eyes fluttered closed. *Screw it.* "Just you, Griff."

Instead of words, his response came in the form of hot lips moving over the sensitive skin inside her knee. Heated breath blew over the path his tactile tongue traced. Progress took him up the inside of her thigh.

A shuddering sigh escaped her when his mouth reached her core. "That'll work just fine."

He chuckled. "It's somewhere to start anyway. We haven't been able to really enjoy the dance until now."

Foreplay. They hadn't had that luxury tonight. As bad as she was hurting now, she didn't know how long she'd last. Anything was better than nothing, though.

He traced the juncture of her thighs, exploring and tasting. Then he flicked her clit.

Her hips rocked forward at the same time she cried out.

Griff wrapped his arms around her thighs, holding her in place. "You're so prime, baby." He nibbled, licked and sucked until she pled for release.

Bowing off the bed, she blindly reached for his head and wound her fingers through his hair. She ground against his mouth as he worked her. His tongue delved deep before moving up to lazily circle that bundle of nerves. A deft pull from his lips would send her over the edge. She moved beneath his hands, encouraging, guiding, silently pleading.

He slid a finger inside her and crooked it, stroking her G-spot with deft movements.

Bailey bit her lip to silence her cries. Pleasure built in intense waves, pulsing through her with every heartbeat. She let go of his hair to fist the sheets. The pressure in her pelvis was too much. "Griff." His name was an invocation uttered with raw desperation.

Then he drew her clit into his mouth and sucked.

Silence be damned. She screamed as the orgasm crashed through her. Control lost, she reveled in the almost electric shocks that traveled through her body as his teeth grazed the tiny bud, the way his heavy breaths skated across skin slicked with arousal, how thoroughly she fractured in his embrace.

Safe. She was safe here in his arms. He wouldn't let her die.

Bailey lay boneless as Griff brought her down from the precipice. The pain wasn't completely resolved, but she also wasn't as desperate as she'd been. Momentarily sated, she smiled when he prowled up her body and paused over her.

He arched a brow. "Better?"

She considered his face. His studied indifference was *too* perfect. There was something behind the facade, something he didn't want her to see. The longer she stared, the more aloof his gaze grew.

"You're thinking too hard, Bailey."

She lifted one shoulder. The urge to pull the traditional female "What are you thinking?" thing ate at her. No way was she that woman—never had been, never would be. Still, she wanted him to see her as more than this, this approximation of a bed partner caught between obligation and desire.

"Would you have ever chosen me?" The blurted question was out and irretrievable before she had the chance to stop herself. *Great. I'm like an emotional Taser. Take him down with one shot, sit on his chest while he pisses himself and then ask the hard questions while he's scrambled.* Her impulse-driven, emotionally needy, come-across-as-desperate-why-don't-you speech center should be surgically removed.

He looked away. Rolling to his side, he grabbed the remote for the room's lights and absently draped one heavy leg across her nearest thigh. "The pain any better?"

Physically? "Some." *Otherwise? I think we're just getting started ripping me apart.*

The muscles in his jaw and throat worked. "You've got to feed, baby. When I come, you've got to let your walls down and pull on my body's *prana.*"

"I assume the 'when I come' means we aren't done." She fought the urge to haul the covers up to her neck. "And what's *prana*, and how am I supposed to feed off of it?"

"We're not done until you've survived your Change. And *prana* is literally the body's life force."

We're not done until you've survived your Change. Well,

hell. If that didn't kick her out of the emotional bog sucking her down, nothing would. The clear expiration date on
this little affair was undefined yet imminent. She blinked
rapidly. Drawing a breath hurt. Creating distance this very
second became critical. But how? *Focus on the prana issue.*
"You're telling me that, to survive, I have to screw men and
suck on their life force."

Griff closed his eyes. His nostrils pinched and lips
thinned. Whatever he'd been about to say got locked down
hard and fast. When he finally looked at her, his eyes were
flat. "Members of our demon class lose *prana* every day.
It's what makes us sexually irresistible to the norms. They
see us as young and vital and sexual. Until the Change,
prana burns off slowly enough that the body can regenerate it without consequence. Then the pre-Change crash happens, and all your body functions get out of sync. Orgasm
will rejuvenate and realign you, but it's temporary—like
eating lunch and expecting to not be hungry come dinner."

She swiveled toward Griff, eyes wide. "You're compar-
ing my need to suck the life force out of someone to a freaking pizza buffet?"

He glared at her. "Your *prana* is dangerously low, which
is why you currently feel so bad. The energy that keeps your
body in sync and your organs functioning is dwindling. If
you don't feed, you're going to go from feeling like death
to praying for it. The feeling will continue until your heart
stops. Then it's game over."

Chills wracked her even though she was burning up. "I
can't drain men of their…whatever."

"*Prana*, Bailey. And yes, you can. Why do you think
you danced on the bar? That's not your speed. Your body's
attracting the *prana* of potential lovers with the intent of

feeding off the strongest. Even if you don't want to survive by the time this is all over, your body's going to do what it has to do to pull through." Griff flopped onto his back, clenching and unclenching his jaw as he stared at the ceiling. "Trust me."

She tried to focus on something, anything, other than Griff, but every path led right back to him. If she was honest with herself, it had always been him. She could have worked any number of places, could have made more money at a different bar before Desire became the city's hotspot. But she hadn't even considered it. When she'd met Griff, that had been it. She felt then just as she felt now—that she'd found her center.

Absently running a hand over her hip, the sensitive pads of her fingers traced the unfamiliar tattoo. *Not tattoo. Marker.* Hesitation stilled her fingers and made her movements sluggish. She looked down and studied the dark circle that bled through raised and angry skin. This was bigger than her past and had everything to do with her future. Continuing to deny the truth was pointless.

She was a succubus.

Griff slid a hand behind his thigh and pinched himself hard enough to bruise. He had to stay focused. Getting Bailey to repeated physical release and encouraging her to let herself go and feed was the priority tonight. He'd see that through and then he'd cut her free and walk away.

The unfamiliar ache in his chest came back. He absently ran a hand over the smooth skin of his pecs, considering. An untold number of unremarkable nights flashed through his mind, every bed partner faceless and interchangeable. Over the past three years, the only thing his one-night stands had

in common was that he'd wished each of the women in his
bed were someone else.

Bailey.

She'd asked if he would he have chosen her. He had. A
thousand times. But his species, being what they were, had
prevented him from inviting her into his life because he
couldn't have invited her into his bed. Incubi didn't differ-
entiate between "good touch" and "bad touch." Their touch
went straight from bad to deadly. More than one woman
had lost her life when he'd waited too long to feed, devolv-
ing into a frenzied bed partner with no stop button, pulling more *prana* from her than she could regenerate. Bailey
would have been relegated to a single, unsatisfying experience, then forced to watch him take a different woman every
night thereafter. She deserved more than that.

*But isn't that what you're doing now? You're just couch-
ing it on her Change.*

Rolling onto his back, he hooked his arm over his head
and stared at the ceiling.

Can't even be honest with myself. Truth, then. Helping
her through this hadn't been an entirely altruistic move.
He needed the opportunity to get her out of his system, get
past this…this…*thing* he had for her and finally move on.

The mattress shifted. He glanced over to find Bailey sitting on the side of the bed. "Problem?"

"This whole thing is a problem." Bitterness tinged her
words, acrid and unnatural.

Hands fisted in frustration, Griff didn't know whether to
reach out to her, speak but not reach out, or hang back and
wait. *Dammit.* Offering comfort wasn't a skill listed on his
personal or professional résumé. Maybe he should just sug-
gest they play a quick game of Twister—keep things sim-

ple. The body parts you had to move were labeled. They'd touch because it was inevitable, and things would go from there. Nowhere in the rules or in the spin of the wheel did the game require players to put their hearts out there only to have them crushed when people crashed. And they *always* crashed.

Her chin dipped forward. "How long does it take?"

"Huh?"

"The Change. How long?" Her arms snaked around her middle.

"Oh. Should be over by tomorrow. But you have to feed. Otherwise? This is pointless."

Her fingernails dug deep into bare skin when she flinched. "Is it that simple to you?"

"It's life or death. Doesn't get much simpler." Silence met his frank assessment. His brow creased. Her fingernails were buried so deep in her skin he was afraid she was going to draw blood. He reached for her. She visibly sagged, startling him into a hasty retreat before he touched her. Her shoulders hunched in a torpid, defeated way that left Griff struggling to form an apology. "Look, I'm not trying to be an ass."

An indelicate snort preceded a minute shake of her head. "You regularly inspire the troops with these brilliant speeches?"

Irritation pricked his pride, swift and sharp. "Cut me a little slack here. I'm doing the best I can."

"Sorry."

"Don't apologize. Just realize shooting the messenger isn't going to get you out of this." He rubbed his forehead. "You've got to at least try to feed."

"Why do I have to have sex to feed?"

"Not just sex. You have to orgasm and so does your partner. Your have to free your instinct to find and feed from your partner's *prana*." The image of her in a stranger's arms made his next words terse. "You have to let go and find a certain level of release to initially loose the instinct to feed during your Change. After that? It's not a conscious decision. Your body will do it naturally during orgasm."

She turned her head just enough to rest her chin on her shoulder. Her eyes focused on some invisible spot in the distance between them. "So that's it, huh? Let go so what I am can take over."

"Pretty much."

"Do you feed every time you come?"

"It isn't something you can control."

"So you do."

The words were soft, not accusatory, but he still felt their impact like well-placed blows. "I told you before—your body will do what it has to in order to survive. It's how we're programmed."

Her gaze jumped to his. "I'm more than this, Griff. I might be a… It might be *what* I am. It'll never be *who* I am, though. Never."

He'd thought the same thing. Early on, anyway. Rolling, he swung his legs over the edge and planted his feet on the floor before lacing his hands behind his neck. Time and experience, the most merciless of teachers, had proved both ruthless and thorough in his education. It had been experience that ultimately broke him, though. The cost had been learning to survive without missing living, and he had.

Until now.

Chapter 7

Whatever turned Bailey into the Happy Humper was winding up, the increasingly familiar need just beginning to stir. Cramps were still mild, so she had time.

"To do what?" she whispered, staring at Griff's back.

He glanced over his shoulder, nostrils flaring. "It's happening again?"

She nodded.

He turned away, head falling forward, hands dangling between his knees.

Somewhere in the apartment a clock ticked, eating up the silence one second at a time. The air conditioner kicked on with a soft rush that drowned out time's passage with innocuous white noise.

He wordlessly stood and rested his palms against the wall. Shoulders rapidly rising and falling with every sharp breath, he leaned forward and rested his forehead against the wall. "This isn't going the way it was supposed to. I can't do this."

Bailey hadn't taken her eyes off that long, strong back as he stood. Now she couldn't look away, and she wanted to. More than anything, she wanted to. "That's it, isn't it?"

"That's what?" he asked, voice flat, almost resigned.

"You're sorry you got into this." The way her voice wavered infuriated her.

She should have known, should have suspected it would end up here. He was clearly sorry he'd made the effort with her. This was the worst part of every affair. With Griff, though? The waiting was killing her. Any moment now, he would turn and look her over with such abject disappointment she'd never recover.

Moving in a nearly blind haze of mortification, she reached for her shorts with a trembling hand. *Gotta get out of here.* If she hurried, she could probably make it to the elevator before the first tear fell. What she wouldn't give for three wishes. The first would make her scathingly witty when pissed off, binding her penchant to cry when angry. The second would deal with scrubbing away her humiliation over this whole debacle. The third—

A hot, hard hand closed over her upper arm. "Bailey, listen."

Panic pulled a total drive-by and yanked her out of the driver's seat before racing off with her sanity. She rounded on him, blindly striking out.

Griff caught her fist and jerked her around. Folding her arm behind her and pressing her against the wall seemed fluid and effortless. The heavy weight of his body pinned her. His hips pressed into her ass, the heavy weight of his cock a heated brand his satin pants only emphasized.

He didn't loosen his hold when he lowered his mouth to her ear. "Want to tell me what that was about?"

Bailey's heart thrashed about in her chest like a wounded bird. She couldn't get enough air, couldn't break his hold, couldn't think. Words wouldn't come. The best she managed was a single shake of her head.

"Okay. Let's try this. Where were you going?"

The way his breath scalded the shell of her ear made her shiver. "Don't know. Thought I'd figure it out on my way down."

"There's nothing to figure out. You need to stay here."

She struggled silently against his hold. It was wasted effort in the face of his strength, but she didn't care.

"Take it easy, Bailey. I'm not going to hurt you."

But that's just it. You will. She didn't need a fortune-teller to spell it out. "I can't do this with you."

He twitched before resettling himself against her back. "I said I'd see this through, and I will."

"Let me go." Her voice broke on the last word.

He relaxed, his weight evolving from a force of nature to a reassuring comfort. "Not happening, Bailey."

Every panted breath pushed out precious oxygen she couldn't seem to recover. "Why?"

Smoothing her hair away from her face, he rested his lips against her temple. "I can't."

Can't. There was that word again. Her throat tightened. "Don't do this to me."

He eased back and turned her around.

She stared at their bare feet. Confusion joined the emotional soup that threatened to boil over.

Griff hooked a finger under her chin. "Look at me."

She forced her eyes up, the move excruciatingly slow.

His pants had shifted and now hung dangerously low on narrow hips. Well-defined obliques created a sharp, suggestive V that disappeared beneath the waistband. Soft light cast shadows across his torso's hard contours. The shallow valleys between pads and ropes of muscle created roadways of temptation she longed to leisurely travel. Heavy pecs sported hard nipples. The blades of his collarbones disappeared into shoulders rounded with muscle.

His Adam's apple bobbed when he swallowed.

It wasn't a conscious decision to reach up and trace the line of his jaw. Stubble abraded her fingertips. She stopped just shy of his chin. Lips, full and firm, distracted her so much that she didn't see him reach for her hand, only felt him gently press her fingertips more firmly against his skin.

She closed her eyes and fought for calm before forcing herself to meet his gaze again.

Brutal honesty rested there, cushioned firmly between sexual heat and undisguised craving. "I'm not going to let you die, and if you walk out of here? That's what's going to happen."

She looked away. "You don't owe me anything."

Letting go of her fingers, he grasped her chin and turned her face to his. "I gave you my word."

"Which makes me a charity case."

His eyes narrowed. "You know better than that."

"Do I? You've made this all about obligation and keeping your word."

"I'm a notoriously bad communicator." He leaned in and pressed a tender kiss to her forehead. "Let me make it up to you, show you just how much I…" Closing his eyes, he leaned in.

Her heart stopped.

He turned aside and rested his cheek against hers. Voice slightly hoarse, he said, "Come back to bed, Bailey."

Her breath escaped in a shaky rush.

"I want you here. With me."

The words were so close to what she needed to hear. But was close good enough? "Griff—"

He slid a hand down her arm, stopping when he reached her hand.

Her fingers laced through his.

A gentle squeeze offered silent encouragement.

Words were pointless. She knew she'd stay. The decision had been made when he first touched her in his office. Wanting him had been a familiar feeling for so long. Now she was here, in his arms and in his bed.

She tightened her fingers around his and let herself fall into the moment.

"I won't do anything you don't want me to."

Then don't break my heart.

Griff led Bailey toward the bedroom. *Too close.* She'd intended to leave him. The thought made his lungs seize. Air became a temporarily irretrievable, priceless commodity. That wasn't what made his pulse thunder and black spots dance across his vision, though. He rubbed his forehead, wondered briefly if he might pass out. All because he'd almost broken his own rule and kissed her.

She tugged at his hand when he continued through the bedroom. "Where are we going?"

"Bathroom."

He didn't pay any attention to the heated travertine floors, copper soaking tub or dark, exotic wood vanities. Nice, but they'd been the interior designer's choices. The shower, though? That was all his doing. A thick glass face revealed a generous teak bench along the far wall. Multiple shower-heads sprouted from the walls and ceiling. Brushed chrome finishes glinted under recessed overhead lights. The pebbled floor lent the space an organic feel.

Griff let Bailey go long enough to engage the digital control panel, selecting the showerheads he wanted before programming the water temperature. Then he slipped his pants off, squared his shoulders and reached for her.

She stepped into his embrace with unfamiliar surety, as if what had happened between them had resolved any lingering hesitations. There was trust in her actions. The realization rocked him, triggering the strangest sensation— a fluttering awareness, soft but persistent. *Look at me*, it seemed to say. But he couldn't, instead squashing it with the boot heel of his determination to manage things better. He'd deal with any consequences later.

The heavy glass door made no sound as he swung it open. "Hop in. The water temp can be adjusted using the sister control panel on that wall."

Bailey moved into the shower, her long, dark hair curling loosely down her back. "I'm sure it'll be fine."

He stepped in behind her. Hot water sluiced over his chest. The familiar smell of his soap was an unlikely anchor in the bog of confusion surrounding him.

Her arms came around his waist.

His abs tightened as he sucked in a hard, fast breath. It was the first time she'd reached for him. Anticipation settled in his pelvis, a hot and heavy weight. He closed his eyes when her hands began to roam the contours of his body. How long had it been since he'd allowed himself to get lost in someone's touch?

The heat of her body molding itself along his back interrupted his thoughts.

He reached behind and gripped her hips. Soft breath

skated along his shoulder blades just ahead of the whisper of lips over his skin. "Bailey—"

"Sh." She ran her tongue down the column of his spine. "Take your own advice, Griff. Just feel."

He wanted to tell her that it had been bad advice, that he'd lost that ability a long time ago, but her mouth was doing invisibly wicked things that scrambled his thoughts. And her hands? They were the perfect combination of soft caresses and scraping nails.

She moved lower, tracing a path down his front that her mouth mirrored on his back. The tip of her tongue found the hollow at the base of his spine, tracing the shallow dip before she blew cool air over heated, damp skin.

Griff couldn't think. Everything he wanted to say and do dissolved in a riptide of sensation. She pulled him down one languorous moment at a time.

"Turn around." Her husky command hardly registered in his haze of desire.

The gentle direction of her hands was all that got him moving.

She sucked his cock in without warning, taking him deep enough that the head bumped the back of her throat.

His shout echoed off glass and stone. Nails dug into his ass and encouraged him to thrust into her mouth every time she descended his length. He slapped a palm against the wall. Fed his other hand through her hair. She groaned her approval. When she slid one hand between his legs and massaged the hard ridge behind his sac, he forgot to breathe.

His head fell back. Every fantasy he'd had of this moment paled in the face of reality. The way her tongue cupped him one moment and teased his corona the next dissolved his ability to form cohesive thoughts. Breathing turned into a shaky, shallow affair.

She slowed the pace, shifting to gently massage his balls. Then she undid him. Wrapping her hand around his root, she slid down his length. And didn't stop. Took him deep. So deep he felt her throat spasm around him.

Release rushed him with more testosterone-driven force than a pro linebacker on Monday night. The magnificent burn of forewarning didn't build. It shot down the base of his spine. There was no stopping it, though. Pleasure followed close on pain's heels, pulsing through his cock and making the ache a sweet misery. So close. He was so close.

Fist tightening in her hair, he managed to growl, "I'm going to come."

Her only response was to take him in again.

"Bailey, if you don't stop…if you don't stop I'm not going to be able to…" Her finger breeched the outer ring of his ass, pressing in gently until she brushed his prostate. Then she flexed against the gland.

The orgasm hit so hard that Griff's eyes rolled back in his head. Bailey drew him deep. A strangled plea left his lips. He let go of her hair to cup her head. And then, hips pumping involuntarily, he gave himself over to the moment. His thighs shook, and his knees bent. He couldn't hear anything but the sound of his own heartbeat thundering against his eardrums like a Southern summer storm.

A strange pull in his pelvis made his eyes flutter open as his body came back online one function at a time. The realization of what had just happened drove him to his knees.

Bailey cupped his face in her hands. "Griff?"

He stared at her, mute. It didn't matter that he spoke six languages. He couldn't have strung together the simplest of phrases if he'd had a gun at his temple. For the first time in his life, he'd achieved an orgasm without getting his partner off. Which meant he hadn't fed. He'd been seduced, had found pleasure for pleasure's sake. *How? And what did it mean?*

"Say something," she pleaded, tracing his lower lip with her thumb.

Water cascaded over him like some kind of blessed benediction and he closed his eyes. Her soft touch stole his breath. What came out of his mouth made sense. It was the depth of emotion, of feelings long dormant in frozen ground that stunned him.

All he could manage was a broken, "Thank you."

Bailey stared at Griff, confused. His words were simple, yet not. The rich emotion seemed over the top. "You're… welcome." She had a hard time not making it a question.

His eyes opened slowly, boring into her with breath-stealing intensity. "Your turn."

"I didn't realize it was about turns," she quipped.

A slow, sensual smile spread across Griff's face. "Baby, it's not. But after that?" He paused and, for just a moment, the facade fell away.

The raw glimpse into him stole her breath. Primal and undiluted, his expression relayed hope and hurt, desire and loneliness, longing and resignation. She'd known, *known*, there was so much more to him than he'd ever let anyone see, yet nothing could have prepared her for the truth. Her heart ached, recognizing each piece of him. He was suddenly a puzzle she'd solved by adding her own pieces to the mix. And wasn't that the terrifying part? What she'd been looking for her whole life had been right here all along.

She moved into him, cautious not to convey her desperation. They weren't only what happened in this moment. Physical connection mattered. Pleasure shared provided what she needed. But they were so much more than this, could offer each other something so much greater.

Arms around his waist, she rested her head against his chest. "Give me a second."

He wrapped her in his embrace with a tentativeness that translated through unsure hands, trembling touches and an overwhelming sense of trepidation.

"I won't bite."

"You sure about that?" His voice rumbled beneath her ear.

She nodded, cheek to smooth chest.

They held each other so carefully, their silence acknowledging that whatever had passed between them was as fragile as spun sugar. Time moved around them like the rush and retreat of the ocean to the shore—unyielding when facing the magnitude that came with self-realization.

Pain drove into Bailey's pelvis with extreme prejudice, ripping her out of Griff's hold. Mouth gaping as she fought for air, she clutched her belly. A second assault doubled her over.

Strong hands grabbed her shoulders. "Bailey?"

She couldn't manage more than a single shake of her head. Her vision wavered. It hadn't ever hurt this bad. Surviving the Change would be impossible if this got much worse. She couldn't take much more. A tear rolled down her nose. Hung there. Seeing it fail to hold on and fall felt so permanent. She closed her eyes.

"Time to feed, sweetheart." Capable arms scooped her up.

Cold air whispered over her skin. Goose bumps rose. "I don't know how."

"Trust me."

Could she bridge the last of the distance that existed between self-preservation and true trust? The answer she needed didn't present itself before the next influx of pain.

Silky sheets scraped over-stimulated skin as he settled her on his bed. She rolled onto her side as she writhed, driven half by insanity and half by clear choice. The affirmation the external pain afforded meant she was alive.

"You ready to give this a try?"

"Please." The breathy answer hardly passed through her lips before Griff slid in behind her.

He nudged her top leg forward, curling his hand under her knee and lifting. The blunt head of his cock stroked the swollen seam of her sex.

She groaned and tried to push down.

"Uh-uh. Let go. Feel. Trust me." Hooking her leg over his hips, he rocked forward at the same time he stroked two fingers down either side of her clit.

"Please." *Had she spoken aloud, or was it all in her head?* The width of his thick erection stretching her walls was absolute agony. She wanted it fast and hard. Craved near violence. Release had to happen. Soon. No doubt her mind was fracturing under pain's relentless onslaught. This position didn't give her the freedom to move, though. She had to rely on Griff to give her what she needed. "Bastard."

He fed his length into her with studied control until the very end. Then he thrust forward, hard. "You undo me." Pulling out, he eased back in, repeating the motion again and again until her walls relaxed. The rhythm he set began with long, slow strokes that fanned the flames of her hunger like well-placed bellows. He pulled his fingers away from her clit. Dug fingers into her thigh. Lifting her leg higher limited her movement even more.

She was at his mercy. Forced to cede control. The idea caused her heart to skip a thunderous beat. *Cede control.* The idea of being so bare to him terrified her. A lifetime spent fighting to survive had taught her to hide, maintain control. And above all? Trust no one.

"Stop...thinking," he grunted. A hard thrust ground their pelvis bones together and wiped her mind clear of anything but the now. "That's my girl."

The luscious tightening of her sheath said she'd find release.

Griff hooked his arm under her leg and reached for her wrist. His grip gave him more leverage.

She arched her back to give him better access.

He pounded into her, unleashing the violence she craved.

Then her heart skipped another beat. Eyes unnaturally heavy, she forced them open and tried to focus. The sounds of sex become as one-dimensional as her sight. She tried to draw a deep breath but only managed a short, hard gasp. The orgasm that had been imminent rolled over her, soft and soothing. Her body tightened around Griff's cock. Her womb pulsed. His shout resonated against her back. The normally hard pulse of his orgasm didn't register. She tried to smell Griff's arousal. *Nothing.*

Her heart skipped twice. *Boom.* Skipped three times. *Boom.* She never would have imagined an absent heartbeat would be so loud.

Drifting, Bailey realized she didn't hurt. Had she fed? Somehow she didn't think so. This felt much bigger than anything she'd ever experienced before. She closed her eyes.

When her breath shuddered out and she didn't feel the need to draw another, she knew.

She knew.

Chapter 8

Griff's arms tightened around Bailey when she went bone-less against him. It wasn't lost on him that he was walking the very fine line of letting this get too personal. He rested his forehead against her neck. Breaking things off wouldn't be easy, but "The Talk" probably needed to happen now, before either of them went too far down this road. Emotional complications aside, they couldn't feed from one another every night without destroying both themselves and each other.

He absently pressed his lips to her shoulder, jerking back when he realized what he'd done. Maybe somebody needed to have "The Talk" with *him*. *What a joke.* He untangled himself before rolling onto his back. If he gave her his whole spiel now it might stop her from feeding. Not happening. *Though it was possible she already had.* One way to find out. He rested a hand on her hip and gave a gentle shake. "Did you feed?"

No answer.

He shook her harder. "Bailey?"

Nothing.

Had she passed out? Griff rose on his elbow and leaned forward. Her eyes were closed, long lashes brushing her skin.

"Angels' kisses," he whispered.

The way her lips were parted gave her a lush, well-loved look. Except...

His brows winged down. The slight blue tinge around her mouth rocketed his heart into his throat. "Bailey!" He scrambled to his knees and rolled her over with jerky motions.

Her limbs moved with a fluid otherworldliness.

"No. No, no, no." Hauling her into his arms, he laid her out on the floor and reached for the phone. "She's coded," he shouted when Seth answered. "Help me." He tossed the receiver. "Think." But he couldn't. Panic flooded his mind with infinite, fast-moving snapshots of her over the past three years—the kid she'd been when she applied, the woman she'd become, the stubborn jut of her chin when angered, the sultry way she moved, her lopsided smile, the way she'd looked at him in the shower. Thousands of things he might have said choked him. "Don't you fucking die." The hoarse command was the best he could do.

Seth materialized at Griff's side. "How long?"

"A couple minutes at the most."

"Shit." He tossed the bag away. "Compressions or breaths?"

Griff just looked at him.

"Compression or breaths!"

"Breaths."

"Then do it."

Griff tilted her head back and hesitated.

"Do it," Seth snarled.

The cold from her lips was a shock. A riot of emotion threatened to drown Griff as he tilted her head back and checked her airway. Sealed his mouth over hers. Pinched her nose and exhaled. He counted the rise and fall of each breath by rote. Then he broke away and hovered, ready to begin again.

Seth took up swift chest compressions.

Air brushed Griff's lips, a result of Seth's efforts. Nothing more. His fingers drifted down her throat to rest over her carotid artery. Each compression resulted in a faint bump against his fingertips. He closed his eyes. This wasn't happening. Not really. Couldn't be.

"Get ready to breathe," Seth ordered. "Now."

Griff silently willed everything he had into each exhale. *Come back to me.* Counting down to the last breath, he broke the connection.

Seth numbered every hand-to-heart compression he made. "Go."

Again, Griff breathed. He stroked her pulse point and ignored the invisible vice tightening around his chest. It had been more than three minutes. They were running out of time.

A small, telltale beat thrummed beneath her skin, faint and sporadic but undeniably there.

Griff jerked back, eyes wide. "I've got a pulse."

Seth's shoulders sagged. "We need to get her to a hospital."

"She'll die." He couldn't look away from her.

"Man, she just di—"

"She hasn't fed."

Seth whistled low. "How long's she got?"

"Not long." Demons he knew he couldn't quell lurked in his eyes. "Her best chance is here."

"Do what you can, brother." Seth stood, brushing at his pants. "Call me and, uh, let me know if…"

"Yeah."

Seth disappeared. No theatrics, no flames, no Disney dance moves. Just a wisp of smoke where the genie had been standing.

Griff gathered Bailey in his arms, focused solely on the pulse that beat in her throat. He nearly dropped her when she spoke.

"Hey." She looked up at him through slit lids, eyes not quite tracking.

"Hey, yourself," he said on little more than a whisper.

She raised a shaky hand to her chest, her brow wrinkling. "I think I feel worse."

"You should. Seth just spent the last few minutes coaxing your heart back online." He looked away, jaw clenched.

"I died." A statement, not a question.

Griff didn't respond, instead settling her on the bed and kneeling at her side. He would have had better luck changing Earth's polarity than preventing himself from running his hands over her. *Proof she's right there.*

Stretching out beside her, he rested a hand between her breasts and openly stared. Her heart beat slow and steady. Sentiment he'd learned to mercilessly suppress crept in. But here he laid, staring at the only woman ever to make him falter, hesitate, wonder. He closed his eyes on a heavy sigh. This had crossed the line into way too complicated.

The faint touch made his eyes flash wide.

Hand over his, Bailey watched him with the most curious

expression. Then he recognized it. She was looking through the bullshit walls he put up and seeing *him*.

The urge to hide, to cover himself, to make excuses for what she might see, made him crazed. He said the only thing he could think of in the face of that brutal awareness. "You'll feed, Bailey. Understand me?" In direct opposition to his tone, Griff tenderly stroked her hair away from her forehead. "Understand?" While softer this time, the command was no less intense.

She nodded and opened her arms.

Drowning in a sea of long-forsaken sensations, he sank into her embrace.

Bailey languidly ran her hands over Griff's body, shifting as he settled between her thighs. Warm sunlight tipped over the windowsills. She turned and watched as it spilled across the room, gilding the man in her arms. *Morning.* For better or worse, her Change was almost over.

Griff's large hand turned her face back to his. "You look at me, Bailey. Only me." She tried to rest her cheek in his palm, but he gently grasped her chin and forced her gaze back to his. "Only me. Understand?"

"Yeah." It would cost her, though whether she would pay out in the currency of joy or tears wasn't clear. It didn't matter. The things that mattered most came with the highest costs and, consequently, the highest risks. This mattered most. "Love me, Griff."

"I…" He looked away. "Find a way to let go, Bailey. If you don't, I'm going to kill you." He snorted, the look on his face nearly panicked. "Again."

She pressed her fingers to his lips and shook her head. "If this doesn't work—"

He jerked his chin away. "Don't." What should have been an authoritative command came out broken.

"Hey." The first wave of nausea rolled through her. "I need you, Griff."

"Yeah." He shifted his gaze back to hers. "Stick with me."

She reached between them, stroking his semi-hard erection with strong fingers. He gently rocked into her touch.

His eyes grew languid.

Sex hung heavy on the air.

Heavy and turgid, his cock kicked in her hand. She rubbed her thumb through the bead of moisture that slicked the broad head. Dragging her fingers down to the root, she reached low to cup his balls. They drew up tight at her caress. His abs clenched when she gripped his shaft again, thrilling her. Thick cords of muscle stood out in arms that trembled beneath her touch.

He looked down at her, eyes wide, pupils dilated. "I want you."

Bailey leaned forward and gently took his nipple between her teeth, flicking her tongue over the hard point. His hiss of pleasure snaked around her.

Pain lanced through her middle. She fell back and fought not to fold in on herself. The empty ache in her womb burned. Her sex throbbed.

Griff kissed the tiny divot beneath her ear. "Let me in, Bailey."

Her sob was saturated with everything she couldn't say. *Take me. Stop the pain. Help me. Don't let me die. Love me.*

He answered wordlessly, guiding his thick erection to her opening.

She pushed her hips toward him as he worked his way in.

Arousal spread from her center. Her nipples pearled. Sensual hunger masked the pain.

He bent low and bit the soft area between neck and shoulder.

Her throaty, wordless approval was interrupted by pain's renewed assault.

Cupping the back of her head, he buried his face in her neck when she arched off the bed and cried out.

Agony. This was what it felt like to be courted by Death. She wanted Griff to push her, to break down the walls that held her back, force her to totally let go and give him all of her. Hell, she needed him to make this happen.

He undulated his hips in a way that started somewhere below the knees and ended around his shoulders.

She gasped and dug her nails into his back.

He did it again. Then he rose up and looked at her.

The unfiltered depth in his gaze drew her in, pulled her under, held her there until she couldn't breathe.

Griff dipped his chin and looked away.

She cradled his face in her hands.

Slipping a hand between them, he stroked her clit with his thumb.

The heavy veil of pleasure didn't lessen the sting of his withdrawal. "Griff." Still cradling his face, she watched him. The way the light played across his body. His unrepentant joy in giving and receiving pleasure. How he closed his eyes to try and rein in the fundamental truths in his stare. That, no matter how hard he had tried to hide, she'd seen him.

Something huge rose in her.

Griff's eyes widened.

A near-brutal storm of base desire crashed into them. He

pounded into her, driving her into the mattress with every down stroke, slave to a sybaritic response neither of them could control.

She clung to him, met his every thrust with violence of her own. Her nails scored his arms.

He pulled out and flipped her over, hauling her hips off the bed before she could protest. "Let me hear you, baby." Teeth sank into her shoulder when he covered her.

She shouted, rocked forward when he buried his cock to the hilt in one hard move. Heat roared through her, intense and primal. Her sheath clamped down on Griff's cock as she charged toward release. All she could think was that she was going to come apart if she couldn't find an anchor. She blindly reached for him.

He met her halfway, grasping her hand and twining their fingers together.

That simple connection blew the walls off whatever prison had trapped her instinct. It rushed out, seeking what she needed to survive. The impact with Griff's essence was so violent it should have, in her estimation, set off regional seismographs.

His grip tightened with bone-crushing force. He faltered. Then he buried his shaft to the hilt and cried out.

She'd been on the cusp of coming apart at the seams. His orgasm sent her careening over the edge. It was what he'd shouted out that sent her heart into the most unbelievable free-fall, though.

Lost in the moment, Griff had called her name.

Chapter 9

The way Griff's heart hammered he had to wonder if a heart attack could kill him, immortal or not. He knew he was smothering her but couldn't bring himself to move. Maybe in a minute. Or ninety. The exchange of life forces had been a total surprise. He'd come away from the experience absolutely energized. At least he *would* be energized—once his heart got off the short track and he could tone it down.

"Geroff." The two words ran together thanks to the way her face was smashed into a pillow.

He flopped over, one arm flung above his head and his legs sprawled out. "You okay?"

She whuffed and blew the hair off her forehead. "Think so."

"How's the pain?"

A catlike stretch preceded her answer. "Pretty much gone."

"Pretty much?" Amusement colored his tone.

"Let it go, lover boy." She rolled onto her side and curled an arm under her head. "Thanks."

He ran a hand through his hair, gripping it at the crown and giving a couple of sharp yanks. That increasingly familiar discomfort settled in his chest. "Yeah. Okay." Her indelicate snort made him glance over. "What?"

"Yeah? Okay?" She shook her head. "Never mind." Rolling onto her back, she stared at the ceiling. "Can I ask you something?"

His stomach cramped. "I guess."

She absently ran her fingernail along the seam of the sheet, shooting him a brief look. "How did you know I wouldn't kill you? When I fed off you, I mean."

Griff closed his eyes. "I didn't."

"I can't believe you would—"

"Leave it alone, Bailey," he bit out. It didn't stop her from drawing in a breath that heralded an argument. He looked over and glared, stopping her before she got started. "I mean it." He let his head roll back before dropping an arm over his face.

Silence settled between them, awkward and charged.

This, *this* was why he didn't do relationships. Ever. It always came down to moments like this. One party ended up wounded and the other was caught backpedaling. There was no parity, no real partnership. It was just an emotional seesaw in perpetual motion. Thinking he could direct the outcome of this little encounter, however brief, had been the ultimate act of hubris. Bailey wasn't—hadn't ever been—controllable. *So stupid.*

The bed moved.

He didn't open his eyes. She'd get up and leave on her own, or she'd force his hand. His stomach bottomed out. Bile burned the back of his throat, and he swallowed convulsively.

The truth of who he was or what he'd become hadn't changed because of this encounter. It only meant it was time to shore up his defenses. He didn't want to think about how many cracks there were or he'd be tempted to find a mason who could repair his emotions. Instead, he closed his eyes and forced himself to center, slowed his respirations and relaxed one body part at a time, all while pretending she didn't exist. Rolling over, he put her at his back.

Sleep slipped in, weighing him down so that, when the abyss opened, he fell into it willingly.

Griff lunged forward, fully awake. He propped his forearms over bent knees. His head hung low. Confusion saturated his thoughts, casting them in a vague, watery light. Sweat dotted his temples. His chest heaved. Adrenaline screamed through him. His muscles twitched. *Just a dream.* He rubbed his forehead, trying to remember details. Something had been chasing him across a plowed field that seemed endless. He'd fought for distance, desperate to get away. Knew that if he turned and faced what pursued him, he'd lose himself. Had to keep it at his back. Soft dirt closed over his ankles and pulled him deeper with every step.

Rubbing his bare feet against the sheets, he swore he could still feel the grit. *What the hell had that been about?*

The mattress moved.

He hadn't.

Hazy thoughts that bled together only moments before now separated like spilled mercury, each scattered sphere a well-formed memory. He held his breath and shifted his gaze.

A slender foot, pale and feminine, peeked out of the covers near the end of the bed. He tried and failed to work up enough spit to swallow. He canted his head. A dark mass of hair came into view. Followed by long, pale limbs. *Bailey. Oh, shit. He'd slept with Bailey.* He didn't *sleep* with women. Sure, he occasionally brought them here for sex, but sex wasn't sleep. Actual *sleep* was never part of the deal. Sleep meant…*sleep.* Vulnerability. Exposure. Unnecessarily awkward "see you arounds." It was bad enough he'd have to see her in the bar, but this? This was an open invitation only morons made. Which made him a capital moron.

He turned around far enough to see the bedside clock. 2:58 p.m. *Son of a bitch.* She was working the first shift this week. If she didn't get her ass downstairs in the next two hours, Friday bar prep wouldn't get done. Not an option. He'd have to wake her up.

The sudden urge to slip out of bed and disappear for a few days made him itch. It would be so easy. Seth could manage the bar while he caught a flight to the Caribbean. He'd check into a resort, do a little surfing, a little dancing and surround himself with a handful of anonymous, oiled bodies. The break would do him good. Things would be normal by the time he got back. It would be like nothing had—

"Hey." The sleepy purr of her voice wrapped around him, sensuous and inviting.

Instinct made his nostrils flare. Nothing. No sex on the air. Drawing his brows down, he chanced what should have been a quick look over his shoulder. Mistake. Epic mistake. He couldn't look away.

She'd propped herself on one elbow. The sheet pooled at the juncture of her thighs, trapped between toned legs. Sheet marks creased her skin. Her abs were drawn taught and created an impossibly long, lean torso. The way she lay exaggerated the dip of her waist and swell of her bare hip.

That wild tangle of loose curls had been swept over one shoulder. Her breasts were exposed. Dusky nipples drew tight as he took her in.

The Marker on her hip had come in, dark and well defined. She traced the circle with one finger. Her eyes never left his face.

Griff cleared his throat. "How, uh, are you—" he cleared his throat "—feeling?"

"Very alive." She bit her bottom lip and grinned, impish yet seductive.

High-def hedonistic thoughts fried his circuit boards. His body instantly became aroused, and he yanked the duvet over his lap. *Chastity cotton. A new personal low.*

Bailey's lip slid from between her teeth and her brow creased. "Griff?"

He turned away. The well of emotion he'd long thought dry began to fill. He couldn't survive this, couldn't live with the overwhelming crush that would leave him bleeding out with every new encounter.

The mattress wiggled. Air moved around him carrying the clean scent that was all her own. "Hey." She settled her hand on his bare shoulder. "Did something happen?"

Yeah. You woke up in my bed. He shrugged her off and stood, kicking free of the bedding. This would go easier if he told her…what? That he'd been weak? That he'd made a monumental mistake? That he'd known her Change was coming and had waited her out, using it to get her out of his system? That she deserved better than him? That this emotional bullshit maliciously violated one of the two rules he insisted his bed partners respect—a rule she had agreed to just last night? That he'd been an asshole for so long, now it had become a lifestyle choice he didn't want to give up? That it was safer for him this way? That he meant it? All of it? That he was sorry? So. Damn. Sorry. He rubbed his chest.

He wordlessly crossed the room and paused to lean over the dresser, bare ass hanging in the wind. It was too damn ironic to laugh over, because he was about to make good on the visual.

His throat tightened. He tried to work out the discomfort, rolling his head back and forth. Nothing helped. *Right. And you know what else won't help? Turning into a pussy.* Schooling his face into a cold mask, he peered over his shoulder with studied casualness.

The sight of her kneeling on his bed, sheet pulled over her breasts, eyes wide, pissed him off. *She had agreed.* If there was an injured party here, it sure as hell wasn't her. "You're going to need to find someone new to feed from every night for at least the first month." An internal fracture threatened to drop him where he stood. "Desire's a good place to scavenge."

Her mouth fell open at the same time she hiked the sheet higher. "Wait, what? Scavenge?"

"If you feed from the same guy more than one night, you'll kill him. If you try to wait it out? Your instinct will force your hand, find the strongest life force for you, and *then* you'll kill him. Might as well choose someone you'll enjoy." He blindly grabbed a pair of socks before shoving off the dresser and heading across the room. The image of her mouth around some stranger's... His fists clenched, but he kept going. "I'm going to grab a shower. You know how to run the elevator."

Bailey moved through a conscious fugue. Everything appeared monochromatic, sounded flat, smelled stale. Shoes dangled from numb fingers. She knew she'd dressed before leaving, but only because she'd checked on her way down. Twice. The elevator doors opened into the employee hall-way. She stood there, undecided. They slid closed. If the car started again, it would be because Griff had called for it. She frantically punched the door open button, shoving herself through the doors the second they parted.

Seth caught her as she careened off the wall. "Hey, slow down. Olympic sprint trials don't start for…"

Full-body shakes chose that moment to materialize.

"What happened?" He held her at arm's length and looked her over.

He shredded me. Truth? Yes. But it hurt too much to say. Instead, she focused on the third button down from his shirt collar and shrugged.

He pulled back, stuffing his hands in his trouser pockets. "You okay?" Genuine compassion infused his words.

She squared her shoulders and forced herself to look up. "I'm giving my two weeks notice. Officially." An aching void settled in her chest, secured by stout threads of despair. "I'll put it in writing after my shift and leave it in your box."

His eyes narrowed. "Come again?"

"I said I'm—"

"I heard you." Seth rattled the change in his pocket. "I'm going to kill him."

Bailey lifted her chin and peered at the ceiling. Tears escaped no matter how fast she blinked, trailing down her temples to disappear into her hair. "Don't." She managed a shaky smile. "I survived, didn't I?"

Tender hands cupped her face and thumbed the tears away. "Yeah. You did. And that's the most important thing."

He gently pulled her chin down a couple of inches so she faced him. "Don't quit, okay? Not yet. Give it a little time."

No doubt her smile was tremulous. "I should go." When he shook his head, she forced a brighter smile and fought to keep her voice level. "You and I both know it'll be more comfortable around here if I bow out."

"Give it two weeks. If you still want to go, I'll make sure you land on your feet." The scowl he sported would have intimidated her three years ago. Now? She recognized it for what it was. He cared.

The realization was just another blow. She'd become a part of the family. Had carved out niches in the business, behind the bar and among the employees. It had taken a lifetime, but she finally belonged. Her chest ached so badly she started to pant.

"Hey." Seth reached for her again.

"Don't." She moved out of reach. "It's good. I'm good, okay? I'll just—" Waving blindly over her shoulder, she backed toward the locker room. "I'm going to grab a shower and fresh uniform before I tackle prep."

His audible sigh said he saw right through her.

Whatever. She hit the door at a run.

Seth understood what she hadn't been able to say, that she couldn't live through watching Griff "scavenge" night after night. Just the thought of getting through the next two weeks made her sick.

The moment the door swung shut, she called out, "Anyone in here?"

No answer.

Bailey sagged against the countertop as hard sobs wracked her body. Mouth open, cries silent, she realized she'd never known a heart could truly break. She did now.

She wrapped her arms around her middle and cradled herself. No more casual untruths. No more excuses. She'd spent three years painting her desire for Griff with broad, careless strokes that never forced her to focus on the details, and there had been so many. She'd tried to ignore the dimple in his left cheek when he smiled, his generosity, the way her heart tripped in her chest when he looked at her, the errant flip of hair over his forehead and how she stopped breathing every time they touched. There had always been plenty of time for the little things, those details.

She'd been such a fool.

The dichotomy of the situation wasn't lost on her, that her last memories of him, her most *vivid* memories, were rich with those very details. But they weren't details she wanted to remember. She didn't want to recall the smell of his cologne, the taste of his skin or the sound of his voice in the dark. To recall them meant she'd miss them, and she would.

She hadn't been brave enough to examine the canvas painted with her experiences. Instead, she'd lied to herself repeatedly, had told herself that the draw was only sexual while she continued to horde the details. Somewhere along the way, she'd fallen in love with Griff. She'd known with a kind of desperate surety that the lies she'd told herself would only hold so long.

Apparently this was the moment the dam broke.

Chapter 10

Anxiety and contempt created a volatile emotional cocktail within Griff as he rode down in the elevator. His senses fired the second the doors slid open. A bass riff flirted with him. Untapped *prana* called him by name, a siren's song of promise. "And those bitches are *so* trustworthy," he muttered. Still, he moved toward the club's main floor, hands loose at his sides, his gait fluid. There was no hesitation when he hit the door.

Hot bodies crowded the dance floor. Artificial smoke twisted and twined around long legs and defined arms as people moved to the music. Tables were full. Cocktail waitresses busted ass to clear the empties, take orders and haul drinks. *Good to see their pockets full of tips.*

The current song wound down. He shot a quick hand signal to the sound booth telling the guy to keep the music hard and fast. The DJ responded with a thumbs up. A hard drumbeat got the dance floor moving again.

Griff moved through the crowd and chatted up the regulars, pocketing a couple of phone numbers. Two hours later he had personally checked out everything but the bath-

rooms. And the bar. He hated the way his stomach shrank
in on itself at the thought. "There's always the Caribbean."

A hard body materialized behind him. Hot breath and a
familiar voice skated over his ear as he turned.

"You planning on bailing again? Because, you know,
things are gettin' real. It's about time you split."

He went chest-to-chest with Seth. This close, it was easy
to see the embers buried in the black flames that were Seth's
pupils. Those embers didn't show up until the guy got righ-
teously pissed. Too bad Griff wasn't in the mood to discuss
feelings. "Nice. Eyes."

Seth smiled, cold and deadly. "Compliment me all you
want. It still won't get me in bed with you."

The crowd around them had stilled, their morbid fasci-
nation acting like some cosmically fucked up reverse ripple
effect that drew spectators in.

Griff leaned in so close his nose brushed Seth's. "Man,
you've got to stop using that as a taunt. Shit has to mean
something to me before it'll piss me off."

The other man's eyes narrowed, smile fading. "Then
you ought to be one happy motherfucker, because I haven't
found anything yet that you give a shit about."

A hard shove sent them stumbling away from each other.
Dominic, head of security and fallen angel, or Nephilim,
stepped between them, planted one plate-sized hand on each
of their chests and stiffened his arms. "Unless you want to
make this a threesome, and you guys know how much I love
threesomes, you need to take this outside."

Griff swept Dominic's arm away. "I'm good." He glanced
at Seth. "And we're done."

In typical fashion, the unflappable fallen angel arched
a brow and grinned. "Glad to hear it. I'd hate to have to

kick your ass then ask for my paycheck. Aaaawkward," he singsonged.

Seth stepped back but never took his eyes off Griff.

"We'll settle this later," Griff said through gritted teeth.

The current song abruptly cut off, and the DJ's sultry voice came over the sound system. "Looks like you guys are in for a treat tonight." Sharp whistles and a round of cheers went through the crowd. "Got a song request, sweetheart?"

Griff followed the other men's stares. He couldn't see over the sea of people from his doubled-over position, so he slowly rose to his full height. All his earlier efforts proved for naught as he found himself facing the bar.

Customers were stacked three and four deep from one end to the other. Most of them were men, and almost all were waving money. Another cheer went up, louder than before.

Like a phoenix rising from the ashes of the mundane, she unfolded. Fresh and beautiful and brutally sensual. Long legs appeared even longer in the tiny uniform shorts. Her company T-shirt had been knotted so high that the edge of her bra peeked out when she moved. That thick tangle of hair had been pinned up with…stir sticks? He snorted. Then she pulled the impromptu pins free.

He wanted to blame the breathlessness on his argument with Seth. He wanted to blame the ache in his chest on heartburn. He wanted to blame the choking emptiness in him on…on… *Shit*. He'd settle for *any* explanation, no matter how absurd. But Griff knew better. "Bailey."

He hadn't realized he'd spoken until Seth moved to stand beside him. "Hurt to look at her?"

The denial hung in his throat. He ran his hands behind

his head and pulled until his arms shook and his neck strained. "Yeah."

The *djinn* crossed his arms over his chest, eyes on the crowd at the bar. "Good."

Dominic moved in beside them before Griff could think of an intelligent comeback. "Any reason I should pull her down?"

Griff said, "Hell, yes," at the same time Seth answered, "No need."

Bailey chose that moment to turn her back to the crowd and swivel her hips.

Griff's jaw hung slack. Lust punched through him leaving massive holes in odd places. Someone grabbed the back of his shirt. That's when he realized he'd started toward the bar. Toward Bailey.

"Hey. You passed on her, remember? Seemed like it was a pretty clear thanks-but-no-thanks kind of pass, too."

Griff shot Seth a hard look. "You talked to her?"

"Tried. She wasn't interested." His eyes narrowed dangerously, and his next words were so harsh and low Griff had to lean in to hear him. "Kind of impossible to miss the fallout, though. Grief has a truly awful sound." He shook his head and looked across the crowd, eyes unfocused. "You had a chance, a real chance, and you pissed it away."

The same thought had haunted every second of every minute of every hour that had passed since Griff had sent her away. "Maybe." At Seth's bland stare, he dragged a hand down his mouth. "Probably, okay? I put my Google-fu to work this afternoon after...well, after. Her *prana* left me feeling better than I've ever felt. Found out an incubus and succubus can sustain each other exclusively, but finding a pair that can be true to each other is less likely than finding an honest politician. No records of long-term anything, though. Only legend."

Seth gaped, and he never gaped. "What did you just say?"

"I screwed up. Should have done my homework earlier. It only proves I don't deserve her."

Seth grabbed him by the front of the shirt and hauled him around. "You stupid son of a bitch. Don't you get it? Love isn't about deserving or not deserving. It's about taking a risk and betting against the house and seizing the moment. It's roll-up-your-sleeves dirty. It's emotionally boggy ground. And it's the only thing that stands even a remote chance of making this life less lonely."

Griff stared at Seth, dumbfounded. He frowned when Seth's face went blank. "You just had a stroke, didn't you?"

The man released him and stepped back. "Looks like you don't need to worry about it."

"Huh?"

"Love." Seth tipped his head toward the bar. "She's headed to the dance floor."

If Griff wondered how the look on his face translated, the way the people nearest him scrambled away provided a pretty universal interpretation. It took only a second to find Bailey because she'd taken the bar show straight to the floor. He watched her move against the stranger. Hands above her head, she rubbed her ass against the guy's zipper.

"Girl can sure as hell move." Seth unabashedly adjusted his cock.

"I can't do this." Griff turned away.

"Can't do what, exactly?"

"This." He gestured blindly over his shoulder. "I have to do...something."

"Looks like it's now or never."

"Huh?"

"She's with another guy on the dance floor."

There was only one reason she'd be with the guy.

She was going to feed.

Bailey moved against the stranger's body, trying desperately to lose herself in the music. No thinking, just experiencing. She didn't know how else to survive what had to happen.

The guy slid his arms around her waist and ground his erection against her. She hadn't done more than glance at him, but she found herself hoping for his sake that he was good looking. Otherwise? His sweaty, groping, rhythm-challenged self didn't stand a chance with a normal woman. Which she wasn't. Not anymore.

No thinking. She blindly grabbed his hand and dragged him toward the exit.

"What's the rush?" he shouted.

"Dying to get in your pants." *How miserably true.*

He yanked his hand from her grasp.

A hard shove sent her sprawling.

"Better be hella good-looking or his genealogy chart just flatlined," she grumbled, pushing hair out of her face as she stood. It didn't really matter what he looked like, though. She couldn't go through with this. "Look, I'm sorry, but I can't—"

The music shut off. She paused. The crowd had closed ranks and gone still. Seth's leviathan form knocked people aside as he headed toward her. *And where Seth was, so was...* She turned with a sense of horror and heartache.

Her jaw dropped. Griff, typically cool and aloof, had the guy by the throat, their faces inches apart. "Touch her again and I'll make sure you're shitting in a bag before sunrise. We clear?"

"Don't." What should have been a command came out flat. Only the residue of pride she managed to scrape together helped her meet Griff's gaze when he looked at her.

He tossed the guy away before taking a step toward her.

She stumbled away, hands held out. "You have no right."

"I'm seizing the moment."

"What moment?"

Another step toward her. "This one."

Seth's voice whispered past her ear. "Roll with it."

She glanced at the *djinn*, an irrefutable friend. He nodded. Turning, she sucked in a breath. Griff stood mere inches away. The smell of his arousal saturated the air. *So that's all this is.* "I danced this dance, Griff. Never again."

He flinched. It was a small reaction, but undeniable all the same.

Seth cleared his throat.

"I've got this," Griff ground out. "You can stop mothering me."

Seth shook his head, one corner of his mouth curling up. "I'll stop mothering you when you grow up. Until then? You're stuck with me."

Griff rolled his eyes before refocusing on Bailey. "Don't leave with him."

The crippling hurt, the one that had been there since he walked away, intensified. *Could a broken heart make someone bleed out?* "I have to go," she croaked.

"Choose me instead."

Traitorous tears slipped down her cheeks. "Don't do this to me."

He held out a hand. "Please."

She took a steadier step back, shaking her head. "No."

Griff closed the distance between them and took her face in his hands. "I'm begging."

"Not good enough." She met his unguarded gaze, left her own pain undisguised.

"I'm…I'm so damn sorry, Bailey." He rested his forehead against hers.

Looking at him proved too hard. An overwhelming need arose, a need to believe in him. Trust him. She wanted the kind of security that chased phantoms from dark corners. The kind of blind faith that never withered, only strengthened. He could give her all of it. Probably. Thoughts and feelings bombarded her. In the end, finding hope proved too hard. "'Sorry' isn't enough."

Lips brushed her cheek, feather-light. Tentative. Seeking.

"Don't do this to me," she repeated. Her voice shook almost as hard as her heart.

"I want you, Bailey."

She slowly opened her eyes. "And right there, that *want* will always be between us. Because I *need* more than that." Funny thing was, she would have settled for "want" hours ago. Not anymore.

Pain decorated his face, only one part of an emotional collage. "I…" He dropped his hands.

"That's what I thought." Whirling, she started for the door, the crowd parting before her as if they were stage curtains lifting for the final act. *How appropriate.* She looked back at Seth, never slowing down. "I quit."

Unforgiving fingers gripped her upper arm. "Get your hands off me, Seth."

"I don't want you to ever call another man's name," that voice growled in her ear. "Ever." He tried to turn her around.

Griff. She couldn't move.

He stepped in front of her and bent his knees to get below her downturned face. "Fine. I'll come to you. Again and again, Bailey. It's always been you."

His hard mouth crashed into hers, fierce and unyielding. The kiss lifted her up and swept her away against her will. He tasted like fine whiskey, smelled like sin, felt so right. *Griff.* Her arms went around his neck.

He picked her up, encouraging her legs around his waist.

A deafening cheer went up from the crowd she'd all but forgotten.

Breaking the kiss, he looked at her. "I need you, Bailey."

She buried her face in his neck, the ache in her chest filled with bitter regret.

"Come upstairs with me?"

"I can't."

He set her down very slowly. "I don't understand."

"I have to feed," she whispered, shame burning in her cheeks. "You said—"

"If I said I found a way around that? Would you come with me then?" His voice had taken on a detached distance she hated.

"Yes." The word was hardly out of her mouth before he grabbed her hand, hauling her through the bar, down the hall and into his private elevator.

Griff pounded on the close button. "C'mon, c'mon." The doors closed and the car began to rise. Then he rounded on her, a wild look in his eyes. "I sent you away because I couldn't see you go through this, couldn't watch you feed and die a little every day. I swear I didn't know until late this afternoon that we could be everything to each other. You have to believe me."

Her forehead wrinkled. "Why check now?"

"I had no idea it was possible. And why now? You. Feeding from you and how I felt afterward. But it was you." He ran a shaking hand across his chest and gripped his shoulder. "I spent lifetimes looking for you. Letting you go isn't an option. Not really." He dropped his chin and snorted. "Who am I kidding? It was never an option."

"Yes."

His head snapped up. "What?"

"I said yes. Before, out there. And now, in here. Yes, to all of it. Yes."

"I need you, baby. Need *and* want. It's always been both when it comes to you."

Her trembling fingers worked at the buttons on her shorts.

He mirrored her motions with hands that shook just as badly.

They finally stood before each other, brutally bare in every way.

"C'mere."

Taking his hand, she stepped into his embrace. Those familiar, capable arms lifted her again. This time, he hooked them under her knees.

She shivered. A sigh of satisfaction escaped her as he slid home.

Pure strength facilitated long, slow thrusts as he gripped her waist. He leaned in.

Bailey met him halfway.

The kiss was nearly her undoing. Tender yet hungry. Patient yet desperate. It spoke to her soul in ways words couldn't. It said he was hers and she was his. It validated months of lusting after him, years of craving what she thought she couldn't have, a lifetime spent needing this very thing. It delivered redemption and sought absolution, all in an embrace that had nothing to do with had been before them and everything to do with what might be between them.

He broke away far too soon.

With her hands laced behind his neck, her gaze slid down their bodies. She watched their coupling, watched his slick cock slide in and out of her as his abs flexed and released with exquisite control. His corona raked across her G-spot. A sense of fullness and pressure settled low in her pelvis. An uncontrollable shiver raced through her.

"I need you to see me." His voice quavered with something she didn't recognize.

"I do see you."

"Really look."

She lifted her eyes to meet his.

He paused, holding her tight against him, buried to the hilt. "I love you, Bailey."

Hope, so elusive only moments ago, came forward on the breath of promise. There was so much she wanted to say, but one thing mattered above all else. "I love you, too."

Griff closed his eyes, and his mouth thinned.

"You okay?" She punctuated the question with soft kisses.

"So damn lucky. I never thought..." A hard shudder wracked his frame. "Never thought I'd end up here, with someone to love, someone who loved me in spite of what I am. With you." Steady thrusts replaced words.

A shaken breath threaded through her chest. "You're so much more than what you see."

He shook his head.

"Yes, Griff." She gripped his chin. "Look at me. Really look."

All movement stopped. His eyes fluttered open, and he took her in.

"What do you see?"

"I see you." His voice, tight with emotion, broke. "Just you."

"And that's what I see when I look at you. Any transgressions you think you have are gone. They aren't part of this, of us, unless you put them in our way. You're the man I love. That's enough." She watched understanding pass through him, deliberate and unhurried.

"But—"

The only way to reasonably silence his self-doubt had her pressing her lips to his. Instinct took over. Rocking her hips, she slid up and down his length. Not as smooth as he'd managed, but she got what she wanted when he began to move.

An appreciative moan escaped her, and he swallowed it down. A symphony of love's sounds filled the elevator— skin on skin, heavy breaths, whispered encouragements, words of passion.

Her need to feed rose. What she was sought his *prana* as orgasm became imminent. His neck became her fulcrum, and she pulled against him to meet his pounding thrusts. She pushed him to near-violence, encouraging him with her own fervor and demanding he hold nothing back. The first flutters in her pelvis stole what remained of her control. The first wave of release crashed over her. Spread through. Burned her alive. She screamed his name.

Bailey thought she might shatter in his arms. He held firm, kept her whole and followed her into depths of pleasure she'd never known. She fed from him as he fed from her. Knew him with an intimacy that had been lacking before.

He pulled her closer as they came down, nuzzling her neck. "If this is what we have to look forward to? I'm *so* in."

"For the long term?"

"Forever."

She relaxed in his arms, the fissures of grief he'd caused healed. And their individual pasts? They'd conquer those together. But there was no rush. Not anymore. Because they truly had forever.

* * * * *

IMMORTAL, INSATIABLE, INDOMITABLE

OLIVIA GATES

Olivia Gates has always pursued creative passions such as singing and handicrafts. She still does, but only one of her passions grew gratifying enough, consuming enough, to become an ongoing career—writing.

She is most fulfilled when she is creating worlds and conflicts for her characters, then exploring and untangling them bit by bit, sharing her protagonists' every heart-wrenching heartache and hope, their every heart-pounding doubt and trial, until she leads them to an indisputably earned and gloriously satisfying happy ending.

When she's not writing, she is a doctor, a wife to her own alpha male and a mother to one brilliant girl and one demanding Angora cat. Visit Olivia at www.oliviagates.com.

Chapter 1

Death must be your heart's desire.

Vidar slammed his glass down on the counter. The crack went off like a shot in the first lull in the marrow-jarring music the mortals had been writhing to since he'd walked into the club an hour ago.

Damn Loki and his riddles.

The bartender's head jerked up, his hand freezing on the way to pour a sixth shot of vodka. "Want something else?"

Vidar fisted a wad of money from his inner pocket, threw it on the counter. "Just leave the bottle. And bring me another one."

The bartender hesitated. Vidar wondered if he'd mention an alcohol consumption limit or ask for his car keys.

Nah. As burly as the man was, he was eyeing him with the wariness he was used to seeing in mortal men's eyes when *they* saw him. This man knew violence, could estimate his chances against other men. Against *him,* he'd rightly calculated them to be none. And that was based solely on the pissed-off vibe Vidar was radiating.

He wondered what the man would think if he knew he

could take out the hundreds of men around them without breaking a sweat.

The way he felt right now, he was itching to do that.

The man must have sensed it, too. He did as ordered, though to his credit, with utmost reluctance.

Vidar fleetingly considered reassuring the bartender that he wasn't breaking any professional code. Having the metabolism of a shape-shifting immortal, he could drink a swimming pool's worth of Midgard's—Earth's—hardest liquor and it would barely smooth his frown. The only time he'd been drunk had been a millennium ago, after he and his team had released Alvar from Fenrir the Wolf's clutches. And then only because he'd celebrated by going through two barrels of mead imported direct from Asgard.

He frowned into the colorless liquid in his glass. His fellow Lokians wouldn't touch *that* stuff at the threat of a hit from Mjolnir. Daven *had* been pounded by Thor's Hammer in a wager between Thor and Loki that he would. He hadn't.

But Vidar's fellow Lokians didn't trawl bars and nightclubs for recruits. They'd taunted him that he did so because puny mortals' liquor was all he could handle. Either that, or he'd grown lazy.

He hadn't volunteered the real reason. That he'd grown indifferent. Finding recruits had ceased to matter decades ago.

And then, he *had* found many of his candidates in such places, where outcasts went to blend in. His days of being creative in looking for recruits were long behind him. The extra effort hadn't proved more effective, and recruits found in joints like this one actually ended up lasting longer. All he had to do while he cast his senses out on search was endure the cacophony and legitimize his presence by downing overpriced, ineffective swill.

He'd better find someone to recruit here. He wasn't in the mood for another wasted night.

But what else was new? He'd had *centuries* of wasted nights. To say he was sick of it all was the understatement of the literal millennium.

That was why he'd invoked Loki at dawn that morning for a one-on-one.

Loki had taken his sweet time answering, had appeared around noon. After an hour of enduring the god talking up his latest TV channel acquisition and how he planned to use it to invade Normals' minds, and showing off his new clothing line's threads, he'd cut him off. Loki had his undying allegiance and all, and for millennia he'd actually enjoyed listening to him plot and brag, but not today.

Today it was over. He wanted to quit.

He should have, centuries ago.

It had been that long since he'd known his job was futile.

He couldn't speak for the others, but being one of the twelve Originals of Loki's Legion hadn't turned out as advertised. He'd signed on thinking it was the ultimate cause, upholding Loki's purpose in searching out Gifted outcasts, recruiting them, fostering them, and swelling the ranks of his army for Ragnarok, the Final Fate of the Gods, where they would help him survive that battle in which all the gods were supposed to kill one another, then take over *this* fucked-up world. All Vidar had managed to do so far was watch his recruits burn in the flames of self-destruction, disintegrate in the maelstrom of madness or wither in the abyss of depression. Rinse and repeat. Ad infinitum.

He was weary of counting the fallen, of the futility of knowing they'd fall. Millennia of that had gotten old. Ancient. He had no more purpose. Not in *this* existence, anyway. His purpose would be renewed when said existence came to an end.

But he was no longer holding his breath for that. Judging from the millenniums that had dragged by with nothing happening, Ragnarok seemed to have been canceled.

After a long moment of studying his perfectly manicured nails and dusting imaginary lint from his ten-thousand-dollar Loki Line suit, Loki had answered. Not out loud.

The words had expanded in Vidar's mind.

So you want death.

Vidar had only nodded. Loki had gotten that right.

He *could* quit without dying. After the first few centuries, Loki had no longer tied the immortality of his Originals to continued service. But without serving Loki's cause, *he* had nothing to live for. He'd lived far too long already. He was centuries beyond ready—hell, beyond rip-roaring *eager*—to hang it all up.

There was only one way to do that. Loki had to strip away his immortality so that his body could die. Or be killed.

But Loki had only flung the cryptic answer at him.

Death must be your heart's desire.

Then, citing a hot date with his wife, Sigyn, followed by a showdown with Thor over some epic squabble between their sons, he'd disappeared before Vidar could probe or persist.

Vidar grunted with a resurgence of frustration and tossed back another swig of vodka direct from the bottle.

What *was* a heart's desire, anyway?

He'd never wanted anything with the all-consuming passion he supposed such a desire should be. And how in Ragnarok's name could death become that to him? Wasn't it enough that he wanted the damn thing, longed for its reprieve?

Evidently, not according to Loki. And knowing the god, he'd said his final word on the matter. That meant Vidar would probably live until Ragnarok and, if they were victorious then, beyond.

He'd often heard mortals moan, *Someone kill me now.*

He *so* sympathized.

He panned his gaze around. Epileptic bursts of colored light sundered the semidarkness. The air was pregnant with odors and emotions, pheromones and hormones, naturally and chemically induced. And the *din*. Only mortals high on one thing or another could find this not only endurable but enjoyable. Mating practices had sure changed since he was a mortal.

He'd give finding a recruit another thirty minutes. His life might be unending, but his patience wasn't. And then...

His thoughts stilled. Noise, followed by everything else, disappeared. The heart that thumped only a handful of beats a minute even in extreme duress hammered.

A woman was sitting in a booth at the farthest end of the club.

And she was...glowing.

Kara winced at the pungent masses, the bone-shaking noise and migraine-inducing strobe lights, and damned herself again.

What *was* she doing here?

She streaked past this joint every day on her way home from the hospital. Tonight, some compulsion she couldn't resist had made her approach, tell the hulking, BDSM-clad bouncers she wanted a peek inside. She'd felt certain that they, who seemed to let in only weirdos, wouldn't open the door for unescorted, boringly clad meat.

To her shock, one had led her to a booth and ordered her

a complimentary drink. Before she could worry that the mass of muscle was hitting on her, he'd left. She was still wondering what that had been all about.

So here she was. Sitting in the midst of what looked like a mass ritual for the exorcism of every inhibition and dress code known to humankind.

She'd never thought places like this existed outside of movies. And though most of the mayhem ranged from ridiculous to repulsive, she had no intention of leaving. Why, she had no idea.

Crazy.

But then, what was one more insanity? Her normal life had turned out to be a lie, and the truth…unadulterated madness.

She reached for the pineapple juice the waitress had snorted at when she'd ordered. She took a sip of the watered down but blessedly hydrating liquid, scanned the light-pulsing, body-packed, crimson-hued psychedelic space over the rim of the glass.

Suddenly the coolness sliding down her throat turned scalding. Her heart sputtered, her every nerve fired.

A man. On the far side of the gigantic room.

He had an elbow propped on the bar and a hip on a high stool, semifacing her. His eyes rose from contemplating the liquor bottle in his hand with disgust, slammed into hers.

If she'd been standing, she would have keeled over.

And that was before a path cleared among the crush, affording her an unobstructed view of him.

Her mouth dropped open, air stalled in her lungs.

This must be what a fallen angel looked like. Or a god. A Norse god. This impossible beauty. This hair-raising aura.

She could swear she *saw* the latter. It had a thousand hues and influences to it, each eliciting images, sensations, wrenching responses. And then came the physical details. The fluid power of his limbs, the pure maleness in his pose, the utter poetry of his proportions, the shoulder-length mane weaved from sunlight and bronze. And his eyes. She shouldn't be able to decipher their color at this distance. But she did. They seemed to emit an azure force field that stormed through her, pillaging and possessing....

The rest of her breath left her with a choppy huff.

Okay. Congratulations. She'd just veered from insane to pathetic. Since when did she think such things exciting? Any man who'd tried such overriding tactics on her, she'd handed his head, right after she kicked his ass. Why would her mind be filling with images of *this* man walking over to her, dragging her into his arms and giving her no choice as he ravaged her mouth and exploited her flesh for his pleasure?

She was getting wet just imagining it. Her core was starting to throb, like it hadn't done in...ever. Not when it hadn't been in response to some seriously well-written erotica. No live man had done this to her before, taken hold of her imagination and libido and churned them into a frenzy this way.

He'd done it with just a stare.

Okay. Any time now. She was more than ready for it. For his eyes to betray a vapid shallowness behind their at-first unfathomable depths.

And that perfect body probably reeked. Those painstakingly sculpted lips probably smelled like a cheap, alcohol-soaked ashtray that spilled guttural vulgarities, and he probably had all the finesse of a phlegm-spitting lowlife and the intelligence of a unicellular life-form.

No one could be that...endowed in more than one arena. And his share of the physical must have kicked him out of line when they were handing out other attributes. The universe wasn't *that* unfair that it would give him more advantages than the…distressingly obvious.

Decimating her expectations wasn't working. She couldn't stop her body from readying itself for all-out sex. Which it must be doing from genetic memory, since she'd never had sex that could be described as all-anything, except maybe all-boring, all-disappointing.

Then she literally couldn't stop her body.

She found herself getting up on legs that shook as she imagined them wrapping around his bulk as he drove into her. Then her feet were taking her closer to him.

Vidar stared at the woman.

She wasn't *really* glowing. But she was. To his senses. And to his more…fundamental parts. She radiated a compulsion, transmitted it on a wavelength that revved dark, dangerous urges inside him. Untempered, unrestrained.

A power he rarely used—making mortals unable to bear the impact of his gaze—emptied a path to her. Then his Lokian vision— another gift he seldom engaged, finding little in this world to warrant its clarity—zoomed in on her.

He magnified each feature of her exquisite face, every strand of spun-fire that framed it, every slope and curve and pore. Her broad, clear forehead bore the mark of intelligence. Her elegant nose and firm jaw spoke of character and strength. Her lips, dainty and dimpled, would be edible smiling or serious, but now, flushed and parted, they invited his ferociousness. Of her body, he could see only the capable, square shoulders, and the heavy breasts, hugged loosely by something out of place and beige.

But it was her eyes, gleaming like Asgard's moons and

as verdant as its seas, that had excesses storming through his mind, sending blood like molten steel to his erection.

He'd thought he'd seen it all. Every kind of beauty, on the mortal and immortal planes. He'd been right. Until now.

Until *this* woman.

Even the gods hadn't been so ambitious as to dream of beauty like hers. Nature, in his experience, had never come close.

And her effect on him wasn't due to a spell or a power.

She was human. Mortal. He even felt that her life force was unstable. She wouldn't have a long lifespan.

He should take her while he could, then.

He imagined himself walking to her, then without saying a word, pushing her back on that bench she was sitting on and mounting her.

He hadn't done anything close to that even when he'd been a barbarian and behavior like that was the norm.

He wanted to do it to her now.

Now *that* was desire. Although of something south of the heart.

And it was reciprocated. She *wanted* him to ravish her.

She was coming to him, the demand for his possession, his pleasures, rising in urgency with her every step closer.

How he would answer it.

Kara neared the man, only the crush of sweating bodies slowing her advance. The emptiness between her thighs throbbed harder with every step.

But along with arousal, anxiety intensified, too.

It would serve her right if he did something obscene when she reached him. Her off-the-charts, out-of-character behavior in walking up to a man who looked like a…a marauder, with drool no doubt trailing behind her, deserved at least a breast grope.

What would she do if he did that, or worse? Slap him? Run away? Rub herself against his rock-solid gorgeousness and beg for more? For everything?

That was it. She'd lost whatever had been left of her mind.

Don't do this. Turn around, walk away.

If she didn't, she'd blow away whatever normalcy remained in her life. After her "family's" recent revelations, she barely had any left. This was just the guy to end "normal" once and for all.

But she could be imagining things. He might be just another mediocre guy, and she'd soon get this will-siphoning lust out of her system with some quickie that didn't involve actual sex or the removal of either of their clothes.

Yeah, sure. Like she'd been imagining things when she'd thought there was something seriously wrong with her. Her "foster family" had set her straight on that.

Next to what they'd revealed, walking up to the most incredible and lethal-looking man she'd ever seen with the intention of asking him to fuck her brains out seemed tame.

To make things worse, he hadn't moved an inch to meet her halfway, just kept staring at her. If you could call that denuding/dissecting/devouring gaze a stare. And if she trusted her senses at all now, she would swear he was getting…bigger.

She was only a dozen feet from him when he suddenly looked away.

Mortification scalded her.

He gazed with even more intensity at whatever had caught his attention. So he looked at everything that way. It hadn't been for *her*. He might even be here with someone. He…

He had men converging on him. Lumbering, black-leather-clad men whose heads were shaved in patterns that looked like gothic runes.

And from their body language, they didn't want to buy him another drink.

Vidar wanted to kick himself.

He'd been so lost in the mortal's eyes, in his fantasies of how many ways, how long and hard, he'd fuck her, he hadn't noticed the minions of Odin closing in on him. Not until they were a dozen feet away. He usually felt them from at least a mile.

He transferred his gaze to them, cursed them most for forcing him to relinquish savoring his mortal vision's approach.

Odinians, like most religious cultists, were sociopaths desperate to belong to something bigger than they were, to draw importance and power from the affiliation. Even if it killed them. But preferably if it killed others.

He wondered how they'd realized what he was. Before arriving at the club, he'd shifted to only three-quarters of his real size.

Maybe the hair? He hadn't shifted that.

Daven always advised him to cut his "goldilocks," shave his beard, ditch the marauding Viking look. As if shaving his own head hadn't made Daven look even more intimidating and conspicuous.

But of course, that wasn't the explanation. These weren't the garden-variety, fanatical mortal fare. They were Endowed. With echoes of the Odinforce. Wonder what they'd paid in return for it.

Someone with Asgard-based Endowment would sense another on the juice. And those with any trace of Odinforce were attracted to Lokians like a negative to a positive charge. They all had this ridiculous belief that they could tap a Lokian's Endowment.

Well, no point hiding in a six-foot body now. Might as well slip into something more comfortable.

He stood, caught the satisfying blip of terror in the men's eyes as he shifted to his full size. But he couldn't engage them here. Especially with the mortal woman in range.

He used their hesitation to cast her a warning look.

Kara froze as the man's gaze slammed back into her.

Before her heart could recover, it stumbled over a new shock.

Either he *had* gotten bigger, or she'd severely underestimated his size. He stood well over seven feet tall.

And as stupid as it was in the circumstances, her eyes darted downward, investigating what mattered to the body that was functioning on auto-nympho mode right now.

Her gaze lingered there for only a moment. But it was enough. Much, much more than enough. If what she'd seen was to be believed.

The moment her gaze moved back to his face, to the scene, air emptied from her lungs yet again. The aggression emanating from the men, the danger rising from him, hit her like a gut punch.

No one else seemed to sense the disturbance, kept gyrating and slithering over one another in oblivious abandon. Maybe she was the one whose senses were scrambled beyond repair?

No. She wasn't imagining it. This would turn ugly. For him. And for who knew how many others in the packed place.

And like she made lightning decisions in the E.R., she made one now. She'd give aborting this a shot. She'd pretend she was with him, and that many others were joining them in moments. Maybe that would make those goons walk away.

Vidar's heart shook off its slow steadiness once more, thudded.

She was moving toward him again. And after he'd given her a look that had given Loki's child, Jörmungandr the world serpent itself, pause.

She must have misread it, must be oblivious to the danger.

And the advantage he'd gained by revealing his true stature was fading. The thugs were psyching themselves up that numbers would trump size and power. He had about a minute to take this away from her. From the rest of the mortals.

He moved before the Odinians could throng around him, force him to engage them here.

He strode toward her. That made her stop, the heat and greed in her eyes replaced with alarm. So she *was* aware of the danger. Then why had she kept approaching?

No time to contemplate this. And he expected her to step aside when he neared her. She didn't. The brush-by he'd intended ended up being a bump and grind against her hot, pliant flesh.

For a split second, he almost forgot the thugs on his tail. He almost crushed that intoxicatingly scented body to him and took those lips that trembled apart on a hungry sound.

He shoved down the urge, resigned he wouldn't fulfill it. Now or ever. He'd never see her again.

He'd tell her something, though.

The only thing he'd ever tell her.

He bumped into her. Kara would have fallen if she hadn't had bodies at her back. She felt as if she'd run into a wall of hot steel. And what she smelled of him during that momentary contact was mouthwatering. Then he was bypassing her.

Before she could swallow the letdown, cry out something, ask if he needed help, he looked over his shoulder and his lips moved.

She shouldn't have heard him over the cacophony. But she did. His hiss seemed to negate every other sound.

"Leave."

She blinked as he receded toward the back exit of the nightclub with the grim tranquility of someone heading to a gunfight. And he'd told her to get while the getting was good.

The men were following him. Ten of them. The rabid gleam in their eyes was explicit with their intentions. They were going to tear him apart the moment they got him alone.

Her gaze shot around. Some dancers had noticed the ominous procession and were nudging one another and commenting. No one was bothering to investigate or intervene.

There might be nothing worth investigating. They might just rough him up a bit over a debt or something.

But even if that was true, ten to one? She wouldn't leave anyone to face those odds alone. Hell, back in junior high, she hadn't even left a tormenting bitch of a classmate alone with the schoolyard bully.

But someone who'd not only jump-started her dormant hormones, but paid her the kindness of worrying about her safety?

The last time someone had done that, they'd ended up dead.

Leave, huh? Good advice. She should take it.

And she would. If she were someone else.

She pushed her way through the crowd in her mystery man's wake.

Chapter 2

Vidar walked out into the bitter cold of Chicago's winter a few steps ahead of his would-be executioners.

That label wasn't much of a stretch. With the collective Odinforce imbuing them, if he let them, they could kill him.

That was, if Loki saw fit to let the injuries they'd cause overcome his regenerative powers.

While he didn't particularly relish the idea of having these bozos be the ones to end his life, death was death. No such thing as a worthy one. They were as good a way to go as any.

The question now was whether Loki would consider this qualified as his "heart's desire."

Knowing the slippery son of a bitch, no. He'd spent millennia in the god's service, but not out of some idealized belief that his lord could do no wrong. Loki did plenty of wrong. So did *he,* for that matter. But all in all, from the proof of eons, Loki stood for better things, did more good, than any of the other gods. It was why Vidar mostly admired him. But he sure resented the hell out of him at times. Loki always pointed out that his exasperation stemmed from the same reason he'd been chosen among the first Originals.

He'd been Loki's mortal reflection. Different, nonconforming and rubbing it in the noses of those who disapproved. And reviled and demonized as Loki had always been for it, too, of course.

But he could try. He'd never accumulated injuries that were beyond his regenerative abilities. Maybe if he did this time, Loki would finally let him go.

Time to find out.

He let the first blow land square on his left cheekbone. He heard the crunch of bones, his and his attacker's, as pain exploded behind his eye sockets.

That was a good punch. Odinforce-boosted strength was something. His bone, harder than steel, had cracked.

He felt another blow coming a full two seconds before his next attacker connected. He had enough time to rip the man's heart out and cram it down his throat. But he didn't even try to block it. Something metal and unyielding crashed against his side. He felt ribs shatter and tear through his muscles and skin. He gritted his teeth on the shredding pain.

"Ooh, he's glaring at us. We supposed to get scared?"

"Is that all you got, you fuck?"

"And we thought a Lokian deserved ten of us, thought shifting was a big deal. All he did was expand. Like a hot-air balloon."

"Is that how your dick expands, too?"

"Seems Lokian is code for Pussy."

At his silence, they attacked again. After more direct hits, the thugs got confident, swarmed around him. He had dozens of openings to rip throats and sever limbs and heads. He took none.

He had to give it to them. They were quick and creative.

They pulverized body parts overlooked by most. His feet and hands were favorite targets. They wanted to cripple him before they killed him. He let them do whatever their twisted appetites for inflicting damage could belch up.

In seconds he was bathed in blood, his left arm all but hacked off, his chest and abdomen punctured in vital areas, his skull fractured. His consciousness was wavering from the pain. He didn't feel the healing kicking in.

Had Loki heeded his request? Would he finally die?

He fell to his knees. He didn't want to get up.

He was ready.

A booted foot kicked his head with enough force to almost take it off his shoulders. Snickers phased in and out of his awareness.

"Is it me or is he enjoying this? You one of those wimps that get off on being abused?"

"But we ain't gonna abuse you, pussyboy. We gonna kill ya, and drink your Endowment."

"What Endowment?"

Rowdy laughter burst out.

They weren't just vicious, they were assholes. One thing an Asgard-Endowed didn't do, mortal or immortal, was humiliate a fallen enemy. Odin should be ashamed of granting such scumbags even the power he wiped off his ass.

He could smell what they'd paid for the Odinforce. Their very lives. They were rotting. Not in flesh yet, but their souls had long putrefied. To them, his Endowment must have smelled like raw meat to a pack of starving hyenas. They thought they could gorge on it and revive themselves. A misconception that held no matter how many millennia passed without one successful incident of anyone absorbing a Lokian's, let alone an Original's, Endowment. Yet power-addicts kept telling themselves they'd succeed where others had failed.

"Hey, hey...look what the cat dragged out."

"Say, isn't that piece of ass from back in the club?"

What were the bastards talking about?

He raised his head, could see nothing. One eye was soaked in blood, the other swollen shut.

But he could smell. Her.

The mortal woman. She was here.

His heart, which that had slowed down to almost a stand-still for the duration of the attack, detonated. What was she *doing* here?

He snapped a crushed hand to his eye, wiped away blood.

She stood two dozen feet away, as tall as most of his at-tackers, her hair a rioting flame around her shoulders in the eddying wind, her outfit flapping around her lush frame. And she hadn't simply stumbled out at the wrong time. Not judging by her confrontational pose and the pipe in her hand.

Another boot whacked his head. "Yo, pussyboy, she one of your Lokian sluts? You sure pick 'em stupid. She came after you like a bitch after her master."

"Can't be for his hot-air dick. He must have her hooked on some Asgardian dope."

"Too bad for her. She got a good look at all of us."

And he roared. *"Leave."*

Another kick to his head. "She ain't going anywhere, wuss."

Another voice chuckled. "Get her, Jack. We'll finish him off."

The thug named Jack charged at her. The moment he was in range, she swung. He heard the crack of metal against bone, saw blood arc in the indirect lights. If the thug weren't jacked up on Odinforce, he would have gone down. She'd hit sure and hard, to cripple, even kill. She understood the danger well.

But if she did, why was she here? For all she knew this was a ten-to-one fight, one he was losing big-time. She was one woman with a pipe. What did she hope to achieve with those odds?

He had no explanation. But he knew one fact.

She was defending him.

Only his fellow Lokians had ever fought beside him, risked injury and pain for him. But that didn't compare.

No one had ever put their life on the line for him.

The thug she'd nailed lunged at her. She evaded him with the grace of a seasoned boxer, hit him square in the throat.

"You're paying for that, bitch," the thug named Jack gurgled. "I was just gonna snap your neck but now I'm gonna rip you some new holes and fuck you in each for days."

The other thugs seemed to consider this a done deal, turned to Vidar, calling to their accomplice over their shoulders.

"Leave us some. I bet a Lokian bitch would love the ten of us taking turns on her."

"Why take turns? Bet she's used to ten at once."

Their intentions jolted him like lightning bolts.

He wouldn't have let them endanger any mortal. But her? Time for heads to roll.

He willed himself back to his feet, forced the words through blood-filled lungs and torn lips. "Here's the thing, you ass-gardian pieces of shit. Torturing and killing me, I would have let you get away with without a scratch. But insulting the lady? Threatening her with that vileness? By Loki's Locket, even thinking it? For *that,* you die."

"Sure, pussyboy, when *you're* two seconds from dead."

"You couldn't raise a hand to do shit when you were in one piece. Now we crushed you like a nut, what you gonna do? Glare us to death? Oh, wait, you can't even do that anymore."

"Here, let us put you out of your misery."

Vidar caught one fist on its way to his gut and another targeting his windpipe. He tore the first clear off, ripped off the entire arm attached to the second.

The disbelief in his attackers' eyes spattered him along with the geyser of blood. Then realization, terror and agony exploded on butchered howls.

"Since I can't raise *my* hands, how about I make do with your buddies'?" He threw the appendage and limb at their colleagues.

They all jumped back in horror. The ones he'd torn apart crumpled to the ground. Two down. Eight more to go.

But first, Jack.

He charged through the now-paralyzed thugs, agony skewering through him with every step. The woman had been holding her own until Jack saw what Vidar had done to his pals. He stopped trying to evade her strikes, took two crushing hits so he could get to her.

Then he had her in a chokehold, screamed, "One more step, you son of a bitch, and I gouge her neck out."

"I wanted to make your death the most protracted and agonizing." Vidar's torn lips pulled back in vicious humor. "Oh, well. Long ago, my mother told me I can't have everything I want." He met the woman's eyes. They were huge, gleaming emeralds in the dimness. Somehow they contained no terror. They transmitted mostly fury. Good girl. He gave her a conspiratorial smile. "Duck."

She didn't hesitate. She exploded in her captor's hold, plowing her elbow into his gut with all she had. He gasped, loosened his arm. She dropped down, giving Vidar a clear shot.

He shifted his working arm into a blade as wide as a broadsword and, in one sweep, lopped off Jack's head.

Without a sound, the woman bolted sideways, escaping the path of spraying blood as the head fell at Vidar's feet with the inimitable sound only heads made on impacting asphalt.

Keeping her behind him, he faced the remaining seven. The horror in their eyes was turning to desperation.

Sustaining another injury was a luxury he couldn't afford. He couldn't go down and leave even one standing to hunt her down. He had to finish them all off, quickly.

He waited until they charged, rage and dread and momentum throwing them off-balance, before shifting his arm into a tentacle as thick as an Asgardian serpent. He lashed it out, reaping them all and lassoing them up in the air. Then he catapulted them to crash down at his feet.

Before any of them could regain his feet, he shifted his arm back to sword-mode. Beheading was one sure way to kill a mortal Endowed. Ripping out hearts and spilling brains worked, too. But those methods were messier and not time-effective. Any other injury could leave the injured able to regroup, reattack.

He finished off the seven, turned to the ones he'd injured first. They'd gotten over their shock and were trying to slink away.

But even armless and handless, they posed as great a danger to her as their now-headless friends had. She could implicate them to the human authorities. They wouldn't let her be. They had to join their gang in death. In moments, they did.

Standing over the scattered body parts, he forced himself to straighten, looked over to her. She was still there.

Her eyes were stricken.

She hadn't looked alarmed when she'd seen him rip off limbs with his bare hands. But seeing parts of him shift into weapons and creatures that existed only in mortal nightmares had probably been too much. Not to mention watching him behead ten men, even if they'd been about to rape her to death.

It was a miracle she hadn't run away screaming long ago.

"God, you're..." She encompassed him with a frantic gesture.

He looked down. His right arm, still shifting back to its natural shape, looked even more grotesque in midform.

Guess that meant ravishing her was out of the question now.

"I-I'm so sorry." She was? For what? No longer being interested in jumping his bones? "I should have followed you sooner." He stared at her. *That* was what she was sorry about? Being slow to attend this massacre? "They...they tore you apart...."

She stopped again, swallowed, a shudder racking her.

His erection, unheeding of any other part of him that was torn or crushed, made its approval of everything about her rock solid. The siren song that flowed from her lips, the beauty that was now a canvas for such vivid emotions, the generosity of the body that trembled with the effect of each.

Her voice caught, cracked. "It's just...I hesitated to call the police. I wasn't sure you'd appreciate their presence."

He sure wouldn't. Mortal scum he could dispatch. Mortal law enforcement he avoided at all costs.

But did she mean that... "You called them?"

She nodded.

Shit.

His hand, which was back to its natural form but felt more shattered than before he'd shifted it, hurt like Odin's sorry ass as he fumbled for his cell phone. He speed dialed Daven.

On the second ring, the line opened. Daven's mocking voice poured into his ear.

"Legion of Loki Lodge. How can I help you, darlin'?"

"You can grab Alvar and get your smart asses down here, stat." He grunted the address, specified the alley. "Get the big truck."

"Clean up detail?" Daven tsked. "And the big truck, huh? You've had a busy night. And you call us when it's over. Serve you right if we made you clean up after yourself."

"Daven, shut up and get down here. And I mean in under five."

"Hey, you okay, man? You don't sound so hot."

"Most of my bones are crushed, my lungs are collapsed, my guts might spill out and my arm is falling off." The woman groaned. He grimaced an apology. "But you should see the other guys."

"I don't care if you hacked the other guys to pieces—"

"I literally did. So make sure you get all the body parts. Ten bodies, corresponding heads, an arm and a hand."

He winced another look of contrition at the woman's gurgle of distress. It was hitting her at last.

"You talk as if you aren't sticking around."

"I'm not. There's...something I must see to."

"Yeah, be cryptic to the man who's cleaning up your mess."

"You'll be the man I hand his ass to if you're not already on the way."

"Texted Alvar during this lovely chat. He's on his way with the truck. I'm on my way, too. Any more orders, O Elder?"

He'd been Endowed ten years before Daven. In one of his more…petty moments, he'd claimed seniority, demanded Daven's obedience. About three millennia ago.

Daven would probably never let him hear the end of it.

"Any more tidbits you want to share?" Daven prodded.

"Law enforcement will be here any minute."

Daven snorted. "The mortal variety, no doubt. Loki's Trickery, man. What kind of mess did you land in feetfirst?"

"Just jacked-up Odinians after my Endowment. And speaking of trickery, their blood is everywhere, so you're in for some heavy-duty illusion until the blue boys leave."

"Peachy. How can I thank you for the hangover I have to look forward to?"

Daven had the strongest illusory power among Loki's Originals. He could create an alternate reality that could con even the gods' senses. But it came at a price. He wouldn't have asked Daven to endure the pain, which was severe and lasted for indeterminate periods according to the extent of the illusion, if he could have done it himself.

"I owe you one."

"With the way I'll feel for the next few months? Make it ten. And I'll collect." He could hear Daven's breathing becoming audible. He must be moving close to a hundred miles per hour now. On foot. After a moment he said, "You still sound bad. Aren't you done healing?"

Daven expected him to be getting back to normal. Agony beyond what any injury warranted notwithstanding—the price they paid for healing without scars—he normally would have been. But then again, he'd never been this injured. Maybe there *was* a limit to their healing abilities. Or Loki, wonder of wonders, had actually listened to him.

But now wasn't the time to tell Daven he might have convinced Loki to let him die. Daven would be livid Vidar hadn't given him the chance to beat him out of that intention before he'd demanded it of Loki. And he didn't want to discuss his possible demise in front of *her*.

He prevaricated. "Just about." And since he might never see Daven again, he added, "Thanks, Dav."

Daven snorted. "Yeah, sure. And if you take a second longer than necessary to report in, I'll hand you *your* ass."

The line went dead.

Vidar looked at the woman. She was still staring at him.

By Loki. How could there be attraction this...fierce? Why now, when he'd thought to end it all? *How* now, when he was all but torn apart? And why was she, after all she'd seen, looking at him as if she'd take anything he had to offer? Hunger was still emanating from her, more empowering than even Loki's Endowment.

"You shouldn't be alive," she finally whispered. "Let alone fighting, and now organizing...cleanup detail." *First it was protection, now it's libido, and both on your account,* he almost told her. "I'm a doctor." Now *that* he hadn't expected. But what about her had he yet? "I *know* you shouldn't be. But that's based on my knowledge of humans. And you're... not."

"Actually, originally, I was human. At least, a subspecies of human..." He stopped. That wasn't likely to contribute to her desire, now was it? Way to shoot himself in the foot. He huffed in self-deprecation. "It's...complicated."

She raised a hand. "You don't need to explain. Just tell me this. You'll be okay, won't you?"

He had no idea. He wasn't dying. He thought. But he wasn't healing at all, either. And he could no longer lock pain away.

But he couldn't tell her that. She was blaming herself for the injuries he'd sustained, for being too slow to come to his rescue. When it was thanks to her that he was alive. If she hadn't come after him, if she hadn't fought for him, made him need to fight for her, he would probably be dead by now.

He just nodded.

She bit her lip, nodded, too.

Then she turned and ran away.

Chapter 3

Vidar watched his mortal savior disappear.

His first impulse was to run after her. Tell her she couldn't run away from him now that she would have died for him, now that he'd killed for her. His world grew colder with every passing day, and he *needed* to wallow in the heat of her life and hunger.

He didn't. And not because the pain he'd tried to ignore had grown overwhelming. It was because she'd run.

He must have mistaken her horror for hunger. She'd probably been processing what she'd done, been through, witnessed. Then her paralysis had shattered and she'd run for her life. She must think she'd been crazy to come after him, probably considered him an even bigger monster than those he'd killed.

Even if she didn't, even if he hadn't looked and felt like an animated corpse from a slasher movie, he shouldn't go after her. All he'd accomplished with this stunt was to possibly maim himself permanently for the eternity he'd still live.

It was better for her to forget she'd ever seen him.

* * *

He hadn't maimed himself.

Seemed Loki had wanted to give him a severe wrist slap by delaying his healing, giving him a taste of what stripping his regenerative powers would mean. For a full week, it had involved more pain than anything he'd ever experienced. But he had healed, fully.

Now he seemed to be just as fully out of his mind.

He was looking for her.

He'd spent the days ignoring the agony as he'd searched, registering only the frustration of each dead end. As he'd healed physically, his mind and senses had come back online. And then, through a mixture of detective work and his ability to absorb psychic echoes—a fundamental component of his shifting power—he'd found her, working in the hospital near the club where they'd met.

He'd shifted to a nondescript mortal form and followed her throughout her day. He'd watched her deal with emergencies in the E.R. with the same decisiveness and fearlessness that she'd shown while facing the scumbags he'd executed. Though dealing with personal danger was a world apart from dealing with that of others, she'd faced both with the resoluteness of a warrior.

Now he watched her walk briskly out of the hospital and into the cold night. Beneath her long coat, she was dressed in another loose, button-down shirt and a flowing ankle-length skirt, evidently her brand of work clothes. With the effect they had on him, the shapeless clothes could have been outrageous lingerie. He was harder than he'd ever been, even more than the other night. Either healing had boosted his libido this once, or her appeal had intensified since they'd shared that experience.

Which wasn't a reason to follow her. He'd never sought out mortal women before. He'd always thought the benefits not worth the risks. To the women. And then, he'd seen the heartbreak Alvar had once suffered—and caused—when he'd gotten too attached to a woman doomed to age and die.

Not that *he* was in danger of forming such a soul-deep connection with anyone, mortal or immortal. But his position had always been that he wouldn't allow his constant battles to invade their fragile lives.

This time, nothing he told himself worked. *This* woman made him realize he'd been able to abide by his code not out of nobility but because no one had appealed to him so much. He wanted her enough to disregard anything, starting with sanity.

And then, the rules that had applied before didn't apply now. He wouldn't live long enough to endanger her. He'd achieve his death, somehow. And the instability he felt in her aura also told him she wouldn't live as long as she should. If she was willing, he would sate this sanity-compromising lust while they had the chance.

All thoughts stopped as she crossed the street to the night-club, tried to make her way through the people milling for a chance to enter.

One of the bouncers closed in on her. Vidar tensed. He'd rather not take another mortal apart.

But to the bouncer's continued health, he just took her arm, escorted her through the crowd with utmost courteousness.

What was going on? Was she a regular here or something?

She sure didn't look like a typical patron of places like this. But she had been there last week, and she'd already knocked his every expectation about her on its ass.

He should wait until she came out, follow her home to be sure she arrived safely, take a few days deciding whether to approach her again....

By Loki's Leer. Who was he trying to kid? Valhalla's hordes couldn't drag him away now.

He shifted to his true shape, had mortals scooting out of his way as he followed her inside, still grappling with unease.

He'd almost gotten her killed. What if further contact with him finished the job, and it—?

The thought sputtered as his senses dragged to her like iron filings to a magnet. She was sitting in the same booth, looking nervous, looking around.

Was she waiting for someone? The same person she might have been waiting for when he'd caught her eye last week? The person who'd have a lust-crazed Lokian on his case if he showed up?

Though he shouldn't be worrying about a contender for her favors or what that unfortunate bastard might be in danger of, anyway. *She'd* probably run away screaming when she saw him this time. That would put an end to this insanity.

Fine. Time to put an end to it.

He started heading for her, and long before she should have noticed him, her eyes snapped around and caught him in their bull's-eye. Her gaze hit him even harder than it had the first time. The heat of it evaporated every intention of letting things end here.

With his every step closer, her eyes widened, her lips trembled. He couldn't bear it if it was with fear and revulsion.

She made a move to rise when he stopped above her.

His hand on her shoulder kept her in place. "Don't run again. I'm not a threat to you."

His conscience barked at him. *Liar.*

He might not be a direct threat, but the indirect threats associating with him could bring her were as, or more, dangerous.

Her lips trembled harder. "I know that."

"Sure." He touched a finger to her pulse, felt her life strong and intoxicating under his touch. "That's why your pulse feels like a trapped bird."

She wet her lips, swallowed. "It's not fear."

His erection jerked. He pressed his finger harder into her flesh, almost groaned with the arousal that sheared through him. "You don't need to placate me."

"I'm not."

His fingers stilled on her frantic pulse. "Then why did you run? If I didn't scare you?"

"Why did I come back, if you did?"

Good question. But when it came to her, the answer might not be the obvious.

He tested her claim. He swept his finger down her neck, the intention not to stop until he claimed the first intimacy clear in his touch, his gaze. He barely managed not to swoop down and catch her gasp on his tongue, drive inside her until he'd drained her of moans for him not to stop, to do anything at all to her.

Her hand came up, covered his.

He raised one eyebrow at her. Too intrusive? Or too creepy, when she'd seen what he could do with that hand, what it could turn into? Mortal in boundaries, after all, eh?

He started to remove his hand.

She caught it, pressed it to her neck.

Feeling his hand sandwiched between the hot silk of her flesh jolted electricity through him, singeing his loins and brain. His erection lurched harder when she pressed her neck into the curve of his palm.

She was showing him that she wasn't afraid of him. More, that she trusted him.

She wouldn't be so trusting if she knew that everything that made him able to pretend to be a civilized, modern man was slipping away, stripping him into the barbarian whose life revolved around plundering and pillaging. And he'd never wanted anything like he wanted her.

Then her earlier counterquestion crackled through his lust-hazed mind.

He blinked. "You mean you're here looking for me?"

She nodded, the bursts of light from the club's strobes highlighting hypnotic jade in the depths of her eyes. "I didn't know if your injuries would truly heal. Or if they did, that you would come back here. I came anyway."

He glided his hand over her velvet flesh, dug his fingers in the depth of her fiery silk tresses. "Why did you come?"

She pressed her head back into his hold, like a cat demanding more petting. "I wanted to thank you."

"*You* wanted to thank *me?*" He shook his head. "Unpredictable is your middle name, isn't it?"

"It could be my family's. My foster family, that is."

So she'd been fostered. That was one tidbit he hadn't learned at the hospital.

He caressed the resolute line of her jaw with one insistent thumb. "And what, by Loki, did you want to thank me for?"

"For saving my life."

"The life that was in danger because of me, you mean?"

"You warned me to get out of harm's way. And you did take the fight away from me and from other...humans."

"And you still walked out after me, pipe in hand." He twisted the heavy locks around his hand, bent over her, his leg now rubbing against hers. "I think I would have died if you hadn't come out."

She tilted her head, giving him a better grip, her face and lips flushing with pleasure when he took it. "That's what I don't get. You let them pulp you. But the operative word here is *let*. You could have...dispatched them at any time. But now that I know your healing power *is* miraculous, I might have thought you let them beat you as some kind of game."

"I assure you, I'm not into pain. Mine or others'. Not the damaging variety."

Her lids grew heavier, her scent stronger. His indirect declaration that he was into the kind of pain that sharpened pleasure heightened her arousal. Her voice deepened, roughened, though her words remained coolly logical. "I said I *might* have thought that, but I don't, since you seem to believe the injuries could have killed you. So...why?"

"Why do you think?"

"You wanted them to get confident before you retaliated? That doesn't make sense, either. So, why?"

He suddenly wanted to tell her. Everything.

He released her hair, straightened. "Because until you walked out and I saw you in danger, I wanted to die."

She gripped his arm in both of her hands. "But you... radiate power and life. Why would you want to end that?"

His chuckle was gruff. "Now you think I'm suicidal."

"Last time I looked, that defined 'want to die.'"

"In my case, it's a bit more complicated than that."

"That's what they all say."

"You get lots of suicide cases in the E.R., eh?"

Her eyes widened, realization dawning. "You followed me!"

"I did. All day."

"You changed into something I wouldn't notice."

She was sharp, learned the rules on the fly, didn't waste time clinging to beliefs once new evidence shattered them, reached the most accurate deduction based on new findings. And he wanted to fuck the hell out of her for it.

"Some*one*," he corrected. "It would have been difficult to follow you as a cabinet or a gurney."

Her jaw dropped. "You can change into stuff like that?"

He cupped it, resumed stroking it, stoking both his and her lust. "Just kidding. I can shift parts of me into inanimate objects. But to shift fully, I have to become something living, even if it's totally made up in my mind. So—still not scared?"

"Because you followed me, or because you can 'shift' into whatever your imagination can conjure?"

She'd latched on to his terminology, was giving it back to him. "According to mortals, both are the stuff of nightmares. We are talking stalker and monster from your worst ones."

Her eyes narrowed. "You want me to be scared, or what?"

"Only for the right reason."

"And that is?"

"That I want to ravish you. Until you're so sore and satisfied you can't even beg for more."

She suddenly rose. Before he could think, move, she slotted her every firm curve into his hard angles, dragged his head down to hers by his hair. Then she closed her lips over his ear in a hot suckle, poured her demand right into his brain.

"Dance with me."

Hunger exploded in his depths, whatever had been keeping it leashed snapping. He dragged her into his arms, slammed her into him, plastered her against his hardness.

People bumped into them as he swept her onto the packed dance floor. He exerted enough influence to empty a circle around them. He didn't want contact with anyone to dilute the feel of her or jar his focus from her. He couldn't bear any touch that wasn't hers.

He bent, kneaded her from the ankle up, bunched her skirt on his way until he had the resilient flesh of her thigh in his hungry grip. He raised her leg around his waist, ground his erection into her tight abdomen. She tossed her head back, arched, undulated against him to the now-languid rhythm. Her breasts rubbed against his chest to the tempo as the thrusts of his hips mimicked the possession he'd soon enact without barriers. Their every inflammatory movement ratcheted the exquisite agony of anticipation.

"Man, you're *big*." She pressed her lushness all over him. He pictured himself tearing those unflattering clothes off her where she stood, driving into her standing up. "Is that real?"

He wound his hand in her hair, secured her head by its tethers. "That's the real me, yes. I can…shrink, if you prefer."

"Don't you dare!" She dragged him closer, her hands greedy on his arms, back and chest. "I've been the huge girl all my life, and it's no fun. Men usually make me feel like the Hulk. Being dwarfed is…incredible. Don't you dare shrink an inch."

"Yes, ma'am." He chuckled, delighting in her candidness, his lips gliding over her velvet flesh, teasing her when she tried to capture them with hers, instead took them to her ear. "So tell me. Why are you not terrified? You act as if what you saw me do and become didn't upset your fundamental belief of reality and the world."

She punished him for denying her his lips, dug her fingers into his arms, gyrated harder against his erection as she poured her answer in his ear. "It didn't. I know weird stuff exists."

"How?"

"I've had some pretty inexplicable things happen in my life, ever since I was a kid, and I am now forced to accept the weirdest explanation for them as the truth."

He didn't want to know details. He would be out of said life by night's end. But he still wanted to know one thing more. "Tell me this, then. How did you fight that Odinian as if you were on the same level? Actually, since he had super strength and speed, dozens of levels above."

"Yeah, sure, that's why he managed to use me as a shield."

He nipped her earlobe in objection. "He would have risked anything to avoid me. Where did you learn to fight like that?"

She rained kisses on his jaw in return. "I wasn't always a respectable doctor. I was once a misfit living more on the streets than in the foster homes that hated taking me in. My juvenile record never made it to my permanent one, since I walked the straight and narrow from seventeen onward."

He pulled back to smile his satisfaction down at her. "You did look like a warrior. And you are. A street fighter, efficient, ruthless, dirty if need be. I should have recognized your method."

She grinned up at him, making her beauty almost unbearable. He wanted to *devour* her. "Since it's the same as yours? Yeah. Once you decided to end the fight, I almost pitied the bastards for how fast and easily you finished them off."

He cupped her luscious ass in his hands, lifted her against him again. "Almost but not really, huh?"

Another reason-annihilating moan of pleasure spilled from her. "One thing I'm not is a bleeding heart. They deserved what you did to them and then some. They would have killed us both, after torturing us. You probably saved endless future victims, too."

He arched her backward, swaying her to the blood-boiling beat. "Don't you put me in shining armor and shove me on a white steed."

"A white knight would leave me yawning. A dark avenger on the other hand…" She kneaded his buttocks, every inch of her rubbing against him, explicit in invitation.

Suddenly he wanted to tell her the whole truth, before he took her. He, who made a calling of conning mortals into doing his bidding.

"I am not that, either. I am a Lokian, and we—"

She climbed him, her arms locking around his neck, her legs around his hips, her lips on his. She thrust her tongue inside his mouth, singed him with her taste, that of freshness, sunlight and vitality, the heat of her hunger. "I don't need you to tell me anything." She wrenched away, impaled him with the urgency in her eyes. "I need *you*. For tonight."

For tonight. Just tonight.

That worked for him.

He'd take her, do everything to her, right here, then leave. He'd never see her again.

Now it was up to him to make it worth the lady's time. Not to mention almost her life.

No problem.

Chapter 4

Kara looked into the eyes of the…man—for lack of a better term to describe him—she'd almost died for last night.

She'd seen him shift parts of himself into lethal weapons and…things; she'd watched him kill ten men with the swift steadiness of a practiced executioner.

If possible, that only made her want him more.

And she'd have him, just this once, if it were the last thing she did. She could literally die replete and happy afterward.

Which, if what she'd learned recently had any truth—and now she was forced to believe it did—might even be soon. It also meant the danger might be as great to him.

She couldn't afford more than this one night. But she *had* to have it. And he hadn't promised it yet.

She wrapped herself around him tighter, tugged on his silken locks. "What'll it be?"

At her heated demand, his painstakingly sculpted lips crooked to one side. "Even though I should say no for your sake, I am at the point where I can no longer pretend nobility. You want me for tonight, you got me. As long as you know what you're getting."

"I have the...wildest expectations." She slid down his body, until she was poised over his hardness. Then she thrust her melting core at him, pleasure spreading even at the impeded contact, and satisfaction at the flare of ferocity in his eyes. "It's up to you to prove me right."

A harsh velvet laugh cracked from him as he shook his head as if at a private joke, his large hand squeezing her buttocks, grinding her into him. "It's up to me to prove you grossly cautious and underestimating."

The coil of arousal tightened another unbearable notch. She nipped that luscious lower lip filled with such promise, such threat. "Braggart. Now, deliver."

He gathered her tighter around him, walked off the dance floor. People melted out of their path as if by magic, even when the place had become so packed everybody seemed to be imprisoned within a cage of bodies and limbs. "Lusty and brazen as well as fearless and ruthless, aren't you?"

"And your point?" she gasped as he slammed her against the upholstered wall by her booth, which was miraculously still vacant, pinned her against it with his weight and hunger.

"Just celebrating my phenomenal luck, my sweet, lethal Kara."

She jerked at hearing her name growled on his lips. Then she remembered. He must have found out everything on record about her at the hospital. Beyond the vital statistics, which now meant less than ever, that wasn't much.

But that was much more than she knew of him. "Do I need to follow you around in disguise to find out *your* name?"

Another laugh revved inside his expansive chest, inside hers, too, as he pressed it against her breasts. His breath as his lips closed in on hers was a blend of pure virility and wildness. "You need only ask anything of me, and it's yours."

He accompanied the last word with a hard squeeze of her buttocks. He took full advantage of her gasp, crashing his lips on her wide-open ones. Then his tongue thrust deep.

She plunged into the taste of him. The flavor of danger and death, but also of power and protection. He'd shrugged off injuries that could have proven fatal last night to defend her. The memory, along with his scent and tang, flooded her bloodstream like a hit of a narcotic, an aphrodisiac. She rode rapids of mindlessness as his tongue filled her, drank her, as his lips and teeth mastered her.

This was no mere kiss. This was an invasion, a ravaging. And it catapulted her into a frenzy.

The music escalated, the thud of the beat rising, the bass rocking the place in miniquakes with each strum. But it wasn't just the music. It was the blood hurtling in her arteries, the heartbeats thundering in her chest, each shuddering through her marrow.

She pulled at his hair with all her strength. "Your name, dammit. Give it to me."

He shuddered as he snapped his head up. "Vidar. Now give it back to me. Moan it. And when I'm riding you, scream it."

She moaned it as he commanded, with a sound she'd never produced, wanton and wild. Every inch of her felt as if it would spontaneously combust. She ground herself against him, crazy for the next level of his onslaught.

He gave it to her, rubbed against her to the escalating rhythm. The abrasion of his hard flesh through her clothes, with that intricate snake locket nestled in his silky chest hair, turned her nipples into pinpoints of agony.

"Vidar," she moaned his name again into his lips, the sensuality and distinction of it adding to her aroused distress.

He obeyed her unspoken demand, yanked up her skirt, cupped her buttocks and opened her core. She keened as she snatched glances to each side where he wasn't shielding her from view. No one was looking their way in the light-pulsing darkness. Maybe because many where engaged in as licentious behavior. Or maybe because…

He angled her hips, and through her silk, soaked panties, wrapped her feminine lips around the girth bulging through his leather pants and she stopped caring about everything but what he was doing to her. She was inflamed, teetering on the brink, the tightness in her loins a stroke away from snapping….

She snatched her mouth away. "Stop…you'll make me come…."

He didn't stop, ground into her, gyrating his hardness against her core. Then it was too late.

Orgasm ripped through her, the coil of need inside her recoiling as it unwound in lash after lash of release, shock waves that rippled and widened until they drowned her, body and mind.

The cacophony enveloping them receded. She could hear only his rough encouragements and her sharp cries of release as he raised her and slid her down his body, had her riding his erection through the barriers of clothing, completing her orgasm.

She finally slumped in his arms, her heart slowing into the sluggish rhythm of satisfaction, all tension dissolved, the warmth of sexual bliss flooding her every nerve.

The moment she regained a measure of volition, she

smacked him. On that chest she'd just finished writhing in ecstasy against. "I told you to stop."

He thrust teasingly at her again, eliciting another shuddering aftershock from her body. "And deprive myself of watching you come all over me from just a couple of kisses and grinds? I'm not into self-denial."

She smacked him again, harder now, this time digging her fingers into his muscles, tweaking the dark gold hair adorning his burnished beauty. "I want to come all over you for real."

He groaned as she twisted harder. "You will. I'm not leaving you until I've made you come half a dozen times. At least. And half of those will be all over me 'for real.'" His fingers sought her still-pulsing core. "That was to get you warmed up." He glided two fingers along her feminine lips. She whimpered as the post-orgasm sensitivity gave way to renewed arousal. It took him just a few strokes to have her aroused out of her mind again.

"Now to get you ready to accommodate me."

She nipped his cleft chin, tried to reach down to release him. "I appreciate the concern, but any readier and I'll revert to the protoplasmic state."

"Oh, you haven't seen, or felt, ready yet." Then he plunged those fingers inside her.

She cried out at feeling their long, roughened thickness slide against her swollen flesh, braced herself between the inexorable surfaces sandwiching her, his torso and the wall, to give him full access, her ankles clamping his hips. She rode his fingers in escalating abandon, gasps bursting from her, pleasure accumulating as he went rougher, faster.

Just as she felt herself overloading, his thumb fondled firm circles on the knot where her nerves converged as his fingers beckoned inside her sheath. She started crying out when he dragged her head back by the hair, plunged his tongue inside her mouth, drinking her desperation, whispering gruffly, "Come for me again."

She did, in one convulsion after another as waves of release buffeted her. Her inner muscles gripped and released his invading fingers, bathing them in an outpouring of pleasure she'd never known her body capable of.

She recovered from her latest bout of stupor only when he lowered her to straddle him in the booth.

She braced her shaking thighs on both sides of his, fumbling with his zipper. "Enough preparations. I want you inside me. And I want you hard and fast."

His hands gripped hers as she tried to circumvent the huge obstacle of his erection. "Easy. Let me do this."

She grinned into his eyes. "Afraid I might damage the goods?"

His smile was unadulterated smugness and sensual threat. "Easy is for your sake, not mine."

She ground herself against him, the demand inside her pounding harder now, shaking her, as if the two mind-blowing orgasms had only fueled her lust. "So which part of 'hard' didn't you get?"

"You'll be the one to get it, as hard as you can stand. Just not to start with. I am not into inflicting pain, as I mentioned before. I'll hurt you if I don't go easy at first."

"You *can't* make me any hotter for you, y'know?"

"You think I'm exaggerating? Wouldn't that only prove self-defeating? My warnings are as factual as those on any potentially destructive tool. Instructions of due care have to precede use."

"And I've been instructed, thanks." She held his head,

rained openmouthed kisses and suckles all over the perfection she wanted to devour. "I'm a big girl. I can...use you."

He captured her roving lips, bit down into them, almost breaking their inner flesh, then laving the pain away. "And you will. When you're ready. For this." He captured one of her hands, guided it inside his briefs.

A frisson of danger slithered down her spine as she felt the reality of what she was inviting, literally, inside her body. His erection was as enormous as the rest of him. The intimidation only sent more fluid heat rushing from her depths.

She sought his eyes, hers widening with a mixture of dread and delight. "Is that the real you?"

He raised one winged dark blond eyebrow sardonically. "As in, am I using my shifting powers to magnify my... endowments?"

She shook her head. "Just a rhetorical question. A stunned one. As unreal as it feels, it's only worthy of the rest of you. But don't you dare expand another inch."

"Will you make up your mind already? First it's 'don't shrink,' now it's 'don't expand.' And this fixation with inches."

"Can you blame me when they're yours?" She pushed his briefs down, let his erection spring free in all its glory. Hard and huge and heavy. And as impossibly gorgeous as the rest of him. It slammed against his abdomen with a slap that made her dizzy with lust. She stroked a shaking hand up and down his smooth, steellike length.

And then she realized. "You're hot!"

Mirth rumbled from his depths as he thrust himself harder into her grip. "And you're wondering why?"

"I mean hot for real. Hotter than a...mortal in high fever."

Surprise flitted in his eyes. "A Lokian reportedly sizzles when he's in the grips of what's called a 'mating fever.'"

"And you've never been before, to know firsthand?"

The look he gave her. She almost came again from that alone. "Not until this femme fatale, no."

"Neither have I, until this marauding Viking." She jacked his length again, shuddered. "Man, you *are* sizzling."

"Don't worry. I've heard the heat intensifies a woman's pleasure."

"I'm only worried that you're not already inside me. Worried for you. Teasing me might not end happily."

"Thanks for the kind warning." He chuckled again, latched his lips over her neck.

Her breath tore through her lungs as he ravaged her in suckles that would leave their mark, that she wished would mark her forever, that sent pleasure hurtling through her with each savage pull.

She'd never dreamed this could happen to her. No boundaries to what she'd want from a man, to what she'd allow him, just raw need, total abandon, unbridled ecstasy. Lightyears hotter than any erotica she'd ever read. Insipid fantasies all, compared to this, to him.

He wasn't meeting her expectations, he was pulverizing them.

He ripped the buttons from her shirt, pushed it aside, and in one flick of those fingers she knew could snap steel like she would chalk, he severed her bra. She cried out at the primal sound that rumbled from him, reverberated through her. A shock of sensation eddied through her as her swollen breasts fell into his palms, as he pressed them together, mitigating the ache, increasing the need. And that was before he bent and took her nipples into his mouth, one by one, showed her there was more suffering, more pleasure.

Between long, hard pulls, he swirled them with his tongue, grazed them with his teeth, blew the stimulation of his steaming breath on them. "I hope you know you got yourself an insatiable Viking on your hands. On every inch of you."

"Promises," she gasped as he squeezed her mound, wound the need inside her tighter before he slipped his hand inside her panties again, spread her open, slid his fingers through her molten folds. She keened, trembling on another edge.

"You're melting." His voice was harsh as gravel now.

She wrenched his hand away from her flesh. She wanted *him,* not release. "State the painfully obvious, will you? So you deem me ready to 'accommodate' you now?"

His narrowed eyes gleamed azure danger as he brought his fingers to his lips, licked them off. "I'm at the point where you'll just have to take your chances with that."

She squeezed his erection as hard as she could. "If you don't deliver on those big-time threats right this second, Vidar, I swear I'll hurt you."

His groaned his pained pleasure, appreciation of her desperation and bravado blazing in his eyes as he tore her panties off her with the same ease he'd ruined her bra. "Wasn't there some provision in your Hippocratic oath about harming others?"

"It's '*First* Do No Harm.' I've given you enough warnings."

"So you did." Something merry and menacing revved from him, had all her hairs on end as he poised her over his length. But instead of driving into her, he glided the scorching, flowing-with-arousal head through the swollen lips of her sex.

She lurched on a shrill cry. The heat *was* incredible, its effect more so. He circled her engorged knot until she writhed, everything focusing where his flesh tormented hers.

She'd never known *anything* could feel this good.

As if reading her thought, he groaned, "It'll only get better."

He broke contact a second before she came apart. Then he raised her with unbelievable strength, made her feel weightless, hovering over him as he thrust up into her in shallow strokes, his face driven.

She tried to crash over him, engulf him. She knew it would hurt. She wanted it to. She wanted him to brand her.

She begged for his invasion. "Now, Vidar, *please*."

He finally obeyed. He thrust up and dragged her down at once, forging through the initial shock and resistance of her body, then plunging past into the depths that yielded for him, feeling like a sword just out of the fire. She screamed his name, with the pain, with its excruciating pleasure.

Her back arched, her head bent back, her mouth opened on the scream that was now silent with the bombardment of sensations. For endless moments she felt nothing, heard nothing, was nothing but overstretched with his potency, invaded, full beyond her capacity, delirious with the carnality of it all, the completion.

He lifted her again, and the receding fullness as he withdrew from her depths had her clawing at him, her demand for him to resume his domination incoherent, fragmented. "*Vidar*...don't...give me..."

"All you can take and more." His face was clenched in what looked like suffering as he pulled her down again.

She'd thought he'd filled her on that first thrust. But he now forged deeper, felt as if he'd never stop. "Nothing has ever felt like this. You're burning me, too. Consume me as I invade you, as I fill you and finish you, Kara. Take all of me, all the way inside you."

He *did* feel all the way inside her, as if he might breach her womb with every thrust. She was trembling all over, as if with the advance tremors of a major quake. Then he lodged himself farther yet, growled, "Come all over me, Kara. Scream my name."

His command was the last straw. Every spark of existence converged into that one point where he was buried deepest inside her, condensed into one pinpoint of absolute being.

Then it exploded.

She screamed his name as the sensations razed through her. She shattered, then reformed around his thickness with every discharge, her inner muscles straining to drain him of all the pleasure he was flooding into her body, of his own release.

From the abyss of ecstasy, she heard him roar her name, felt him stiffen in her arms, ram her deeper than ever, breaching her completely, before jet after jet of his seed flooded her. Her orgasm spiked at feeling his hot release inside her intimate flesh. She shook, writhed, pleasure almost damaging in intensity inundating her.

Time ceased, stretched, streaked. All she knew was that she was draped all over him, a nerveless mass, replete to her last cell, her heart hammering over his, her lips open on snatches of air and on the burning flesh of his neck.

She'd just been fucked out of her literal mind in a crowded nightclub. And no one was even looking at them.

Or she'd been too far gone to notice if somebody had been

watching, and she'd raise her eyes to find an avid audience of hundreds recording videos and waiting for an encore.

She didn't give a damn about them. Only about the encore.

Still feeling him undiminished inside her, she pulled back to look at him. His eyes were heavy with pure male satisfaction, his lips filled with dominant arrogance and the promise of more.

She rested her buzzing palms over his hot, hard, moist chest. "You were right to warn me. It was…beyond endurance."

His eyes darkened. Then he began to raise her off him. He'd misunderstood.

She clung to him, inside and out. "The *pleasure* was. More, Vidar. I have to have more."

Vidar looked into the flushed face of the woman he was still buried to the hilt inside. The woman in whose body he'd just experienced the first complete pleasure of his endless existence. She was devouring him with the same stunned voracity that raged inside him, demanding more.

He had to have more, too. He'd thought he'd walk away after he'd sated them both. But this encounter had just whetted his appetite for her until it felt like a sword twisting into his vitals. In fact, a sword had only been agonizing. But *this* was also maddening, will-sapping, and all around far more dangerous.

For now, he could only succumb.

He lifted her off him, shuddered with her at the pain of separation. "And you'll have more, Kara. I'm only halfway through fulfilling my promise." He reached for the coat she'd discarded on the bench, helped her put it on over the clothes he'd ripped apart. He adjusted his own clothes with difficulty before standing up, pulling her to her feet. "I pledged the night, too. And that's still young."

As soon as they exited the club, she tugged at him. "Where are we going?"

He hadn't even considered where. But he could only think of one destination. "My place."

She stopped, pulled her hand from his. "No."

He frowned. "Your place?"

She shook her head. "Neutral ground."

She was right. This had to remain…neutral. And it had to end with the night. It didn't matter that something corrosive was eating away at his euphoria and reason. A voice that demanded he override her, take her to his place. And keep her there.

He wouldn't. For all the reasons there were.

He forced a smile to his lips. "Neutral ground, it is."

Chapter 5

Vidar chose said neutral ground with care.

Instead of doing what he could to ensure that she'd relegate this night to the shelf of her one-night stands, he was going out of his way to give her a night to remember.

He wasn't doing what he'd done with his own one-night stands, either—keeping them out of focus, so that by the time day dawned, his memory of each had blurred before it was mostly deleted. He was committing Kara's every nuance to the damned indelible part of his memory.

He watched her greedily now as she looked around the twenty-thousand-a-night suite of the zillion-star hotel. Not that he'd pay a cent. He had money, too much of it, but he almost never needed it. As a Lokian, everything this world had to offer was his for the taking at the flash of a locket. Loki's Locket. The manager of this establishment, a wannabe Legion recruit, had taken one look at it and given them the suite that spanned half of the uppermost floor. They could stay here forever if Vidar wished.

They'd stay only tonight.

She turned to him, her expression whimsical. "So you're obscenely rich as well as criminally sexy."

"Look who's talking." He bent and swept her up in his arms. She clung immediately, met his kiss halfway, dueled with his tongue with the same urgency and ferocity, giving him back his hunger on the same level.

She murmured into his mouth. "I'll spend the night with you anywhere. Don't spend that much money here. Donate it to the hospital instead and let's go to a motel or something."

"I'm not taking you to some sleazy dump."

"Not coming with an astronomical bill doesn't mean it would be a dump."

"I'm not paying a cent here. Money isn't the only way to pay for things. And I'll donate to the hospital, anyway."

"Should have known you'd have influence and connections, too. Okay, you may proceed."

He grinned, pinched her buttock. "Yes, ma'am."

In seconds he took her across the threshold of the expansive en suite bathroom. He placed her on her feet in the middle of its marble floor, brooded upon those clothes he hated. She'd commented on his animosity with amusement, insisted she loved his "bodice-ripping" tendencies, was delighted when he'd insisted only she had inspired them, but was adamant about not accepting replacements. Knowing she relished his ferocity, he had her standing in a heap of tattered clothes in seconds.

Then he looked down at her. Towering barely a foot shorter than himself, her breasts were a feast, her waist and tummy trim and firm, her hips lush with femininity. Her limbs were long and smooth, her shoulders square and strong. Every curve and line and swell of her was the epitome of womanliness.

He skimmed his hand from the curve of her shoulder to her breast, blood roaring in his ears, his loins, as its warmth and resilience overflowed in his large hand. "You wear those clothes like I do my disguises."

She thrust her breast into his hold, inviting a more aggressive possession. "But you saw through them."

He pinched her nipple, bent for a compulsive suckle. "I didn't see anything near the truth." He raised his head, gathered her against his length, groaning as she melted into him. "You're beyond glorious. A goddess."

Her face flushed with pleasure as her hands treated his clothes with the same hostility. "Look who's talking."

Delight expanded through him as he surrendered to her impatience, wallowing in it as she exposed his body to her hunger.

Then he had her inside the shower stall, melding their nakedness below a steady jet of hot water, plundering her fragrant mouth in wrenching kisses, his hands seeking all her secrets, taking every license, owning every inch. He brought her to another orgasm around his fingers, before going down on his knees and draping her legs over his shoulders. She wantonly plastered her back to the steamy tiles, arched her hips at him, opening herself wide for his devouring. He suckled and tongued her to two more orgasms, growling like a beast as he drank her overflowing pleasure.

When he finally let her melt off his shoulders, she hugged him around the hips and engulfed his erection, what she could of it, in her mouth.

He'd never enjoyed giving or receiving oral sex. Seemed that was because it hadn't been her sex he was devouring, or her mouth that was devouring his. He'd never felt such a purity of desire from a woman as she delighted in his texture and taste. The look of blissful voracity that adorned her face as her lips wrapped around his girth, murmuring and moaning her pleasure, soon had him stripped down to his savage male component, blind with lust, with the need to dominate his female completely.

He still tried to pull away when he felt his seed about to burst from his loins. She keened in protest, dug her fingers hard in his buttocks, kept him lodged inside her mouth. And he climaxed in torrents of scalding come, the pleasure agonizing as he watched her drinking him.

When she'd made sure she'd drained him to the last drop, she reluctantly slipped his intact hardness out of her mouth, pressed her flushed, wet face to his thigh. "You feel and smell and taste incredible, addictive. Another Lokian power?"

Something ugly slithered down his spine. The thought that another Lokian might appeal to her, arouse her as much.

But no. Her lust was specific to him. Just as his was to her. He knew it.

He dragged her to her feet, crashed his lips on hers, drove inside the fount of her taste in ferocious rhythm. She clung to him, lips and limbs. He pressed her against the slippery wall, wrenched her thighs open around his hips and plunged inside her. By now he knew she craved his aggressiveness, could accommodate him, even if barely, that the edge of pain only made her pleasure more explosive.

She screamed his name with his every slam inside her fluid heat, clung to him harder, opening wider, demanding that he take everything, do everything to her, hold nothing back.

They exploded into orgasm together. He jetted inside her with almost his full strength behind each thrust as she smashed herself against him, her muscles a convulsive vice around his cock, milking him dry as ecstasy tore through her, pushed them both into a seizure of devastating release.

A long, long time later, he set her back on her feet, supported her when her legs buckled, lathered and rinsed her lushness, and licked and suckled her to another soothing orgasm. He was addicted to her taste and pleasure already. And he mustn't even *think* it. This ended tonight.

But the night still had many hours. He'd use up every second.

He gathered her, wet and sated, took her back to the bedroom.

He threw her on the bed, watching her bounce on it in a sinuous arch of sensual madness. Desire roared at full blast all over again.

He crawled on all fours over her, looked down at her as she spread herself for his exploitation and pleasuring.

"Now, Kara. Now I take you as you should be taken, on a bed worthy of your satin flesh, servicing your magnificent body until it is numb with pleasure."

She opened her thighs for him, hooked her ankles around his waist. "You did that when you had nothing to work with but a narrow wall, a cramped bench and a slippery shower stall. So don't knock uncomfortable and inconvenient."

"My apologies." He cupped her buttocks, mounted her, smiled into the emerald fire and desire that were her eyes. "But for the rest of the night, you'll have to put up with comfort and convenience with your pleasure."

"Oh, that works, too. I'd put up with anything at all as long as I can have *your* magnificence."

"You have it all, my glorious Kara."

He rode her for hours this time, in every position. And as

promised, he made her come all over him in each. The fiercest had been this last time, when he'd had her on her side as he took her from the back, stroking her with his fingers at once. As she seized and shook, he finally joined her in the depths of pleasure, poured the fuel of his come on hers.

He wanted more, but she was finally too drained, too replete, to arouse again. He remained buried inside her, turned her head, drowned them both in a leisurely mating of mouths until she drew a fraction away, her swollen lips spreading in a smile of bone-deep satisfaction.

"Overachiever." Her voice cracked, shivered down his every supercharged nerve. "You far surpassed your promised projections. I lost count of how many times I came. I think I've lost the ability to move ever again, too."

He almost said he'd crammed too much in too little time, since this one night was all they'd have.

He didn't. He wouldn't shatter the perfection by bringing up an end that was still a few hours away.

He pulled her back into him, contained her body in the curve of his and counted her breaths as she fell asleep.

He debated falling asleep himself.

Should he waste his remaining time with her sleeping?

But this would be the one time he could sleep with her in his arms.

He hugged her closer, closed his eyes.

He woke up as soon as she moved.

He remained still, pretending to sleep, watched her through slit lids. She tiptoed around the lushly carpeted room, gathering her ruined clothes. As soon as her coat safely covered her and she'd finger-combed her wild curls into a semblance of order, she sat down at the desk.

For a long moment, she stared at the notepad. Finally she wrote what must have been only a couple of lines.

Then she rose. She stood there, looking at him across the distance for what felt like forever.

The temptation to go to her, drag her back to bed, tell her she was going nowhere, ever again, was brutal.

He maintained his sleep pretense. She finally turned and walked to the door. Her shoulders were slumped, her steps impeded.

She didn't want to end it.

He was grateful that she did.

He wouldn't have had the will to walk away.

Chapter 6

Thank you for the best two nights of my life.
   I'll never forget you.
   Vidar read the note again. As if he'd find new words, more meanings. Something he'd missed the first thousand times he'd read it.
   It had been a week since Kara had written it. He'd grabbed it the moment the door had closed behind her. He still couldn't stop taking the note out every few minutes to reread it.
   The words remained the same. The meaning, too.
   She'd added the night of mortal danger to her life's best. Because she'd found him then.
   Yet she'd walked away. She hadn't tried to find him again. He knew. He'd gone to the nightclub every night since.
   He'd thought that if she did seek him out, he'd let them have another night. Or two. Or ten. He'd been telling himself that they might have enough of each other by then. That it wasn't wise to let something so fierce go unassuaged or it would eat through them. As it was eating through him.
   But as each day passed, his disappointment intensified.

How could she not wish for more of him, when he was in agony for more of her?

In disguise, he'd followed her from work to where she lived alone in a loft downtown, searching for evidence that she hoped he was trailing her in her glances, her movements. He'd thought sometimes that she looked around, expectation in her eyes, then seemed let down when she thought none of those around was him.

Maybe he'd seen what he was longing to see.

The only thing that held him together was those words.

I'll never forget you.

But they were no longer enough.

He had to find out if she'd meant them.

If she hadn't, he'd just say hello and move on. He'd have certainty, closure. He was going insane not knowing for sure.

He folded the note along the line she'd made, stowed it with reverence beside his other vital possession, Loki's Locket.

Then he rang her loft's intercom.

In seconds, the line opened. He heard clanging followed by her breathing as if she'd come running. Then her voice poured from the machine, stripped of its inimitable nuances, but still her voice. It cascaded over him in a wave of violent longing.

"Yes?"

It took him seconds before he could only mutter, "Vidar."

Everything ceased. Time. The sounds in the background. Her movement. Her breath.

He gritted his teeth, bracing against the answer he dreaded.

Please go away.

What would he do if she said that? He couldn't walk away.

But if she said it, he had to respect her wishes.

The intercom line went dead.

His heart punched his ribs, the blow feeling it would leave both bruised.

What had he expected? She'd asked for just one night, insisted on neutral ground, woken up first and left. Her silent rejection now told him all he needed to know. His presence was unwelcome. He should leave her alone. It was over.

A tidal wave of black dejection crashed on him.

And he finally admitted it to himself. Finding her had rejuvenated his will to exist. More. Sparked something unprecedented, an unquenchable desire to *live,* an unknown kind of life, with passion as its fuel, with her as its driving force.

It didn't matter that he wouldn't have had much time with her. Any time he could have had would have felt like forever. Far better than eternity without her.

He'd thought he'd reached his lowest point when he'd invoked Loki and demanded death. He hadn't. She'd been able to drag him out of that abyss, just by wanting him. Now that she no longer did, nothing could bring him back.

He turned, descended the dozen stairs leading to the building's porch.

The door burst open, slammed against the wall.

"Vidar."

He swung around. *Kara*.

She flew down the stairs, literally. She knew he'd catch her.

He did, crushed her to him, feeling as if he'd caught everything worth having, the whole world.

Her hug and the kisses she stormed over his face were frantic.

Shaking with the reprieve of knowing she reciprocated his desire in full, he felt everything fall away as he carried her up to her loft, homing in on her bed. What followed was a new level of abandon, their lovemaking frenzied, their pleasure blinding.

Endless hours later, she stirred over him, raised a head unsteady with the enervation of fulfillment. Her curls tumbled over his chest, those eyes that had rekindled his soul pouring emerald fire and the absoluteness of her desire over him.

Then she blew every expectation out of the water all over again when she murmured, "You shouldn't have come."

A disconcerted moment passed. Then he said the same words she had the night he'd sought her out again. "I came, anyway."

She gave him back what he'd asked her. "Why did you come?"

When he'd asked, he'd already known the answer, wanting to hear it from her. She wanted the same now.

He'd give her anything she wanted. "Because I couldn't stay away. I've starved for you. Have you for me?"

"Were you here these past six hours while I was bingeing on you?"

His delight with her honesty rumbled from his depths. "You can binge on me in an open-ended buffet."

"No, I can't. You know it can't work. It's why I walked away. It's why you let me."

"I have another explanation for why I did. I was an idiot."

"No, you weren't. The problem is, together we're so mind-blowing that you want more, against your better judgment."

"Judgments change, and mine wasn't better—I just *thought* it was better. It isn't. Also, mind-blowing is a problem I want indefinitely. I want us to be together."

She stilled, frowned. "Define together."

"Be together. *Live* together."

Those elegant eyebrows rose. "On the strength of one night?"

"Two now. Three. We started our relationship by almost dying and killing for each other. Then we proceeded to almost die or kill each other with too much pleasure. I think we've hit on the perfect combination."

She shook her head, started to put distance between them. "Vidar, I've spent the past week writhing in withdrawal. I want you with such an intensity it's a literal pain...."

He plastered her against his sizzling flesh. "And now I can be there to relieve that pain day or night."

She again braced her palms against his chest. "It's not that simple, and you know it. You're...immortal, a warrior of some sort..."

"And you're afraid I'd drag you into mortal danger."

"Will you let me complete my own sentences?" He raised a hand in concession. "From the way you call people 'mortals,' it's clear this...perishability is what defines us to you. I'd be a liability to you."

That was her concern? Would he ever chart her unpredictability? He gathered her tighter. "You were a lifesaving asset that first night."

"Only because I put myself in 'mortal danger,' and you survived to save me. What if next time you had to die to do it? I can't be your Achilles' heel."

"You won't be. I'll take every precaution so that no one will ever tie you to me." She began to shake her head again and he stopped her with a solemn look. "I'll walk away in only one instance. If you don't want me."

"Oh, I don't. As I just spent hours proving." She bent for a compulsive kiss, drew away, sighed. "We *were* foolish to think one night, or two or ten, can quench this fire." Exactly what he'd thought. "So if you promise I won't be a handicap, we can be…together until it burns itself out."

Exactly what he *didn't* think would happen. This would only burn brighter.

But he'd let her find that out for herself. And that he'd keep her safe.

She threw him another curve. "And promise, if I leave again, you won't come after me."

His heart compressed. She was already planning the next end.

But he had to promise her freedom. If one day *her* desire burned out, he had to let her go.

"You have my word." She nodded, her tremulous smile tinged with melancholy. She knew her desire wouldn't end, too, was only making provisions for his best interests. His heart expanded again. "Now, don't you want to know everything about me?"

Her lips quirked. "Being together doesn't mean poking my nose into your affairs."

He glided a hand indulgently up and down her silky back and bottom. "What if I want that delightful nose there?"

She arched into his caresses like a feline. "You don't strike me as the kind who opens the book of his life to others."

He laughed at the understatement. "You could say that again. One of my job descriptions is Trickster."

She grinned at him. "Then this truthful compulsion has to be a side effect of a blow to your head that night."

"I want only you to know the truth. To know me."

"I know enough, so don't sweat it."

As she started kissing him again, he stopped her. "What do you know?"

She sighed, as if in resignation that she had to satisfy him before he would her. "You call yourself a Lokian, and since you're a Viking and a shifter, you clearly follow a religion founded around Loki, the trickster, shape-shifting Norse god."

"It's not a religion, but a Legion, sworn to uphold Loki's code. That of protecting and fostering outcasts."

"Loki was—or, now that I know he exists—*is* an outcast himself, right? According to the comics and movies, he's also a villain."

"That's what is advertised by his rival Asgardian gods, mainly Odin and Freyja. They, and those who believe in them in Midgard—Earth—consider Loki and his followers abominations."

"Because of their shifting, right?" He nodded. "So the villain part is bad press that stuck."

"Pretty much. Loki's eternal battle isn't about gaining power through deceit, as they say, but fighting for his right to be different, to maintain his rightful place among the gods without conforming. To that end, he formed his Legion of like-minded mortals a few millennia ago. He started with the Originals, twelve Legionnaires with the strongest shifting and illusory powers. I am one of those. He granted us immortality and sent us out to recruit outcasts like us, to foster the Gifts that had made Normals reject them, and bring them under Loki's protection."

"And that's something, I bet."

"Loki is very generous to his followers, yes. The problem is, throughout the ages we've had to initially gain our recruits' trust through trickery. Apart from the paranormal element that would make most freak if confronted with the truth up front, the paranoia against Loki is very well established."

"And that helps your enemies paint you as villains."

He squeezed her breast in appreciation. "You got it. Sharp and brilliant. Is it any wonder I constantly want to ravish you until you faint with pleasure?"

She reciprocated by nipping his chest. "I constantly want to ride you to oblivion, too, so we're even. So, you trick people into signing on to your Legion?"

"No. Once the hurdle of approach is over, it's our code to leave them free to make the decision, even though that ensures that few throughout the ages pledge allegiance, even with the possibility of immortality as one of the perks."

"So not everyone in the Legion is immortal?"

"Being a candidate for immortality takes specific power levels, personality traits and something that only Loki can determine. Most recruits with psychic and shifting powers are candidates for one level or another of longevity, though."

"So how many immortal Legionnaires are there? Beyond the twelve Originals?"

He exhaled in remembered frustration. "Too few. Though mortals dream of immortality, few can handle it. Among the thousands I have recruited, only dozens had survived beyond a couple of hundred years. Only *one* of the dozens I judged capable of being inducted into the Lokians' inner circle survives to this day. The others gave in to insanity, excess, depression, and ended their lives or caused their own death, most times along with that of others'."

Her eyes grew thoughtful. "You feel you've failed them, and Loki, don't you? And since you've lived for millennia, the toll of time and loss has grown too much. That's why you wanted to die the night I first saw you."

A surge of fierce emotion spread inside his chest. He cupped her cheek tenderly. "Seems you do know a lot about me."

Her smile was impish, even as her eyes misted. "Told you. I also know that you more than foster the Gifted. You fight other gods' followers. The night we met they were after your 'Endowment.'" She suddenly giggled. "Oh, the mental image *that* brought!"

He tasted her smiling lips. "They thought they could suck out the part that makes me immortal."

She went still. "And that's not possible, right?"

"No. Not that it stops goons from trying. But when they're not coming after us like junkies, they go after our recruits, to prevent Loki from gaining more followers."

One eyebrow rose. "What does Loki want with followers, anyway? He sounds like a cool god and the ego trip of amassing worshippers doesn't suit him."

"Followers are not worshippers. Loki is not my god but my lord and general. I swore allegiance to him, and I believe in his goal. For the Gifted to have their rightful place in the world."

"Ruling it?"

He shrugged. "Just leading it where their Gifts make them fittest for the job. Certainly ending discrimination against them. To that end, Loki needs to survive Ragnarok, which is allegedly the Final Fate of the Gods. It's supposed to be a showdown where all gods end up killing one another and dying. We're working on making sure Loki walks out of it alive and victorious. And though we remain a tiny minority, with all of us being Gifted, we are a huge threat to the other gods' masses of worshippers. Even those they Endow are originally Normal and no match for us."

"Wow. Just wow." Her look of wonder gave way to teasing. "And you are a white knight, after all."

"Oh, no, I'm not. We Original Lokians take 'the end justifies the means' to very dark-gray realms."

She grinned at him. "Sounds like my kind of guys."

He swung her around, flattened her beneath him, loomed over her menacingly. "Guy. Singular."

"You *are* that." She wound herself around him, seeking his invasion. "And you are that to me. Now fill me. Singularly."

He slid inside her, bottomed out on that single thrust she demanded, swallowed her cry of welcoming shock, shouted with exultation as her flesh enfolded him like it was made to fit him.

This woman. This flesh. This union. *This* was what he'd waited an eternity for. A good thing he hadn't known, though, or he would have gone insane while waiting.

But now that he'd found her, he wouldn't lose her again.

And if reason insisted he would, one day, to mortality, he silenced it.

For now.

Chapter 7

Vidar watched Kara saunter into her loft. He'd entered through the window as usual, observing the secrecy of their relationship. For the past six weeks, it had worked perfectly.

They did.

They synchronized their working hours, sharing every minute between. When she had a long shift, he arrived before her to pamper her when she came home. He had her favorite lasagna waiting for her tonight.

"Mmm." She inhaled as she approached him with a smile that made his very being tighten. Sensual and wicked, delighted and delighting. "Now what do I devour first?"

He bent to take her lips. "Food will get cold. I won't."

"Let's eat fast, then, since you get hotter."

He chuckled, swept her off her feet and took her to the table. He sat her down, served her.

She looked up as he started massaging her stiff shoulders. "Won't you join me?"

"I snacked on endless rubbish while on stakeout with Daven."

She grinned. "Good thing you have this nuclear metabolism, or Daven and his atrocious eating habits would get you fat over a weekend."

She turned her attention to her meal, dug in appreciatively, hungrily, and started telling him about her day. He told her about his, marveling yet again at how she discussed his battles as naturally as she did her cases. She wiped her plate and rushed to shower.

He watched her streak away, sighed his pleasure. She was more magnificent than any goddess. Addictive passion on two gorgeous, endless legs, between which he'd found a heaven far better than any mortal had dreamed or god had promised.

He'd never truly lived before she'd wanted him.

And he now understood what Alvar had gone through. Wondered how he'd recovered. If you could call being a morose, unstable son of a bitch "recovered." But Alvar *had* survived.

He wouldn't survive losing Kara.

He had to make her immortal.

But to become so, she had to be not only Gifted but one of a rare minority. Even if she was all that, not many had been able to withstand the reality of living indefinitely. He himself, before he'd met her, had been ready to end it all. And he didn't even feel a Gift in her.

But he was working with the conviction that her effect on him eclipsed his Gift-detecting ability, that a part of what had attracted him to her initially, and her to him, had been her Gift. Why else had she been there? She'd admitted she hadn't known why she'd entered the nightclub, had no idea why they'd let her in. He was betting it was something she didn't realize she had, pulling her to him, swaying those bouncers.

What remained was to uncover that Gift. He'd then make sure she was one of the few who could attain and withstand eternity.

She'd come back, was lowering herself over him, fresh and hot and urgent, her knee rubbing his erection, her eyes devouring before her lips sank into his. She always came home from work starving for him, didn't want foreplay in that first slaking of hunger, wanted him wild and rough and assuaging. He always gave her what she needed.

But after the nightmare he'd had last night, he had to settle this tonight. He'd dreamed himself standing at her window, gazing down as she looked up to wave goodbye. Out of nowhere, a car had hit her.

It had driven home that he couldn't assume he had time to find a solution, counting on her youth and health. An accident could rob him of her. He needed insurance, right now.

He weaved his fingers through her hair, pulled her from worshipping her way down his body to the cock that wanted nothing but the embrace of her hot, talented mouth or her snug, welcoming body.

"Hey!" She looked up in protest. "I'm hungry." She rubbed him through his pants. "You...feel ravenous, too."

"That's putting it mildly. But we need to talk."

The change that came over her was spectacular. One moment she was the incendiary lover who drove him out of his mind with a glance, the next she was a stranger. In another second she was sitting at the far end of the couch, her face unreadable.

"You don't need to talk. You don't owe me a talk. You want to leave, just walk out and never look back."

He blinked in stupefaction. "What? That's not what I

want to talk about." His heart thudded in disappointment. "By Loki's Leer, Kara, you'd just let me go that easily?"

She shrugged, face still shuttered. "You'll leave sooner or later. I accept that."

"Well, I don't accept it. I don't want to leave. And I don't want you to leave me, either. I won't let you go."

She tipped her face. "Are you going to hold me captive?"

"A very willing one. But I meant I won't let you go, *ever.*"

"Uh, you do know I come with an expiration date, don't you? And if that's in fifty years, I doubt you'll hang around till then. You'll maybe stick with me to my sell-by date."

He gritted his teeth at her cavalier attitude to what was tearing him up inside. "Don't be ridiculous."

"You mean you'll stay with me till I'm ninety? Let's get real here and admit you'll at best stay until my menopausal mood swings send you flying out that window."

"I don't intend for you to reach menopause."

Her lips twisted. "I do intend to take hormone replacements."

"Cute. I mean, I won't let you age."

"You think you can make me an immortal, don't you? I thought that was reserved for an elite selection of Gifted."

"You might be one of them. I believe part of why I was so violently attracted to you was because I sensed you have a Gift."

Her headshake was adamant, final. "I don't."

"That you don't realize that you have one doesn't mean you don't. It might be buried deeper than usual."

"How can it be buried deep and at the same time be so apparent it drew you so strongly?"

He felt his brain overheat with the validity of her question, with the contradictions, the desperation to find a way. "I don't know. Yet. But it can't have all been sexual."

"Why not? Our sexual chemistry is way off any chart. And then every other sort of passion and emotion was involved, too. I think I fell in love with you the moment you took that guy's head off for me."

His head almost exploded. To hear her say she loved him now, when she was cornering him into admitting and accepting he would lose her...

He almost ground his teeth to powder. "How romantic of you."

"I'm just trying to explain the overwhelming thing you feel from me. Not that it's anything you should concern yourself with. What I feel is my responsibility, my business, not yours."

His heart shriveled. "And how accommodating of you."

"Listen, Vidar, I'm a big girl. I knew what you were from the first night, and still a horde of your Norse mythology creatures couldn't have dragged me from on top of you. I've loved every second we've had together. What I feel doesn't change a thing." She came over him, hunger flaring in her eyes. "So if you don't intend to leave just yet, shut up and let me have you. I'm mortal, so don't you dare waste my time talking."

He held her away, desperate to find a hope, an answer. "But you *may* be more than mortal."

"No. I'm nothing special, and one day I'll die." She undid his pants, took out his cock, straddled him. She wore no panties beneath her skimpy nightie. Her moist heat scorched him as she undulated over him. "But not today, so enjoy me while you can."

He held her by the hips, stopped her from impaling herself on his erection. "I want to enjoy you forever. If I can make you immortal..."

"You can't. This is hard enough for me without you harping about it. I have no Gift you can foster—the only thing you're fostering is bitterness about something I was okay with, my inevitable death." She tried to scramble off him. "Okay, congrats, you've managed the impossible. I don't feel like screwing your brains out anymore."

He tugged her back. "Fine. Whatever. I'll do it to you, anyway." He thrust inside her in one hard, long stroke. She screamed at his invasion, wrapped him inside and out in a vice of hunger and welcome. He growled at her captivation of him.

Then everything disintegrated in the inferno of pleasure.

It was after she'd collapsed in his arms, sated and shuddering with the aftershocks of her last orgasm, that reality crashed over him again.

If she had no Gift, then she was lost to him.

No. He wouldn't accept that. He would find a way.

Loki. If he wanted his precious Originals to remain a round dozen, he'd better cough up a special provision for Kara.

If Loki couldn't, he'd find someone who could.

He'd sell his soul to have her forever.

Vidar had barely put a foot down from the car when Alvar floored it. He had to bail out, roll on the ground, avoid two incoming cars, before he got to his feet, chuckling.

In two days he'd forced Alvar and Daven to conclude a mission that should have taken five, so that he could go back to Kara. The rush job had involved a lot of pain and injuries. They weren't happy.

They now stuck their heads out of their windows and sneered at him at the top of their voices. "Whipped," "Lapdog," "Doormat."

He chuckled again. Poor guys were still in shock. And denial. They couldn't get their heads around the fact that their shining beacon in uncommitted bachelorship had fallen in love.

In far more and deeper than love.

And he had fantastic news he couldn't wait to share with the woman who had him fathoms-deep in her thrall. Loki had consented to do all he could to make Vidar's "beloved" immortal.

They'd kept prodding him to tell her over the phone. But he had to have her in his arms, wrapped around him as he did.

He changed into the flying creature he preferred, entered her loft through the window. The moment he landed, changed back, a terrible sensation hit him between the eyes. A combination of nausea, aggression and antipathy.

A vibe that screamed Asgardian.

Horror exploded in his head and chest.

Someone from Asgard was here. He'd somehow messed up.

His first instinct was to charge in. But the aura he sensed was ancient, frighteningly powerful. This wouldn't be like with the Odinians. His attack might not be swift enough to save Kara.

He had to think. Learn all he could about his adversary before he made a move. Kara's life was at stake.

His default was to cloak his presence from detection, but he shifted to phantom/invisible form, too, so the entity in the loft with Kara wouldn't pick up on him.

He neared Kara's bedroom, heard her voice. He detected no fear in it. That meant nothing. She was too brave for her own good. Images of her attacking the entity, pissing it off...

Everything inside him froze as he overheard part of what she was saying. What she'd called the person with her.

Aunt Sigrun.

He couldn't have heard right.

Maxing his cloaking powers to make sure he wouldn't be detected by whatever Kara had called "aunt," he looked inside.

And saw her. A woman who looked like a bank CEO. Petite, elegant in an immaculate skirt suit, caramel hair in a smooth chignon. She looked to be in her mid-thirties. As did he.

But while he was a few millennia old, she was a few dozen.

She was a Dís. An ancient Norse deity of fate.

And she was having tea with Kara.

Her expression was that of an admonishing parent as she said, "You're way off schedule, Kara. We did our part directing you to the Lokian. You've had him eating out of your hands from day one. When will you bring in his soul?"

Chapter 8

Kara jerked as something slammed outside.

The wind from the window she kept open for Vidar must have knocked something over.

She grabbed for the distraction. "How about I go check the damages and you see yourself out, Aunt Sigrun?"

Sigrun eyeballed her. "How about you give me an answer? A ballpark date?"

"How about sometime around never?"

Full, crimson lips twisted mockingly. "Don't get pissy with me, missy. I have no stake in this matter. It's for your own good."

Kara huffed. "Yeah, sure. You're a saint. Just go, okay?"

"Tell me you're working on it, at least. You need this big guy dead, and all you've done so far is fuck him nearly to death." Sigrun paused, cracked out a laugh. "Say, is that your plan?"

Kara rolled her eyes. "God, for someone older than the pyramids, you've got one juvenile sense of humor."

Sigrun eyed her sardonically. "Tsk. Bringing up age when you're just a millennium or so younger? *And* when you have a schoolgirl crush on your mark? Granted, the Lokian is luscious, and we don't begrudge you using him for all the raunchy sex you can while you can, but no matter how hot his hide is, you know it's his or yours. So step up your schedule, hmm?"

Kara moved pointedly to the bedroom door. "Weird that you could live for millennia and still think repeating yourself makes what you say more effective. Thanks for the visit, Aunt Sigrun."

"Drop the 'aunt' bit already, would you?" Sigrun rose serenely, decked in brand-name elegance and tossing her five-hundred-dollar haircut. "It was cute when you were a fifteen-year-old urchin and under six-foot, but now you're scaring all my hot guys away."

"Haven't you eaten enough already?"

Sigrun let out another merry laugh. "Only those scheduled to be devoured, sweetie. And there's no such thing as gorging yourself on enough hunks. As you're now in a position to judge. By now you realize there's no getting enough of a hot guy who knows how to use his hot bod. But you know you'll do it sooner rather than later, so give that stud of yours one last ride for the ages, then put him out of his misery."

Kara sighed in exasperation, shook her head again at the incongruence of the fragile figure that she now knew wielded the power of a thousand men.

Sigrun pecked her on the cheek on her way out. "Thanks for the tea. Even if I made it myself." At the loft's door, she threw over her shoulder, "Clock's ticking, Kara. Get on the ball."

Kara gritted her teeth as the door closed behind Sigrun. Her "aunt" even managed to make it click condescendingly.

She had to put an end to this, get her "family" off her back....

"So...how are you planning to take my soul?"

Kara's skin almost pooled to the ground. *Vidar.*

She swung around in an arc of vertigo and dread.

He materialized on the sofa. Endless shoulders stiff, cabled forearms braced on his thighs, fists balled, knuckles white. But it was his face that squeezed her heart until it almost ruptured. It was as if bleakness and betrayal had seeped into his essence, snuffed it out. His eyes seemed focused into the depths of something devastating and macabre.

He'd been there all the time.

He'd seen Sigrun, heard everything.

She swayed a step toward him. "Vidar..."

He raised his eyes, sent her supplication backlashing in her throat, detonating in her chest with a flare of desperation.

"Let's skip the shock and denial. The protestations, too, that I misunderstood what I overheard of that little 'family' chat you were having with 'Aunt Sigrun.'"

She tried to swallow shrapnel from the heart that had shattered at his pain. "I'm...sorry you heard that."

The despondency in his eyes deepened. "I'm sure you are."

She attempted another begging step toward him. "I'm not sorry it's out in the open, just that you found out that way...."

Words congealed inside her again.

God, he looked, *felt,* so...desolate.

He exhaled as she expelled every ounce of air from her own lungs. "So your aunt is one of the Dísir."

That made her find her voice. "How did you know that?"

"After millennia living among Norse mythology figures, I can sense one a mile away. But those so-called 'gods' have their own place at the top of my Reviled List. Their judge-and-executioner-of-fate shtick got old long before the Dark Ages and having one in the vicinity gives me hives. But you always blind me to anything but *you*. I felt her only when I was a few feet away. And all I felt then was terrified for you." His eyes were black now, as if everything inside him had been extinguished. "You had me so totally fooled, it's tragically funny. I really have to give it to you. We were seamless. You could teach Loki himself advanced courses in deception."

The need to scream denials boiled her blood. "I didn't deceive you. At least, I didn't mean to—"

"Spare me." His growl was so hurt it made her plunge deeper into despair. "The charade is over. So just tell me. How did you intend to get my soul? And you want to barter it for yours? How did you lose it? To your aunt? What did you get in return?"

She hung her head. "It's…it's a long story."

"So far, I'm still immortal. I have nothing but time. Entertain me."

It was a shearing moment before she could bring herself to say the terrible truth out loud. "I'm…I'm a Valkyrie."

He jerked up straight, his eyes flaring a frightening azure. "Enough lies. You're a mortal. I can feel it."

"I'm that, too. It's really complicated."

His gaze radiated distrust and disillusion. "I'm listening. Don't skip a detail."

She gave a painful nod. "From the time I was around six, I've been having flashes of…other lives. My parents thought it was hyperactive imagination until the fact that

I 'remembered' only dying people disturbed them enough to seek help. I was diagnosed with high-functioning autism at ten, and strangely, that put their minds to rest. Not that it mattered. At my twelfth birthday party, a huge fire engulfed our home and Mom, Dad and older brother saved me and all the guests, but died themselves from smoke inhalation."

Her tear-filled eyes overflowed, her heart twisting all over again with the loss and guilt that had never stopped hacking at her. Vidar's face hardened. He now believed that every word she said, every emotion she displayed, was a lie. She couldn't blame him.

But this terrible development had its upside. Being able to come clean at last was as relieving as it was agonizing.

"I felt I was responsible for their deaths, and no matter what counselors told me about survivor's guilt, I withdrew into myself, had to be dragged into foster homes from which I ran, one time after another. That's when I did my street time.

"When I was almost seventeen an all-female family took me in. I thought they were weird, but that made them perfect for me, since I believed I was a weirdo myself. They offered me a roof over my head and left me to my own devices, which was all I wanted. I could fend for myself, just wanted the system to forget about me. The casual company worked for me, too. I left when I was eighteen to go to college, but they'd become sort of my family, and I went back to them every chance I got.

"Then, last year, on my twenty-seventh birthday, they revealed a truth that made my fears that I was possessed or had an evil, split personality seem like a laugh. They started by telling me what they are, though they didn't say they're gods, just 'agents of fate.' They made it sound as if they had nothing to do with fate's decisions." His vicious snort put paid to that claim. "They told me Valkyries are a subdivision of their kind. I thought they'd mentioned them because they were famous ones. Turned out, they were telling me *I* was the famous one."

His eyes widened. "You're *the* Kara?"

She'd researched extensively since her aunts' revelations. She'd found many contradicting stories concerning "her," "the wild-haired, stormy Valkyrie."

She nodded, forced herself to hold his now-burning gaze. "Not that I remember anything. They said I was too traumatized, because I subconsciously chose my family's souls for Valhalla when they died heroically. I wasn't ready to learn of my true nature when my aunts took me in. So they kept an eye on me until I could access my powers consciously and deal with my fate."

"The fate that involves swapping my soul for yours."

At his lifeless statement, another surge of tears rose from her depths. "I only wish I was soulless, like you think."

"Too late to go all poignant on me. Stick to the facts."

Anything she said in her defense would only enrage him more. And would be pointless. She'd lost him. But she owed him the truth. It was all she could give him anymore.

She inhaled shakily. "They told me my troubles started when I aroused Odin's lust and all he aroused was my antipathy. But it seems I was always too blunt, and my rejection humiliated him so much, I gained myself a godly enemy who devised an original chastisement for me—fragmenting my immortality. Ever since, I have lived on Earth in one incarnation after another, having a shorter lifespan and hazier memories of my past lives in each.

"In this last incarnation, I was reborn a baby to human

parents, oblivious to my past and powers. According to the shrinking pattern of my previous lifespans, this one is expected to be...real short. But the kicker is that this time, when I die, I won't be coming back. Through the fragmentation of my immortality, Odin has managed to end it. Then he'll have me, after all. Since no Valkyrie has ever died, he'll have an unprecedented soul in Valhalla as a bonus, and I won't find a hero's welcome like those I've been sending there. Apparently I kept complicating my plight by refusing his offers to end my curse by succumbing to him, and after an eternity of rejection, he has a lot of wrath to wreak on me. To escape his clutches, I have one other option—oblivion."

"That son of a bitch."

Her heart gave a thunderclap at his savage growl.

Her bruised gaze wavered on his beloved face. He looked wrathful enough to go after Odin and execute him like he had his minions. Was he outraged on her behalf?

"At times like these, I remember that being in Loki's service was an eternity well-spent. That bastard will get his ass divinely kicked in Ragnarok if it's the last thing we Lokians do." His savagery was painful even when it wasn't all directed at her. "But how does that tie in with the Dísir fostering you to one day harvest my soul?"

She struggled to continue. "The goddess Freyja sent them to offer me either an escape from Odin or oblivion with a place in Fólkvangr. They said I'd get a hero's welcome in *her* afterlife. Or if I don't fancy that, maybe a restoration of my immortality. She wants one thing in return, though. The soul of a Lokian."

He gave an ugly laugh, disappointment ratcheting in his eyes. It broke her heart into tinier pieces. "So it's not even me in particular. But what, by Odin's Damnation, does she want with a Lokian's soul?"

"It's the only kind of warrior soul impossible to harvest. Lokians always refuse the lure of either Odin's Valhalla or Freyja's Fólkvangr, choosing oblivion instead."

He frowned, digesting this. "We never knew where Lokians went when they died, but they sure as hell wouldn't go to Valhalla or Fólkvangr and help that bastard and bitch prepare for Raganrok."

She gave a difficult nod. "They said I would be the one to change that, bring the first Lokian to Fólkvangr, because of my mortality. No Lokian would be on his guard when he met me, making it possible to come close, fulfill what no other Valkyrie has ever been able to. Freyja believes having a Lokian's soul would tip the odds in her favor in her eternal conflict with Odin and Loki."

Bitterness burst in his eyes. "So you searched out not only any Lokian but an Original. I bet that will gain you extra points with your goddess."

"She's not my goddess," she protested. "I don't know who the hell she is. I didn't even believe most of what they told me, not even when it explained so much of the weirdness in my life. I didn't fully believe them until I saw *you*."

"And you realized what I was on sight. That is why you approached me, why you followed me."

"I had no clue what you were until I saw you shift."

"Are you pretending that you were attracted to me for real?"

"Why do you find that hard to believe? You took one look at me and wanted me, too."

"*I* was playing into your trap like the gullible mark you managed to make me." She shook her head, but he pressed

on. "But why didn't you want me to die? Your mission would
have been accomplished...." Words died on his lips, a new
suspicion blossoming in his eyes, like blood from a fresh
stab. "But that wouldn't have served your purpose, would
it? A Valkyrie can only take a soul if its owner volunteers
it. So has everything since then been part of a plan to get
me to trust you, to lose my mind over you, so I'd make you
a willing offer of my soul? Was it all to prolong your time
with me so you'd be there when I finally managed to kill
myself?"

"If I wanted to do that, why did I leave that first night?
Then the second? How could I have known you'd look for
me?"

"Are you kidding? You had me by the balls after one look
and you knew it. Dangling your carrot made me go to any
lengths to have you, twisted me into too many knots to notice anything was wrong."

She gaped at him in mounting horror. "Don't you see
the gaping plot holes in this scenario you're concocting?"

"I see only the irony. That you didn't realize you didn't
have to go to these lengths. I went out to die that night. And
with the way I felt about you already, I would have given
you my soul. And to think it was the sight of you that made
me cling to my soul, so I could protect you with it."

His agony mutilated her. "God, Vidar, don't saddle me
with more than I'm guilty of. I told you the facts you demanded, which I had no part in. There's still *my* side of it
all."

His huff was undiluted dejection. "Should be interesting."

"It isn't. It's just the truth. When I saw you, all I knew was
that you were the only man I'd ever wanted on sight. Then I
rushed to help you, but I thought I was too late, that they'd

kill you. I threw myself into the middle of the fight even when I thought they'd kill me, too. If you hadn't turned out to be far stronger than what they or I expected, they *would* have killed me. You sensed I was a mortal, and I am. I have no powers left beyond, allegedly, the soul-harvesting one, which I've never used consciously.

"Afterward, realizations swamped me. Everything my aunts told me was true. I ran because I was afraid you would realize what I was. I couldn't bear to see your hunger turn into revulsion.

"But I went out of my mind worrying you wouldn't heal, or that you would but I'd never find you again. I went back the next night praying that you would, too, told myself if you did, I'd have just one night with you. I was afraid that if we had more, I'd put you in danger. But you came after me, and I was weak, kept taking one more day, one more week. Then today I discovered my aunts pushed me to go to that nightclub, opened doors for me there. But my attraction to you was all me. I loved you...*love* you with all of me."

Tears were a steady stream now, and it felt as if her life force were hemorrhaging.

"I only wanted to have whatever time I could with you, then leave you with fond memories. But to prolong my time with you, I blinded myself to the dangers and I ended up losing you now, not later, and erasing anything beautiful you ever felt for me. My only consolation is that however much you hate me now, you will live forever, and in what will be a blink to you, I will be dead. And you'll forget me. Or if you ever remember me, it'll be with mild pity when you look back and realize that being with you, loving you, was the only real life I ever had."

Chapter 9

Kara teetered around, sent a tear, tiny and cold, splashing on Vidar's hand. It felt as if it was a torrent of molten lead, eating him through, body and mind.

Moments later, he heard her bedroom door close with a defeated, final click.

He could have sat there forever, buried under the avalanche of realizations, his whole being gripped in a maelstrom of agony.

After what felt an eternity, he rose, went after her.

On his entry, she jerked up from a ball of misery. She looked at him with eyes as bruised as his very soul felt.

He braced one knee on the bed, stabbed his aching fingers into her fiery locks, cupped her precious head. "Being with you, loving you, has been the only real life I've had, too. And that when *I* remember every minute of the eternity I lived before I found you."

"Vidar…"

He devoured her choking surprise, groaned into her trembling lips. "I love you, Kara. I far more than love you. And I believe you. I believe *in* you. I was never into worship, but

I worship you. You're the reason I'm alive today, the only reason I ever wanted to really live. And now I realize what Loki meant when he told me death has to be my heart's desire. Now it is."

She jerked hard. "What the hell do you mean?"

"I mean I'll go out tonight to die in battle."

"What?"

"You heard me. And I will give you my soul. I've lived too long, have known no happiness until you came into my life. Now it is my heart's desire to pay with the soul you ignited inside me so you'll live forever free."

After a long moment of horrified shock, she gritted out, "Okay, tell me this—are you *nuts?* You want to buy my *alleged* immortality with yours, the *bona fide* thing? And you think for a second I will agree to this insanity because...?"

"Because if your aunts give up on your cooperation, they'll use another Valkyrie to get my soul. And then both of us will lose everything."

"Remember the part about willingly volunteering your soul? If they could have used another Valkyrie, they would have long ago."

"And now that they know what you mean to me, they can. They'll make me an offer I can't refuse. Your life for mine. And for you, I will let anyone take my soul and anything else I have anywhere."

"See?" she cried, eyes filling. "I *am* your Achilles' heel!"

He stoked her head lovingly. "And it's my pride and privilege to have you as my fatal weakness."

Two fat tears arrowed down her trembling cheeks. "And in which moron's book is my life more important than yours? I'm the one who's mortal and who'll die, anyway, so leave it at that. I always feared something exactly like this happening, but now that it did, and all's out in the open, just give me your word you won't let anyone use me to black-mail you, and let's live as long as we can together. I have many good years left."

He shook his head. "We had the time we had together because your aunts were waiting for you to fulfill your mis-sion. Now that they know you won't, we're out of time. One of us will die. And in *this* moron's book, your life is more important than mine."

She smacked him, in tears again. "Stop it. Just stop it."

He captured her hands, dragged her into a fierce embrace. "Let me love you the best I know how, my Kara. You've suffered too much in your existence, and I am the only one who has the power to end your suffering. How can you pos-sibly ask me not to do it? How can you think I'll let you fall into that sadist's hands?"

She shook her head frantically. "I'll opt for oblivion. Ceasing to exist isn't such a bum deal. I wouldn't know if it is."

"But oblivion *isn't* ceasing to exist. You'd know, and you'd go mad, every single second. It's *not* a reprieve. I have first-hand accounts from a few...acquaintances who've come back from there. While I would be their trophy Lokian in Fólkvangr, would probably be treated as a prize. It might not be my afterlife of choice, but the worst of it is that I'll have a boss I hate."

"And you want me to live forever to do what? I wouldn't even want a mortal lifespan without you. No life would be any life without you."

"You'll find plenty of worthy causes to fill your time. And I'll live on inside you. I would have died a meaningless death if you hadn't saved me. Now my death will serve an ultimate purpose—your eternity and freedom."

"No, Vidar," she wailed. "I won't let you do it."

"You have to, my beloved Kara. It's the only way."

Vidar cast the silent Kara a sideways glance.

She sat beside him in the car, looking ahead into the night, her eyes unseeing, her lips clamped together.

At least she was no longer weeping.

He wished he could have had more time with her. But he knew the Dísir. Sigrun had pretended nonchalance as she'd left Kara, but he'd felt her chagrin. And her fear. She knew Kara wouldn't come through and dreaded Freyja's reaction. They wouldn't have left them in peace another day, would have forced his hand.

And like Kara had said, once she was immortal again, the pain she was feeling now would fade. It never would have for him, but he hoped it would for her.

He regretted only having to inflict this final injury on her.

He was taking her to his battle. She had to be nearby when he died so that she could harvest his soul.

He brought the car to a stop.

In the warehouse in front of them, there was a sort of a low-life summit between Odin and Thor worshippers. All Endowed. And all hated Lokians with a rabid passion.

Crashing their meeting was a sure way to go.

He turned to Kara. She remained staring ahead.

He should just go. He couldn't. Just one last kiss.

He dragged her to him, took her stiff lips in a kiss where he poured all his love. She didn't reciprocate. She wouldn't say goodbye, letting him know what he was doing was one-sided. She hated him right now for depriving her of himself.

He hoped this anger would help her until she could start healing and forgetting.

He left the car, didn't look back.

He entered the warehouse, and after the initial stupefaction, it was very much a déjà vu of that first night he'd seen her.

He was soon accumulating too many injuries, feeling his life force deserting him. He knew this time Loki would let him go.

He was willing his soul to leave his body and go to her, when suddenly among the haze of agony he felt a disturbance spreading like wildfire, through his abusers, through his abused body.

He raised his head. And she was there. Kara.

He watched in horror as the déjà vu congealed. Some of his attackers charged her. This time she stood there, made no attempt to protect herself. The first one who reached her ran her through.

He heard her cry, watched her fall to her knees, and knew.

She would die. Right here. Before his eyes. They had killed her.

And he went berserk.

He felt nothing more until he was panting over the hacked bodies of his enemies. Kara's killers.

Then he was crashing to his knees by her side, shuddering apart with heaves of desperation. He gathered her in shaking arms, madness and grief pouring from his eyes, spilling all over her.

Her lashes fluttered. His heart ruptured. She was still alive. But not for long. He felt her essence ebbing, only moments' worth left to power her last breaths.

Her eyes opened and impaled him with a look of serenity.

Then she smiled. *Smiled*. "You didn't think…I'd let you carry out this harebrained idea…did you?"

He wanted to shake her, strangle her for doing this to him, to herself. He could only choke, "You're insane, insane…."

"Not really. This will work…you'll see. I've been doing research…and this is one way out my aunts and Freyja conveniently forgot to mention…and you didn't think of. As a willing sacrifice…I've cornered both gods. They won't be able to force me into anything. Odin can't claim me…and Freyja has to accept me in Fólkvangr without your soul as a ticket in."

"Why wouldn't she restore your immortality?"

"That was only…on offer…in return for your soul. I only want eternity if you're with me…and we can't be alive together…. It's a catch-22. So this is…the best solution."

"There's another solution. Take me with you."

"I can't. But I'll be fine in Fólkvangr. I've existed way too long, too, and even if I don't remember it…I feel the weight of time in my bones. It will do me good to get off this merry-go-round. Also my job as tour guide…to the fallen is nowhere…as noble as yours…as guide…to the outcasts. I'll end my existence with reversing my role…saving a mighty warrior instead of selling him on Valhalla and…trapping him into helping…that Odin oaf."

And he roared, "I'm not leaving you to those psychopaths. They'll find a way to punish you for thwarting them. So if *you* can't take me with you, if I can't be with you, I want anyone who covets my soul and anything else I can give to take it all wherever they wish. If they release you from this vindictive curse *and* restore your immortality."

A sudden wind tore through the stifling warehouse, eddying madly in thickening smoke clouds.

As abruptly as the vortex formed, it dissipated.

Sigrun appeared with two other women, reeking of that inimitable Dísir bouquet, dressed as if for a board meeting. They walked toward him and the now weakly gasping Kara with tranquil steps.

Kara's eyes grew taunting. "It's over, aunts. You can't have him."

Sigrun smiled indulgently at her. "Oh, but it's no longer up to you, sweetie. It's up to him." She turned her eyes to Vidar. "Did you mean what you just said?"

"I did," he gritted. "I do. Now quit wasting my time."

Sigrun raised perfectly manicured hands. "Just a second, big boy. We don't appreciate it when anyone comes complaining that we didn't give them time to read the fine print. You understand the significance of granting us such a carte blanche?"

"I do. My soul, and anything else you want."

"You do know what 'anything' means, right?"

He nodded tersely. "Do it already."

Before he could draw another breath, oblivion claimed him.

As he faded away, he heard Sigrun exclaiming excitedly, "Wow, Kara, you've gone where no Valkyrie has gone before. I thought you were being overconfident when you said you'd get us better than his soul. You not only made him volunteer it, he literally signed to anything of his. This means his Endowment, and anyone he's connected to through it. The other Lokians, and even Loki himself."

Awareness returned like an incoming train.

It impacted him, left him decimated and scattered.

His senses coalesced from the whiteout of agony, converged on a realm that pulsed with power, everything enveloping him indeterminable, beyond his grasp.

So this was Fólkvangr.

Then he ceased trying to decipher what bombarded him.

Kara was there. Whole. Heartbreakingly beautiful.

She was staring at him, her face void of expression for the first time. She looked so near. She felt as if she were in another realm.

"You're just sensing her real feelings at last, y'know?"

The Dísir. Those bitches were here, too? Great.

"Isn't it? We'll make your afterlife so…interesting."

Were those pests reading his mind?

"Here we can do that and more. We can do anything, really."

"Then you can literally fuck yourselves," he growled.

"Tsk. Don't be a sore loser, Vidar."

"You're losers, period."

"We'll excuse you, poor man. You must be feeling so stupid, so used right now. But don't feel too bad. Kara's convoluted plan and her seamless execution of it would have fooled any of us. It was a con for the ages. I bet Loki will teach her methods in his Trickster University for eons to come. If he doesn't join us here soon."

Vidar turned his eyes to Kara's impassive one.

He turned to the Dísir. "Play another one."

"Which one? The game where we try to pretend that you're not the laughingstock of the afterlife? The master trickster who was taken in like a wet-nosed chump?"

"Save it, hags. As we Lokians say to females we wouldn't touch with a realm-long pole, that's one itch I'm never helping you scratch. You'll have to live with the excruciating fact that Kara and I gave our lives for each other. But then, that would imply that you actually feel. You don't. You're defective models who came onto this immortal coil stripped of vital components, so you'll never understand why we did what we did for each other."

"You got a mouth on you, boy. We have an eternity to… put it to good use, though."

"Save your threats for someone who gives a shit, or looks at you and sees anything apart from pathetic jokes."

The Dísir looked at one another, then burst out laughing.

Sigrun pretended to wipe away a tear of hilarity. "Oh, boy. Taming this one will be major fun."

Vidar grunted in disgust. "Dream on, crones. And do your worst. All I care is that you spare Kara. Since she's here, then you reneged on your deal, took my soul and won't release hers. I guess I walked right into that. But at least do this one thing that *might* excuse your existence. End her torment."

"You *still* believe the sob story she told you? Priceless."

"Shut *up* and give her peace."

"Oh, fine. Let's go along with your delusion about what's happening here for a minute. How do you propose we do that?"

He looked back to the indifferent Kara. Then he turned solemn eyes to them. "Make her forget me."

"Wow, dude, stupid and stupidly noble, unto eternity and beyond." Sigrun's eyes twinkled at him. "You want a side order of the same mercy for yourself?"

Vidar snorted. "No, thanks, and hold the taunts."

"You sure? We're feeling generous in celebration of netting ourselves a first-of-its-kind life-form here, so we advise you to make use of this one-time offer—two amnesias for the price of one."

"Don't you dare come near my memories. Not that you can. We Lokians have parts of our memories fueling the souls you so covet. That's where my memories of Kara and my love for her reside. Mess with those and the whole package degrades. Your choice."

The Dísir went silent.

Then Sigrun probed, "But you can do it, can't you? You can wipe out the memory of her and that of your love for her. Why not do it and spare yourself an eternity of kicking yourself for being such a fool?"

He looked at Kara. Her eyes were no longer impassive. There was such…condescending pity in them.

He turned to Sigrun. "That's another thing you have no hope of grasping with your deficiencies. But if you want my answer for your records, the memory of Kara, of loving her, will be the one thing to make my afterlife worthwhile, just as they made my life for the brief time I had the blessing of having her in it."

This time the Dísir's silence lasted longer.

When Sigrun finally spoke, her sneer had lost some of its corrosiveness. "You're so cute when you're in denial. You can't face it that you, the ultimate trickster, are trapped for eternity because you fell into her honeytrap. You cling to your belief in her like a five-year-old in Santa. But if she's so true, why isn't she saying anything? Why is she looking at you with such pity in her eyes?"

"You're keeping her silent, but she doesn't need words to communicate her emotions. You're making me *see* indifference and pity, but I *feel* her turmoil and desperation, for what she considers my sacrifice, when giving up anything for her is a privilege."

The gloating in the Dísir's eyes wavered.

Then disappointment crashed in its place.

One of the other two exclaimed, "By Freyja's pigtails! All this effort and all we get is this intractable mule."

The other one huffed in exasperation. "We might have eternity, Sigrun, but with this one it means only that he'll have that long to drive us insane. He's a lost cause."

Sigrun finally leveled fed-up eyes on him. "Congrats, you big lout. You've thwarted us. If you loved Kara any less, if you had the least distrust in her, we would have kept both your souls. But contrary to what you think, we didn't write the manual of fate, we just abide by its letter. On the first page, it says it is people who damn themselves by their weaknesses and actions. And damn your blue eyes, you acted only with ridiculous resoluteness, while Kara, that silly girl, did everything with infuriating selflessness. By the Dísir's own rules, we have to issue you a full refund of your souls."

The brunette Dís nudged her. "Tell them the rest already."

Sigrun exhaled in chagrin. "We have to issue you a reward along with those, too, dammit. Your hearts' desire."

The blonde Dís quirked an eyebrow at him. "What will that be? Or shall we guess?"

"I have one desire." He looked back to the still Kara. "To be with Kara. If 'in life' doesn't work, then I'll take in death."

Sigrun huffed. "So which part of 'hearts' desire' didn't you get? You want to go back to life with her, you got it."

He stared at the Dísir. "That's it? You'll bring us back to life, and let us be?"

"Give the man an extra life." Sigrun pulled a thick, fraying-at-the edges tome out of thin air, opened it. "But according to the Rewards Section, Resurrection Chapter, said life can only be as long as the shorter-lived among you was supposed to live. So you have only around a couple of centuries. And don't complain. We did tell her her last life would be ridiculously short. But then, you might even have less—as long as your 'love' lasts. *Or* as long as your new choices let you live."

The brunette Dís handed him a cheap plastic pen. "Before you sign, you do understand that you'd be throwing away certain eternity in the limitlessness of Fólkvangr, for the uncertainty love and life will bring you? That you'll take your chances with both?"

He snatched the pen from her hand, stabbed his palm with it, signed his name in blood where Sigrun indicated.

"You can be Kara's proxy. But if it turns out it wasn't what she wanted, expect her to hate you till her dying breath."

He looked at Kara, reached for her hand, kissed it before he nicked her finger for a drop of blood. Then he signed her name.

He added something in both their blood before he turned to the Dísir, hands on hips. "I put a little provision there that keeps your...agency at bay. I'm not letting you mess with Kara's life ever again. Now let us out of this dump."

The Dísir grunted something to one another, eyeing him with disappointment and something like admiration tinged in challenge. Then he felt himself fading.

Vidar phased back to awareness to the glorious feeling of Kara throwing herself at him.

Before he could get his arms to work, to wrap around her, she was climbing him, smothering him in hugs and kisses.

He sagged down where he stood, which turned out to be on her bed, relief like he'd never known inundating him.

When she'd expended the impetus of urgency, she looked

down at him with eyes melting with love and flowing with tears. "Oh, God, Vidar…you believed in me when you had every reason not to."

He caressed her precious cheek. "I had *every* reason to, since you *are* my every reason."

She charged him with another bout of frenzied passion and gratitude before she pulled back, looking apologetic. "But, uh, don't expect my aunts to leave us alone. I bet Sigrun is already looking for a loophole to circumvent your provision. Not to mention Loki. I don't see him relishing having one of his Originals shacking up with a Valkyrie."

He wrapped her wild locks around his hands, dragged her in for a wrenching kiss, before raising her face to smile assurance at her. "I already told your aunts what to do with themselves. As for Loki, he understands passion and values the rare, let alone the unprecedented. You should see him with his wife. He's like a delirious puppy around her. He'll understand what we have."

Then he was tearing their clothes off, melding their flesh, groaning long and loud at the soul-deep pleasure and poignancy. "But if Loki doesn't, he can also help himself to the same activity I recommended to your aunts. As long as I have you, I don't care who thinks or does what. Your fateful aunts said we'll take our chances with love and life, and I can't wait to start taking every one with you."

She pulled him into her depths as he thrust to merge them, cried out her exultation, her eagerness for anything with him.

After he took her over the first edge of endless ones to come, he looked down at her face, flushed and blazing with love, feeling replete, complete.

Suddenly, he laughed.

She wound herself around him. "What?"

"Do you realize your ridiculous aunts thought this was a punishment? Especially the limited edition part of it? Two centuries of this?" He hugged her exuberantly. "Hell, I would have done anything for two years. I would have taken two days. Two *hours*."

"Hush, don't give them ideas. And don't rub it in." She rose over him, delight and devotion lighting up her impossible beauty. "But two centuries sounds just about right. That works for me. And boy, will I make it work for you."

He spread himself for her to take of him what she would, to show him what he'd survived that long for. To be hers. Far more than he could have ever been on his own.

And he groaned his ecstasy and thankfulness. "Work away."

* * * * *

PLAYING WITH FIRE

MICHELE HAUF

Michele Hauf has been writing romance, action-adventure and fantasy stories for more than twenty years. Her first published novel was *Dark Rapture*. France, musketeers, vampires and faeries populate her stories. And if she followed the adage "write what you know," all her stories would have snow in them. Fortunately, she steps beyond her comfort zone and writes about countries she has never visited and of creatures she has never seen.

Michele can also be found on Facebook and Twitter and michelehauf.com. You can also write to Michele at: PO Box 23, Anoka, MN 55303, USA.

Chapter 1

"Just a few more tweaks..." I entered a final password into the security database for the Council's new storage facility, located in the seventh quarter of Paris behind the former military school, and clicked return. "And you'll be up and running."

"Thanks, Cinder." Certainly Jones, the Council's chief archivist, slapped me across the back and propped up his booted feet on the table next to the security panel that featured six HD screens that would broadcast from all cameras. "Where you headed next?"

"Not sure. I might have some downtime here in Paris."

I was the Council's one and only systems technician and securities advisor. Computer algorithms and mathematics? Such innate skill ran through my veins. You might even say I was the originator of numbers. And despite the Council's tradition of observing and respectfully guiding as they oversaw the paranormal nations, they were aware a more high-tech method of watching must be utilized in this day and age.

Certainly was a witch who practiced dark magic, and

had given me the name Cinder after I'd escaped from Beneath, and had been a friend and advisor regarding this mortal realm since.

"Here you go. The storage facility is now online." I clicked Return and we both leaned forward to study the security screens that flickered on to show various places within and without the ultra-warded facility. Certainly was the first to notice the blur on screen six.

"Is that a person?" he asked. "Coming *out* of the storage facility? I'm not aware of scheduled access today, other than you."

My heart sank, because it would be too insane that someone had infiltrated the place while I had taken the wards and security down for a mere two hours to set up the cameras.

"Can't be." I eyed the dark figure. Looked small, like a kid, dressed in black. The person slinked along the back wall of the building. And then the figure tugged off the black hood to reveal a fall of long blond hair.

"It's a chick," Certainly said. "Robbing us!"

"Not for long." Shoving away from the desk on the roller-wheeled office chair, I stood and spread out my arms in preparation to smoke on out of there. "Be right back."

I'm a fire demon from Beneath. I wield fire as my own personal weapon. I can do cool things like mist to smoke or fire, and traverse great distances with but a thought. But apparently, I can't prevent a thief from taking opportunity of security downtime.

I smoked to human shape outside the storage facility. Wisps of emerald smoke lingered at my feet. A lush perfume hit me like a bouquet of "I'm sorry" roses in a cheating boyfriend's face. Anger rising, flames wisped from my hands as I ran around the corner and spied the blonde figure dashing down the Metro stairs.

Smoking to the top of the stairs, I didn't bother that mortals would notice. It was well after midnight and this Metro station appeared empty. I raced down the concrete tunnel, my boots thudding in rhythm to the arriving train. I could smoke faster than run, and did so, insinuating myself onto the train car just as it braked.

The thief jumped on and collided with my chest as I assumed solid human form.

"Gotcha," I said, grabbing her wrist.

Hollering out an impressive karate-like "hiyah!" she kneed me in the groin.

Whoever this guy was, he certainly did not have me. Sexy, though. Even wincing and bent over as he clutched his jewels. Poor thing. I may be tiny and unassuming, but I can wield a punch that'll knock a werewolf flat. Attribute that to my mortal genes; my father was once a welterweight boxing champion. Add to that the fact I've been vampire for ten years and have possessed witch magic for eight, and I'm the complete danger girl package.

"Is that how you pick up women?" I asked, leaning against the steel pole behind me as the subway car zoomed forward. The guy righted himself, all nearly seven feet of him. A leather choker around his neck clasped a silver circle right over his Adam's apple. "You're cute and all, and my goddess, those shoulders are impressive, but I like my men a touch more romantic. Flowers. Platitudes. Sweet nothings whispered in my ear. That's how you'll win my heart, buddy."

Sneering, he lunged and gripped my shoulders. My reaction time slowed by observation of his sigh-worthy muscles, he managed to wrap his arms around my chest and arms so I couldn't push him away. Now he seemed impervious to my kicks that landed on his shins. Should have worn my steel-toed Doc Martens, but low ballet flats were necessary when sneaking around.

"You have something that belongs to me," he hissed. His breath was hot with a hint of mint, and his arms felt even hotter, like he was made of molten steel. "Rather, you took something from the Council."

Ah. I understood now. Had there been cameras on sight? I'd received intel there were no security measures in place. What the heck?

"Don't know what you're talking about, McSteamy. Seriously you have a fever? Ouch. You're burning me!"

He released me like that. "Sorry." The sexy bruiser stepped back, shaking out his hands. A few flames fell from his fingers to the floor of the train and flickered out in red cinders.

Wriggling my back, because I felt sure he'd burned through the black turtleneck and to my skin, I asked, "What the hell are you?"

"Fire demon."

Well, well. That explained the smolder in his mesmerizing brown eyes.

"And you are vampire."

"Who has witch magic," I said, because I wanted him to know exactly what he was dealing with. A demon? I could take him, no problem. Unless he was able to shoot flames at me. Hmm...

The next stop was mine. I shifted my hips and turned a

foot in preparation to dart as soon as the automatic doors slid open.

"What did you take?" he asked.

He didn't know? Then I wasn't going to tell him. Not even if he licked me from belly to neck and spent a lot of time suckling and kissing in between with that hot tongue of his.

Whew! *Where had that come from, Parish?* You are not attracted to the demon's smoldering gaze. Well, maybe a little. Combine the smolder with his solid, muscled form and that messy dark hair that hung over one eye—okay, I was attracted! This fine specimen would coax even a nun to tear off her rosary. But I was the furthest thing from a nun.

The train stopped and the doors opened. I sprang out and ran toward the exit, expecting the demon to tail me. Since when had I ever been attracted to the demonic breed? Their black blood was rumored to taste nasty. Still, muscles and smolder rated high on my scale.

I met my gorgeous pursuer at the top of the stairs that opened onto a cobbled avenue. How had he—?

Lowering his head, his dark eyes smiled in triumph, though his perfect lips did not move. Kiss me with those thick bowed lips, Mr. Sexy Demon.

Nix that. He wanted something I couldn't—wouldn't—give him.

And yet, when the going got tough, I could slip into sneaky sensual mode with an ease that made others in my tribe beg to take lessons. All men could be controlled with a wink and a flirtatious touch, if not a little magic.

I took the last two steps slowly, walking right toward the alluring hunk of oh-so-fine. My apartment was close but I guessed he'd trail me, so I had to make sure he didn't have the capacity to do so. What I knew about demons is they liked to sin and they never refused the carnal pleasures (or so I hoped).

He was well over a head taller than me—easy for any man since I barely toed five feet tall—and his shoulders were twice as wide as mine. Strong, powerful and able to eat little girls for lunch. The notion of this man eating me...

Parish, your mind is in the wrong place!

But not wrong for my impromptu plan to work. I'd been practicing a submission spell, but it did require blood. Guess I was going to have to take one for the team.

Tilting up on tiptoes, I landed the demon's mouth with mine. Clinging to his shoulders I delivered my seductive wiles with a firm, explorative kiss. I licked his lips and tugged out the bottom one with my teeth. Man, he tasted like dessert. Yeah, run your hands down my hips and derriere, you horny demon. That'll make the spell sink in deeper—and my teeth.

I snagged his lip with a fang and blood spilled across my tongue. Hot, thick and probably black, but it didn't taste bad, rather caramel salty and dark. Before he could exclaim, I swiped my finger through the blood and then pressed it against his throat above the choker and smeared it in a black circle. "Cedo!"

The demon soared through the air, away from me. He transformed to green smoke midflight, which hadn't been part of the spell. If the spell was successful, he'd only want to please the one who had just kissed him. And a submissive man would never take what didn't belong to him, especially from the girl he adored.

Not about to stick around to see what came next, I dashed down the narrow cobbled alleyway, congratulating myself on a successful nab tonight. If all went well, tomorrow

I'd be back in Venice at my father's bedside. And his soul would be saved.

I raced through the apartment building lobby, decorated in the old art nouveau style with acanthus leaves and half-naked women climbing along the walls, and up the stairs to the second floor where I'd borrowed an apartment from Zara Destry, the Lilith tribe leader. I love that vampiress. A fine replacement for my long-dead mortal mother, she took care of me as if I was one of her own. I had only my father left, but that wouldn't be for long. I needed family to help navigate the paranormal world I'd been thrust into against my will.

Punching in the digital code, I swung the apartment door inside, and let out a chirp at the sight of the smirking demon whose hair smoked and whose palms were filled with flames.

Chapter 2

The vixen had the audacity to run her tongue along those bright white fangs. Add that to the lifted brow and her rose-kissed cheeks and I instantly lost the anger that blazed in my hands. Rubbing my palms along my thighs sifted off the after-smoke in emerald wisps.

This little thief would undo me. I had sensed her attempt to bespell me at the top of the Metro stairs, to somehow make me want to submit to her. Hadn't worked. I am impervious to witchcraft. Though the kiss had been worthy of another go at it. And very well, the spell had sent me flying. How had she been able to do that? Vampires could not maintain such powerful magic, could they?

She boldly approached me, the tip of her finger stroking the corner of her bow lips, eyeing me up and down with pale gray eyes that held a diamond twinkle.

Straightening, I set back my shoulders, because she walked behind me now—was she checking out my ass?

"This apartment is warded," she said. "How'd you get in?"

For the same reason witchcraft had no effect on me: I

could cross any and all wards thanks to the devil's mark carved into my back. But she didn't need to know that. "Just lucky. Now hand over what you took or—"

"Or?"

She swung around in front of me, a teasing glitter sparkling her eyes. Everything about her was pale yet bright, and energized with a heightened sexuality that I could feel enter my pores as if an enemy invader I'd like to embrace. I rarely turned down opportunity to dally with a gorgeous woman. The sensual pleasures were meant to be indulged.

Impervious, Cinder, remember that. You do not want to submit to her.

"Just what did you have in mind, handsome?"

If she thought flirting would distract me— Was she wearing pink lipstick, or were her lips that lush and petal soft? Kissable. The compulsion to kiss her arose and—

I grabbed her wrist and slid my hand along the waistline of her tight black pants. Her small frame was lost against my greater bulk, but I distinctly noticed the hard press of her nipples below mine and the heat of her breath that landed on the base of my throat.

What had I come here for? And why was my hand now sliding with sensual ease along her back and around front where I felt no bra beneath the body-hugging black shirt?

"Find something you want to play with?" she cooed. "I know I have."

Her tongue touched the skin at my throat where the white business shirt gaped open, and I sucked in a gasp. Delicate fingers tickled along my pectorals. The feel of this tiny thief seeking to overpower me did not surprise so much as make me want her to succeed.

"What's your name, sexy?" she asked.

"Cinder," came out on a throaty hush that startled me.

What the hell, Cinder? You're being played by a sneaky vampiress.

I gripped her wrists, abruptly stopping the futile seduction. "What's the name of the thief I caught red-handed?"

"Parish," she said, her kissable lips curling to an even more irresistible pink bow. "What makes you think I stole anything?"

My hand dropped to her derriere where the pocket wasn't formed like a soft womanly curve. Still holding her wrist securely, I slipped the heavy piece out from the pocket and held it before her. "What's this?"

She narrowed her gaze, but gave no indication she was at all flustered. "What does it look like to you?"

I inspected the heavy disk, about half an inch thick and three inches in diameter and etched with indiscernible runes on what looked like black carbon fiber. I had no clue what it was, but if the Council had chosen to store it in a high-security facility, then it must do something bad. I was familiar with the measurement scale of all things from *bad* to *really bad* to *oh fuck this is going to leave a permanent mark*. I'd guess this thing landed somewhere between bad and the permanent mark range.

"You have no idea," she said on a ticklish peal. Snagging the disk, she danced away from me and around behind the black velvet couch. "Who are you, Cinder?"

"I am the Council's security advisor."

Chagrin heated my neck when she gave me the "seriously" look.

"The security wards were down for two hours," I explained, "so I could set up the system. How could you have possibly known the window in which the system would be shut off?"

"I didn't. Guess I got lucky." She strolled down a hallway, and I knew she was going to hide the evidence.

I smoked ahead of her and landed beside a dresser, but too close to the dainty whitewashed piece of furniture, which caused me to stumble and land ungracefully sprawled across a low platform bed.

Parish giggled at my faux pas, and I could but shake my head at how out of my senses this vampiress made me. *Me*. The demon of hellfire, the Flaming One. It was as if wherever she went, I felt compelled to follow, whether or not I'd gain the stolen device. I simply wanted to be near her. Had the spell worked after all?

This was going to be a long night.

There was no way the demon would leave with *ritrovatore d'anime* in his hand. I'd been planning this heist for weeks, and had succeeded thanks to a little reconnaissance help from my tribe members who wanted only the best for me and my mortal father. Now, if the fire demon would get out of my way, I could hop a plane for Venice.

But the distraction of his insanely muscled body and those eyes that couldn't seem to do anything but smolder at me, made me wonder if a little focused seduction wouldn't go a long way in getting the demon on my side. A smear of black blood had dried above the leather and silver choker. Apparently the submission spell had not taken. Though he was following me around like a puppy dog. Hmm… No, I didn't sense unconditional abandon on his part or even a smidgen of undying worship.

But he wasn't as staunch as he liked to think. I knew I

couldn't physically defeat him, so I'd have to dig deeper into my wiles.

Opening the dresser drawer, I dropped the device onto a stack of silk panties and closed it. A flick of my finger and a whispered, "Claustro" restored the lock spell to the drawer.

Before Cinder could pull himself up to sit, I leaned over him, on the bed, and pulled open his button-up shirt with a daring rip. Mmm, crisp white cotton against deeply tanned flesh. I loved the white-collar corporate raider look on a man who could literally toss flames through the air. And his pants were midnight-black. Oh, baby, what a sexy combination.

"What the—?"

"There's a handsome man lying on my bed," I cooed. "Wouldn't want to let this opportunity pass. Mercy, that is more than a six-pack. I didn't know they made demons so sturdy."

"I was forged Beneath. Of course I'm—"

I tongued his nipple, and he hissed with pleasure. "You won't start on fire if I do this, will you?"

The whole fiery hands thing had freaked me, but I figured it's because he was a fire demon. I didn't have a fire extinguisher nearby, so I hoped he could keep his cool.

"Parish," he rasped. "Not wise."

"Maybe I should keep a bucket of cold water by the bed?"

"No. Won't flame."

I licked down his abs to his stomach. Oh hell, no belly button. What the heck?

"Beelzebub and all the demons in Beneath, what are you up to?"

I maintained seduction mode, but only by not looking at his smooth belly. "Up to? Only your stomach," I said, then licked a trail higher to a hard pectoral. "Now I'm at your chest. A little higher?"

He gripped the back of my hair tightly, which pulled my tongue off his skin, but I could work with his angry vibe, and bracketed my knees around his hips.

I hadn't realized demons could look so physically different from other paranormals. If he didn't have a belly button, then he may not have a birth mother. I could buy into that. Corporeal demons were summoned from all sorts of nasty, or so I suspected.

"Your spell didn't work," he said through a clenched jaw, "so now you think you can distract me?"

"I have been known to distract." Though it was much tougher going the more I thought about his unholy origins. Tossing my head to the side slid my long hair over his bare chest.

He hissed again in pleasure. "I'll call your bluff. Let's do this."

Flipped around, I soared onto my back and landed the pillows with a cushy pouf. The demon crawled over me, his fingers sneaking up under my top. I knew he would get what he wanted—what we both wanted—before the night was over, and what I wanted was a distracted demon.

As he kissed a path from my belly button up toward my panting breasts, I wondered where, exactly, I'd sink in my fangs.

Chapter 3

The vampiress wanted some?

I glanced to the drawer where she'd tucked the device, of which, I still had no idea for what it was used. It wasn't going anywhere, and I was getting harder by the second. She rubbed her body all over mine, and I was no angel—well, not anymore.

Gliding my hands up under her shirt, I tugged it over her head and bent to suckle her nipple. Parish squirmed with delight, and I'd never get tired of the sensation of a woman's fingernails raking my scalp and pulling me in for more.

She felt like the fire I could bring up with my anger and she tasted like something even demons would be forbidden to touch. I never imagined I could get so quickly turned on and want to plunge myself inside a woman more than I did now.

What were we doing? The chase had been set aside. Both believed we could distract the other. And I—hell—I wanted her like I'd never wanted another thing on this earth. All senses were focused on her sighs and coos, her skin's sweet rose scent. I had to have her.

Her legs wrapped around my hips and tugged me against her soft belly. My cock ached, and I had to unzip to relieve the tight tension strapping it to my body. It sprang out and the little vixen grasped it firmly, making me clench the pillow near her head.

"You're playing with fire," I growled and lashed her other nipple roughly.

"You're not going to burn me, are you, Cinder? That would be far from the sweet nothings I prefer. Mmm, you're so hard."

"I only make flames when I'm angry, vixen." I shuffled down my pants and she nudged them from my legs with her feet, and followed with her pants. "What are sweet nothings?"

With a dismissive shrug, she said, "I'll know it when I hear it."

"You really think you can distract me and get away with what you stole?"

"What I— Oh. Right. Forgot about that."

And I honestly think she had forgotten.

Slipping a hand behind her back, I drew her up and knelt on the bed, bringing her into my embrace. She licked my skin and neck and poked her tongue through the silver circle lashed around my neck on braided leather. Oh, yes. There. Ahh... Gauging my pulse with her tongue to my vein, she then made way to my mouth with her sweet pink lips that kissed with a passionate fierceness of which, I couldn't get enough.

My hands skated on her silken skin. She arched her back and tilted her hips to match my movements, and when I slid a finger over her smooth mons she hummed through our kiss, signaling I'd found the sensitive bud that topped her folds. The tiny jewel was slick and hard. I stroked it slowly, then faster, a little harder, then softly, reading her coos and moans as a roadmap to her pleasure.

"Cinder, yes." Her head tucked against my neck, and her fingernails digging into my chest, I winced at the delicious pain. Her other hand stroked my cock, luring the swollen head to her wetness. "Feel my fire," she whispered. "Claim it if you can."

I was all over that challenge.

Lifting her by the hips, she wrapped her legs around mine, and I lowered her onto my shaft, groaning deep in my throat at the hot, tight connection that blasted through my senses with an atomic surge. Rational thought fled. I wanted the fire this vixen could give me, and shudders racked my body with impending climax.

"Yes," she said on a gasp. "Demon, you are incredible."

When I felt the prick of her teeth at the vein on my neck, I should have shoved her away. Instead I pulled her in because the sharp intrusion rocketed my pleasure off the scale. I wanted to drown her with my darkness and hold her close as I succumbed to the depths along with her.

I had come to Paris with the intent of stealing *ritrovatore d'anime* and escaping the city without notice. Yet here I was, impaled upon a gorgeous fire demon's shaft, my legs and arms wrapped around him, and my teeth sunk deep into his smoky flesh.

There wasn't any other place I'd rather be. No other moment I'd want to experience.

Whoever had told me demon blood was nasty had been wrong. Cinder's blood seeped into my mouth on a hot ooze. It tasted like a decadent treat that melts onto your tongue and lingers. Salty sweet like caramel, yet dark, and tinted with something I couldn't discern. I wanted to drink him until I drowned.

But even as I licked his flesh, he pierced me deeply with his hot penis that felt as if it had been fire-forged and hammered to a skillful weapon. So good, he fit me perfectly and every glide up and down disturbed my clit and, combined with the taste of his blood, I couldn't hold on to reality much longer.

Fingers losing hold of his shoulders, the hum of an incredible orgasm shivered through me. My body shuddered, tingled and danced for the demon. He possessed me. I wanted to be possessed by him.

Head tossing back, I gasped on the blood filling my mouth as the pleasure overwhelmed me. Cinder cried out at the same time. We came together in an illicit bonding of demon and vampire, fire and blood. Thoughts slid away. Exquisite shocks of satisfaction encompassed my body and spilled me backward to land on the plush pillow and sheets in a giggle of triumph.

I hummed and touched my mouth, tracing the blood from my lips and licking it clean. Another giggle escaped because I had never felt more satisfied. I'd forgotten something… What was it?

I didn't want to waste this bliss, so I didn't even try to summon what I'd forgotten.

Cinder collapsed beside me, declaring allegiance to a tiny vixen with teeth. That would be me, the tiny vixen who had conquered the big bad demon. Heh. Fist bump for me.

I sighed and curled onto my side, the lush swoon that accompanied the bite granting me a giddy high that, accompanied with the after-sex high, I felt sure would remain for a long time.

The fire demon sighed and green smoke misted into the air. I waved a hand through the sigh. "You are one hot number."

"I like numbers. Mathematics are my thing."

"Is that so? Never would have guessed. You always been a demon?"

"Why do you ask?"

I shrugged. "I don't know. I was born mortal. Only been a bloodsucker for a decade."

"I've been demon for..." His sigh hushed over my sex-warm skin. "Ages. You ever hear of *l'homme vert*?"

"The green man? Isn't he some forest myth? I thought you were from Beneath?"

"I am. *L'homme vert* was a myth created by mortals. You know Paris experiences sinkholes a few times every year that fall many stories into the underlying tunnels?"

"I'm from Venice. I'm not much up on Paris, other than the Eiffel Tower and the banana and Nutella crepes. Man, do I miss eating."

"A rather large hole sunk into the tunnels in the seventeenth century, and went down forever. Or as close to Beneath as you can get. Mortals fell in and died in the fall, but some did not. Those that were rescued reported seeing a green man."

"You? Because you've got that cool green smoke?"

He nodded. "I had come up to reconnaissance, and some saw me."

"Did you...take them Beneath?"

"I used to guard the gates to Beneath. I have only ever received souls destined for my gates."

"Oh." I turned onto my back and closed my eyes. Souls destined for Beneath. Ugh. I'd needed that reminder. Papa waited for me. How could I have forgotten? I had to get out of here. "Now that you're not Beneath, who takes the souls?"

"Not my concern. I'm done with that nasty business. Trying to live on the up-and-up now."

"With numbers?"

"Security and IT work does demand a love for numbers."

Cinder sat and turned his legs off the other side of the bed. He reached for his clothes. Feeling a strange loss, I turned to touch him, and for the first time, saw the massive tattoo on his back. It was thick and black and curved in wicked arcs and scythes, seeming to almost clutch his spine.

And then I suddenly knew it wasn't a tattoo. "Himself's mark!" I gasped.

He turned abruptly, but didn't twist around enough to hide the mark.

"You belong to…?" I clutched my throat. Saying the dark prince's name was never wise. Say it three times and he'd invite himself over for dinner—and food would not be the menu. "But you said you didn't work Beneath anymore?"

"I don't. I escaped a decade ago, but I still wear his mark. He owns my soul. But he hasn't come to claim me since I've walked mortal ground, so I'm of a mind to keep quiet and live my life while he turns the other cheek."

"I'm sorry for you."

"Why? I'm a demon, Parish. Most of us are in Himself's ranks, and those who are not, are deemed worthless."

"But you work for the Council."

"They don't know about my alliance with Him—the dark guy. Former alliance." Pulling on his shirt, he glanced to me. "You won't tell anyone, either."

"I won't." And, despite his warning tone, I meant it. I shuddered, because having no soul was all too familiar to me. "Without a soul you can never love."

The demon cast a smirking gaze over my naked body. "Love isn't necessary to lust."

And suddenly I felt cold. Discarded. *What did you expect, Parish? You were both using each other for distraction.* Until… It had changed to something more than a distraction.

Wow. I can't believe I'd admitted that to myself.

Cinder leaned in and kissed me. Gently, tenderly, brushing his lips over mine to linger. What was he about? Telling me he couldn't love in one moment then kissing me like he loved me in the next?

Like you would know if love bit you on the neck, you silly vampire.

"I've never been bitten by a vampire before," he said. "That was amazing. Made the orgasm twice as strong. I'd thought vamps were disgusted by our black blood."

"I've been told the same, but you taste like every treat in the book all rolled into one. So good."

And I looked aside, because I'd just experienced heaven in the guise of hell. Not that I deserved a fair shake. Vampires weren't exactly upstanding citizens. Even those of us who had never asked for the transforming bite.

Cinder pulled up his pants. The man had no soul. Which meant, I could never let him get his hands on the device locked in the drawer.

"So I just had sex with the green man," I mused, in an attempt to detour my thoughts. "This paranormal realm and immortality are still so new to me. Were you always a guardian of the gate?"

"Not until after I fell and was changed to demon."

"Fell? What were you before demon?"

"Angel."

"An angel. But…"

Vampires couldn't drink angel blood. The divine blue blood entered their system then—bam! Bye-bye vampire.

Feeling my throat close up, I pushed up onto my elbows. "I drank your blood," I said on a frightened whisper.

"I said I was *once* an angel. My blood is black now, vixen. And you haven't exploded into bits."

"Yet." Panicked, I clutched the sheets, but again, tried to maintain a calm head. But if I overlooked the small detail about drinking his blood, there was another, even bigger connection that suddenly cemented. "How did you make that incredible fall? Why did you do it?"

"I fell with my angel brethren millennia ago. We lusted after mortal women."

I closed my eyes tight. No. He couldn't be. A fallen one?

"My brethren sought out their mortal muses on this earthly realm. But I fell too far, you might say. Been working for Himself for a couple thousand years."

"But you escaped Beneath…"

"Through a sink hole about a decade ago," he said.

"And now you're searching for your muse?"

"Parish, I'm demon now. Even if I once had a muse, I'm not interested in her. I'm a soulless dark demon trying to make his way in this realm by flying under the dark prince's radar, and to hopefully earn some respect from the Council."

"A soul is the only thing a being has going for them. Without one you're just a…"

"A what? A mindless, unfeeling thing? Do you think me mindless, Parish?"

"I was able to seduce you rather easily."

Man, I should have gotten all the details about his history before sliding between the sheets with him. I pressed a palm over the skin on my forearm that was thinner than the rest. Why hadn't I stuck to the plan?

"But you weren't successful in distracting me. I'm still not leaving without the device you stole."

Oh, no, he wouldn't. The last being on this earth who should touch *ritrovatore d'anime* was this demon—who had once been a freakin' fallen one with a muse.

I took a few deep breaths, filling my lungs and gathering courage and fortitude.

"I took it for a reason. I need it. Just for a day." I would have no use for it after that. "You're not the keeper of it, are you?"

"No, but it was stolen on my watch. I'm responsible for its safe return."

"I'll return it safely. Promise." I kissed him, wishing it was longer, deeper—but no, I had to be smart. "I really need to go. I have to catch a flight to Venice."

"You're going to use the device in Venice? For?"

"It's for my father. He's on his death bed."

"So it's something that'll restore life? Bring him back to health?"

Oops. No more details. "Not even close. Goodbye, demon lover. Can you do that smoky thing and leave?"

He nodded, but I'd be a fool if I hadn't recognized the regretful tug at the corner of his mouth. Green smoke misted at his feet, which was weirdly impressive, and within seconds his entire form smoked and wavered out through the window as if sucked out by a vortex.

I hadn't much time. The demon was just amusing me; I knew he would be back. The situation had gotten much worse than I could have anticipated. But so long as Cinder remained in the dark about the device, I would be safe. Fingers crossed.

"I'm coming, Papa. Just need to gather a few things."

Chapter 4

I smoked back to the security lab in the archives of the Council building. Certainly Jones was still there, in fact, I had my suspicions he lived there sometimes. He flashed me a raised brow, but didn't comment. I looked down. Forgot to put on my boots and button up my shirt.

"I tracked the thief," I offered, "but she's got the piece locked up." In a dresser drawer fashioned from wood. Stupid, Cinder. I should smoke back, flick a flame onto the wood and...

"You don't know what it is, do you?" Certainly asked.

"What was stolen? Does it matter?"

"Not in the overall scheme of saving our asses for having lost the damned thing, but my guess is it's something that might interest you."

"I had it in hand. Made of carbon fiber?"

"No, something ineffable."

"Really? It's a small, thick disk with runes on it."

"Hallowed runes. It's an angelic device called *ritrovatore d'anime*. We call it the Retriever. It's a soul retriever."

I slapped a palm over my heart, for no other reason than

it had started to beat rapidly. The words, angelic and soul, struck a chord within me. Which would place its origins Above, and that meant I should have gotten a read on the thing having come from that place. A twinge of regret tightened my muscles. I'd never thought to miss Above, yet maybe I did and didn't want to admit it.

"It can only be used once a century," he continued. "It retrieves a lost soul. Human or paranormal can use it. I suspect the thief is missing a soul, or knows someone who is in dire need of theirs. You have a soul, Cinder?"

Parish had asked me the same. Taken aback at his question, because Certainly had never delved too deeply into my origins since we'd met a decade earlier, I could but shake my head.

"'Spose not. You being fallen, and all."

"I am no longer angel. Completely demon," I muttered, though my thoughts raced.

Himself owned my soul, and had marked me duly to show the world I was his, as Parish had seen earlier. The devil's mark dug deep into my being, and at times when Himself sought to punish me, it felt as though it wrapped its thorned talons around my spine.

Ritrovatore d'anime? Could such a device return *my* soul?

Palm sliding down my chest to fall away from my body, I stood there. Did I want my soul? Did I need it? I'd done perfectly well without one.

Though I'd only been in the mortal realm for a decade. I couldn't know what a missing soul would give me. I hadn't felt as if I'd missed out on anything. Parish seemed to think a person could not love without one. But I'd been in love before. Surely. Well, there must have been a time when I had experienced love.

Hmm... Nothing jumped to mind. Not an image of any particular woman I had dated over the years, or shared a tumble between the sheets. I'd seen two or three women exclusively. But love?

"Get it back," Certainly said. "I don't care if it comes back slightly used, either. I don't want to catch hell for losing one single item from the archives."

"I'll return in a snap."

I smoked back to Parish's bedroom. The drawer wouldn't give, but of course it was locked with whatever warding spell she'd used on it. While witch's magic had no effect on me, if an object had been bespelled it was completely effective.

Scent of the tiny vixen's rose perfume stirred me and I turned to spy the vampiress stuffing clothes in a duffel.

"It's warded," she stated the obvious.

"Yes, but it's also made of wood." I lifted the dresser and smashed it on the floor. Wood shattered. The Retriever disk skittered across the floor and landed at my bare feet. I snatched it. Full of smug satisfaction, I winked at her. "Guess vampires who steal magic from witches aren't so powerful as they like to think."

She chuckled and approached me, the sexy red dress that ruffled out at her thighs slinking over curves I'd tasted less than an hour earlier. I held the disk before me, daring her to take it from me. She would try, and I invited the sensual tussle that would ensue.

"You think you're so clever?"

"Not so much clever as using common sense. You smell like roses. Freshen up your perfume?"

"I'm beyond seducing you, Cinder. I'm on a schedule. Things to do, places to go."

"A soul to retrieve?"

"You figured that out?"

She swallowed and I guessed she'd hoped I wouldn't learn that detail. Did she believe the object would hold some value to me, a soulless entity? She was right. I could use a soul. Might come in handy if I ever did want to know the experience of love.

She tilted up on tiptoes to kiss my chin. I bowed my head to catch her touch on my mouth, but she was too quick. She stepped back and I reached for her, but my hand slapped the air before me as if an invisible wall.

I hit it with the hand that held the disk, and it again stopped in midair.

Parish took the disk while I was stunned enough to not have a good grasp. I groped for it, but my hands didn't extend farther than a foot before me. Nor could I step out of what seemed a column around me.

"Backup ward," she said, and kissed the disk, then returned the smug wink.

"This won't hold me for long," I growled. "Witch magic has little effect on me."

"Seems to be working well enough right now."

Yes, and why was that?

"It will hold you long enough to give me a head start," Parish said. "Thanks for the good time, green man. Wish the situation were different and we weren't both in it for ourselves. I could have really gotten into us."

Us. The word resonated in a waver through my being. It felt...right. "We can have an us," I said, knowing it as truth before my brain could even argue.

"Give it up, lover boy. Ta!"

The vampiress stepped into a pair of sexy black high

heels, grabbed a purse emblazoned with a skull on it and then exited the bedroom. I heard the front door slam, and then I kicked, but stubbed my foot on the warded wall.

I'd been played by the thief. This was some powerful magic to contain me. Although it hadn't been placed directly on my person—and I stood within a perfect chalk circle drawn on the floor—so that could be a reason it was working. Circles. They had power over me for reasons related to my angelic origins. But now the tiny vixen had only fired my desire to find her again, and next time, make her pay.

With kisses and sex. Because I wanted her again. For reasons that were as unexplainable as my knowing we could be an us.

Demon, what in all Beneath is going on with your cold, soulless heart?

I landed by the Piazza San Marco in Venice as the sun rose on the Veneto, and realized I hadn't a clue where to find Parish, and what was her surname? Flipping out my cell phone, I dialed up Certainly.

"Parish Marazetti," he said as he searched the Council database that I had designed to categorize, sort and order all known paranormals. "Her parents are mortal. She was born in 1978 and was changed to vampire in 2002. Ah. She's a member of tribe Lilith."

Certainly's groan echoed the same groan I felt rise upon hearing that fact.

"Ball busters," Certainly said.

I nodded. I'd heard the derogatory term about the all-female tribe, and had bought into it, but until now had never met one personally. Parish certainly was a tough little number—and quickly becoming my favorite number—but I wouldn't place her as a man-hating vampiress with a vengeance as Lilith members were painted. She'd been too receptive to my touch for that, and does a cooing vampiress who comes with a few strokes qualify as a ball buster?

I think not.

"You got an address for her?" I asked. "I'm in Venice. She's got the Retriever."

"Dude, you seriously let one small vampiress get away from you?"

Make that a tiny vixen.

Fine. So I'd let her get away. She had magic. I had some wicked demon magic and hell, *fire* but something about the sneaky yet sensual blonde had made me forget that fact.

"I'll send you the coordinates. It's her father's house. Her mother died fifteen years ago. Looks like the father, Lanzo Marazetti, isn't doing too well, either. Cancer."

"Thanks." I clicked off and then used the GPS to locate the address.

A vampiress visiting her dying mortal father? I wasn't sure how to approach the scene, but if I focused on grabbing the device, I could be out of here and back in Paris within the hour. But not without first checking the usefulness of the soul-retrieving device.

I had grown up in the cozy palazzo that was decorated on the exterior with fading Istrian tiles. As I approached, I saw the demon lurking outside and cursed that he'd beat me here. I'd expected him to follow. Indeed, my weak magic was ineffective against him, but I guessed magic not aimed directly at him had some power.

Apparently not for long.

With an exhale, I felt courage leak from my pores. I just

wanted to get inside and check on my father. I'd called ahead and the maid said he'd been sleeping for three days with little wakefulness, and he hadn't asked to eat. His breathing was raspy and shallow. Not long, the maid had commented.

My heart crumbled to papery pieces as the demon stepped toward the main door to block my entrance. I slid a hand inside my purse to clasp *ritrovatore d'anime*. The cool disk reassured me for a moment, and I lifted my shoulders.

As I neared Cinder, his overwhelming presence softened my resolve and knowing how strong he was, and how tenderly he had held me when we'd had sex, stirred up want and desire, yet also fear and caution.

He'd said we could be an us. Really? Had the demon fallen for me?

It wasn't so bizarre to go there. I certainly felt something toward him. But not love. Lust, as he had implied, was easier. And there was his history, which scared me for reasons he must never learn. Is that why he kept following me? Was he *compelled*? Couldn't be. And such a compulsion had nothing to do with my poor spellwork. What were the odds that two destined for one another would meet after thousands of millennia? And I had only been born decades earlier.

A teardrop splattered my nose. I hated to show him weakness, but it was impossible to prevent with father so close, and Cinder unaware of my urgent task.

"Just go away," I said, my voice breaking into a hush. "This is family business. You can't understand."

"You think you can get back your father's soul with that device?"

I met his gaze. Dark eyes that had seen thousands of years

and things Beneath that I didn't want to imagine. "How do you know that?"

"It's a guess. Putting two and two together." He stood his full height, arms crossed high over his chest. So imposing. And smelling like he belonged…to me. I could taste his blood on my tongue right now, and it prodded at me as if it were an addictive substance, of which I needed one more taste.

Christ, but I needed strength. And my soul sprang for that need.

I plunged against Cinder's hard, steely form and clung, allowing the tears to fall, and my heart to open. "Papa's dying. I want him to have his soul back before he dies. I don't want him to go…"

I couldn't say Beneath. Papa didn't deserve that punishment. Not when he'd ransomed his soul for me.

"How did he lose his soul?" Cinder asked softly.

I shook my head, unwilling to discuss this and only wanting him to close me in a hug. Yet he remained unyielding, his arms still crossed beneath my embrace.

"Demon, if you've an ounce of compassion, let me pass."

"I'm not familiar with that emotion."

"You are, you just don't want to admit it to yourself. I have to get inside. He's failing. You can have the device back when I'm finished."

"Have you the code to use it?"

Code? I hadn't considered I'd need a code. Yet *ritrovatore d'anime* was a solid chunk of dark metal. Of course there must be a means to open it. Why hadn't I thought of that until now?

"I'll figure it out. I've magic." I tilted back my head to meet his gaze. Finally he dropped his arms, yet still didn't embrace me. Demons were supposed to be emotionless and cold.

If he wasn't going to yield, I'd do it for him. Summoning an air spell, I flung the demon aside—but his body merely swayed. Right. Forgot the magic had no power against him personally. "Just give me a head start, please," I pleaded.

With a tilt of his head, he nodded, and looked away down the cobbled street. Just long enough to allow me to punch in the digital code and rush through the cool, shadowed house to my father's bedside. Cinder would follow, I knew, but I blessed him for the chance.

Lanzo Marazetti was awake and breathing roughly when I sat on his bedside. Golden light from the rising sun danced on the windowsill and the canal water's reflection cast wavy shapes across the ceiling. Papa looked at me but showed no sign of recognition. His salt and pepper hair had grown long over his ears, a prideful adornment he'd always carefully combed because he knew how it had attracted the women. He'd waited five years following mother's death before dating again. I'd wanted that happiness for him. He was a man who thrived in the love of a good woman's arms.

I held his hand and felt the slow pulse at his wrist. His skin was cold and his fingertips were bluing.

"You're a good man, Papa. I've brought something to make your transition easier."

Digging the device out from my purse, I placed the heavy disk on Papa's chest, then waited. For what, I wasn't sure. What code? Shouldn't the thing just work?

I searched my memory for the spells I had stolen from witches over my decade of training with tribe Lilith. I'd initially thought taking magic from a witch through blood-sexmagic so evil, yet the majority of the witches had been cooperative and had actually participated willingly, thanks to my vampiric thrall and sensual wiles.

Cinder was aware of a code? I would have to make him talk.

Kissing Papa's forehead, I whispered that I'd return. It was difficult to leave the dark bedroom, but when I heard the commotion below, I quickened my pace.

Chapter 5

The blonde spitfire blazed into the study and hissed in a whisper, "You don't have permission to enter this home!"

I set down the marble globe I'd been studying with care and turned to lean against the ancient mahogany desk that might have been around for centuries. "I'm not a vampire, vixen. I can enter any dwelling I choose."

"Generally a person waits to be invited in if he means to be in the least nice."

"Never confessed to being a nice guy, either."

"You're an ass."

"And you should be nicer, seeing you've got some big favor you want to ask of me. Yes?"

Fists chugging at her sides, she blew out a breath of frustration instead of another argument. I had guessed correctly. And I immediately felt awful about it. Someone had taken the wind out of her sails, and that someone had been me.

I shouldn't feel bad. She was a thief. But standing here in her father's home, with him upstairs—dying—would never put me in the running for sainthood.

Defeated and quiet now, Parish pulled the Retriever from

her pocket and held it before her on a shaky palm. "Please, help me. I need the code to make it work."

"Tell me how your mortal father lost his soul?"

"I don't have time for this, demon."

I winced because I preferred her to use my name and not the label that suddenly made me feel dirty and lesser around her brightness.

"Do you even care?" she continued. "He's dying. He's so close…" She tilted her head down and I looked away before I could see the teardrop. Too late. I smelled the salty sadness. My chest squeezed oddly. "Fine. Papa sold his soul for me."

"For you? But what…?"

"I didn't want to tell you this, but apparently you've not a clue."

"A clue about what?"

"About what I really am, or rather, what I once was, and how I believe we were destined to meet."

Now she'd lost me. She was vampire, who I assumed had once been mortal due to the mortal father. Destined to meet? I bought into that crap about as much as I believed in fate and soul mates. Life was what you made it; it was not foretold before you set foot on this earth. Unless…

"Cinder, I was born with a sigil on my forearm." She displayed her forearm, but where she stroked it the skin appeared paler, thinner.

A sigil? That was an angel thing. And as she spoke, I started to shake my head, not in disbelief, but in utter awe.

"I was born a muse," she said. "A female who would attract a fallen one to mate with me and give birth to a monstrous nephilim. My father learned what the sigil meant when I was eight. And believing if it wasn't there, it wouldn't lure an angel, to have it removed…Papa sold his soul to the dark prince."

Not one to ever be taken by surprise, that detail stunned me. I dropped my jaw open.

"Himself flayed it off right then and there. Without anesthesia. I've never felt so much pain. Ever."

I clasped a hand over my heart. *Why had it begun to hurt inside my chest as if wounded?* Himself was the great tempter, and that little bargain didn't surprise me at all. But to know Parish had been a muse—or rather, still was—took me aback. Removing the sigil couldn't change what she had been born to, could it?

You're thinking in terms of destiny, demon. Stop it.

And yet, I *had* felt compelled to her all this time. Hadn't been able to keep my head on straight and go right for the stolen device. Had allowed her to seduce me because I'd wanted her more than I'd ever wanted a woman in my life. And I'd allowed her to escape, because seriously? I could have wrangled her outside the storage facility if I'd wanted to.

Oh, bloody dark demons. Maybe this destiny stuff had some merit.

"What was your sigil?" I asked quickly, and touched the choker at my throat. "The shape of it. Do you remember?"

Heaving out a big sigh that wavered through my skin, Parish collapsed on the big leather easy chair beside the window overlooking the canal. I empathized with her heartache. "Why do you want to know? Is it because you now suspect the same thing I suspect?"

Her big gray eyes flashed up at me and I felt the flash in my heart, hard and forceful, yet it tendered away some of the ache, and a bright flame ignited there and knew it hadn't been started with anger.

"Labatiel," I offered.

"What?"

"That was my angel name. Labatiel, the Flaming One. I'm no longer angel, Parish. You've nothing to fear from me should your sigil match..."

I couldn't say it. The fallen ones bore a sigil to match that of their muses. I didn't have one on my body since I'd been changed to demon, but I knew what it had once been, because I'd been haunted by the shape all my life. In fact, I loved the shape.

"A circle," she said. "Just a simple circle."

I fell to my knees before her.

The demon on his knees before me was enough to stall my heart, and not because it was some great romantic gesture that should win my heart.

Without a spoken word, I knew his sigil was a circle. The fallen one had found his muse.

I had believed when the sigil was removed—as had my father—I was no longer a beacon to the fallen one. I had further believed, after becoming vampire, I'd left that horrible nightmare of someday becoming a nephilim baby mama behind.

Yet here he knelt, the one man on this entire planet who could fulfill that horrible destiny.

Unless it was truth that when Cinder had been changed to demon he'd lost all angelic qualities. He seemed to think so. Could I hope for that?

"Show me yours," I said quietly.

"I don't have a sigil now. It was once here." He turned his head, revealing his neck where I'd bitten him. He stroked a finger right there, where the vein pulsed temptingly. No sign of any skin having been removed or even the faintest circle. The leather choker brandished a brilliant silver circle. All this time. And neither of us had been the wiser.

I could scent his blood. It tempted like perfume to my soul.

"You've no need to fear me, Parish. I will not harm you. Nor can I make you pregnant with a monster."

Smoothing a palm over my belly, I now regretted the sex without a condom. But he couldn't know everything. "What if you're wrong? What if some innate angelic part of you remains?"

"Look into my eyes, tiny vixen. You know what an angel's eyes should look like?"

They were supposed to be all colors, kaleidoscopic and ever changing. Cinder's gaze was dark brown, pinpointed with spots of white. No depth, and yet, unimaginably fathomless.

Swallowing, I stroked aside the hair that hung over his left eye. "We were once destined for one another. How weird is that?"

"I'd say it's off the scale. But you're not frightened of me? Please don't be. I want to help your father, Parish. I swear it to you."

"But if you used the *ritrovatore d'anime*— Don't you want your soul?"

"I have decided to have a soul would be most favorable. Yet it would render me mortal. Not sure I'm up for that. Mortality is so…final. You were once mortal. A muse, yet mortal. How did you become vampire?"

Not the most upstanding moment in the history of Parish Marazetti's great life adventures. But since Cinder had been so open with me, I owed him.

"I decided to move to New York after I'd graduated because I had an independent streak a mile wide. Much to my father's protests, I took off with stars in my eyes. The night I arrived in New York City I went to a club and I had a drink that made me tipsy too quickly. I think something was in it—no, I know there was something in it." I sighed and hung my head. "I hooked up with a man that night and woke up in his coffin the next morning."

"A coffin?"

"I know, right? So old school. I also had a bite on my neck, and the vampire wanted me to become his eternal lover. I never ran so fast. Never saw the creep again. But what I didn't expect is that I'd transform to vampire weeks later. I couldn't tell Papa. I didn't want him to know I'd become a monster, probably an even worse monster than the one he'd sold his soul to prevent. Everything he had sacrificed for me had been lost. I couldn't afford New York for long, so I moved back to Venice where I was inducted into tribe Lilith. They have become my family. Yet I tell my father I'm taking night classes to cover for my need to hunt for blood."

"You think lying to him is the way to show your love?"

I looked up abruptly and sniffed back a tear. "It's the only way. As if you would even know, demon who doesn't believe in love. If Papa knew I had become vampire it would have killed him on the spot. He'd thought he'd saved me from one horrible fate, and then I walked right into another."

And this was getting too complicated. Me, empathizing? I don't think so. I had only to grab the Retriever and smoke back to the Council storage facility.

Or, I could—for one moment—give the woman what she needed. Compassion. I wasn't sure how to do that, but

I suspected listening, offering her quiet reassurance, might be the thing.

I nodded. "I'm sorry. I have no insight into mortal matters of the heart."

She stroked my cheek and it surprised me she could find such tenderness when it was her heart that was obviously breaking. "You've the capacity to feel, Cinder. I know that about you, and I've only met you. Please. Will you help me to give my papa back his soul before he dies?"

I stared at the device she held on her palm. It would work once a century, Certainly had explained, and would give back a mortal or paranormal their soul.

Even mine.

I didn't need a soul. Did I?

You want a soul if it can allow you to love. Because I thought I was falling—again—only this time it was for the vampiress who had once been a muse and probably still was. And she was *my* muse. At one time I would have walked this world seeking only her, and would have walked for millennia until finally she was born and I could claim her.

And it would have been an evil compulsion, born of my rebellion to fall.

I was suddenly thankful for my demonic nature. It had changed me. Made me less a monster than I had been when an angel, if anyone could believe that.

Love Parish? It felt too precious, too much of a long shot. But if a soul could grant that emotion...

"I'll see what I can do." I accepted the disk from her. "Perhaps my mathematics knowledge can unlock the means to operate this device."

Parish plunged into my arms and I held her close, feeding off her vibrant energy. She felt right in my arms, and I wasn't sure if that was a good thing or something that would have me unlocking the device for my own use.

Hell, I already knew the answer to that one.

Chapter 6

It was difficult standing back and letting Cinder handle the soul retrieval device. Yet if anyone could break the code, he could, thanks to his skills.

I wandered into father's quiet room where he slept, and I didn't have the desire to wake him. It seemed a peaceful rest, and I prayed when he did go it would be in his sleep and not painful—and with a soul.

I owed Papa that much for what he had done for me.

Stopping in the hallway that looked out over the tiled foyer before the open study door, I stroked a finger along my forearm where Himself had flayed off the mark. Foolish of me now to accept that simply removing the mark would actually change my destiny. I'd been born a muse. I would remain so.

And yet, I hadn't been born vampire. Nor had Cinder been born demon. We were both something different now. Change wasn't always good, but maybe in Cinder's case it was.

Closing my eyes, I could feel his presence. *Another man*

in my life without a soul. Suddenly it occurred to me how unfeeling I had been.

I had asked Cinder to crack a code that would give my father back his soul, without even considering that perhaps the demon would like his soul as well. Sure, he'd implied he could do without, but he was the sort of proud demon to put up a front.

How could I be so callous? Cinder had years, centuries, hell, probably millennia ahead of him. A man who lived so long without a soul couldn't be much of a man. And yet, he was. Perhaps because humanity still clung to him?

But he'd not been a part of humanity until recently. He was an angel by origin, a demon by creation. Mortality, as he'd said, was so final. A creature who had lived for so long must think it the ultimate punishment.

I wondered what he could do with a soul, and suspected it would be great, fathomless, wondrous. He held knowledge of millennia within him. And I suspected he wouldn't use it for evil, as I'd yet to see an evil move on his part.

I glanced up the stairs to Papa's room. He had a few days at most, perhaps only hours or minutes. A soul would ensure his passage to heaven, or as the paranormal nation termed it, Above. Or would it? I felt sure Papa had lived an upstanding life, but I didn't know much about him from when before I was born. Mama had never spoken of their lives, or probably, I had never asked. Parents don't talk about stuff like that, it seemed.

Could *ritrovatore d'anime* give back two souls? It was doubtful since the thing only worked once a century.

Oh, my heart. What to do? I wanted to save my father, and yet, how could I overlook the man I had begun to care about?

Stepping bravely forward, I entered the study and found

Cinder sitting facing the window where sunlight glinted sharply in a crack that demarcated the glass. He held the disk upon his chest, his eyes closed, though I sensed he was not asleep, just concentrating, going deep.

A thin white crease glowed around two edges of *ritrovatore d'anime*. He had accomplished something? Was it ready to open?

"Cinder?"

He held up a finger, prompting my silence. I pressed my back to the wall to keep from rushing to grab the thing from him. As much as I had little means to do so, I truly did trust him. He'd given me all those head starts. Talk about sweet nothings. And I could still revisit the taste of his blood on my tongue, and that was enough to quiet my anxiety.

He sighed and looked to me. "Sorry. That one didn't work." The disk went dark. "Wish there was a written spell for this thing. I'm nearing the end of ideas."

I wandered over and sat on the arm of the easy chair next to him, and tapped the dark metal disk. "I imagine millennia ago this thing came with instructions carved on a tablet, eh?"

He chuckled, and pulled me onto his lap in a casual move. I curled up my legs and snuggled against his warmth.

"I'm sure at one time there was a written manual, or spell," I continued, "But you know modern times. Nothing comes with instructions anymore. I can never figure out a new cell phone. A person usually ends up going online to find the manual."

"That's it." Cinder's body tensed but he didn't move to push me from his comfortable lap. "Why didn't I think of that? Everything is online."

"You think? I don't know about that. This is ancient magic."

"But if it was ever written down, there is the slightest chance... Hell, the Council archives are vast, and all computerized, thanks to me. Do you have a laptop?"

"No, but I've an iPad in the desk drawer." I retrieved the tablet computer and returned to Cinder's lap.

As we waited for it to power up, he stroked a finger along my chin and tilted my head to look at him. "How is he?"

"Still alive. Peaceful, it seems."

"That is good."

"You don't really care about him. You just want to get this done so you can bring the disk back to where it belongs. Will they be upset it's been used?"

"The archivist implied I could bring it back used. And you're wrong about me not caring. It surprises me to say this, but I am concerned for anyone who means something to you."

"Did you just confess to having feelings for me, demon?"

"Yes, maybe. I do have feelings, but I hadn't thought to embrace the gentler, more empathetic ones. Hell, I think I could cherish you. Perhaps I already do. Perhaps I have for millennia."

The meaning in that statement held us in silence for long moments.

"I was sitting here concentrating on the disk," he softly said, "but at the same time I was dialed into your every step through this house. I wanted to know where you were, how you moved, what your emotions were. I could feel your sadness, and your vacillation to confusion. What confuses you, tiny vixen?"

I was no longer confused. I couldn't imagine not giving this man the opportunity he didn't know he wanted. As for Papa? I prayed he could accept the choice I had made.

"I want you to use this," I said, placing the disk in his

palm and holding my hand over it. "You've more use for a soul than my father. He treads Death's threshold. You, on the other hand, have thousands of years to enjoy a soul."

Instead of protesting, he clasped the Retriever and nodded. My throat went dry as I wondered if I'd made the correct choice. But then Cinder shook his head. "A mortal man's soul is worth a thousand demon souls, surely." He placed it in my hand then kissed my cheek, my nose, my eyelids.

I didn't want the sweet connection to stop, so I pushed away thought to protest his refusal, clutching the disk to my chest, and tilting my head to kiss his mouth.

Demon sweet heat claimed me with his intense kiss. I moved into him as his hand slid along my side and coaxed me closer. Easily we joined and easily we accepted. Perhaps we were both weary and bonded by a strange quest when neither should be helping the other. Didn't matter. I admired Cinder and I wanted him desperately.

He stopped the kiss and stared into my eyes until I whimpered softly because I couldn't speak or make my hunger known without biting him. And I wanted to bite him and drink his dark blood, be damned the urgency to save my father's soul.

"After this is all done, when we've unlocked the Retriever and made your father safe," he said, and my heart fluttered in anticipation. "Would you consider me as…?"

"A lover?" I kissed him deeply, lingering in the heat of him, the impossible sweetness. "My boyfriend?" Another kiss and I straddled his lap. "Someone I could fall in love with?"

"Parish, I can't love."

"You could if you had a soul."

"I won't take what belongs to your father."

"It doesn't belong to him. I stole *ritrovatore d'anime*. It's any man's soul to claim."

"And if I took the soul this device could give me, you'd forever wonder about your father. Where he is? If he is in eternal unrest? Be honest. You would."

He was harshing my sensual vibes, pulling me down to reality when all I wanted to do was avoid the truth and soar on bliss. And rightfully so. This demon did care. And that made me love him.

"I'll give the soul to my father," I said, "but I want you no matter what happens. As a lover, a boyfriend, the man I think I can love."

"You could accept a demon?"

"You could accept a vampiress who craves your dark blood?"

"Your bite does things to me that nothing else can do, sweet one. Do you think that is the reason you can bite me and not be offended by the taste of my blood? Because you are my muse?"

"It's weird, but possible." I stroked my forearm. "You like circles, don't you?"

He tapped the leather choker joined with a silver circle. "I do. I've been haunted by them all my life. It's the only reason I know that was my sigil."

"I think that's why I was able to trap you in the ward, too. Can you forgive me for doing what I had to do to help my father?"

"Forgiveness isn't necessary." He turned the Retriever around between us. "Let's take care of this and then deal with what our hearts desire."

"Deal." I grabbed the iPad, and turned on his lap so the both of us could search the internet together.

Chapter 7

Hours of online research finally netted results. I kicked myself mentally for not thinking of this in the first place. And where did I find the spell to unlock the Retriever? Inside the Council's archives, nestled deep within a collection of grimoires that had been scanned but never sorted, obviously, for the scatter of unordered information I'd had to sift through.

Parish handed me the colored jpeg we'd printed from the archives. It was blurry but the handwritten text was remarkably neat so I could read the Latin words with ease. But I didn't read them out loud because this was an action spell that required specific movements of my fingers around the cube. The right sequence would unlock it.

"Let's do this." I grabbed Parish's hand and marched her out into the foyer, but paused, unsure about charging into her father's room and taking control. "You lead."

She kissed me, and I realized I couldn't get enough of her kisses, and was happy we'd decided to continue this following what we were about to do. But I wasn't stupid. I didn't think it would last. The angel I'd once been did not compel me to have sex with her to create a monster, yet I had been compelled, there was no doubt about that. Yet when in demon form, well, I had wings of fire, which were not at all like my former angelic wings. So I had to hope all that was in the past.

Parish led me by the hand to stand beside her father's death bed. I could smell impending death, and knew it was so near we'd best hurry. Signaling to her that I would stand on one side of the bed and work the device, she nodded and walked around to the head of the bed and stroked her father's hair.

The old man roused and murmured his daughter's name. I ignored the touching scene and began to read the instructions, placing my fingers as instructed on the disk. The first sequence lit up the runes.

"I love you, Papa," Parish said, and I paused.

The disk went dark. *Concentrate. If you care about her, then get this right, even if you want the soul for yourself.* Because with a soul I could fall in love.

But with a soul I'd surely become mortal.

It would be worth it to have Parish's love. Hell, I wanted to know what love felt like!

She caught my eye and the wondering innocence I saw there redirected me back to the task.

Forget the soul, be happy with the consolation prize, demon. It's more than you've ever had. It's more than you deserve.

"I'm ready," Lanzo Marazetti rasped, "to move on."

"To heaven," Parish whispered and kissed her father's forehead.

I moved my index finger across the disk. The device suddenly hummed and the top portion turned a quarter turn, flashing out a bright beam of blue light. A gasp caught in my throat. I'd unlocked it.

Quickly I placed the Retriever on Lanzo's chest and stepped back in preparation to be awed by what I expected would happen.

Parish, too stepped back, yet still held her father's hand. "Go in peace, Father," she said.

And the blue light spread out in a circle, glancing through the entire room, and moving through Parish and me. It hit me directly in the heart, and toppled me from my feet, and suddenly I was flying through the air. My back hit the plaster wall and I dropped. I cried out, I think, but I didn't hear my voice.

Something had gone wrong.

The blue light hit me with an intense feeling of love. Bathed within the cool sensation I stretched out my arms and took it all in. In that moment I knew my father's soul had reunited with his body, and in the next moment, I knew he had drawn his last breath. And that knowing filled me with peace.

The blue light lingered for seconds, as if a rippling water pool suspended midair, and it was then I noticed Cinder sitting against the wall, as if tossed there. His head hung forward and above his crown of dark hair floated a small blue circlet.

I made a small cry. It looked like a halo. But it couldn't be. Well, it could be. He had once been an angel. I wasn't sure how angels worked, and what their haloes meant beyond that the halo held their earthbound soul.

"Oh my," I whispered. "His soul?"

I glanced to Papa. His face was peaceful; his mouth had

fallen open in death. I knew he had gotten his soul as I knew I must drink blood for survival.

But what had happened to Cinder?

I rushed to his side, and as I did, the blue halo dissipated and the entire room went dark. A gleam of twilight shone across the tiled floor, highlighting the demon's downturned face.

"Cinder? What happened?"

I smelled sulfur, a sure demonic odor, yet I had never scented it on him before. And in the next instant he lifted his head, slapped a palm to his chest and looked around. "I got it," he said on a hush. "A soul."

"You did? But...?" Had it granted souls to both Cinder and my father? Perhaps the device sensed anyone who had not one and retrieved both? "You know it?"

He nodded and clasped my hand to press over his heart. I felt it beat, proud and strong, but that was nothing new. "Your father, too?" he asked.

I nodded.

And then Cinder cried out and his body lunged forward. The sweep of what sounded like a thousand crow wings crushed the silence. Dark wings tore away his shirt and swept out behind him, growing from his back. They were not of feather, but rather a mix of roman and modern numerals tightly fit together in what seemed a hologram but I couldn't determine the substance.

Was he returning to angel form?

Cinder cried out in myriad tongues, ancient and revered, yet indefinable by modern ears. It hurt my skull, but it only lasted a few seconds before dead silence muted the air. And he collapsed forward, his wings sweeping the air. They swept my face and it felt as if I'd been touched by something so soft and liquid I would never define it in my lifetime.

The wings of glowing numerals folded over his body and then...dissipated to a fine crystal ash over and around his prone form.

I lunged forward and plunged my fingers into the cool ash. His wings. Gone. Destroyed. Because he had so boldly received his soul? He would not have asked to have the divine taken from him if he'd known he still possessed it, but this was proof he'd carried it with him. Always.

The fallen one had indeed found his muse.

Another cry alerted me he was still in pain. Wanting to touch him, to help him in some manner, I could but hold my hands over his back as I watched the thick black devil's mark glow bright red and appear to curve into his body as if to clutch his lungs. Cinder shouted, his fingers digging into the wood floor. And then the mark flashed out to nothing, leaving behind burned flesh in the shape of the cruel symbol that had once marked him as Himself's slave.

Truly his soul must have returned to him.

"Cinder, I'm so sorry," I said, but I wasn't sure if I really was.

His hand slapped the floor, through the angel wing ash, and he lifted his torso and shot me the sexy smolder that had initially won my heart.

"Don't be sorry. I'm mortal now." He dropped his head to the floor. "Like it or not."

He did not want mortality. Cinder had sacrificed immortality to give my father the same. Everlasting life beyond the mortal coil.

A disturbance of light caught my attention and I swung a look to my father's bed. A man clad in black stood before the bed, his arms outstretched and face tilted back to accept the glittering light that popped out from Papa's chest.

"The soul bringer," Cinder commented quietly. "Come to ferry your father's soul…"

At Cinder's pause I looked to him, only to catch him hiding a wince. Was he in pain? I switched my gaze to the soul bringer. The two had exchanged a silent conversation.

"What was that about?" I asked. "Where is he taking my father's soul? Cinder?" I clutched him by the shirt lapels, but his eyelids fluttered and he passed out, falling forward into my arms. "Papa?"

The soul bringer had gone. My father's body lay in repose beneath the smooth white sheet. My happiness wilted.

Chapter 8

A *week later...*

I waited outside as Parish made a last walk through her father's palazzo. She hadn't plans to sell it because she preferred to live in Venice, but we intended to spend a few months together traveling. The funeral had been a few days ago. I had been forced to concoct a lie of silence in response to Parish's question about her father's soul by giving her a nod and a kiss to her forehead.

Easier that way, than to explain what I'd seen in Reichardt, the soul bringer's, eyes. He had collected a dark soul stained with much sin. It mattered little that Lanzo Marazetti had gotten his soul restored. Once blackened, there's no going back.

I knew Parish suspected the same, but we would not discuss it. It was better that way because neither of us can know anything for certain. Look at me: my origin was angel, I'd been changed to demon, and I was now pitifully mortal.

Never expected any of that. Destiny was a crock.

And yet, destiny had somehow lured us together, and for that, I would be forever grateful.

When my tiny vixen appeared and locked the front door, she turned a bright smile to me, and my heart expanded. I know now that I had felt love toward Parish when in demon form. Because my heart felt the same way now, but even more, greater, brighter, if that was possible. This was love.

Opening my arms, I tucked her close and led us down the street to the hotel where she'd wanted to stay away from the memories of her father. It was close to midnight and streetlights reflected across the white bedsheets. I pressed a kiss behind her ear where she smelled like roses, and whispered, as sweetly as I could manage, "Nothing."

"You think so, demon?" she said, but it was hardly a protest. Nor was her next move, as she pushed up my shirt and tugged it over my head. Her fingers burned into my skin, but it was never as hot as when I'd the power to produce actual fire.

"No longer demon," I muttered as she flicked open the fly of my jeans.

"And not entirely pleased about that." She moved up to bracket my face and I'll be damned if those soft gray eyes weren't the very stars that I sought every night. "We haven't said much about you getting your soul back. But I can sense you'd rather be anything but mortal."

Curling an arm around her back, I pulled her closer. Not about to get into anything hot and heavy until we'd had a conversation. The vixen had a manner of always getting her way, and I was good with that.

"I will die and you will live on. That sounds like the worst possible situation to me. I love you, Parish."

"You do?"

"Yes, and I even know what that means now. I loved you before I got my soul. I know it."

"Oh, Cinder. I love you, too. We were meant for one another."

"In a roundabout way, yes. So I hope you'll understand when I make this next request. I want something from you. Something that will give us forever."

"Anything. I'd give you my heart if I could."

"I already have that, as you have mine." I pressed a palm over her heart and I think our pulses synched. But if she would grant me my request, then I knew they would synch, ever after. "Bite me," I said. "And transform me to vampire."

He was asking for something that I'd initially thought a curse. That was, until I'd been taken in by tribe Lilith and taught to hunt and exist as a vampire. It wasn't a bad gig. And for a man who feared mortality, it could be good.

For the two of us, it could prove even better. I wanted to bond with Cinder as only two vampires could, in blood and soul. So I dipped my head to his neck without a second thought, and punctured his skin with my teeth.

No dark demon blood this time, just plain red mortal blood. But it still possessed the caramel sweetness of the man with whom I was falling in love. So decadently dark, too. If this is what my future held, bonding to Cinder in blood, then I was so glad he caught me outside the warehouse.

His magnificent body arched against mine as I sucked his blood, taking communion from his new soul. It was tinted with shades of the divine and darkness, and all colors in between, and I felt the power of his former being surge through me and brighten my body.

I drank until I could drink no more, and my lover's hand gripped my hips, rocking his groin against mine as the swoon overtook him, and blood orgasm overwhelmed us both. I did not lick the wound to seal it. The only way he could transform would be to now drink mortal blood and the vampiric taint would do the rest.

Together, our souls would bond and he would take a part of mine into his soul, as I would take a part of his into me. We would not become soul mates, but something so much more, fire and blood, forged in love.

* * * * *

RESURRECTION

Lisa Childs

Bestselling, award-winning author **Lisa Childs** writes paranormal and contemporary romance for Mills & Boon. She lives on thirty acres in Michigan with her two daughters, a talkative Siamese and a long-haired Chihuahua who thinks she's a rottweiler. Lisa loves hearing from readers, who can contact her through her website, www.lisachilds. com, or snail-mail address, PO Box 139, Marne, MI 49435, USA.

Chapter 1

Centuries ago...

The rhythmic beat, beat, beat of the drums echoed in Anya's blood as it pumped hot and heavy through her veins. Sand shifted beneath her knees where she knelt beside the trickling stream. She cupped her hands in the water, splashing it onto her face and throat. But the water didn't cool her heated skin. Nor did the wind that rustled the branches of trees in the woods looming all around her, nearly blocking out the glow of the crescent moon.

Beat. Beat. Beat.

Her hands trembled, and she clasped them against her throat where her pulse pounded in tandem with the drum. Although she was far from home and in a foreign land, she still recognized the natives' music for what it was. *A war cry.*

Would they wait until morning to attack the invaders? Or would they, with their intimate knowledge of the terrain, use darkness as a cover to defend their land? She could not find fault with protecting what was theirs. But how did they know that the strangers had come to conquer? Or did they treat every intruder as a threat?

Beat, beat, beat...

She had no answers to her questions. The only thing she knew for certain was that a battle would be waged. Anya closed her eyes, reliving the devastation of previous wars. The scent of blood, sweet and strong, filled her nostrils. Blood, thick and sticky, clung to her skin as she laid hands on the fallen warriors, bringing them back to life.

Resurrecting the dead.

That was *her* special ability. Such a *gift* was bestowed on every other generation of females in her family. Anya's grandmother could predict the future. Nana had already seen Anya's fate: the long arduous voyages across oceans, down straits and over lakes, to a faraway land...a land with powers nearly as unique as every other female generation of Anya's family.

Because it was special, the conquerors had to have this magical land—had to claim it as theirs as they had claimed Anya.

From the shadows in the forest, Gray Wolf studied her. With her hair and skin as pale as the luminescent crescent moon, she appeared more an ethereal woodland creature than a flesh-and-blood woman. She had slipped away from the invaders, past even their watchful guards, as if she were an apparition. Yet the Wise One claimed she was not a spirit.

The shaman had picked the special flowers, and after dividing the poisonous blossom from the stems and leaves, he'd eaten the poison. Not enough to kill him, just enough to invoke the visions that had warned of the invaders...and the woman. She was more powerful than the men with whom she traveled—because she made them invincible.

Yet *she* was not.

She leaned over again and cupped her palms in the trickling water of the stream. As she lifted her hands, water escaped through her fingers, dripping from her delicately featured face onto the bodice of her gown. The wet material appeared nearly as translucent as her skin, molding to every swell and curve of her body.

He held the breath that burned in his lungs, struggling to escape in a groan. But he could not betray his presence. Not yet. The drums pounded, echoing the heavy throb of each beat of his heart.

Gray's fingers slid over the smooth tip of his spear. His mission was to turn her from flesh and blood to spirit. Some other warriors thought him brave for accepting the mission, for sneaking into the enemy camp to kill the woman. Some thought he had chosen the mission out of vengeance for the death of his woman at the hands of previous invaders.

But he had not accepted just the mission; he had accepted his fate. He did not need to eat the poison flower to know that *she* was his fate.

Not a twig snapped nor an animal rustled. So it was the extreme stillness of the night that alerted Anya to *his* presence. Kneeling yet in the sand, she turned away from the stream, and he was there. Even before he touched her, she *felt* him.

Then one of his arms slid around her waist, pulling her to her feet and back against the hard sculpted muscles of his bare chest. Moonlight glistened on his skin, reflected in his deep-set dark eyes and caught in the shock of white hair that fell across his forehead. The rest of his hair, hanging long around his face and impossibly broad shoulders, was as deep a black as the shadows in the woods.

She opened her mouth to scream, but something cold and hard pressed against her cheek. From the corner of her eye she caught the glint of moonlight off metal—the tip of a spear. He slid the spear over the line of her jaw, down the arch of her throat to where her pulse pounded madly. Then the metal tip slid farther down, the sharp point slicing away the damp bodice of her robe. Moonlight bathed her bared breasts and glanced off the spear as it ran down the cleft between them. The tip moved across the swell of her left breast until it pressed against the flesh under which her heart beat hard.

He wielded the weapon with skill, with just enough pressure that she felt the threat but no pain. Not even a scratch from that sharply honed point marred her skin. She arched her neck, so that she could see his face, meet his gaze and try to read his intentions.

Did he only want to scare her? Or did he actually intend to kill her? Or seduce her? No matter his intentions, he exuded danger and was certain to harm her.

His dark gaze held hers, but she could read nothing in the fathomless depths.

She licked her lips, drawing his attention to her mouth. "Wh-what do you want with me?" she asked.

Muscles flexed in his forearm and biceps as his large hand tightened around the handle of the spear. Did he intend to plunge the weapon into her heart?

"No," she murmured, the protest weak when she needed to fight. Yet she dared not move too much or breathe too hard for fear of the spear tip piercing flesh. But she reached out to clasp his forearm with her fingers, her pale skin a stark contrast to his. Muscles hardened beneath her touch.

He released a breath, which stirred her hair. Despite the heat of his body pressed tightly to hers, goose bumps lifted her skin, and she shivered.

"Please don't hurt me," she pleaded, tears stinging her eyes, because she knew her efforts were futile. She doubted he could understand her words. She couldn't reason with him or threaten him as she had the warriors with whom she traveled.

But maybe she could seduce him.

She slid her fingers along his arm, stroking his dark skin. And she moved her other hand from her side to his, smoothing her palm down the hard muscle of his bare thigh. He expelled another breath—this one ragged.

Gray's body grew taut, aching with the desire to take her. But the Wise One's words echoed in his head. "Kill her quickly, lest she trick you. The woman is a sorceress."

She shifted in his grasp, pressing against him. And the lushness of her body roused his to life. He hardened and throbbed—and swallowed a groan.

Her hand clutched his thigh, her nails digging into his skin—marking him as he wanted to mark her—as his.

She turned her head, her soft hair brushing his chest. Then her lips followed, trailing across his skin as she pleaded again. "Don't hurt me..."

He understood her. From the invaders who had come before, he had picked up the language. But that wasn't the only thing he had learned from those earlier visitors. He had learned that the ones with the pale skin were not to be trusted.

Kill her quickly...

The Wise One's voice grew fainter in his head, drowned out by her soft whisper. "Please..." The warmth of her lips brushed his skin again.

Beat, beat, beat... The drums, pounding out the war cry, reminded him of his mission. He stepped back, releasing her so abruptly that she dropped to her knees on the sand again. Then he raised the spear. If his people had any chance of defeating the invaders, this sorceress could *not* live.

She lifted her face toward him. Tears shimmered in her light blue eyes; one broke free and trembled on her thick black lashes. "Don't kill me. I'll do anything...you want me to..."

He had never seen such beauty. Her hair, her face, her body...she seemed too perfect to be of this world. To be real. Unable to help himself, he reached out to touch her hair again. Soft pale gold tendrils tangled around his fingers; he clenched his hand in her hair.

She turned her head, and her lips glided across his forearm. "I'll do anything..."

She reached out, sliding her hands up his thighs to the loincloth under which his erection throbbed. Her fingers closed around him, and he jerked.

"I can be your woman," she offered. "I can pleasure you..." Her golden brows drew together over her light eyes, her unshed tears turning from terror to frustration. "You don't understand me..."

Even if he hadn't been able to comprehend what she was saying, her actions spoke louder than her words. She pushed aside the buckskin and leaned forward, brushing her lips along the length of his shaft.

His fingers, still clutching her soft hair, fisted. A woman had not touched him—in so long. And never like this...

As passion flooded him, his grip on the spear eased, and he buried the tip deep into the sand. As he wanted to bury himself inside her.

She closed her mouth around him, her teeth scraping over his most sensitive skin. Then he felt something else sharp, the point of a weapon at the base of his shaft.

She pulled back her head and lifted her face to his.

"You may not understand me, but you'll understand this," she said, her eyes glittering with determination and desperation as she increased the pressure of the weapon—literally threatening his manhood.

His body tensed even more as anger surged through him, along with the passion. She might not be a sorceress, as the Wise One had warned but the woman was definitely dangerous.

Chapter 2

With the taste of him on her lips, in her mouth, Anya struggled to focus. Her hand trembled, and she nearly dropped the weapon—the one she always hid beneath her gown, bound to her thigh with a leather thong. She kept it just in case she couldn't reason or threaten her way out of harm.

"I will kill you," she promised, tightening her grip on the weapon. "Or I will make you wish you were dead..."

"I have wished myself dead many times," he told her—in a deep voice and in her language.

She jerked with surprise. "You can understand me?"

He stared at her, his gaze dark and penetrating. "Every word."

She lost herself in his eyes. Perhaps he understood *more* than her words. She did not end lives. She resurrected the dead.

"Do it," he advised her. "Kill me."

Her hand shook, and she tightened her fingers around the crudely carved handle of the dagger that Nana had helped her fashion, as if knowing the dangers Anya would one day face. But Anya could not drive the blade into him. She could not stain his beautiful skin with blood. Her voice cracking with fear, she pleaded again, "Let me go…"

"Back to the men who will fight us tomorrow, trying to steal what is ours?" he asked. He shook his head, sending his hair falling around his handsome face. "The only way they can triumph is if *you* are on the battlefield with them."

"H-how do you know?" Did he have the same gift as Nana? Could he see the future? What did he see as her fate—death at *his* hands?

He gestured around at the woods and stream. "Like you, our land is special, has herbs and flowers that can be eaten and then empower the one who eats them. That is why your warriors want our land."

She nodded her admission. "True."

"Yet how will they know," he asked, "which herbs will empower and which will kill them?"

"I—I don't know…"

Distracted by his words, by his ability to speak in *her* language, she didn't notice when he moved. His hands wound around her wrists, yanking her to her feet and knocking the dagger from her grasp. Shackling both her wrists in one big hand, he reached into the sand and extracted her weapon.

"You travel with warriors, yet you know not how to fight," he taunted her as, like with the spear, he ran the tip of her dagger from her cheek, down her throat to where her pulse pounded madly with the rhythm of the war drums.

"I am not a warrior," she admitted, although he could have no doubt that she did not possess the killer instincts of the men with whom she traveled. Or of fearless warriors like him.

"My name is Anya." She had distracted him once with feminine wiles she had not been aware she possessed.

Guided by those same instincts, she ignored the knife at her throat and leaned forward, so that her breasts, bared by her torn gown, pressed against the wall of sinewy muscle that was his chest. "I am a woman."

His voice a guttural groan, he agreed, "You are a woman."

"I can be *your* woman," she said to tempt him. She told herself she only offered her body in order to save her life. But her pulse quickened as excitement coursed through her. His body, all dark skin and hard muscle, fascinated her as no other man's ever had. And she was around men, warriors, all the time now, since she had been taken from her family.

"My woman?" he asked. As if by magic, a flower appeared in his hand, replacing the dagger. The white petals were luminescent against his dark skin. He lifted the flower to her mouth and rubbed the silken petals back and forth across her lips.

Anya's heart slammed against her ribs, then raced. She stared up into his face, fascinated, too, by the strong features. The nose, which was nearly as sharp as the blade of his spear. The deep-set eyes, and cheekbones that looked as though they had been carved from teak. Then his image began to waver in and out of focus, and her head felt light.

He hadn't rubbed the flower across her mouth to seduce her but to kill her.

"No...," she murmured weakly as her legs folded beneath her. But she didn't fall—he caught her up in his arms. Did he want to carry her off somewhere and bury her? Or was it true what some of the men had said, that these natives burned their dead?

Her last lucid thought was of flames, scorching the flesh from her bones.

* * *

Kill her quickly...

His people would want proof of her death. Her body. Or at least her blood on his hands.

He tightened his grip on her, holding her higher against his chest as he moved with swiftness through the woods. Branches rustled and voices rose as her war party finally discovered that she was missing. With knowledge of every trail through the trees, he moved sure-footedly. Not toward his village but away.

And silently. Not one of the invaders canvassing the woods caught a hint of his presence. Not as she had sensed him. He had chosen this mission, and his people had agreed he was best suited to carry it out. Until his tragic loss had turned a lock of his hair gray, he had been known as Silent Wolf.

Her weight was slight and his arms barely strained as he carried her to a place so secret not even the Wise One knew its location—deep in the woods, on the rocky precipice of a steep ravine. He dropped to his knees at the base of a pine tree and pulled her with him beneath the low-hanging boughs. The canopy of branches provided the same amount of shelter as one of the village dwellings. On a previous visit to his private sanctuary, he had brought blankets and other provisions. He fumbled with a torch that bathed the space in faint flickering light.

Then he laid her upon the blankets, her long hair spreading like sunlight across the dark material. With reluctance, he pulled his attention from her and rummaged around the canopy until he found an urn. He removed the stopper, poured some water into his palm and, kneeling beside her, splashed the water onto her face, making sure to wipe the last trace of flower petal from her lips.

Her lashes fluttered, then lifted, her light eyes focusing on his face. "Am I dead?"

"If you are, so am I." But he had been dead—for a long time. Ever since the earlier invaders had killed his woman. Like Anya, she had gone off by herself. To escape him? Theirs had been a union arranged by the elders and the Wise One. Had she regretted their match, their son? He would never know. The other men had found her before he had.

And since losing her, he had been dead—until he touched *this* woman.

"What did you give me?" she asked, her eyes wide with fear. "Poison?"

"Then you would be dead," he stated. "I gave you a flower—an aid for sleep. As well as the plants for special powers, this land yields flowers and herbs for every ailment." Except death. Not even the Wise One knew how to resurrect the dead.

Was that why the shaman wanted *her* dead? Because she had more knowledge—more power—than he possessed? This was not the first time Gray had doubted the Wise One's motives. The man already had the chief's ear, replacing the elders as primary council. Gray suspected the shaman wanted the chief's power, as well.

"This *land* is special," she said as she glanced around the surprisingly spacious area he had found beneath the canopy of pine boughs.

"It is special," he agreed. But he looked only at her. "And it must be defended against *all* enemies—by whatever means necessary."

"I am not your enemy," she claimed as she propped herself on an elbow and leaned close to him. He was kneeling beside her.

"You travel with enemies," he reminded her, "with invaders intent on stealing what is ours."

"But yet you have stolen from them first. You have stolen *me*." Her eyes sparkled in the warm glow of the torch.

"It is my mission," he said, "to take you from their camp."

"I made your mission simpler," she said, "by venturing off alone."

"Why?" He asked aloud the question that had haunted him since he'd found her alone by the stream.

"Sometimes I need to get away," she said, without explaining what he needed most to know.

Was that why *his* woman had gone off by herself? Had she needed to get away from him, from their child?

"Why?" he asked again, more curious about *her* now than about his past.

Tiny lines furrowed her brow as her eyes darkened with painful memories. "You are not the first to take me captive."

"These invaders—they hold you against your will?" he asked, studying her beautiful face intently so that he might discern if she spoke the truth or was attempting to trick him again.

"They took me from my *home*, from my *family*, when they learned my gift."

"I am not like them," he said. "They took you for life. I take you for death." It was his mission. And no matter what he learned about her, honor bound him to carry out the mission he had accepted.

"You are *not* going to kill me," she said, leaning closer, so close that her lips nearly brushed his. "You would have killed me by the stream. You would have run your spear through my heart."

Kill her quickly...

The Wise One had known Gray needed to kill her—before he touched her. Before he connected with her. He cupped her face in his hand, his fingers as dark as a shadow against her pale skin.

Pale skin and hair. He closed his eyes as the memories crashed over him—of the men who had claimed to want friendship, who had offered trades and knowledge. But they had taken more than they'd given; they'd taken lives and destroyed destinies before they had disappeared again.

The Wise One had assured Gray that they would not make it back to the land from which they'd come. With them, they had taken more poison than power.

Yet they still held power over Gray. The power of hatred and vengeance. They had taken his woman. Now he had taken theirs.

"I will kill you," he promised her and himself. He had to carry out his mission. He could not risk the safety of his people again—not even for her.

Her breath caught, and her eyes widened with fear.

"But before I kill you, I will have you..."

Chapter 3

Beat, beat, beat...

The heavy pounding of the war drum echoed the frantic throbbing of Anya's heart as blood rushed through her veins. While she was no warrior, she could not calmly accept the fate he had decided for her. She had to fight him.

Hoping her people might hear her, she opened her mouth to scream, but his mouth covered hers, stealing her breath and her desire...to fight. Despite the hard pressure of his mouth, his lips were soft and full against hers. Then his tongue slipped into her mouth, tasting her while giving her a taste of his passion.

Anya lifted her hands, intending to claw at his shoulders, but instead, she clutched at the broad expanse of his chest. Muscles rippled beneath her touch. And he moved so that instead of lying beside her, he lay over her, his weight levered on his hands, which he braced on either side of her. Then slowly he lowered his body, so that his chest pressed against her breasts, bared by her torn gown.

Her nipples, teased by his sleek skin and sinewy muscles, hardened, and she moaned into his mouth. So he lowered the rest of his body, his erection straining against his loin-cloth and the thin material of her gown. She shifted beneath him, arching her hips as restlessness stirred inside her. And pressure began to build.

And still he only kissed her, his mouth feasting on hers, his tongue stroking in and out of her lips. She lifted her hands from his shoulders to his hair, clutching at the silky black strands to pull back his head.

His dark eyes glittered in the torchlight like sparks dancing on a fire. "Do not fight me, woman," he warned, his voice gruff with passion. "I do not want to hurt you…"

Yet he intended to kill her? Hope flared that she could distract him from his mission. That she could make him fall…for her.

"Anya," she reminded him breathlessly. "And what do I call you?" Besides her fate.

"Gray…"

She touched the lock of white in the hair falling across his brow, and she found the strands even softer than the black. "Because of this?"

"Wolf," he finished. "I am Gray Wolf."

"And are you?" she asked, shifting beneath his hard-muscled body. "A beast?"

He pulled her hands from his hair and lifted them over her head. Then he lowered his head and slid his mouth down her throat, his teeth scraping her skin.

She shivered, tingling everywhere from his touch.

He flicked his tongue over the hollow of her throat where her pulse pounded like the beat of the war drum. He moved lower, over the exposed curve of her breast. Despite the heat of his breath and the warmth of his mouth, she shivered again. His lips closed over the hard peak of her nipple, suckling, then tugging with his teeth.

Anya moaned as the pressure in her body built. She pulled on her wrists, trying to free herself from his grasp. But his hand held tight while his other hand moved over her body, pushing aside the bodice of her gown. While his mouth stayed at one breast, his palm cupped the fullness of the other, his thumb scraping across the nipple.

The intensity of passion crashing through her body made tears sting her eyes. Never before had she experienced such sensations, such torture.

"Please," she begged every bit as desperately as she had for her life. "Gray…"

His name on her lips snapped Gray's fragile grasp on his control. He released her wrists but only to pull the tattered gown over her arms and head, baring her beautiful body to his hungry gaze and mouth. He explored every inch of her pale skin and discovered where she had hidden her dagger, in a leather thong tied around her thigh. Scratches from the blade marred her otherwise flawless skin.

And she marred his skin, her nails scraping and digging as she clawed at his shoulders. But she wasn't fighting him off—she wanted him closer. He wanted them closer, too, as close as a man could get to a woman. Yet he held back, almost reluctant to bury himself inside her, despite the insistent urging of his tortured body, for fear of losing himself in her.

So while he focused on tormenting her, he tormented himself. He tugged at the leather thong with his teeth, pulling it from her thigh. Then he soothed the sensitive skin with his lips and tongue. Her flesh quivered beneath his mouth. And she tried to press her knees closed as she squirmed on the blankets. But he opened her legs, his attention drawn to the pale gold curls at the core of her womanhood.

Like that of the wolf he was named for, a growl, deep and low, emanated from his throat. And he took her with his mouth, kissing and licking and teasing her most sensitive flesh. She clutched his hair, then his shoulders, as she writhed beneath him.

He slid his hands up her body, pressing her back against the blankets. Then he cupped her breasts, stroking his thumbs over the hard pink nipples that begged for his touch.

As she begged, "Please..."

Did she know for what she pleaded? Did she know the pleasure that awaited her? With his tongue he delved into the heat of her body, lapping at the sweetness as she came apart in his arms, crying his name.

He pulled back as she curled onto her side, sobbing into the blankets, her hair tangled across her face. After pulling off his loincloth, he reached for her and brushed that pale curtain from her face so that she could not hide from him what she felt.

Devastated. Had no man ever given her pleasure before?

"What was that?" she asked, her damp eyes wide with fear—as if he was the one with the power now.

And maybe he was.

"There is more," he promised her.

She shivered and her nipples hardened again, her breasts tilting toward him. He lowered his head, first brushing his mouth across hers. Her lips opened for his tongue, and he imitated with her mouth what he'd just done to her body.

She clutched at him, first his hair, then his shoulders, then her nails scraped down his back to clutch his buttocks. "More," she breathed against his lips.

His mouth fused to hers, he parted her legs again and in one swift stroke—so as to not prolong the pain he suspected she might feel—he drove into her. Her body tensed and she cried out again, this time in that pain he suspected. And more tears rolled down her face. He kissed away the salty moisture. "Even your tears are sweet," he murmured, awed at the completeness of her beauty.

Lightning had struck the ground near him before, and the powerful current had shimmered in the air. That was how he felt now, connected to her, as if a powerful current shimmered between them.

Sweat beaded on his lip as he fought to control the pounding of desire in his body, of the urgency to pound into her until he achieved the release he wanted. He needed...as he had never *needed* before.

Anya fought him now, when she should have fought him before. Her body stretched, hurting at the invasion of his thick manhood. She pushed at his shoulders and arched her hips, trying to buck him off. But he sank deeper. And she stretched more, skin burning. "No!"

"Shh," he said, his lips moving over her face, kissing away the rest of her tears. Then he touched her lips with his, reigniting the passion that fear and pain had chased from her body.

His hands moved between them, smoothing over her breasts, tugging at her nipples. Then his fingers shifted lower, over her navel, through her curls. He pressed a fingertip against her most sensitive area, rubbing gently until the pressure built inside her again. Not the pain, but the pleasure.

And he moved, pulling out. But now she wanted him to stay, and she locked her legs around his lean waist and clutched at his back. He drove back inside. In and out. In and out. Her body tensed again as the pressure spiraled out of her control. And she shattered as pleasure poured out of her.

Gray drove in one last time; then he tensed and shuddered as he pumped his hot seed into her. "Anya..." He rolled to his side, with her locked in his arms, their bodies still joined, and he fell asleep with her name on his lips.

In the faint light of the torch, she studied the sharp angles and strong lines of his face. It was a face of more than character, a face of honor. Despite having taken her, he would carry out his mission—because he had no doubt given his word to his people.

When he awoke, he would kill her—unless she killed him first. Despite her body's protests, Anya wriggled free of his arms, of his possession. As they parted, an aftershock of pleasure rippled through her. She bit her lip to hold in the small cry of satisfaction. She had never known such pleasure existed. And she doubted she would ever feel it again.

Having been asleep when he'd brought her to this spot beneath the tree, she had no idea where they were. Or how to find her people. If she ran, he could find her or he would let her die alone, lost in the woods. Through the provisions with which he'd stocked his hideaway, she rummaged, but she found no weapon—until she knocked aside his buckskin. And found her dagger. She picked up the weapon, the crude handle fitting with comfortable familiarity against her palm.

When she and Nana had created the weapon, she had known that she might need to use it someday. But she had never dreamed that the first man she had to kill was the only one she would ever love...

Realizing the depth of her feelings, she studied his face again—the beauty of his dark skin and strong features. And she accepted that she could plunge the dagger into her own heart more easily than she could his. Hiding the dagger in the sand beneath the blanket, she curled against his side, her head on his chest. Beneath her ear, his heart beat in tandem with the never-ending war drum.

Sunlight glimmered through the pine boughs, bathing her skin golden. He stroked his knuckle along the delicate curve of her jaw. Then he ran his thumb over her chin to brush across her full bottom lip. Even in sleep her mouth pursed in a kiss that was both soft and sexy. His skin tingled at the brief contact.

Every time desire had awakened him and he had reached for her in the night, she had met his passion with her own— and with a generosity he had never known. He had never had a woman with such spirit or such beauty.

With her pale hair and skin and delicate features, she was so beautiful and so fragile. All he had to do to fulfill his mission was press his hand over her mouth and nose and deprive her of breath. He slid his fingers across her cheek, and her thick lashes fluttered. Her eyes opened and her gaze met his.

And his breath fled his lungs as his heart raced. He had to do it. He had to protect his people, his land. He had failed them—and *her,* the mother of his son—before. He could not fail them again.

His hand shaking, he clasped it tighter over Anya's mouth and nose. Panic filled her pale eyes as she realized his intention…to kill her.

Chapter 4

Her lashes fluttered again as her eyes rolled back. And as the life began to leave her body, it left his, too. His strength ebbed away, and he pulled his palm from her mouth. She lay limply in his arms. So he lowered his lips to her cool ones. Her breasts arched, brushing against his chest as he breathed life back into her. Then she kissed him back, lifting her hands to tangle her fingers in his hair. And his heart knocked against his ribs.

He pulled back, wrenching himself from her arms. "You won't seduce me away from my mission, woman." He tied on his loincloth and tossed her ragged gown at her. "Cover yourself."

She dragged the gown over her head. As she hid all that silky pale skin from his hungry gaze, he stifled a groan of regret. But that was not his only regret...

"I *have* to kill you," he said.

"If you kill me, you are killing yourself," she said, then nodded as if she knew something he did not. Just how powerful was this woman? "But that is what you want."

He wanted *her*. Even though they had made love through-out the night, he wanted her again. Still. Always.

"Death," she said. "You told me so last night, before we... before you brought me here. Why do you want to die?"

"I have barely been living," he admitted. "Ever since men with pale skin and hair like yours killed my woman, the mother of my son."

She released a ragged breath. "I'm sorry..."

"And because I did not protect her, I should be dead, too." As a warrior, he was honor bound to protect his people and especially what was his.

"But you have a son..."

"By not protecting his mother, I failed him." His heart clutched with regret for all that he had lost. "Her people are raising him now."

"He needs his father," she insisted with a longing that reminded him she had been taken from her home, from her family, in order to serve the warriors with whom she traveled. Alone with those men, how had she remained un-touched—until him?

"Your son needs you," she urged him.

He shook his head, unwilling to let go of the guilt he had carried for so long. "My people need me to carry out this mission."

"To kill me." She opened her hand, and the dagger lay across her palm.

"You found it." He had hidden the weapon in his loincloth. "Why didn't you kill me?" When he had slept—finally—after so many sleepless nights, she had had opportunity to leave. But she had stayed, at his side, in his arms. She had not left him as his woman had—even though Anya had had more reason. Could she care about him…as he feared he cared about her?

"I thought about it," she admitted. "Last night when you were sleeping…"

"What about when I had my hand across your mouth?" he asked, his stomach knotting with regret that he had hurt her.

"You will not hurt me," she said as if she had read his mind.

Was bringing back the dead her only gift, or like the shaman, did she have other powers?

*Kill her quickly…*The Wise One's command rang in his ears. He had already failed part of his mission. He could not fail his people entirely. "I have to…"

She shook her head. "You will not hurt me because I love you. I want to be with you. Forever."

He dropped onto his knees beside her on the blankets. "Anya…"

"And you love me."

His chest ached; he felt as if his heart was being ripped apart—torn between his loyalty to his people and his growing feelings for her. He reached for her, closing his hands around her throat.

Anya held her breath, waiting for the pain of his fingers crushing her windpipe. But instead, he stroked her skin and tipped up her chin with his thumb. Then his mouth covered hers, and he kissed her with all the passion he had shared with her the night before. But his lips gentled, and he shared the love she had only hoped he felt for her.

The love that matched the power and intensity of her feelings for him. Her lips clinging to his, she ran her hands over the rippling muscles beneath tawny skin. Smoothing her fingers over the hard slope of his chest, she discovered nipples, smaller and darker than hers, but no less sensitive, apparently, as he sucked in a breath when she flicked a fingernail across one. Then she pulled her mouth from his, slid her lips down the straining cords of his neck, then over the sleek skin of his chest. She flicked her tongue over his nipple.

And his fingers tangled in her hair, pulling hard enough to make her scalp tingle but not hard enough to hurt. Her teeth scraped his nipple, threatening. And a chuckle rumbled in his chest.

Then she moved her hands lower, tugging off his loincloth. And when she wrapped her fingers around his straining erection, his laughter died.

"Let me do to you...what you did to me," she said, easing back so that she could sprawl across his hard thighs. As her lips closed around him, his hands clutched her hair. She slid her mouth up and down his shaft, taking his length as deep in her throat as she was able, and she ran her tongue around his smooth skin.

"Anya," he growled, his breath harsh. He pulled her up and dragged her gown over her head, nearly tearing the fragile fabric again in his haste to bare her skin. Despite the warm air and heat of the passion they shared, Anya shivered.

His hands smoothed over her, as she had done to him. He cupped her breasts in his palms and lifted them to his mouth. Then he suckled and tugged at her nipples.

Pleasure streaking through her, Anya arched her back and moaned. His hands slid down her body, over her hips, down her thighs...then he eased her legs apart and stroked through her damp curls.

"You are so hot," he groaned, easing one finger, then another inside her.

Anya's muscles went taut at the invasion, and she came, her head lolling back as she keened. He kissed her, then licked the slickness of her passion from his fingers.

"You are so sweet…"

"Let me taste you. Spill your passion into my mouth," she offered.

He pushed his thumb against her full lower lip, as if considering her offer. But he shook his head and lifted her so that she straddled his lap. Then, his hands shaking as he gripped her hips, he lifted her higher and impaled her on his throbbing erection.

Anya bit her lip at the force of his invasion, stretching to accept all of him. She had thought he'd buried himself deep inside her last night. But she hadn't realized how big he was, how deep he could reach into her. She wrapped her legs around his waist and her arms around his shoulders, and she rode him, sliding up and down his slick hot shaft.

He gripped her hips again, helping her rise, then pushing her back down. Up and down, she slid, their bodies rubbing together. Her nipples scraped his chest while the hair around his erection teased that most sensitive part of her.

Her body tensed as the pressure built, winding tighter and tighter inside her. "Gray…" she begged, wanting that pleasure only he had given her. Greedy for more…

He tilted her chin so her gaze met the hot intensity of his. He watched her as finally the pressure eased, her body shuddering with sweet release. But he did not stop moving, driving up the pressure again, building it higher and tighter than before. And as it began to break, she opened her mouth to scream, but he covered it with his, driving his tongue between her lips as he drove himself deeper and deeper into her body.

She shattered, breaking into a million scattered pieces of pleasure, and he grasped her tighter, pounding into her with quick thrusts until his erection pulsed, filling her with his hot release.

Finally, both of them gasping for air, their lips parted. But not their bodies. He leaned his forehead against hers. "This is impossible...our *love*..."

She blinked back tears. "You love me?"

"Like I have loved no other," he declared. "You have seduced my soul. It belongs to you now."

"And I belong to you," she vowed. "Heart and soul."

He kissed her again, just a soft brush of lips against lips. "You will forever be a part of me, but we cannot be together in this life."

She shook her head. "We can," she insisted, unwilling to give up what they shared. "The warriors—the invaders—without me to resurrect them will fear a fight. They will leave..."

But still the war drums pounded out a beat that seemed to have grown louder and closer.

"It's not your people who will make it impossible for us to be together," he murmured, and he tilted his head, as if listening. Then he pressed a finger to her lips.

Yet it was too late for silence. They had been found. He put her gown back on her, knotting the bodice to cover her breasts. Then he dressed quickly. And before they could be dragged from the canopy, he helped her out with him. She blinked against the brightness of the sun, but he gave her no time to get her bearings before he pulled her along behind him.

Twigs snapping in the woods betrayed the arrival of the warriors—not hers, but his. Despite knowing the trails so

well, he could not bring her into the forest with him. They
would be discovered. Behind them boulders lined the mouth
of the steep ravine. Too steep for retreat? He had nowhere
else to go, nowhere else to hide the woman who meant more
to him than his own life. But it was too late for him to risk
the ravine—too late for retreat.

His people stepped from the woods, the shaman leading the warriors. Blood smeared the man's face and chest.
If the blood was human, Gray doubted the Wise One had
killed any of the invaders himself. He was more apt to use
herbs or roots than his spear. Instead, he manipulated others to do his killing for him.

Just as he had manipulated Gray to kill Anya.

"You had to know that I would find you," the Wise One
said, pointing his spear toward Gray. "And that I would
know you had not killed the woman. There is *nothing* I do
not know."

"There is no reason to kill her," Gray said, but he spoke
to the warriors, not the shaman. Trusting that Anya knew
her people the way he knew his, he said, "The invaders have
left. There is no threat."

"*She* is a threat!" the shaman insisted, shaking with fury.
And with fear?

"Only to you," Gray accused him as he stepped in front of
Anya. He reached for her hand, so that she would not tumble
from the rocks into the steep ravine. But something sharp
jabbed into his palm. The blade of her dagger. He wrapped
his fingers around the vicious little weapon.

"She was not traveling with the invaders by choice. They
had taken her against her will. She has chosen to be with
me," he said, still awed by the depth of her love. "She has
chosen to *stay* with me."

"No!" the shaman yelled, his voice vibrating with rage, cords standing out in his neck.

"She is no threat to *us,*" Gray promised his people. "Only to *him*. The Wise One wants all the power—to control us."

"Do not listen to him!" the shaman screamed. "She has bewitched him. She is the danger! We must kill her. *Now!*"

Gray stared out at the warriors at whose sides he had fought off invaders and vicious animals. Bound by honor and loyalty, he would have given his life for any one of them. Now he would *take* the life of any who threatened the woman he loved. He lifted his chin and declared, "You will have to kill *me* first."

"What…what are you all saying?" Anya asked, her voice quaking with fear. Although she did not know his language, she had to have recognized the threat.

"She will not harm us," Gray insisted as the gazes of his fellow warriors slid from his to the shaman, "but *he* will. If we keep following him, if we keep *blindly* doing what he says, eating what he wants us to eat, smoking what he wants us to smoke, he will kill us. And if she's gone, no one can bring us back to this life. She can bring us back—"

"No!" the shaman shouted, rage and madness setting his eyes ablaze as he focused on Gray and hurled the spear.

Pain pierced Gray's heart as the blade penetrated skin and flesh. But he could not die yet. He could not die and leave Anya at the mercy of a madman. Empowered by his love for her, Gray raised his arm and sent the dagger flying through the air.

He did not see if the weapon connected with his target. He saw nothing but the trees overhead as he staggered back. Soft hands gripped his arm, nails biting into his skin. But she wasn't strong enough to hold him up. And he could not take her with him.

Summoning the last of his strength, he pushed her back. Jagged edges of rock sliced through the soles of his feet as he slipped, then fell. Catapulting through the air to the depths of the ravine, the last thing he heard was Anya's scream.

Chapter 5

Throat burning from the force of her cry, Anya stared into the ravine, trying to catch a glimpse of the man she loved as he disappeared into the abyss.

"Gr-Gray!" Her voice cracked on his name. And her heart cracked, breaking apart, as she realized she could not reach him…to resurrect him.

She turned to his people. But the warriors shrank back, afraid of her, despite their weapons. "Help me!" she pleaded. But she did not know if they could understand her any more than she had understood them.

She'd had no idea what Gray or the other man had been saying. But she had known the leader of the warriors had meant her harm. By taking away Gray, he had hurt her more than if he'd taken her life. He'd taken her love.

But Gray had taken the leader's life. The warriors lifted his bleeding body. His eyes open in death, he stared, in shock and accusation, at her as they carried him away through the woods.

"Help me!" she screamed after them. "Help me get Gray. I can save him." But only if she could find him.

She scrambled over the rocks at the lip of the ravine, desperate to reach him. But her feet slipped on the steep slope, knocking pebbles and dirt loose. She fell onto her stomach and slid, branches and weeds catching her gown and clawing at her skin. Tears of pain, both emotional and physical, dripped from her eyes.

"Help me! Help me!" she pleaded weakly. If she died trying to reach him, she would not be able to help him. So she fought her way back up the bank. But the warriors were gone, leaving her alone with her despair. She had no idea which direction they had gone, so she had no way, no hope, of finding their village. But could she convince them to help her even if she could find them?

"Gray!" she screamed his name again. But nothing stirred in the dark depths of the ravine. The war drum silenced, the woods were oddly still but for her sobs.

Frustration and panic gripped her, leaving her only enough strength to climb onto the largest boulder. Then, clinging weakly, she wept, her tears running from the rock to drip into the ravine.

Hours or days later, small dark hands tugged at the skirt of her gown. Too weak to lift her head, she could only turn her cheek against the rock. Two boys stood at the base of the boulder. The younger of the two stared up at her with eyes swollen from the tears rolling down his face.

Hers had dried some time ago, although sobs still convulsed her body—she had no moisture left to shed tears. The older of the two boys lifted a bowl toward her. Her hands trembling and stained with blood, Gray's and hers, she reached out and took his offering.

"Drink it," the smaller boy told her—in her language.

This boy was Gray's son; she saw the father in the son's eyes and in his indomitable spirit. And she glimpsed the gentle nature of the woman Gray had mourned.

"Thank you," she murmured as she lifted the bowl to her lips. The drink, thick with crushed herbs and roots, tasted bitter against her lips and tongue. If it was poison, she did not care. If she had the strength, she would hurl her body into the ravine with Gray.

Without him, with her people gone, she had no reason to live.

"Drink," the boy said again.

"You can understand me?" she asked.

His dark eyes serious, he nodded. "My father, he taught me—to protect me…"

From people like her? The ones with pale hair and skin? Yet she detected no trace of fear in the boy's eyes, only sadness.

"Tell the warriors to come back, to find your father," she urged him. "I can help him…" But how much longer? How long could he be dead before her ability to bring him back to life was lost?

"They sent me to you," the boy explained.

"To kill me?" Had the son inherited his father's mission?

He shook his head. "To bring you back to our village."

She turned away, staring into the depths of the ravine. "I cannot leave him."

The boy followed her gaze and shuddered. "No one has ever come back from there. The elders believe it is the other world…"

"Why do they want me…at the village?" she asked. "I thought…I thought they wanted me dead."

"The Wise One wanted you dead. They know that, now

that he is dead and cannot fool them. They believe my father's words—that you are no threat to us."

His last words. That was what he had said. With his last breath, he had defended her. Loving him more, she felt her heart contract.

More tears streaked down the boy's face. "And they believe *me*."

"But you do not know me."

"I know the Wise One, the shaman. I know that he was the one who killed my mother—not your people."

Anya's breath caught at the sorrow and guilt on the boy's small face. He was so much his father's son. "How...?"

"I saw him." The boy shuddered again. "And I did not protect her."

"But you are just a child."

"But I did not tell...what I knew."

His word against the shaman's? "You would not have been believed. You were right to say nothing." But she feared he would struggle for a long time to accept that his silence was not cowardice.

"I was afraid," the boy confessed, his voice soft with shame.

She shook her head. "You are a brave warrior," she assured him. He did not fear her as his people had.

But the boy did not need her, either. He had his mother's people. He needed his father, though. And so did she.

Her tears fell again, replenished by the potion the boys had given her. She wept and wept, her tears dripping from the boulder into the ravine.

And rain began to fall, joining her tears. Cracks of lightning and booms of thunder chased away the boys. But she did not move from her boulder, the water soaking her hair and gown.

When the storm moved off, she fell into a fitful sleep, tears still streaming down her face. A while later she awoke to the gentle lap of water against the rocks. She lifted her head and stared with disbelief at the lake that now filled the deep ravine.

Had her tears or the rain filled the abyss? She did not know. Wondering if she dreamed still, she leaned off the boulder and dipped her fingers into the water. Her skin tingled and warmed. The lake was more than real; it was *magic*.

And it brought him back to her. His body bobbed to the surface, his dark skin pale with death and stained with his blood. She stretched out her arms until she caught his shoulder and dragged him onto the boulder with her. The spear still impaled him. She fisted her hands around the wooden handle and pulled the spear free of his chest, of his heart.

How had he had enough life left to hurl the dagger and save her?

"And you thought I was the one with the power," she murmured as she pressed a kiss to his cold lips. "*You* have all the power," she insisted. "And all my love. Come back to me."

She laid her hands on his chest. Through her palms, heat radiated from her to him, warming his cold skin. The flesh sealed over his wound, leaving his skin sleek again over hard muscle.

And his heart beat once. Then twice.

"Gray!"

His lids lifted, and he stared up into her face, his eyes dark with confusion, which turned to desire. "Woman…?"

"Your woman."

"My *magic* woman." He shifted against the rock, sitting up. Then he pulled her close. "You brought me back to life."

She shuddered. "I thought you were lost to me forever. You were dead for days."

"I was dead for *years*," he corrected her. "And the first time I touched you, you brought me back to life." He lowered his head and covered her mouth with his, kissing her with all his passion, all his love.

The last time, he had given his heart out of obligation and honor. Now he gave it only out of love, love more powerful than any herb or root grown on the land of his people.

"We will be together," he promised her, knowing now that nothing was impossible—with this woman. "Even if we have to leave this land, we will be together."

"Yes," she agreed with a soft sigh of contentment. "But we are not leaving this land. Your people have accepted me."

He gazed around the woods, but they were alone. "They have?"

"They sent your son. He told me they believed your words…about the Wise One." Her throat moved as she swallowed hard. "And they believed the boy, too."

Gray furrowed his brow, confused. Had death slowed his thought processes? He could not understand what she meant. "About what do they believe him?"

She drew in a quick breath, her eyes dampening with sympathy and concern for the boy. "He saw his mother's death…at the hands of the shaman."

Gray nodded as his world righted itself. His son had not withdrawn from him out of anger that his father had not protected his mother. Like Gray, he had withdrawn out of guilt, over being unable to save her. A ragged breath slipped through his lips. "That poor little boy…"

"He's a strong boy. A smart boy," Anya assured him as if she already felt for his son what she felt for him.

"Can you...do you..."

"Love him?" she asked, and nodded in response. "Yes. And I think he belongs with *you*. With *us*."

His heart, healed by her touch, swelled with love for this woman with her generous spirit. "Yes, with us."

"Here," she said, gesturing at the lake filling the ravine. "On the shore of this lake."

"Lake?" Awed, he glanced down at the water, shimmering with the reflection of the sun, that had filled the expansive width and the depth of the ravine. Most his people had believed it a bottomless abyss. "How..."

"Maybe the rain," she said, her pale skin flushing with color. "Or my tears."

"Your tears?" Regret for causing her pain made his heart clutch. He brushed his fingertips across the silky skin of her beautiful face.

She nodded. "I wept my eyes dry. Then your son and another bigger boy brought me a drink." A slight grimace distorted her delicate features, and she shuddered as if reliving the flavor.

"The bigger boy—he is the shaman's son."

"I am lucky it was not poison," she murmured, then lifted her gaze to Gray's. Her pale eyes were lit up—much like the surface of the lake, but with love and gratitude rather than sunlight. "The shaman—he's dead. With the spear already through your heart, you killed him. Already dead, and yet you saved my life."

Gray nodded, satisfaction filling him that his spear had not missed its target. "Not even death can stop me from protecting or from loving you," he promised his woman.

She lifted a trembling hand to her lips. "Not even death," she murmured, then asked with fear, "What if the boy did give me poison—to avenge his father's death? To be so happy only to have it snatched away again..."

Gray shook his head, his body tensing as he remembered the man's cruelty toward his own son. "No. He feared his father most. He gave you a special drink—"

"That made my weeping never end," she said.

"Until you filled the ravine," he mused, awed again at the depth of her love for him, "with your tears...and brought me back to you."

"Forever," she said, wrapping her arms tight around his shoulders. "Never leave me again."

"Never," he promised. "We will build our life here by the Lake of Tears—with my son."

"With *our* son," she corrected him, already claiming his motherless boy as hers, too. Then she pressed a palm against her stomach. "And with our children to come."

"Will they have your powers?" he asked, thinking of how the shaman's son had instinctively inherited his father's knowledge of the land.

She shook her head. "Not our children. But of our children's children, a daughter will be born with a special ability. But I know not what."

"And if we have only sons?" he asked, smiling at the image she had painted in his mind of their family, of generations of descendents to carry on their legacy of love.

"All our children will have power," she assured him, "the power of their warrior father. They will be strong and brave and honorable—"

"And happy."

"And happy," she agreed, lifting her mouth for his kiss.

As he pressed his mouth to hers, Gray felt the power of the woman in his arms—*his* woman. But her power wasn't her ability to bring the dead back to life. Her true power was love.

* * * * *

NOCTURNAL WHISPERS

CARIDAD PIÑEIRO

Caridad Piñeiro is a multi-published and award-winning author whose love of the written word developed when her fifth-grade teacher assigned a project—to write a book that would be placed in a class lending library. She has been hooked on writing ever since.

When not writing, Caridad teaches workshops on various topics related to writing and heads a writing group. Caridad is also an attorney, wife and mother. For more information, please visit www.caridad.com.

Chapter 1

She came to him as she always did, her exotic kohl-lined eyes dark as midnight, her full lips stained blood red as she taunted him. "You know what I want."

Lord Alec Wright trembled with both fear and pleasure, well aware of his visitor's desire. He tried to speak, but she covered his mouth with her cool, smooth hand, silencing him. The sweet, spicy perfume of myrrh, which had been rubbed into her skin when she'd been entombed centuries earlier, nearly overwhelmed him.

"No more empty promises," she said, a sad smile slipping onto her lips, her eyes fathomless. She ran her free hand across the smooth lines of Alec's chest, rousing the desire she used as punishment for his crimes.

Alec steeled himself against her touch, fighting the arousal she stirred so easily with her luscious beauty. Death had forever sealed her exquisiteness, and, with his selfishness, he had condemned them to be bound together until he fulfilled her one and only wish.

She snaked her hand downward until she reached the

head of his erection. Encircling his engorged length with her palm, she stroked up and down, dragging a moan from him.

"Such strength." She bent her head to kiss the side of his face, still covering his mouth with one hand while tempting him with the other. Her power kept him pinned to the mattress as she wrought her torture.

Alec murmured a protest and fought against the desire threatening to consume him, but she only laughed and tenderly bit the side of his neck before working her way down his body. Soon her lips were poised just above the head of his cock. The bittersweet smile turned wicked as she licked the tip of his foreskin and dragged a moan of pleasure from him. "You cannot resist, even though you know what will follow."

No, he couldn't resist her. He had never been able to resist the allure of his darkest needs. As the "spare heir," he'd found his parents had cared little for what he did. No matter what, their attention had always been on his older brother. Alec's failure to earn their approval had led him to try ever more outrageous activities to snare their notice, even if his behavior resulted in disapproval. That self-destructive bent was what had brought him to this: a life of pleasure-pain spent searching for a way to satisfy a mummy's desire.

She took him into her mouth then and moved on him, working him with her tongue and lips. Her full, generous breasts rubbed along his thighs, creating even greater need.

He wanted to touch and taste, to feel their lushness in his mouth, but he was caught in the web of her power and could not move, could not truly enjoy her. Because the passion with which she dominated him was her punishment for his misdeeds.

She aroused him even more, drawing out his need until he was shaking beneath her.

With a satisfied laugh, she left him poised on the edge and faced him, determination in eyes black as midnight.

"You know what I want."

She finally released him from her dominion so that he could whisper a sibilant, "Yes."

Before his eyes, her skin lost its creamy olive hue and became pale as alabaster. A heartbeat later her striking features eroded as her skin became dust as dry as the Sahara. An unseen wind rose up, blowing away her features until she was a faceless entity above him.

She opened what was left of her mouth and keened with centuries-old pain. The sound ricocheted inside his skull, bringing distress so powerful that it pulled him from the nightmare.

Alec bolted up in bed, breathing heavily. His body was hard and aching from the desire she had awakened—a brutal desire he was cursed to endure, alone, until he fulfilled her one and only yearning: to reunite with her child.

In his head came her keening cry once more, reminding him of the loss she had suffered not once, but twice. First when her toddler had died of a fever, and then again when Alec had taken the child's preserved body from beside the woman's mummified remains.

Gritting his teeth against the agony of her wail, Alec rose from the bed and shuffled over to a table, his erection almost painful. He drew in a shaky breath, willing his desire to subside as her presence faded, leaving him with some semblance of peace.

Only when he found her child, the mummy he had traded for money to pay off some gambling debts, would he finally have true tranquility and an end to his lonely existence.

At the Formica-and-metal kitchen table that was nearly

an antiquity itself, he shuffled various papers and notes. He preferred staying in older, out-of-the-way locations to avoid the paparazzi who were forever trying to hunt him down. This little walk-up had been the perfect place to conduct his investigations, he thought, reviewing his papers yet again and arriving at the same conclusion that he had weeks earlier, when he had begun his trek to New York City.

Her child was here, likely stored away in the New York Center for Antiquities' basement like many other dusty pieces of history. Much like the mummy's remains were now in a British museum, visible to one and all who wished to view the collection of ancient treasures spirited away from Egypt's sands.

So close, he thought, planning how he would get his hands on the tiny bundled child so he could return it to its mother.

Leaning a hand on the tabletop, Alec shifted more papers and unearthed the recent article he had printed from the internet. He stared at the picture of the lovely, dark-haired curator who had just come on board at the museum.

Dr. Kate Morton. Fresh-faced and full of a zeal that radiated even in the posed photograph.

No doubt one of her tasks as a new hire would be to familiarize herself with the museum's collections and review the inventory in storage.

A perfect opportunity for him to use his skills to seduce the young curator and convince her to give him what the mummy desired.

Maybe then Alec would finally be free of the mummy's curse. Maybe then he'd secure an end to a solitary life that had grown too tiresome to endure.

Chapter 2

Dr. Kate Morton eased on a lightweight lab jacket to protect her from the chill down in the museum's storage area, and picked up the clipboard from her desk. Glancing at her list, she gave a satisfied smile at the progress she had made. She already had a number of artifacts she might drag out of the bins and shelving to freshen up a few exhibits, including the Egyptian area.

Key card securely fastened at her waist, she headed out of her cubicle-size office and down to the lower levels. With a grin at the security guard manning the entry, she swiped her card and the security system disengaged the lock on the door. Besides the rare artifacts, quite a number of priceless paintings, sculptures and works of art were safeguarded in another section of this area, necessitating the tight security.

Kate returned to where she had left off the night before, picking through the shelves and bins to check the items against the inventory list the head curator had provided. The records indicated the last time each item had been on public display, and quite a number of relics had been stored away for quite a while. As Kate reconciled the items with the inventory, she also used her cell phone to snap photos of those she wished to use to assemble a few new displays.

Hours passed as she worked in the row filled with a plethora of Egyptian pieces. Although her stomach grumbled as lunch hour came and went, Kate was determined to reach the end of the row before returning to her desk, where she'd commence work on a fresh exhibit. Her mind was already whirling with ideas, and she was eager to show her new bosses that they had made the right choice in hiring her.

With a final check of the last item on the list for that area, she was about to return to her office when she noticed yet another box. It was tucked behind a large crate containing a chunk of an obelisk rescued from the area flooded by the Aswan Dam project. The weight of the stone inside made the crate impossible for one person to move, which was likely why someone had not bothered to reach the other box. But Kate refused to be as lazy.

Dragging out the items next to the obelisk, she half climbed onto the lower shelf and grabbed the cardboard box. Shimmying it from behind the heavier crate, she crawled out into the aisle and pulled the box into the light.

A fine layer of dust covered it, a testament to how long it had been since anyone had touched the carton. The yellowed cardboard was another sign of age for the roughly two-and-a-half-foot-long package. Kneeling before it, Kate peered at the handwritten note on top.

"Do not open."

There was no signature or date on the warning, and the writing was rather erratic, as if the words had been scratched in haste, or by someone not in full possession of his faculties.

Kate didn't need a knife to cut the tape sealing the top; it was so old it had long ago lost its ability to stick.

She hesitated as she grabbed hold of the box flaps, a combination of nervous excitement and trepidation gripping her. A chill erupted at her core from that mix of emotions, but she pushed aside her fear and opened the box.

Inside was a small but carefully preserved sarcophagus. The human features painted on it were not quite realistic, as if the artist had been struggling to capture the youth of whoever lay within. Judging from the size, it had to be a rather young child, possibly even a toddler. Despite the age of the inhabitant, green eye makeup enhanced the face depicted on the coffin. Kate recalled that several historical texts and hieroglyphics showed Egyptian children wearing such makeup. It hinted at the fact that ancient Egyptians had thought certain colors possessed sacred energy.

Kate sat back on her haunches, examining other details on the sarcophagus. Gilding covered a good portion of the burial piece, and at its center, a series of small green amulet stones had been set into the surface.

It was in such pristine shape and so unusual due to its size that for a moment Kate wondered if this wasn't some miniature replica created for display purposes.

Reaching out, she laid her hand on the sarcophagus in the hopes of determining if it was of modern origin. But as she did so a shock snaked up her arm and traveled to her center.

Longing arose, so sharp and powerful that Kate cried out and fell back, breathing heavily. Physical need had her wet and aching, but that response was twisted together with a yearning so deep it made her want to weep.

This is no replica, she thought, sucking in deep, measured breaths to control the emotions that had seized control of her at the first touch.

Because it was an antiquity, she knew she couldn't open the sarcophagus and attempt to either x-ray or scan whatever was inside without being in one of the museum's clean rooms, to safeguard the relic.

How about protecting yourself? a little voice in her head warned, and Kate couldn't deny that a major dose of fear lurked within her.

If just a touch could create such sensations, what would happen if she opened the container? Would she be like Pandora, opening the proverbial box and unleashing untold horrors?

Totally illogical, she scolded herself. The relic was just another piece of the past. But even as she said that, she couldn't deny that she had experienced some kind of power when she'd touched the sarcophagus.

She rose shakily to her feet and snapped a few photos of the antiquity. Then, careful not to make contact with the item, she slipped the box back into its hiding space on the shelf and replaced the other items around it.

Kate didn't want any of her colleagues at risk handling the relic until she'd had a chance to explore its provenance and better understand the power she had sensed hidden within it.

But even as she walked away, the emotions that single touch had unleashed remained within her, threatening to swamp her with their physical demands.

Clenching her teeth against the need that had her insides quivering and wanting release, she rushed away, determined to satisfy both her curiosity and her desire.

Chapter 3

Alec waited in a chair before the museum director's desk, confident that his plan was perfectly designed.

It had taken him days to reach out to various sources who owed him an assortment of favors. After all, the curse had made him virtually immortal, and in the nearly two hundred years since he had discovered the mummies, he had amassed quite a lot of information on some very influential people and their families.

Thanks to that, he had a letter of introduction from someone on the board of a top British museum whose grandfather had engaged in more than one indiscretion the family wanted to keep secret. Alec was a major benefactor of that particular museum, which happened to hold the remains of his tormentor. He hoped his influence there might make the return of her child easier. He had no doubt the board member he had come to see could assist in a number of ways.

If Alex was forced to steal back the child, the board member would assist in covering up the sudden appearance of a mummified baby within the museum's inventory. But Alec was hoping to find some other way to secure the child's remains. Preferably a more legal way, since he now had means that he had not had a century and a half earlier.

Ironically, his brother had died just a few scant months after Alec had sold the mummy's child. His brother's death had made Alec the sole heir to their family fortune. Alec had built up those assets over the course of his long existence, but had also spent considerable sums searching for the mummy's baby. Often, he had come close to finding it, though it had slipped from his grasp time and time again.

But not this time, Alec thought, certain that he would soon have the mummy child in his possession. He had enough funds to purchase an item from the New York museum's vast collection, but likely not enough for something as rare as what he sought. Such an item was so unusual as to be virtually priceless, and it was unlikely that any museum would willingly part with such a treasure.

Not that that would deter him, Alec thought, as the director laid down the letter and narrowed his eyes as he considered Alec. When the man spoke, a slight chill laced his voice.

"I'm not sure what our institute has to offer, Lord Wright."

Alec smiled slyly. "A museum as magnificent as this must have some small item stored away with which it might part. Or possibly you would consider a loan of some pieces for an exhibit, if the price was right."

At the mention of money, the administrator's eyes glittered with interest. Tight budgets were regularly an issue at many institutions.

"What kind of price are you envisioning?" the director asked, in a friendlier voice.

"That depends. Possibly a cut of the ticket sales, if we're talking about a loan for an exhibit."

All earlier frostiness melted away, and the director rose and held out his hand.

As Alec stood and shook it firmly, the man said, "I think that's a definite maybe. In the meantime, I'll take you to meet Dr. Morton."

Alec smiled at the mention of the pretty curator. "Kate Morton? She did a stint at the British Museum, didn't she?"

"You've heard of her?" the director asked as he stepped around his desk and motioned toward his office door.

Alec ambled beside him to the entrance. "I've read some of her publications and seen her work on various exhibits. We considered trying to woo her, but when we heard your museum was offering, we knew we couldn't compete with such a prestigious organization."

The director nearly preened as he took the lead. Vanity always responded well to praise, a lesson Alec had learned painfully over the decades. In his brash youth, he had misunderstood such insincerity, considering it to be true respect. Now he knew better, but he wasn't averse to using it for his own gains, or in this case, to right the wrong he had done.

They reached Dr. Morton's office in just a few minutes. When she came to the door, a flush on her cheeks and looking rather flustered, he felt gobsmacked.

Kate Morton wasn't just pretty. She was gorgeous.

The various photos he had seen of her on the museum's website and in an assortment of scholarly journals had seriously not done her justice.

She was tall for a woman, but with the kind of full figure that was sadly no longer in style. Women were meant to have curves, and Kate had them in dangerous abundance. He fisted his hands to keep from reaching for them and exploring their generous contours.

As she turned her dark cocoa gaze on him, intelligence radiated in the depths of her eyes, but it was also impossible to miss the look of instant distrust. He wondered what man had instilled it within her.

"Lord Wright," she said, as she held out her hand after shooting a nervous glance at the director.

Alec stumbled, realizing that he had clearly missed the introduction because of his perusal of the sexy curator. He took her hand in both of his, and a blast of desire slammed through him. Apparently, given the trembling of her fingers and the gasp she barely contained, she felt it, too.

The mummy's desire or something else? he wondered, but drove that thought immediately away. He had stopped believing in the possibility of anything real for himself. Kate Morton's reaction, the smidgen of want she had revealed at his touch, had to mean that she had been in recent contact with what the mummy wanted.

After sucking in a deep breath to control the arousal he told himself was brought on by the curse, he met her gaze directly. "Dr. Morton. It's an honor to finally meet you."

Clearly taken aback, she carefully extracted her hand from his and pushed away a stray lock of dark, silken hair. A furrow marred her brow as she considered him. "Have we met before?"

"I doubt I would forget someone like you," he said, pitching his tone to the intimate level women had regularly succumbed to during the course of his long life.

The yearning that had been dogging Kate ever since she had touched the sarcophagus responded to the sexiness laced through his voice. Between her legs, she throbbed with need, and her nipples tightened into hard, sensitive nubs. Even the slight rub of her suit jacket fabric brought increased desire.

As she gazed into Lord Wright's glittering, glacial-blue eyes, she knew he sensed her want and would gladly satisfy it.

He was a handsome man, although not her type any longer. Blond, bright and brawny, he reminded her too much of the ex who had stolen one of her papers and published it as his own. The theft had delayed her doctorate by nearly a year, as she had been forced to produce a new thesis.

"Are you okay, Dr. Morton? You look a little flushed," the director said from beside her, eyeing her with curiosity.

"I'm fine. It was just a little warm down in the storage area," she lied, her gaze never shifting from Lord Wright's face. As she examined his features, she once again thought there was something familiar about him, but could not quite place him.

"I'll have to speak to maintenance about that. It's important that area stay at a proper temperature," the administrator replied, before quickly adding, "I'll leave you and Lord Wright alone to discuss his intentions."

As her visitor's heated gaze settled on her once again, Kate suspected his intentions were not quite what the director pictured, not that she would complain. She was a modern woman, after all, and it had been too long since she had experienced such need, much less fulfilled it.

"Lord Wright," she said, and motioned him into her office.

He stepped inside, and as she closed the door, she realized that his very masculine presence dwarfed the tiny space, forcing her to lean back against the door to create some distance from him.

"Intimate, isn't it?" he said, peering around her office before firmly settling his gaze on her. The intensity in those icy blue eyes once again ratcheted up the want within her, making it almost painful.

"I prefer to think of it as comfortable," she replied, and dragged off her suit jacket to battle the warmth in her body.

A mistake, she realized, as his probing gaze settled on the hard points of her nipples visible through the fabric of her blouse.

"Do I bother you, Dr. Morton?" he said as he took a dangerous step closer.

She jerked her head up a determined notch, and his attention was drawn back to her face. "Not in the least, Lord Wright."

"Alec," he said, and inched toward her until he was so close she could feel the spill of his minty breath against her lips. It only made her want a taste of the firm mouth barely inches from hers.

"Alec," she repeated with a soft sigh, relinquishing her normally logical self to the visceral feelings swamping her.

He groaned then like a man in pain, but immediately said, "Say it again. Say my name."

She wondered at the need in his voice, which went far beyond the physical, but did as he asked, while tossing her suit jacket onto her desk. She wanted her hands free for other things. "Alec."

A shudder shook his body before he took a final step, bringing that hard muscular body flush against hers. The long and very hard ridge of his erection pressed into her belly, leaving no doubt about the desire he was feeling.

Alec knew the mummy's curse was at work here, creating the attraction that gripped them both in its spell, yet he was powerless to prevent his reaction. In the past he had been able to control his response, in part because he knew that his partner would inevitably suffer a visit from the mummy's spirit if they made love. But there was something about Kate, something in that both wounded and wanton gaze, that had touched him. That made him want to touch her, both physically and emotionally.

"You feel it too, don't you, Kate?" He nuzzled his nose along hers, avoiding the full lips he wished to taste. Fisting his hands to keep from cupping her lush breasts.

"I do," she replied, slightly breathless as she returned his simple caress, her probing gaze locked with his the entire time.

It scared him, the intensity of her examination. For the first time in his life, he wanted her to see a man different from the one he had been for so long—a reckless, selfish man who had brought ruin upon himself. He wanted to think he was a better man now, one who was trying to make things right. And yet to do so, he had to lie to her. Maybe even cheat her. That fact twisted his gut into knots, but couldn't drive away the need he was feeling. A need that went far beyond the physical.

Dragging his gaze from hers, he focused on her lips for the barest moment before he closed his eyes and unerringly found her mouth.

It was soft as rose petals against his, and warm. With a soft sigh she gave herself over to his tentative kiss. For long moments he explored the contours of that fullness, savoring her response. Trembling, she slipped her tongue out to taste his lips, and then opened her mouth to allow him entry.

He groaned then. In response she reached up and laid her hand over the center of his chest, as if trying to gentle him with her touch.

No one had ever done that before, not even his mother.

To his parents, he had been merely a throwaway child, and they had shown him barely any hint of kindness or love. Now a virtual stranger was showing him that and more.

He raised his hand and gently cradled her breast, wanting to give her pleasure. Wanting to treasure her as she deserved. Tenderly, he plucked at the tight bud beneath the fabric, earning a ragged sigh and a shift of her legs that allowed him to slip his thigh between hers. He applied a slight pressure upward, against her center, and she rode along his thigh, seeking release.

"Let me touch you," he whispered against her lips, wanting to gift her with pleasure. Needing to feel the heat and wet of her passion, and hear her soft cries of satisfaction. It had been too long since he'd experienced that kind of response from a woman.

"Please," she almost keened. He immediately undid the buttons and zipper on her pants and inched his hand down past the tiny scrap of lace barely big enough to call panties, to find her damp center.

While he continued to pluck at her nipple with one hand, he circled the swollen nub between her legs with the other, applying pressure to bring her to release. With each tender pass of his fingers, her desire grew, until she broke away, breathing heavily, to glance down to where he was pleasuring her.

He followed her gaze, watching as he moved his hands beneath the fabric. He caressed her clitoris before dipping inward to slip the tip of his finger into her vagina. She cried out then and gripped his wrist, as if afraid of the pleasure she was feeling.

"Sssh, do not worry, love," he whispered, and brushed his lips along hers. Then he bent his head and took the tight tip of her nipple between his teeth, teasing it with a gentle bite that had her crying out with want.

"Alec." She cupped the back of his head, holding him close, and shifted her hips into his hand to ask for more.

Alec could barely suck in a breath as his cock and balls tightened almost to the point of pain. How he wanted to be inside her, experiencing the wonder of her body, but he knew he could not risk the mummy's revenge. But even if he could, it was too soon for Kate. He could sense it in her almost virginal wonder as her body responded to their love-making. Because of that, he held back his own needs, wanting to pleasure her, needing her to trust him.

As he continued to fondle the damp, heated cleft of her sex, dipping his fingers within her while caressing her clitoris, he undid the buttons on her shirt. Pulling aside the demi-cup of her bra, he exposed the luscious fullness of her breast and her tight, pink-brown nipple. It was hard from his ministrations, but so warm as he closed his lips around it and suckled her. He alternated licking the sensitive tip with nipping it in a teasing way that had her holding his head to her and rocking her hips against his hand as she sought her release.

He urged her on with soft words of encouragement, wanting her to explore her own needs, asking her to tell him what she desired.

"Bite me," she said, surprising him with her request.

He complied, gently teething her hardened nipple.

She climaxed then, her body shaking against his. Her wet juices drenched his fingers and made her cleft slick and hot with her release. Her reaction nearly made him come in his pants as he imagined what it might be like to be immersed in all that damp heat.

Kate cried out his name and gripped his shoulders as he gentled his touch. After a swift brush of his lips against her breast and a last glide of his hand along her sex, he took a step back. His gaze focused on her face as she hurriedly rearranged her clothing, restoring order as guilt settled in.

"I don't normally do this," she said as she awkwardly closed the last button of her blouse.

With a sad smile, he said, "Neither do I."

She doubted it, but as she examined his features, she saw a hint of something—loneliness, possibly. It reached deep within her, awakening emotions more dangerous than the desire she had just experienced. It made her cup his cheek and stroke her thumb across his rough beard, offering comfort.

"Thank you," she said, wanting him to know that despite her earlier words, she had no regrets over what had happened.

With a smile that was slightly brighter, and which lightened those stunning crystalline eyes, he replied gruffly, "You're welcome." Then he gestured to her desk and added, "Should we get to work?"

Chapter 4

Kate had barely finished changing into her comfortable jeans and a plain white T-shirt when the knock came at her apartment door. Puzzled by who it could be, she peered through the peephole to find a pair of already familiar blue eyes staring back at her.

She yanked the door open and said in exasperation, "Lord Wright. I should ask how you got my home address—"

"But by now you know that I'm a man used to getting what he wants." He breezed into her apartment, his hands filled with an assortment of bags. From one of them drifted delicious smells that dragged a low rumble of hunger from her stomach.

She quickly covered her midsection to muffle the sound, but Alec merely arched an eyebrow and said, "I love a woman who's not afraid to admit to her needs."

Heat raced across her body and along her cheeks, since there was no denying that his reference was to more than her tummy's pleased sound. When his gaze settled on her unbound breasts, her nipples hardened. She was seemingly unable to fight her response to him. But she tried.

"Lord Wright—"

"Alec, please. I thought we were past such formalities," he said as he continued into the small dining area in her apartment and laid down the bags he was carrying. Without waiting for her approval, he began pulling out an assortment of take-out containers, which he set on the table.

Her stomach grumbled again, and since she had no other plans for dinner, she reluctantly gave in. "I guess you're used to getting your way."

Despite her words, she went to the small kitchen adjacent to the dining room and pulled out plates, forks and glasses, which she set on the table as Alec removed the lids from the various dishes, unleashing more savory aromas.

"It smells wonderful," she admitted, and took a seat while he expertly uncorked a bottle of wine that he had brought along as well.

"I hope so. I understand Tao is one of the better restaurants in New York." He poured her a generous amount of white wine.

Kate had dined at the trendy and expensive Asian restaurant only once, but it had been enough to prove to her that its reputation was well-earned. "It is, but how did you know—"

"You strike me as being selective and discerning. It seemed like an appropriate choice," he said, taking a seat beside her, but not before removing an elegantly packaged, foot-long box.

"Or maybe it was the matchbox from the restaurant you saw on my desk."

"Maybe," he admitted with a wry grin. When she shot a look at the foil-wrapped package, the smile turned sexy.

"Wondering what's in the box?" He split the order of

crab cake appetizers and offered her the mango chile dipping sauce.

Because he was a man of surprises, she suspected the gift box contained another one. Once again she thought of Pandora and the dangers of too many revelations. Kate had already had more than she'd expected in one day, from her encounter with the unusual sarcophagus to her earlier abandon with Alec. Somehow she suspected the present would yield yet another moment of wickedness.

Her logical mind warned her of the threat of such actions, but it was difficult to heed the admonitions when everything about Alec screamed of pleasure.

They shared the meal, feeding each other from the assortment of dishes. The crab cakes with their sweet-spicy sauce were an elegant way to begin the meal. The dumplings and crunchy cucumbers that followed were a pleasant palate-cleanser for the main dishes he had selected.

Crispy orange chicken and a Kobe sirloin so tender it melted in her mouth satisfied her physical appetite, but throughout the meal, another kind of hunger had been growing.

She told herself it was a mistake to be so attracted to Alec. He was too smooth, too handsome, too rich, too everything.

But the nagging sense within her that warned that he couldn't be trusted was having a hard time battling the part of her that wondered what it would be like to be possessed by a man like him.

It was impossible for Alec not to see that Kate was interested. It was there in the sexy tilt of her smile and the occasional glance at his mouth as they ate. It was there in the husky notes of her voice, which stirred awake his own desire. For most of the meal he had been painfully hard as he imagined kissing those enticing lips or exploring every curvy line of her body.

He imagined that she made love much like she had savored the meal they had just shared, with each bite and taste bringing a new sensation and enjoyment. She was clearly a sensuous woman, and his balls tightened at the thought of exploring that sensuality with her.

A hundred years ago he might have done just that, throwing caution to the wind and allowing himself the pleasure of making love to her even though it would bring the mummy's wrath down upon her. But not this time.

In the short while since he'd met Kate, he had grown to like her. She was smart, witty and so sexy that he found himself imagining the impossible.

But he had to remember it was just that—impossible

He might have to betray her to accomplish his ends. Once he did so, and reunited the two mummies, it might be time for his long life to finally come to an end.

"I'd offer you a penny for your thoughts, but that doesn't feel like it would be quite enough," she said, and he realized he had stopped eating. Not that there was much left of the meal.

A moment of honesty seized him and he blurted, "I'm not sure you really want to know what I'm thinking."

Seeming to sense the discussion might become far weightier than she had expected, she sat back and wiped her mouth with her napkin. After carefully folding it and laying it on the table, she asked, "Why is that, Alec?"

"Because we both know we want each other, but you don't trust me."

He already knew her to be direct, so her answer was not

unexpected. "You're right on both counts. I am attracted to you, but you're not the kind of man who inspires confidence."

A funny thing for her to say, really, since for most of his adult life he had taken advantage by instilling false confidence in one person after another. But then again, he suspected Kate was familiar with con men.

"So who was he? The man who took advantage," Alec said, wanting to understand her. For the first time in his life he wanted someone's trust.

Kate sucked in a long, hesitant breath, but then blurted out, "My ex-fiancé. We were both doctoral students at the time and, unbeknown to me, vying for the same position at a local museum."

"He beat you for the job—"

"He stole my thesis, but the museum was wise enough to realize he wasn't the right person for the position. Not that it made my life any easier, since I had to redo all my work," she admitted, plucking at the napkin on the table in a nervous gesture.

Alec reached out and covered her hand, hating that even after so long, the memory had the power to disquiet her. "It's in the past, and the truth of the matter is you were the one who won the day."

The barest hint of a smile passed across her lips. "What doesn't kill you makes you stronger," she said, and met his gaze in challenge.

No, the mummy hadn't killed him, although more than once in the hundred or more years since she had begun her curse, he'd wished she had. But the experience had definitely made him stronger. Possibly even a better man, something that his parents and a host of others had not thought possible. For that reason, he said, "You're right not to trust me."

Chapter 5

Kate narrowed her eyes and considered him, surprised and confused by his blatant honesty. But she had no intention of denying what she was feeling, because she wanted to explore the desire sizzling between them. "You're quite direct, aren't you?"

"Would you rather that I take a different approach? Possibly cajole or flatter?" He dropped his voice to that sexy low tone he had likely perfected during years of seduction.

"I wouldn't fall for that," she admitted with a casual shrug.

They had been sitting kitty-corner to share their meal, their knees occasionally brushing beneath the table. Now he inched closer until his leg was cradled between both of hers and there was no escaping the touch of his thigh. The muscles were rock hard, and heat spread through her as she imagined the press of those legs naked against hers.

With a shake of his head, Alec chuckled and said, "No, you wouldn't fall for that, but it might be nice. What woman wouldn't like to hear that a man finds her attractive?"

The heat in her cheeks deepened and her voice quavered as she answered, "This woman doesn't need to hear it."

"Bullshit," he retorted, and immediately reached out, cradling her face in a hand that was surprisingly work-roughened for an aristocrat. "You are stunning even though you're afraid to acknowledge that."

"I'm not afraid, just cautious of men with glib tongues and Greeks bearing gifts," she said, and motioned to the finely wrapped package still sitting on the table.

Alec peered at it from the corner of his eye before yanking it over with his free hand. "Caution can be good, so I'm forewarning you that opening this could be...dangerous."

Wonderful, she thought. She'd been right. Another Pandora's box for her to explore. "Then maybe I should wait a bit. Until I trust you a little more."

"Or until you trust yourself," he dared her, those intimate tones continuing to stir up all kinds of needs within her. But as his thumb stroked the contours of her lips, she admitted that she didn't want to wait to explore some of what she wanted.

She opened her mouth and let her tongue slip out to taste his thumb. The pad was salty, and she took his finger between her teeth and licked it again. She closed her lips over it and sucked it into her mouth.

He shuddered against her thigh before she released his finger and murmured, "Tasty. Maybe we should think about dessert."

After another quick glance at the table, Alec replied, "Sorry to say I hadn't thought of that."

Kate smiled and stroked her hand along his leg, stopping just shy of the very noticeable bulge beneath the pressed khaki of his pants.

"I think I may have something in the freezer. Why don't you go to the living room and I'll be out in a second?"

She didn't wait for his reply before she hurried to the refrigerator in the small galley kitchen off the dining area. Yanking open the freezer, she spied the unopened pint of French vanilla. Probably pedestrian to royalty like Alec, but by the time she was done, he would never think of ice cream in the same way again.

She pulled the pint out, ripped off the cover, grabbed a single spoon and strolled out to the living room, where Alec had settled himself on the couch. A strategically placed pillow in his lap hid the erection she had noticed earlier. She wondered why, after all his earlier sexiness, he was suddenly shy.

Not that she would allow that to keep her from what she wanted.

Kate put a little extra sway in her hips and smiled as she noted the way his gaze followed that motion, before trailing up her body to settle on her unbound breasts beneath the soft fabric of her T-shirt. His visual examination was an almost physical caress, and her nipples tightened into hard points.

He gulped and shifted on the sofa, laid one hand over the pillow to keep it in place.

She ambled toward him and slipped between the V of his legs, to sit on the coffee table in front of him, where it would be impossible for him not to see her. Where his thighs and knees would be in constant contact with her and where, with one short move, she would be in his lap.

Alec seemed to understand her intent, and went all gallant on her. "Are you sure about this, Kate?"

The way he said her name, so low and intimate, made

her sex clench and throb. Made her go wet at the thought of hearing him say it again as he came.

"I'm always sure about dessert," she replied, and shifted to the edge of the coffee table. The action made her knees intimately brush the apex between his legs and the hardness of his balls.

A rough groan escaped him, but she didn't pause in her game plan, digging out a bit of ice cream with the spoon and holding it up to his lips.

His clear, icy gaze was filled with heat as he locked it on hers, opened his mouth and closed his full, sexy lips over the spoon and ate the ice cream. She quickly spooned up a larger bit and brought it to his lips, but made a point of smearing it along the edge of his mouth.

"So sorry. Let me clean that for you." She leaned close to lick his lips clean. The cold sweetness of the ice cream was a direct contrast to the hot saltiness of his skin.

"May I have a taste, as well?" he asked, dropping his gaze to the hard nubs of her breasts before firmly settling his attention on her face once more.

"Maybe later, after I've had *my* taste," she replied, feeling empowered by the little game they were playing.

"You're being a bad hostess, you know," he teased, and laid his big strong hands on her thighs, stroking their length before settling his palms at her waist.

"Very bad," she admitted, and motioned to his shirt with the empty spoon. "So bad that you may want to take that off so it doesn't get messy."

He tightened his hands at her waist, hesitating for a fraction of a second before he went to work, unbuttoning the expensive Egyptian cotton dress shirt. He ripped it off to reveal the broad muscled planes of a truly magnificent chest and the defined ridges of his flat abs. Despite his blond hair, his skin was deliciously tanned. Fairly smooth except for a smattering of golden curls at the center, which narrowed and descended in a straight line obscured by the pillow still sitting unceremoniously in his lap.

"That has to go," she said, grabbing the pillow and tossing it aside to reveal the final path of that enticing swath of fair hair.

She gulped in a breath as she took in the sight of the immense bulge beneath the fine khaki. When she dragged her gaze away, back to those very masculine features, they once again struck her as being familiar.

On one shoulder he had a birthmark about the size of a palm print that looked like a sprinkling of cocoa powder on his skin. Unusual, but she felt as if she had seen it somewhere before.

When he noted where her interest had been drawn, he shrugged carelessly. "The birthmark is a Wright trait. My brother and father both bore similar stains."

She embedded the spoon in the ice cream and left it standing there. Then she traced the edges of the birthmark with her index finger, almost memorizing the shape, until he reached up and took hold of her hand, forcing her attention back to his face.

"Dessert, remember?" he urged with a wicked grin, and opened his mouth wide.

Kate indulged him, spooning up a large helping of ice cream, only some of which made it to his mouth. A large glob fell off and landed on the upper plane of his pectoral muscle.

"So sorry," she said with false apology. The heat of his body quickly melted the confection. A trail dripped down his skin to the edge of his hard brown nipple, providing her with the perfect excuse.

"Let me," she offered, bending to lick all around it, savoring the contrast of sweetness with rough, salty male against her tongue. When he groaned and cupped the back of her head, she continued her caress, licking him again before covering him with her mouth and sucking on the hard nub. She teethed it gently, which earned gentle pressure at her waist to urge her closer.

She did as he asked, climbing up onto his lap until the hard ridge of his erection was nestled tight to her center, and he groaned again.

His gaze followed her movements as she spooned up another dollop of vanilla and offered it to him. As soon as he had taken the bite, she leaned forward and covered her mouth with his, licking at the remnants on his lips, slipping her tongue in to dance with his after he had swallowed.

His mouth was cold for a millisecond before the heat of their kisses chased away the frostiness.

Over and over they kissed until, well aware where this little game was taking them, they broke apart, breathing heavily.

Alec swallowed hard and stared at the dark tight nubs poking against the thin cloth of her T-shirt before shooting her a half glance. "I want another taste, but of something far sweeter."

Kate released a laugh tinged with unexpected nervousness, but didn't hesitate to help him as he slipped his hands beneath the hem of her shirt and dragged it up and off her body.

She sat in his lap, exposed, visibly trembling as she cupped her breasts and leaned forward. "You wanted something sweet," she said, her voice husky with need and anticipation.

Alec smiled, pleased by her offering—and by something else he had suddenly realized. The passion between them was intense, but unlike their earlier encounter, it was untainted by the power of the mummy. He wanted to understand why, but not now, when for the first time in over a century, a warm, willing and totally fascinating woman could be his.

As she rose up on her knees to bring the tips of her breasts to his mouth, he cradled her back and skimmed his lips along those sensitive peaks. The action dragged a ragged sigh from her, and the bump of her hips along his erection.

He fought the urge to toss her to her back and plunge his cock into her, because this moment they were sharing was too rare in his tortured lifetime. He wanted to savor every second of it, and of her, before the mummy came to torment him again.

Because of that, he took his time pleasuring her, plucking her tender pink-brown nipples with his mouth and hands. Enjoying her soft cries of pleasure and the heat and damp of her as he dipped one hand into her jeans. He swirled his index finger around the swollen nub of her clitoris before exploring her nether lips with his hand, applying gentle pressure as he stroked her. She moved on him while he continued to suck and lick her delicious nipples.

The throb of her impending release came against his hand and he tempered his actions, wanting to return to their earlier playfulness.

He broke away from her, earning a muffled protest as he moved her to the couch. She lay there, confused for a moment, until he reached for the buttons and zipper, opened them and dragged her jeans and panties off.

He sat back for a moment, appreciating all the feminine beauty he had exposed. Her sex glistened, flushed an enticing deep pink. He wanted a taste and a tease, and reached for the pint of ice cream. Spooning up some of the half-melted dessert, he dribbled a line of it from her navel to the edge of the dark curls at her center.

Kate jumped when the chill hit her belly. From the look on Alec's face, she guessed that he planned to eat her up, not that she would complain. He had gifted hands and a talented mouth, and she knew he would bring satisfaction with both. But it made her wonder if he was as good with his cock. She reached forward and covered his bulge through the fabric of his pants. Hard, thick and oh so long, it made her drip in anticipation.

Alec chuckled then and moved her hand away. "Not yet, love. Not until you've had your satisfaction."

She shivered at the possibilities, but then all conscious thought left as he dipped his tongue into her navel and licked his way down to her clitoris. She almost came at the first stab of his tongue against that hyper-charged nub, but knew it was too soon. She wanted to experience the pleasure he could bring.

Closing her eyes and arching her back to give him greater access, she became a creature of sensation, exhorting him onward with determined entreaties until she was shaking and drenched from his mouth and her own juices.

He pulled away for a moment and she protested, cupping the back of his head with her hands and holding him there. His sexy chuckle vibrated against her vagina before he inserted his fingers into the slick canal and stroked more insistently, bringing her to the brink. She hung there, suspended, until he raked his teeth along her lips and clitoris, dragging her over the edge.

Kate called out his name and pushed up into his mouth, but his actions gentled, willing her back to earth and to his arms. He scooped her up into his lap and tucked her head beneath his chin, running his hands up and down her spine in a soothing motion.

Kate's release had stolen her will and energy, so she was content to recuperate in his arms. Although even the slightest brush of the crisp hairs on his chest against her sensitive nipples was enough to slowly rouse her desire once more. Not to mention the insistent and continuing push of his unforgettable erection against her.

She wanted him. Wanted to satisfy him as he had her. But when she reached to undo his pants, he laid a cautious hand over hers.

Holding her back was probably the most honorable and stupidest thing Alec would ever do, but he couldn't make love to Kate and risk having the mummy's curse extend to her. Trying to explain without giving away that he had been less than honest, he brushed his hand across hers and said, "I don't want to rush things."

A strangled laugh escaped Kate. "Don't want to rush? You've taken me twice now—"

"And I trust it's been as pleasurable for you as it has been for me," he replied in a perfectly level and cultured voice. If she knew that what he wanted to do was throw her back onto the sofa and plunge his dick into all that delicious femininity, without any gentleness or thought to the consequences, she might not be eyeing him the way she was now, clearly wondering if he was for real.

"Not that I think it should be tit-for-tat—"

"I'll never complain about the tit part, especially not ones as lovely as yours," he said to distract her, cradling her breasts once more. Her nipples instantly hardened, and she sighed raggedly, grabbing hold of his wrists.

"So not fair. I can't think when you do that," she complained.

Her heat and moisture registered through the fabric of his pants and his erection jerked in response, so powerfully that she could not fail to notice it. Once again she laid her hands against him, only this time he couldn't find the will to stop her.

She quickly undid the buttons on his pants, then took hold of the zipper and dragged it down the length of his erection. Alec's anticipation was almost excruciating, as was the delay while he raised his hips to allow her to pull down both the khakis and his briefs.

His erection sprang free, jutting from the triangle of golden curls at its base.

"So different," she said as she stroked his length with both hands, exploring his shaft and the foreskin covering its head. Fascinated by the look of his penis, she seemed unaware that each movement of the skin created almost unbearable friction beneath.

"Hopefully not too different," he said, and tenderly cradled her hands, tutoring her in how she could please him.

She was an enthusiastic student, working him with her fingers, then slipping them beneath the edge of his pants to caress his balls until he was trembling, his body tight as he fought against his release. He was enjoying her touch too much to let go. He wanted something else from her.

As her gaze met his, Kate must have realized that, for

she gave a knowing half smile. "Lie back. Relax. I'm just getting started."

He groaned at her words and almost lost it, barely holding back as a pearl of release crowned the tip of his penis.

With a bold swipe of her tongue, Kate licked it, but then turned her attention to dragging his pants and briefs completely off him. She paused then, kneeling in the V of his legs, her gaze traveling from his knees to his powerfully muscled thighs.

She bent at the waist and ran her hands across all those muscles and the golden hair covering them, loving the sensation of rough and smooth beneath her palms.

Pausing at the juncture of his thighs, she bracketed her hands around his groin. His cock rose proudly above curly, dark gold hair and his magnificent balls. Dipping her thumbs downward, she ran them across the hard orbs in his sac, massaging them as she inched her hands ever closer to his dick.

Alec moaned and pushed upward with his hips, silently pleading for her touch. For her kiss, she thought, as she finally encircled him with her hands, dropped her head and took the tip of him into her mouth.

A ragged sigh slipped from him, and beneath her hands she felt the release of some of his tension. But as she made love to him with her lips and tongue, caressed his balls and the root of him with her hands, the tightness in his body increased until he was shaking beneath her. Until she was likewise quivering, imagining how he would feel inside her, all that immense masculinity filling her.

She moaned against his cock and the vibration was his undoing.

With a rough cry, he came, spilling himself into her

mouth. She ate him up, licking and sucking at his salty release, gentling him with her hands and mouth even as she
fought the desire still raging inside her.

Alec reached for her, undone by her caresses and yet
aware of her state. It was impossible to miss that she was
fully aroused again, and he wanted to offer her release.

Gently, he urged her to rise until her breasts were close
to his lips. He moved from one to the other, suckling them
as he reached between their bodies and shoved his fingers
up into her vagina. The position of his hand allowed him to
place pressure on her nub, and she took advantage of that,
rocking her hips and riding his hand to a rough, fast release.

She collapsed on him then and he tucked her in tight,
tenderly stroking his hand up and down her side as she pil-
lowed her head on his shoulder. The musky smell of their
desire scented the air, along with the vanilla of the melting
ice cream on the coffee table, as they recovered from the
pleasure they had shared.

Kate brushed her hand lazily back and forth along his
chest, feeling at peace and yet also wired. She had never before experienced such satisfaction with a man, but in these
quiet moments, logic returned to warn that she knew nothing about Alec.

Certainly not enough to trust him, she thought, as she
peered toward the dining room table, where his gift sat unopened.

Her mind continued to ponder a rapid-fire series of con-
flicting thoughts as the sounds of a New York evening
reached into her third floor walk-up apartment. The rattle
and rumble of the subway that ran beneath the street directly
outside her door. The screaming siren of a police car, followed by the blare of a fire engine. A moment of silence

followed, but soon the bells of the church up the block tolled the coming of midnight.

Alec stirred at that, sleepily mumbling, "I should be going."

He should, she thought, raising her head and propping her elbow on his broad chest. But as she examined his features, one word escaped her lips.

"Stay."

Chapter 6

"Stay? You want me to stay? The night? In your bed?"
Alec said aloud, needing to convince himself that she hadn't
just made the unexpected offer.

With a gamin-like grin, she motioned to the sofa where
they lay, half on, half off after their earlier activities. "Where
else? This wouldn't be all that comfortable."

"Stay," he repeated, not in question this time, but in wonder. He couldn't remember the last time he had actually
spent the night with a woman. Certainly not in the last century, and before that....

The last woman he had actually spent the night with and
made love to had been driven mad within a week by nightly
visits from the mummy.

But he hadn't made love with Kate--although their interlude had been incredibly satisfying. And he could think
of dozens of ways to satisfy her during the course of the
night that would protect her from what consummation would
bring. If she even wanted more, that was. He tempered his
male ego in the hopes of convincing himself that staying

the night was a totally logical, sensible and honorable thing to do.

"You don't have to stay if you don't want to," Kate blurted, in response to his prolonged silence, and made a motion to leave his side.

He grasped her arm with light pressure and laid his index finger against her lips to silence her. "I want, Kate. It's just that…what I'm feeling for you is something I didn't expect," he confessed.

She called to him on so many levels. Made him think of things that were no longer possible. Even if he would eventually leave her, maybe even betray her, for tonight he wanted to experience what being in love might be like.

Her grin was rueful. "You're not quite what I imagined, either."

"Should we retire to your room?" he asked, with such decorum that his mother would have at least been proud of his manners if nothing else.

"Let's." Kate slipped off him to stand on the carpeted floor. She held her hand out to him and he accepted her invitation and followed her into her bedroom.

It had been a long time since he had been in a woman's boudoir, and yet some things didn't change. The jewelry she had worn that day lay scattered across the top of the dresser, beside some makeup and perfume bottles.

Funny, he hadn't smelled any foreign scent on her. For good measure, he took another sniff. Only the slightest hint of a flowery fragrance lingered beneath the aroma of woman and sex.

He tamped down the desire her scent aroused, and stopped at the side of her sleigh bed. Queen-size, although with his stature they would still be sleeping quite close.

If they slept.

Kate eased beneath the covers and waited for him to join her.

He did, climbing onto the mattress. It dipped with his weight and had Kate rolling against him.

Alec didn't mind. He wrapped an arm around her back as she tucked her head beneath his chin. She rested one hand over his heart and slid her thigh over his with the ease of a longtime lover.

The action brought comfort and despair.

They would not have enough time together to become that familiar with each other.

"Good night, Alec," she murmured, and then yawned.

"Good night, Kate." He focused his attention on the feel of her beside him, and her breathing as it gradually slowed and lengthened.

Short minutes later, a soft snore confirmed that Kate had finally fallen asleep. Only then did Alec close his eyes and allow himself some rest.

A melding of fear and desire roused her into that netherworld between dreams and consciousness.

Bits of an image swarmed before her eyes as her heart pounded in her chest and a chill crawled across her skin.

As Kate watched, the pieces of the image fit themselves together like a jigsaw puzzle, until she was staring into the kohl-lined, midnight eyes of a beautiful, ebony-haired woman.

The woman searched Kate's features, clearly confused. Her crimson lips twisted with annoyance before she raised her hand and skimmed it down the side of Kate's face.

"Who are you?" The woman's voice hissed like wind-blown sand.

"Kate," she said, trying to move away as the stranger trailed her hand down Kate's neck to her shoulder. The touch was cool against her skin, but raised the undeniable heat of passion.

Seemingly satisfied with that response, the dark-haired woman said, "You know what I want."

Only Kate didn't have a clue what the woman desired, or why the dream seemed more real than not. "I don't know—"

"You know what I want!" she cried more forcefully, the sibilant hiss in her voice becoming stronger, and grating against Kate's ears.

She tried to cover them, but found she couldn't move. She was trapped in this weird waking dream, pinned beneath the woman as she ran her hand down Kate's body. But as Kate followed the path of that violating hand, it was not her body she saw. Instead the vision was one of a powerful male body smattered with golden hair.

Alec's body? Kate's doubt lasted only a second. Her captor skipped her hand upward to a shoulder, and a chocolate-colored birthmark confirmed Kate's suspicions. But Kate didn't understand why she seemed to be inside Alec's body and mind, experiencing the arousing touch of this ghostly woman. Hearing her determined pleas that made no sense to Kate.

"Who are you?" Kate asked, wanting to know the identity of her tormentor.

The woman ignored her, trailing her palm upward and covering Kate's mouth to silence her. The perfume of myrrh nearly overwhelmed her senses, so powerful was the aroma. Although she thrashed her head back and forth, the woman maintained her fierce grasp with little effort.

"Help him or join in his misery," she said, once Kate had quieted down.

"His misery?" Kate mumbled against the palm covering her mouth.

The woman's eyes were fathomless as she ran her free hand across Alec's chest. As she had before, Kate experienced the touch of the woman's hand against Alec's body as it were her own, caught up in Alec's nightmare. Suffering the desire that was more punishment than pleasure.

This can't be happening, she thought, and closed her eyes against the sight, steeling herself against the unwelcome touch. Fighting the arousal the vision seemed to stir so easily.

Her captor snaked her hand downward until she reached the head of Alec's erection. Encircling it with her fingers, she stroked up and down his engorged length, and Kate heard Alec's moan in her head. Experienced his need as the woman's power kept them both pinned to the mattress while she wrought her torture.

Alec's breath caught in his chest as he awoke and finally realized he was not alone in his nightmare. Kate's voice and thoughts jumped around in his brain as the mummy's desire bound them together.

He murmured a protest and fought against the passion threatening to consume him, which Kate was likewise battling. The mummy only laughed and tenderly bit the side of his neck, before working her way down his body until her lips were poised just above the head of his cock.

As she had for over a century, she warned, "You cannot resist, even though you know what will follow."

But he had resisted, Alec thought. Even earlier that night, as tempting as Kate was, he had not sought the pleasure of making love to her because he had known how wrong that would have been.

He was no longer the callow man who had sold a woman's child to pay off a bet.

Mustering every ounce of his determination, he drove away the image of the mummy working his dick. Ignored the way her full, generous breasts rubbed his thighs, trying to create even greater need.

"I am not that man any longer," he shouted out to her. In that instant, something broke her dominion over him and Kate.

The mummy's image faltered for a moment, but then a wave of power flowed from her, restoring the vision.

"You know what I want," she urged yet again, almost fearfully, as if sensing her control over him was suddenly waning.

"Yes, I know. I will not disappoint you," he said, with more conviction than he had ever felt in all the years she had been tormenting him.

With that admission, her skin lost its creamy olive hue and paled to the color of a bright moon. A second later her features lost all definition as her skin dried up and an otherworldly wind blew away all traces of her. But not before her pitiful keening rattled his brain, reminding him of the pain he had wrought with his selfishness.

Alec bolted up in bed, breathing heavily. Beside him Kate did the same.

He turned to face her, wanting to explain, but she yanked the sheets up and scrabbled away from him.

"What the hell was that?" she cried.

Chapter 7

"That was Amunet. She was the wife of a very rich merchant in ancient Cairo," he said, much more calmly than he had thought possible. He sat up against the headboard, never breaking his gaze from Kate's.

"And she's here because...?" Kate asked, holding the sheets to her nudity as if they were armor against him.

"I stole Taweret, the child she had lost to a fever only weeks before her own death from the disease."

"You stole her child?" Disgust colored every word.

"It was 1857. On a lark, I decided to go on an expedition—"

Kate waved a hand to stop him. "You say you went on an expedition in 1857. That would make you, like, one hundred and fifty-four—"

"Actually, one hundred eighty-four. I was thirty at the time. As the 'spare heir'—"

Kate gave an angry slash of her hand. "Stop. This is crazy. You're crazy if you actually believe this."

And because she clearly thought he was possibly insane, she scrambled from the bed and snatched up a robe, belting it around herself tightly and jerking her hand in the direction of the door.

"I think you should go."

Alec understood, but he had to give his explanation another try. Now that Amunet had made a connection with Kate, she would not stop until she either had what she wanted or had driven Kate insane.

"I never wanted to involve you like this. All I wanted was to get back Taweret."

With a huff, Kate spread her hands wide and shook her head. "What do I possibly have to do with…"

Her voice trailed off, and he had his confirmation of what he had suspected after first meeting Kate. She had found the mummy's toddler. She had found Taweret.

"You've seen Amunet's child. Touched her. You can help me break this curse." He slipped off the bed and stood there, hands outstretched. Pleading his case.

He was insane, she thought, and yet she couldn't battle the blast of yearning that shot through her from the sight of all his beautiful masculinity.

Treacherous longing—to which she'd already succumbed. Again. He had used it to get close to her so he could find the mummy. He had used her just like her ex had.

"Get out," she said with cold fury. She needed distance to try and make sense of what was happening. Make sense of whether or not what Alec was saying could possibly be true.

"She'll be back, Kate. She'll be back every night until Taweret is returned, or until she drives you mad."

Kate could not dismiss the profound sadness and fear in his words, nor the regret. But was that emotion for his torment or because he had involved her in his nightmare?

Drawing a deep breath, she calmed the emotions rolling around within her like marbles, and said, "Please leave, Alec. I need time to think about all this."

With a reluctant nod, he acquiesced, but not before saying one word.

"Robinson."

With an almost militarily precise about-face, he left the room. The rustle of clothing told her he was dressing, followed scant seconds later by the quiet snick of the lock as he closed her front door.

Kate started shaking then, so hard she had to wrap her arms around herself as if that could somehow keep her from falling to pieces.

But it didn't.

She dropped to the floor and leaned against the side of her bed, buried her head in her knees and cried—huge, sobbing breaths that shook her body.

How could she have given herself to him so recklessly? Had she not learned her lesson about men like Alec?

Over and over she flagellated herself for her poor judgment. But just as she hadn't sat back when her ex had screwed her, she wasn't going to now.

Wiping away the trails of tears, she rose and stiffened her spine, collected herself as she went into her living room and tidied it, straightening the cushions on the sofa. Cleaning up the empty take-out dishes and avoiding the gift that Alec had brought. The gift they had decided was best left for when she had trust in him.

She left it in the middle of the table, but not as a hopeful gesture. She left it there to remind herself of the foolishness of trusting handsome, charming men.

Then she went to work.

* * *

The chirp of her alarm clock drifted in from her bedroom, growing more insistent the longer she ignored it, until it finally fell silent.

Kate had been staring at the photo for so long, it blurred before her eyes until she had to squint to bring it back into focus.

The Robinson expedition.

In 1857, armed with what were then newfangled cameras, Robinson and a group of Englishmen had headed to Egypt, then hired a boat and a crew of locals to guide them to the various ancient ruins of the Nile. The expedition had captured prized images of many of the temples, which were later either moved or lost due to the construction of the Aswan Dam and the resulting waters of Lake Nasser.

After discovering the mummy child the day before, Kate had begun some preliminary investigations into its origins, but she had skimmed over this particular British team, since there had been no mention of any of the group members entering the tombs.

If Alec was telling the truth, that bit of history had clearly been in error.

Despite her initial reaction to his late night confession after the mummy's visit, long hours of research had led her to these photos and to the proof of at least part of Alec's story.

Second from the left stood a beautiful bare-chested man who looked remarkably like Alec. He had that same sexy grin, the same lean, muscled body, and on his right shoulder, a dark, uneven smudge. A birthmark much like the one she had discovered last night during their very passionate interlude.

Just the thought of all they had done roused fresh desire, but also despair.

How could she have been so stupid? Alec had been way too charming and determined in his pursuit. Clearly, it had not been about his attraction to her, but a desire to get close enough to confirm that her museum possessed Amunet's child.

And then what? Kate wondered, raking her fingers through her hair as she continued to flip through various photos from the Robinson expedition. Had Alec planned on stealing the mummy, or did he have some other idea about how to reunite mother and child?

Kate reached the end of the photos posted on one website and then found a link to the British museum Alec had claimed to represent. Not so false an assertion, it seemed. His name was on a list of the museum's top benefactors. Maybe he was high up enough that the administrators would not question him if he suddenly showed up on their doorstep with a rare mummy.

A virtual visit through the museum revealed an exhibit with Amunet's mummy, as well as other artifacts the Robinson expedition had apparently brought back with it from their journey to Egypt. Clearly, Kate should have delved deeper in her earlier research, but then again, she hadn't had much time. Only a few hours to try and find some mention of an unusual mummified child. She had not had the opportunity to really dig into the various references.

The museum website had more photos taken by Robinson and his group. As she scanned them, she detected Alec in a few others, full or partial views. And then one snagged her attention.

Alec was in the background with a group of locals, huddling next to something. Something small. And although the item was mostly obscured, enough of it was visible for Kate to discern that it was the coffin for Amunet's child, Taweret.

Opening a new tab on her browser, Kate decided to find out more about the man who had intrigued her so, something she should have done before giving most of herself to him.

But this search proved more elusive than the one for the Robinson expedition. Although there was a wealth of information on the Wright family leading up to Alec and his brother, Thomas, from that point on the facts grew sparse. Various references indicated that after the death of Thomas, the elder son and heir, Alec had become the next lord, and the family had grown more prosperous, but reclusive.

Understandably so if Alec was what he claimed—a 184-year-old man living with a mummy's curse.

Amunet's words repeated in Kate's brain: *You know what I want.*

Although she hadn't come out and said it, Kate had no doubt now about what she desired: to be reunited with her child.

Kate wasn't a mother yet, but she couldn't imagine the pain of losing a child at so young an age, and then a second time to grave robbers. She couldn't think of Alec in any other way right now, so great was her anger at him.

Anger for what he had done to Amunet and Taweret.

Anger at what he had done to Kate herself.

The chirp of her cell phone yanked her from her thoughts.

The museum, she realized, after she checked the caller ID.

She answered, and the director's assistant didn't wait a second before saying, "Are you okay, Dr. Morton?"

From the corner of her eye, Kate caught a glimpse of a clock and realized she was nearly an hour late for work.

"I'm fine, Sarah. I was just doing some research this morning and lost track of time."

"That's good to hear. You're so reliable we could set our clocks by you, so we were worried."

Reliable, predictable and a workaholic. Those had been the benchmarks of her life until now.

Until Alec.

"I'll be in shortly, Sarah. Does the director have any free time today by any chance?" Kate had to discuss the mummy with him and try to find a way for Amunet and Tawaret to be reunited. Not because of the curse, but because it was right for mother and child to be together once again.

Chapter 8

Alec sat in Kate's office, waiting for her arrival.

He had gotten to the museum as the doors opened, after spending a sleepless night thinking about all that had happened. Recalling the joy he had experienced in Kate's arms.

His body hardened, but the call of passion was tempered by an abyss of loss.

He had lost her last night after the mummy's visit and his revelation. He had seen the realization of betrayal steal the light of love from her eyes.

For over a century he had been trying to make things right with Amunet. He was close to doing that. Just a few more calls and the pulling of several more strings and he might be able to make up for his selfishness and end the curse.

And then what? he wondered.

He had lived well after the death of all his family and friends. Outlived the England he knew, with its genteel ways, and watched it suffer through not one, but two cataclysmic wars. Punishment enough to see all that he loved and cared for vanish.

What would happen now if he ended the curse? Would he finally be allowed some peace in his life? Would he be able to finally grow old, or would he just fade to dust like Amunet did virtually every night?

The creak of a floorboard warned him that someone was near. The doorknob turned and Kate flew into the room.

As she had been yesterday, she was professionally dressed in a smart pantsuit that did nothing to hide those delicious curves he had explored at length the night before.

There was no holding back his need now. It slammed into him, making him painfully hard. Making him want to rise from the chair and touch her again. But her do-not-think-about-it vibes kept his ass nailed to his seat.

"What are you doing here?" she said, closing the door behind her and leaning against it to avoid coming near him.

"I wanted to explain," he replied, his tone as neutral as he could manage, considering how much she meant to him. He suspected that she would misinterpret any emotion as just being another ploy to try and deceive her.

"What's there to explain? You're a thief. A seducer. A liar."

"And a beggar," he interjected, determined to prove he could change and be the kind of man she would want in her life. If he was meant to have a life, after all.

His comment clearly threw her. Narrowing her eyes to consider him, she shook her head, her shoulder-length dark hair gleaming as it moved. "A beggar? You? From what I gather, when your brother passed—"

"I would have traded anything for him to have lived. He was the one destined to lead. Not me."

Alec wished he'd had the opportunity to tell his brother that before Thomas had died from influenza. But he'd been filled with animosity and resentment back then. Only when he'd been forced to assume responsibility for his family's holdings had he understood all that his brother had sacrificed to fill that position.

Alec's words and the emotion in his voice must have chipped a small crack in the icy shell encasing Kate. "From what I read, you did well by your family and subjects," she said.

Alec looked away from her and up to the ceiling, recalling those first few months after his brother's untimely passing. His parents hadn't failed to remind him that he was second best. That they hoped he wouldn't fail them and the people who depended on him.

He hadn't failed, even with Amunet torturing him. He had managed the estates and businesses while searching for Taweret everywhere he could imagine and beyond. He had been shocked by how quickly the trail of the mummy's child had disappeared.

But no longer.

"I made some calls this morning. The museum. Bankers and lawyers," he said, beginning his explanation for what he had done. It wasn't what he had originally planned, but having met Kate, having fallen in love with her at first sight, it was the only thing he could do.

"I don't understand," she said, wrapping her arms around herself defensively.

"You were right with what you said before. I lied to you. I intended to seduce you and, if all else failed, I was going to steal the mummy's child."

She arched a brow and focused her gaze on him like a laser. "And now?"

He finally rose and tossed his hands up in surrender.

"I've had my people set up a foundation that would allow our two museums to reunite the mummies and share them for exhibition. One year here, one year in Britain."

Kate shook her head again, vehemently. "Even if you could somehow get both museums to agree—"

"I already have my board's approval to proceed."

That stunned her into a long silence, although the gamut of emotions churning within her was evident on her expressive face. "What you're proposing would cost a great deal of money."

With a nonchalant shrug he said, "That's why I'm a beggar. I've pledged my personal assets to fund the project. But there's another reason I'm a beggar."

Alec took the two steps across the office to bring him directly before her. He shoved his hands in his pockets to keep from touching her. Leaning close, he whispered tenderly, "I would do anything for you to forgive me. Beg for you to give me another chance."

"I'll help you convince my director to consider the collaboration, but as for you and me..."

She didn't have to say more. He could see it on her face, and he couldn't blame her.

"Have a nice life, Kate."

"What about your life, Alec? What happens to you when Amunet gets her child back?"

That she cared enough to ask gave him hope that eventually she would forgive him. If there was to be an "eventually" for him after mother and child were reunited.

"I don't know, Kate. But I have to do it. For them and for you. I don't want Amunet to bother you."

His words touched Kate's heart, softening the anger that

had been riding high from the moment she'd discovered him in her office. "Thank you for that truth at least, Alec."

He dipped his head slowly and a sad smile spread across his lips. "Take care of yourself, Kate."

"You do the same, Alec." She stepped aside and opened her door.

He walked out without any further appeals, and she closed the door to keep herself from calling out to him. Then she focused her mind on what she would explain to her director about what she had found during the inventory, and why their museum should agree to Alec's proposed plan.

When her phone rang nearly half an hour later, she knew who it would be. She even had an idea what she would say to her director at the meeting he'd requested.

Her one hope was that Alec would not be there, because she wasn't sure she could deal with seeing him again. At least not so soon.

There was too much hurt there. Too much emotion for her to casually sit across a table from him as if nothing had happened between them.

Girding herself for the meeting, she mustered a calm facade and headed to the director's office.

Six months later

Kate was pleased as she eyed the lineup for the exhibit, which snaked through the museum and out the front door. The public had responded overwhelmingly to the hopeful story of the reunion of mother and child after being apart for nearly two centuries.

Tickets were sold out for months for the exhibit she had put together with materials at her museum, along with others on loan from Alec's. The monies coming in would help pay for a number of new items, and prevent layoffs, which had been looming due to a decrease in charitable donations in the current economic downturn. Ticket sales would also help defray the costs Alec had pledged for the transport of the mummies and the setup of the exhibits.

Kate told herself time and again that the pledge hadn't been generosity on Alec's part. He had done what was best for himself. Only she knew that he could have gone about reuniting the mummies in a number of ways that hadn't involved the possible loss of a goodly amount of his assets.

For months, as the two museums haggled back and forth about the terms of the agreement, she had wondered why he had done it, unwilling to believe that their short interlude had been part of the reason. But deep in her heart, Kate had hoped that she was the cause of his sudden generosity and honor. That in that brief time together Alec had begun to feel as much for her as she had for him.

She thought she might be in love with him. No matter what he had done a century and a half earlier, or what he had planned to do just months before, she'd come to believe he had truly changed. That he'd become a better man.

As she was heading back to her office, she stopped short as she noticed that the director had entered the exhibit, trailed by half a dozen or more reporters and camera people. He paused in front of the display holding the two mummies and then stretched out his hand, inviting someone else to join him.

Kate's heart sped up, almost knocking against her ribs when she saw Alec step reluctantly into the limelight. He wasn't one for such public displays; she had learned that over the months as she'd read up on him and his family.

He looked well, she thought as she ambled closer, staying out of sight because she wasn't sure she could face him yet. Through the many weeks she'd spent arranging for the transfer of Amunet's mummy and setting up the exhibit, she had worried about what would happen once mother and child were brought back together. Worried that Alec's life might hang in the balance, even though she knew reuniting the two was the right thing to do.

Apparently, the reunion had done him well, she thought as she stood behind the group. There was a lightheartedness about him that he'd lacked during their first encounter. His smile, sexy as always, came more easily and a bright gleam lit his gaze—until he turned and caught sight of her.

Heat immediately filled those ice-blue eyes, but his attention was pulled away when one reporter asked him a question.

"I can't take credit for this wonderful event. It was Dr. Katherine Morton who discovered that the mummified child in this museum's collection was related to Amunet. Thanks to her diligence, mother and child are finally at peace," he said. And before anyone could ask another question, he excused himself.

The sea of reporters and camera people parted before him as he walked toward Kate. When he stopped in front of her, so tall and imposing, her breath hitched in her chest as she remembered how it felt to have all that masculine beauty beneath her hands. Between her legs, her sex grew heavy and wet, remembering how he could please her.

"It's good to see you, Kate," he said, his voice pitched low so only she could hear him. Those deep tones roused even more yearning.

"You look well," she replied, eating him up with her eyes and wishing they weren't somewhere so public. As much as she had tried to deny that he hadn't touched her heart, he had. She couldn't lie to herself any longer.

He smiled broadly and held out his hands. "Not bad for almost two hundred, don't you think?"

"Not bad," she admitted with a chuckle.

"It's nice to see you smile again, Kate."

The way he said her name caused an ache in her heart and heat along every nerve in her body. How she wanted to hear him say her name when he came.

"I'm glad you're here, Alec," she said, unable to hide her true emotions any longer.

He arched one blond brow and that heat crept back into his gaze. "How glad?"

She didn't get to answer, as the crew of newspeople broke away from the director and swarmed in their direction, clearly sensing something might be up.

Alec smoothly took control, introducing her and helping her field questions, until one female reporter, apparently picking up the vibes between them, asked, "Are you and Lord Wright an item?"

Kate shot him a nervous glance, not sure how to answer, but he stepped in quickly. "Dr. Morton and I have a relationship based on mutual respect and admiration."

That mollified the reporter for the moment, but to avoid any further probing, Alec excused them from the interview, slipped his arm around her waist and guided her toward her office.

She knew what would happen once the door closed behind them. She knew she could refuse, but wouldn't. She craved him the way a landlocked sailor yearned for the ocean. Worse, she wasn't sure that just one time would be enough to satisfy her longing.

His back hit the door with a resounding thud as she pressed herself against him, hungry for the hardness of his body. She plundered his mouth for the taste she had longed for so many months to sample.

"Sweet Kate. I've missed you so," he said, as they broke apart for a rough breath before kissing again.

She couldn't explain how, but that one night with him had not left her. If anything, the yearning for him had grown during their separation, and it had nothing to do with the mummy's desire. In fact, Amunet had not visited her again, seemingly satisfied that Alec would finally keep his word.

Kate was so needy, she was almost violent as she tore at the buttons on his shirt and pants, wanting to expose the masculinity that had burned itself on her brain. As the shirt gaped open, she licked her way to his flat brown nipples and bit them.

Alec slipped his hand beneath her blouse. With one quick twist he undid the front clasp of her bra, then covered her breasts, tweaking and rubbing her nipples into hard points. But that wasn't enough. He wasn't sure he could ever get enough of Kate.

He urged her away so he could slip off her suit jacket and the fine silk sweater beneath, exposing her lushness to his gaze. Then he reached behind him and locked her door before gently leading her forward to sit on the edge of her desk.

As her gaze met his, she knew what he wanted.

While she worked the buttons and zipper of his pants, he undid hers and pulled them down, exposing a surprise.

Her clean-shaven pubis allowed him unhampered views of her sex. It was already flushed with passion, and drenched. He could smell her arousal as he bent and dropped a kiss on her navel, before working his way down to lick that smooth surface.

She held his head to her and lifted her hips, offering herself up to him.

He dipped his tongue to taste the swollen nub and then covered it with his mouth, applying gentle suction until she was writhing on the desktop. He wanted to keep on pleasuring her, but he was too close to the edge. Already he could feel his climax swelling his balls, wanting to wash over him.

And it had been too long. Too long to wait any more.

He rose and positioned himself at her center, cradling her buttocks in his hands as he slipped the first inch into her slick vagina.

Her breath caught in her throat and her gaze locked with his as he pushed forward, filling and stretching her inch by inch until he was buried to the hilt. Her warmth and wetness welcomed him, making him never want to leave the wonder of her body.

He stood there, trapped in the sensations, imprisoned by the feelings she evoked in him.

She must have felt the same, for she wrapped her legs around his waist to hold him deep.

"You feel—"

"Amazing," she finished for him, and smiled shyly. "I could get used to this."

With a wicked smile, he trailed his hands up her sides to cup her breasts. Tenderly he caressed them, testing the weight in his hands, tweaking the tips until he couldn't wait another second for a taste.

He bent, and the action drove him ever deeper, dragging a moan from Kate.

"Did I hurt you, love?" he asked as he brushed a kiss

across her lips before dipping his head down to suckle her breasts.

"No, you're just so... big," Kate replied, arching her back to give him freer access to her breasts, and to move her hips against that long, thick length that was filling her so completely.

Now it was Alec's turn to moan, and she shifted her hips again, moving him in and out of her, urging him with words of encouragement and her hands grasping his buttocks.

He reared back and drove forward, making the desk creak and shudder beneath them as he pushed them both ever higher. His motions were almost brutal, fueled by the desire that had been simmering during months of separation.

His thrusts pushed her to the center of her desk, sending her blotter and papers flying. Kate bent her legs and braced her feet on the edge, raising her hips to meet his. Something inside her gave way as she accepted the pumping and rocking that were stealing her breath and sending her flying higher, until with one last push her release washed over her.

Alec sucked in a deep breath and stilled, his body shaking and his dick throbbing in her warmth. Her muscles milked him as her climax coaxed him to his own pleasure. With one last thrust against the slick friction of her vagina, he came, spilling his seed inside her.

Slowly, breathing heavily, he lowered himself onto her, lightheaded from the passion they had just shared.

She stroked him, running her smooth hands along his back. The brush of her lips against his temple were tender as she said, "I think I love you."

Alec smiled and raised himself on one arm to look down at her. "You think? You're not sure?"

With a wry grin, she swept back a lock of his hair. "I may take a little more convincing," she said.

"How about tonight? Maybe I can convince you then," he said, well aware of how they would spend their time together if she agreed.

"At eight? My place?" Kate offered readily.

"I'll be there."

Chapter 9

Alec knocked on the door to Kate's apartment, and at her muffled, "Come in," he entered.

The living room was dark except for the light spilling in from the dining room. Even that illumination wasn't all that strong, since it came from dozens of lit candles arranged on the table, and on the sideboard at one end of the room.

An assortment of plates on the tabletop were filled with familiar dishes, as well as one surprising item: the gift he had brought her on that fateful night so many months ago.

He realized as he examined the food more closely that she had recreated their first meal.

"Kate?" he called out, wondering where she could be.

She walked in a second later, wearing a crimson silk robe that clung to every lethal curve, and shifted like a second skin with each step she took.

He immediately grew hard at the thought of touching her beneath that silk.

She smiled and gave him a wicked glance as she detected that her efforts had reaped the desired results. But then she surprised him yet again by holding out a similar robe to him, this one in a very masculine midnight-black.

"I thought you might want to get comfortable."

She thought right; he was so hard and swollen already that the pressure of his dress pants was almost unbearable. In a rush he went to her bedroom, undressed and pulled on the robe. The silk slid over his body like a caress, and he had to grab his cock to tame his desire lest he come right then.

With a few strangled breaths, he restored control, then returned to the dining room, where Kate was spooning food onto their plates.

As they had what seemed like a lifetime ago, they shared the meal, telling each other what they'd been doing over the many months apart. Finally, they reached the end of dinner, and Kate said, "I missed you, Alec. I didn't think I would."

"Me, either, Kate. I never expected to come to care for you the way I did," he admitted, no longer afraid, now that the mummy's curse was gone and Kate was safe.

She smiled and reached for the elegantly wrapped box he had left her months earlier. "You said I should open this when there was greater trust between us."

Something broke free inside Alec as she slowly undid the ribbons on the box and then peeled back the paper. Hesitantly, she lifted the lid to reveal his gift to her.

Her shocked gasp was followed by a sexy chuckle. "You were right about the trust part," she said as she set the lid on the table. Inside the box, a carved jade phallus rested on a bed of pink tissue paper.

"I picked that up on a trip to China nearly one hundred years ago, while I was searching for Taweret. I didn't choose it for anyone in particular. There was never anyone I felt would appreciate it," he explained, almost shyly.

"Will you help me appreciate it?" Kate asked, rubbing her hand up and down the cool surface of the jade dildo, while at the same time reaching beneath the silk of his robe to touch him. She encircled his dick and stroked him as she traced the delicate carvings on the cool stone.

Alec nearly lost it at her touch, and had to stop her in midstroke. "You'll unman me, Kate."

"Sweet, Alec. Why don't you show me what you want?" she said, snatching up the jade phallus. Grabbing his hand, she led him to the bedroom, where she scooted to the center of the bed.

She undid her robe, letting it fall off her shoulders to pool beneath her. As in the dining room, the only light came from some strategically placed candles creating an intimate glow.

Her body was pale against the crimson of the robe as she lay back against her pillows and picked up the dildo.

"Show me what you want, Alec," she said again, clearly the one in control.

Alec couldn't talk. His throat was too tight with emotion as he realized the trust she was placing in him. Instead, he showed her by taking hold of her hand and guiding the tip of the phallus to her center. Slowly, he slipped it inside her as he knelt between her legs.

"So cool," she purred, as he urged her to take in the nearly ten-inch length of the dildo.

With his hand covering hers on the handle, he began a slow and steady stroking. Building her passion, he bent and kissed her tits, biting and sucking on her nipples until she was mewling with need and shifting her hips against the silken puddle of her robe on the bed.

He kept on, mindful not to hurt her with the hardness

of the jade as he kissed her nipples and breasts, until he needed more.

Easing back, he took her free hand and urged it over the silk covering his cock. "Touch me!" he commanded, and she did, encircling his erection with her fingers, rubbing the fabric up and down his length until Alec was reeling from the desire overtaking him.

He slipped the dildo from her body, earning a protest, until she realized his intent.

When he eased onto his back, the black silk of his robe fell open to expose the magnificent length of him, which made the jade phallus pale in comparison.

Kate dragged in a breath to steady herself as he guided her over him, gently grasping her buttocks. He drew her down slowly until he was filling her, stretching her to the point of pleasure-pain. She sat there, impaled on his dick, her sex throbbing and clenching around him.

"Touch yourself, Kate. Touch your breasts. Touch your clit," he said, clearly so near the edge that the slightest action might take him over.

She raised one hand and took hold of her nipple.

His gaze fastened there as she rotated it between thumb and forefinger, creating a sympathetic twist and tightening between her legs.

He moaned like a man in pain. In husky tones he said, "I feel it, Kate. It feels so good."

His words urged her on. She tweaked the tip harder, and gasped. Lowering her hand to her smooth pubis, she parted it to find her clit, and pressed there with her fingers, creating another wave of unbearable pleasure.

His cock jerked inside her and swelled, pressing against

the walls of her vagina, unleashing a torrent of dampness that revealed she was near her own limit.

Slowly, she rose upward, her juices slick against his skin, before roughly sinking back down.

"That's it, love. Ride me," he said, and she did, shifting her hips to take him in and out of her vagina, savoring the warmth of him, so different from the cool kiss of the jade dildo. As Alec's gaze settled on her breasts, she knew almost instinctively what he wanted, and reached up, caressing her nipples until she was trembling and nearly undone.

He rose then in turn and sucked on her tits, kissing and gently biting the peaks. Reaching between their bodies to find her sensitive clitoris, he pressed his thumb against it and rotated, shattering her control.

She came with a violent shudder and ground down into him, swiveling her hips one last time as her release swamped her senses.

Alec relished the motion of her muscles along his length. Surrendering to his passion, he allowed her warmth to pull him to his climax. His arms wrapped around her to keep her close as he came, reluctant to release her.

As sanity returned, they fell back onto the pillows, cradled in each other's arms. Their bodies were still joined when, scant minutes later, Alec grew hard once more.

"Really?" Kate teased as passion ignited again.

"I don't think, if I live another hundred-and-fifty-some years, that I'll ever get enough of you," he confessed, and skimmed his mouth across hers.

Kate returned the kiss, whispering against his lips, "I think I know now, Alec."

"Know what?" he asked, even as he rolled her to her

back and slowly moved his hips, seeking to satisfy them both once more.

"I know that I love you," Kate answered.

Alec smiled and made love to her again, certain of one thing.

As painful as the torment of the mummy's desire had been, he'd do it all again for the love of a woman like Kate.

* * * * *

MILLS & BOON®

Why not subscribe?
Never miss a title and save money too!

Here's what's available to you if you join the exclusive **Mills & Boon Book Club** today:

- ✦ *Titles up to a month ahead of the shops*
- ✦ *Amazing discounts*
- ✦ *Free P&P*
- ✦ *Earn Bonus Book points that can be redeemed against other titles and gifts*
- ✦ *Choose from monthly or pre-paid plans*

Still want more?
Well, if you join today we'll even give you
50% OFF your first parcel!

So visit **www.millsandboon.co.uk/subs**
or call Customer Relations on 020 8288 2888
to be a part of this exclusive Book Club!

MILLS & BOON®

Why shop at millsandboon.co.uk?

Each year, thousands of romance readers find their perfect read at millsandboon.co.uk. That's because we're passionate about bringing you the very best romantic fiction. Here are some of the advantages of shopping at www.millsandboon.co.uk:

* **Get new books first**—you'll be able to buy your favourite books one month before they hit the shops

* **Get exclusive discounts**—you'll also be able to buy our specially created monthly collections, with up to 50% off the RRP

* **Find your favourite authors**—latest news, interviews and new releases for all your favourite authors and series on our website, plus ideas for what to try next

* **Join in**—once you've bought your favourite books, don't forget to register with us to rate, review and join in the discussions

Visit **www.millsandboon.co.uk**
for all this and more today!